Born in London, Alan Fenton was educated at Mercers' School in the City. Having won an open scholarship to Oxford he did two years National Service in the Royal Air Force, becoming a Pilot Officer, before going up to St Edmund Hall to read English Language and Literature.

On graduating, he worked as a trainee in business for a couple of years before writing a sketch for a children's television programme starring Ronnie Corbett. This led to a career writing comedy sketches and scripts for T.V. comedy series, Saturday Night Spectaculars and Sunday Nights at the London Palladium for most of the top comedians of the day, including Ronnie Corbett, Bruce Forsyth, Dickie Henderson, Roy Castle, Arthur Haines, Jack Douglas and Joe Baker, Dick Emery, Irene Handl, Des O'Connor and many others.

After several years of comedy scriptwriting, he drifted back into business. Working for a large American trading organisation he travelled the world, until he and a few friends set up their own company trading in metals and minerals, and ultimately in oil.

Leaving business a few years later, he wrote the *Shadow of the Titan*, his first novel, based loosely on his business experiences. Subsequently he wrote *The Call of Destiny*, the first book in the *Return of Arthur* cycle, and its sequel, *The Hour of Camelot*.

Alan Fenton lives in London with his wife and nine Pekinese dogs.

The
HOUR OF
CAMELOT

Alan Fenton

THE DOVECOTE PRESS

First published in 2010 by The Dovecote Press Ltd
Stanbridge, Wimborne Minster, Dorset BH21 4JD
ISBN 978-1-904-34979-2

Designed by The Dovecote Press
Printed in Spain by GraphysCem, Navarra

All papers used by The Dovecote Press are natural, recyclable products
made from wood grown in sustainable, well-managed forests

A CIP catalogue record for this book is available
from the British Library

1 3 5 7 9 8 6 4 2

THE SWORD IS DRAWN

Prologue

Rising from the edge of the world the full moon laid a silver trail across the sea. A knight on a white horse trotted along the path that skirted the clifftop, turning his mount inland by Castle Rock, through fields of long grass, across the drawbridge, and into the courtyard of Camelot Castle.

From the shadows came a soft whinnying; hooves clattered, striking sparks on the cobblestones. A black horse moved into the flickering light of flaming torches, on its back a knight clad from head to foot in black armour.

'I challenge you to a joust,' he said, his voice expressionless.

'Who challenges me?'

'The Black Knight.'

'That tells me nothing.' The knight on the white horse raised his visor and removed his helmet. His hair, like his suit of armour, was the colour of gold, his blue eyes sparkled in the torchlight. 'At least let me see your face.'

The black knight hesitated, motionless on his horse. Then he too raised his visor and removed his helmet. In the light of the moon the eyes in the bearded face were cold.

'Why do you challenge me?' asked the knight on the white horse.

'Men say you are a great champion.'

'That is no reason for us to fight.'

'Reason enough for me.'

'You and I have no quarrel,' said Arthur. 'Instead of trying to kill each other, let us drink wine together in Camelot's feasting hall.'

'Never. We are enemies.'

'How so? I never saw you before in my life.'

The black knight laughed scornfully. As if sharing its master's contempt, his mount snorted, its hooves clopping restlessly on the cobblestones, horse and rider moving together as one.

'It is written,' he said. 'We must fight.'

'I will not fight you.'

'If you do not,' said the black knight, 'the world will know you are a coward.'

Arthur gripped the pommel of his sword. 'So be it,' he said. Beckoning the black knight to follow him, he guided his horse through the portcullis, across the drawbridge, and down the steep path that led to the foot of the cliffs.

Taking up their positions on the beach, the adversaries lowered their visors and levelled their lances. Moonlight glinted on gold and black armour as they hurtled towards each other. In the same instant both spear points struck home, and the two knights, jolted sharply back by the impact, fought to regain their balance even as they wheeled round and sped away before turning to face their opponent.

A second time they spurred their horses to a gallop, a second time lances battered armour. For a moment it seemed they both would be unhorsed, but again they pulled themselves upright, spun their mounts round and trotted back to the starting point.

Yet again they raced towards each other, and this time the clash of spears on breastplates was so fierce that their lances shattered into a myriad of shards that floated in the darkness, transformed to silver by the moonlight. Hurled to the ground the two adversaries lay stunned, their horses steaming in the cold night air, pawing the sand impatiently.

Arthur, the first to recover, struggled to his feet, raised his visor and removed his helmet, waiting patiently for his opponent to do the same. 'I congratulate you, sir knight, on your skill and valour,' he said. 'The contest is even. There is no victor and no vanquished. Honour is surely satisfied.'

Slowly the black knight nodded, as if in agreement. But instead of taking the hand held out in friendship, he drew his sword from its scabbard, swung it high and whirled it in a circle of scything steel. At the last instant Arthur dodged the terrible blow, though not entirely, the sharp blade cutting through his shoulder armour, slicing the flesh and splintering the collarbone above his left arm. Crying out in pain and rage, he staggered and almost fell. Then, swift as lightning, Excalibur flashed in the moonlight, and the black knight's head rolled in the sand.

As the warm blood oozed from the headless trunk, the black knight stooped and grabbed his head by the hair. Cradling it in the crook of his right arm, he grasped the bridle in his left hand, stepped into the stirrup and pulled himself up and onto his horse. The cold eyes in the decapitated head looked down, the lips moved. 'This day is yours, Arthur. My day will come.'

And turning his horse away, he disappeared into the night.

One

THE ISLAND OF Camelot lies in the middle of the ocean, its white buildings shimmering in the bright morning sun – pyramids, squares and pentagons, columns and spires, rectangles, hexagons and spheres – each structure unique, yet each blending with the others in perfect harmony. At intervals of a hundred metres around the island's perimeter clusters of white columns soar, tall and slender, crowned with a halo of antennae moving silently and purposefully, like the feelers of giant insects probing the sky. This could be a city far out in space, light years into the future, if there were not one notable exception to the scrupulous order of its layout and the geometrical precision of its architecture – the ruins of an ancient castle, with one surviving ivy-covered corner tower, crumbling walls, a dry moat, and the remains of a gateway and drawbridge.

Along a path that led from Transport Maintenance to Command Control two men strolled – one in his mid-fifties, tall and spare, with shoulder-length white hair and robe trailing behind him in the breeze, his companion in his early-thirties, slim and of medium height, with sapphire blue eyes and blond hair. On the chest of his dark blue uniform embroidered in gold was the insignia of a hand drawing a sword from a stone.

Eclipse, a huge cigar-shaped aircraft, rose vertically from its launch pad, flashed in the sunlight and vanished.

In Merlin's smile there was more than a hint of the inventor's pride. 'An operation?'

Arthur shook his head. 'War games.'

Three man-size robots rushed by, eyes winking furiously.

Merlin's eyes asked the question.

Arthur touched the metal disc on the lobe of his left ear, activating his earcom. 'Robot technicians,' he said, 'back from servicing Nimble fighters.'

A hovercart, the island's favourite means of transport, floated towards them a few feet off the ground, the troop of soldiers on board saluting Arthur smartly as they passed.

'Actives on their way to Kraken,' said Arthur, anticipating the next question. The ocean equivalent of Eclipse, Kraken was a sub and supra-marine Titan. Again the corners of Merlin's mouth lifted in a self-satisfied smile.

Overhead, four ungainly looking craft with stubby wings appeared from nowhere and bumbled playfully about the sky like giant puppies before disappearing again as they mantled.

'I love my Scuttles,' chuckled Merlin, ducking only just in time as three technicians sped inches above his head powered by mini-backpacks known in Camelot as seven league boots.

'Military operations?'

'So far only two,' said Arthur. 'The first to eliminate a stockpile of chemical weapons in the Middle East, the second to stop militias massacring refugees in North Africa.'

'World reaction?'

'We have the people's support, and compliments from the media too, all with the usual exceptions of course.'

'How about world leaders?'

'They're sceptical,' said Arthur. 'They don't really trust us. We need to convince them we're on their side.'

'And how will you do that?'

'Talk to them,' said Arthur.

Merlin's lips twitched. 'That should be interesting.'

A harsh screech echoed from Castle Cliffs as a barn owl swooped and perched on Merlin's shoulder, dangling a dead mouse in front of his face. Merlin's nose wrinkled distastefully as Virgil squawked, swallowed the mouse in one gulp and glided off to look for more.

Command Control was flanked by a gently sloping grass verge on which the two men, comfortable in each other's company, relaxed for a time without speaking. 'Now tell me about this dream of yours,' said Merlin without preamble.

Scouring his memory for every detail, Arthur recounted the story of the black knight's challenge, the jousting contest and the ghastly end of the dream that still haunted him.

'Is that it?' Merlin enquired.

'Yes.'

His head drooped on his chest, his big green eyes shuttered, Merlin, to Arthur's dismay, began to snore loudly. A couple of minutes later he opened his eyes, yawned and stretched. 'What is it you want to know?'

'Who was the knight in golden armour?'

Merlin directed a baleful look at his beloved protégé. 'Please do not insult my intelligence. Or yours.'

Arthur blinked. 'Then who was the black knight?'

'The personification of evil,' replied Merlin.

'Why did he challenge the knight in golden armour?'

'Because evil sees good as competition.'

'The black knight didn't die,' said Arthur, 'even when his head was severed from his body. He picked it up, and the head spoke.' His forehead furrowed. 'I'm trying to remember his exact words.'

Merlin's green eyes glowed. 'This day is yours, Arthur. My day will come.'

Even after all these years Arthur could still be astonished by the powers of the Magus. 'How did you know that?'

'It was on your monitor.'

'You read my mind?'

An airy wave of the hand. 'Something like that.'

'Tell me, Merlin. Why didn't the black knight die when I – when the knight in golden armour – cut off his head?'

'No one can destroy evil,' said Merlin, adding softly, 'not even you.'

'Why not?'

'If good were able to destroy evil, there would be no people left on the planet.'

One of Merlin's riddles.

'Because...' murmured Arthur, his mind grappling with the answer, 'because all men are part good, part evil. Is that it?'

'Exactly,' said Merlin. 'And that is the mystery and the tragedy of creation.'

'Are you saying good can never overcome evil?'

'There will be an end,' said Merlin, 'but who knows when, or how it will be. Your dream showed you the road you must take, but it did not show you what lies at the end of it. How could it? Only one thing is certain; man can never change his nature. No one can do that – no one but God.'

'Then why doesn't He?'

'Who knows? Perhaps He isn't ready. Perhaps He doesn't want to.' The green eyes were sombre. 'Perhaps he can't.'

As the two friends sat in silence, Arthur's thoughts ebbed back to the days when he and his brother, Keir, fished by the stone bridge at Ponterlally – or rather when Keir fished, and he lay on his back reading his future in white wisps of cloud strewn across the sky by the fitful wind. What dreams he had dreamed! How many alien invaders challenged in a beam of sunlight! How many enemies overcome in mortal combat! How many spaceships flown to galaxies at the outermost extremities of space and time! If only life were as simple now as it was then. What use was it to fight the forces of darkness if God did not, or could not, change man's nature? 'My dream,' said Arthur, 'is that the meek will inherit the earth. Is that all it is, Merlin, just a dream?'

Merlin's green orbs softened. 'Listen to me, Arthur,' he said. 'You were born at the winter solstice, the time when the sun is at its lowest point, the longest, darkest night of the year, when the world lies in waste and people long for redemption. So were the solar gods, like Mithras, the god of light and truth; so was the saviour, Jesus Christ. In that time of greatest despair new hope is born and will be born again and again.' He laid a loving hand on Arthur's shoulder. 'You are that hope, Arthur.'

A young woman appeared from behind Command Control. Beckoning Merlin, she called him by name. As he hesitated, unwilling, it seemed, to obey the summons, she tossed her head and was gone.

'Who was that?'

'Nimue.'

'Who is Nimue?'

'The one who has me in her spell.'

Surely the Magus was joking. 'You are the one who casts spells,' said Arthur.

Merlin's eyes gleamed. 'Nimue is possessive. She wants to imprison me in a cave and roll a boulder over the entrance.' To Arthur's surprise the Magus sounded more than a little intrigued by the prospect.

He looked to the sky and raised a hand. Virgil flew down, spread his wings and landed softly on his master's shoulder. 'I must go,' said Merlin, avoiding Arthur's eyes.

'Stay, Magus, I have so many questions.'

'They will all be answered in the circle of time.'

And before Arthur could say another word Merlin was striding away, hair and robe streaming behind him in the breeze, Virgil clutching his shoulder, his wings fluttering as he struggled to keep his balance. When he was about thirty metres from Arthur, Merlin turned, and framing his face with his hands, patted his left thumb with his right index finger as though he were taking a photograph. 'Remember the photo I never took,' he called, waved twice and loped off in the direction of the sea.

What was all that about? One of the Magus's little jokes? Or something more significant? Arthur was puzzled. For a few desolate moments he was a child again, the wretchedness of abandonment oppressing his spirit, his fingers straying to the scar on his left cheek. 'Merlin!' he cried, 'Come back! Come back!'

But the Magus had disappeared. Determined to find him, though uncertain which way he had gone, Arthur walked on, slowly at first, then faster, through the concourse of white buildings into fields of long grass, until he stood at the edge of the cliffs overhanging the island's beaches.

Far below, the Atlantic waves, tormented to white crests by the approaching storm, curled to the shore. Standing firm, legs braced against the fierce gusts, he looked and listened for the Magus. But there was nothing to see but the deserted beach and the fretful ocean, nothing to hear but the plaintive cry of gulls and the wash of the incoming tide.

Two

IN THE SMALL HOURS of a midsummer morning the sky above Richmond Park was overcast, moon and stars obscured. In the distance lightning flashed, illuminating the plump underbelly of cloud. Thunder growled. A herd of deer huddled under the sheltering branches of an oak tree, reacting nervously to every sound, the stag snorting and stamping the grass, the females peering anxiously into the night.

At the edge of a clearing a middle-aged man and two young women waited, from time to time looking expectantly at the sky. Around them on the grass lay a few small items of hand luggage. One of the women, tall and gangling, with protruding teeth, paced back and forth. 'What time is it?'

The man consulted his watch. 'Two-thirty.'

'How will they find us?'

'They'll find us.'

If they were aware of anything, it was of the sudden silence that cocooned them. They had seen and heard nothing, when there it was, a dark presence looming over them. Sinking slowly to the ground, the Scuttle bounced twice on huge wheels, its belly opened, steps slid smoothly down, powerful lights blazed, flooding the clearing, and a stockily built man with a thick neck and flaming red hair strode towards them, hand outstretched.

'Lord Grant?'

'Please call me Leo,' replied the older man, reaching out his hand and noting that the hand that enveloped his was big and the grip firm, though not aggressively so.

'I am Gawain.'

'This is my daughter, Guinevere.' Then, indicating the gangly young woman, 'And her friend, Gertrude Lancaster.'

As Gawain bowed courteously to the women, his eyes focused on Guinevere who acknowledged his bow with a slight smile. 'My friends call me Lanky,' gushed Gertrude, flashing her buck teeth.

'I must ask you to hurry,' said Gawain. 'We are not mantled on the ground.'

'Not mantled? What does that mean?' asked Leo.

'It means we can be seen.'

'Ah,' murmured Leo, still looking mystified.

They were scarcely in their seats when the Scuttle rose vertically a few hundred feet above the trees, banked sharply, and headed across London in a fast climb to the north, though still slow enough, as Gawain explained, to reduce force 'G' to a comfortable level.

'How long is the flight?' asked Leo.

A terse response. 'Not long.'

It was clear from the tone of Gawain's voice that on this point there would be no elaboration. For a few minutes he sat near them, explaining what they needed to know about the Scuttle, whilst Lanky darted flirtatious glances at him, to the obvious embarrassment of Guinevere.

'Control yourself,' she whispered, as Gawain moved forward to the flight deck.

'I'm sure I don't know what you mean,' said Lanky, piqued. Her habitual good humour almost instantly restored, she snuggled into her seat. 'Have you noticed his lashes?' she hissed, 'They're blond! White blond!' Receiving no answer she continued unperturbed, 'And that gorgeous red hair. Bet he's got a temper.'

Not in the mood for chattering, Guinevere turned her head away. Discreetly, Lanky observed her friend, wondering what was going on in that beautiful head. She was taking a massive step, was Guinevere. Did she know what she was doing? Could she be getting cold feet? It must be more than four years since she turned down Arthur's first proposal of marriage, and then two weeks ago he had proposed again, this time by videolink. Five long days she had reflected before accepting him. Five days! Admittedly Arthur was thirty-three, and ten years was quite an age difference, but what did that matter if you loved someone? Besides, he was special; handsome, brave, charming, famous – more than famous – he was an international hero, the darling of the world! And this brilliant man, this catch of the century, doted on her! So what was there to think about? Nothing. Not five days. Not five seconds!

But then Guinevere had never been one to act spontaneously. She considered everything she did before she did it. She wouldn't buy a pair of shoes on impulse, let alone accept a proposal of marriage. Above all things, she prided herself on being sensible. So what was so great about being sensible? There were times when Lanky felt like grabbing her friend by the shoulders and shaking all that sense right out of her.

Guinevere was thinking about the man she had agreed to marry. Though far from getting cold feet, she was, nevertheless, a little apprehensive at the prospect of meeting Arthur again. Committing herself entirely to a man was a new, and yes, disturbing experience. She reassured herself with the thought that she was reasonably, not recklessly in love. For some – perhaps even for most women – love without passion was unthinkable. Not for Guinevere. Hardly a day passed when she did not thank her lucky stars that passion was not in her nature. Life was so much simpler for a woman able to control her emotions. Being in love was wonderful, but not if it involved abandoning common sense.

The door of Scuttle's control deck was open. On the left of Gawain sat the pilot. For most of the short flight all they saw of him was the back of his head silhouetted against the dim blue light of the cockpit. When once he glanced back at his passengers, Guinevere glimpsed a long face, a straight nose, and dark, brooding eyes that seemed to observe her with something like disdain.

Lanky's eyes popped. 'Did you catch that dreamy man? Now that's what I call a dish!'

Guinevere's chin lifted disdainfully. 'That young man could do with a lesson in good manners. Not so much as a word of greeting. And did you see that superior look he gave us?'

Gawain, moving back to prepare the passengers for landing, could not help overhearing. 'Don't let him bother you, ma'am,' he said, 'he doesn't mean anything by it.'

Embarrassed that her comments had been overheard, Guinevere pretended not to understand. 'I'm sorry?'

'It's the way he is.'

'The way who is?'

'Lancelot.'

'Hmm.' The name meant nothing to her.

Three

IN ARTHUR'S APARTMENT the two lovers talked happily of times past.

'I loved you from the first moment I saw you,' he said.

Guinevere blushed, something she rarely did. 'Do you remember when that was?'

'Indeed I do. It was in the library of your father's house, and you were angry because he had let slip that you were only thirteen.'

'I was nearly fourteen,' said Guinevere, 'and it was really important to me that you knew it. '

'You asked me how old I was,' recalled Arthur.

'That's right. And you said you were almost twenty-four.' A mischievous smile. 'You didn't seem too happy about that.'

'Ten years seemed such a big age difference,' he said, reflecting that it still did.

'And then I never saw you again until my eighteenth birthday party.'

'That was when I fell in love with you. Was it the same with you?'

It was a second before she answered. 'Of course it was.'

That slight hesitation thrust to the surface of Arthur's mind a question he could not resist asking. 'Why did you turn me down when I proposed to you the first time?'

A question she had expected, and for which she had her answer prepared. Several answers in fact – she had been afraid of marrying such a prominent man, she was too young, she had not understood her true feelings. Somehow though, when it came to it, none of these explanations seemed either adequate or entirely truthful, so that in the end all she said was, 'I was a fool,' slipped her arms round his neck and kissed him tenderly.

But then suddenly she stiffened and drew away from him looking almost frightened.

'What is it?'

'There's something you need to know.'

Now he was worried, seriously worried. Did she not love him? Had she changed her mind about marrying him? Though if she had, why had she come all the way to Camelot to tell him so?

'A few months ago I saw a gynaecologist.'

Guessing immediately what she was going to say, he almost felt relieved. 'Medical science today . . . ' he began, but she cut him short.

'I went for a second and a third opinion. Both confirmed the first. I can never have a child. I wanted to tell you when you phoned but somehow I just couldn't. I had to see you . . . to tell you face to face.' Her hands clasped and unclasped nervously in her lap. 'I know how much you want a family,' she said, her voice low. 'When you phoned to propose, you had no idea that I couldn't . . . so what I mean is – I would quite understand if you . . . ' Her voice dropped.

'It makes no difference,' said Arthur. 'None at all.'

'We have to talk about it.'

'There's nothing to talk about,' he said firmly. 'All that matters is that we love each other.'

Tears brimmed in her eyes. In Arthur's arms she was truly happy, knowing that she had made the right decision, and that she loved Arthur as she never had, nor ever could, love any other man.

The next morning, the sun shone, the Atlantic waves jumped for joy, the warm breeze whispered its congratulations, and the slender trees lining the avenue that led to the House of Prayer bowed a gracious welcome. Early in the morning the crowds began to gather for the wedding. The sun was high when Arthur walked up the steps of the House of Prayer, followed a few minutes later by Guinevere on the arm of her father, Leo Grant. No one, it was generally agreed, had ever seen a more beautiful bride nor a handsomer groom.

The marriage ceremony was simple and moving. As it drew to a close the couple exchanged their vows. Then, placing the wedding ring on Guinevere's finger, Arthur kissed his bride. The congregation stood and applauded as the happy couple made their way down the aisle, through the doors, and out onto the steps. Bells pealed, startled doves scattered from the tower of the House of Prayer, and the cheering crowds were filled with an exhilarating sense of optimism and well-being. For every man, woman and child on the island of Camelot the union of Arthur and Guinevere was both the perfect expression of ideal love, and a symbol of hope for the future.

Four

Both of them young, talented and opinionated, Lancelot and Gawain clashed swords on almost every issue, their rivalry intensified by the mutual conviction that each was the better man, infinitely better qualified to be Camelot's Chief of Staff – an appointment Arthur was expected to make shortly. Since Arthur himself was not permitted by the code of the Round Table to participate actively in military operations, it was generally expected that either Lancelot or Gawain would be handed the baton. The question was, which one?

The door panel buzzed, the speaker crackled.
Name?
'Lancelot.'
In a nano-second the computer matched voice and iris with its records.
Enter, Lancelot.
'You sent for me, sir.'
'Ah, yes. Take a seat. Be with you shortly.' Arthur tapped his computer keyboard, and the white dome above his apartment slid open uncovering a high resolution twenty-five metre telescope. Pointing at the big eye-level monitor, his eyes shone with excitement. 'See that, Lance,' he said. 'Know what it is?'
'The night sky?' said Lancelot vaguely, his mind focused not on the monitor, but on Arthur's reason for summoning him.
'What you are looking at, Lance, is our solar system.'
'Indeed.'
Arthur tapped the keyboard, realigning the telescope. 'Any

idea what that is?'

Lancelot made a show of studying the big screen. 'Some kind of – um – galaxy?' he ventured.

'A supernova,' said Arthur, 'actually in the process of exploding about a billion years ago. The light from that explosion is only just reaching us. It's probably a black hole by now.'

'Amazing,' said Lancelot without conviction.

'Current thinking,' said Arthur, 'is that the universe is about thirteen and a half billion years old – based on the Big Bang theory, that is. Of course, some favour the zero point energy theory. You've heard of it, of course.'

Crossing one leg over the other, Lancelot agitated the dangling foot furiously. 'No, actually, I haven't.'

'Really?' Arthur seemed surprised. 'Well, anyway, it's the theory that energy just bubbles out of nothing and disappears again, meaning that our universe runs along happily for a time and then collapses and makes way for another universe, and so on.'

'Interesting,' said Lancelot, striving unsuccessfully to match his expression to the word.

Once more the door panel buzzed.

Name?

'Gawain.'

Lancelot frowned.

The computer matched Gawain's voice and iris with its records and invited him to enter.

'You sent for me, sir.' Seeing Lancelot, Gawain's freckled face flushed. 'What are you doing here?'

'I might ask the same of you,' said Lancelot.

The two men glowered at each other.

Whilst Gawain scratched the back of his leathery neck and Lancelot's dark eyes smouldered, Arthur, seemingly unaware of any tension in the room, continued to expand on one of his favourite topics. 'Astronomy teaches us that underlying the apparent confusion of the universe there is order,' he said. 'Without order there would be chaos. The same is true of our little planet.'

Turning off the telescope, he considered his two young friends affectionately: Lancelot vain, outspoken, occasionally arrogant or even downright offensive, but intelligent, honest and independent-minded, a man to be trusted; Gawain sociable, loyal, generally even-tempered – though liable to sudden temper flares – and tough, both mentally and physically, a safe pair of hands. Both exceptional young men, in their nature nothing mean or underhand, their virtues and vices there for everyone to see.

'Which brings me to the point of this meeting,' said Arthur. 'I have invited the two of you here to help me make a difficult decision. You want to know what it is?' he asked, observing their bewilderment with some amusement.

A blank look from both men.

'Which of you to appoint as Camelot's Chief of Staff.'

The outraged silence that followed was broken by Lancelot. 'I am, sir, as everyone knows, the last person in the world to blow his own trumpet. Nevertheless, I think I may say without fear of contradiction that no one in Camelot can match my qualifications, no one has my experience of military strategy and tactics, no one has my knowledge of the art and science of war.' He coughed self-deprecatingly. 'It would be wrong of me to list my personal qualities – intelligence, courage, determination, creativity; those I leave for others to praise,' he concluded with a complacent smile.

'In that case,' observed Gawain tartly, 'you'll be waiting till hell freezes over.'

'Forgive me, sir,' said Lancelot, with a withering look in Gawain's direction, 'but why this charade? Why not confirm my appointment now?'

Even in the full glare of Lancelot's stern scrutiny, Arthur did not blink. 'Because, Lance, there is another candidate with comparable qualifications.'

'Comparable qualifications!' Lancelot's eyebrows arched steeply. 'And who might this paragon be?'

'I am speaking of Gawain,' said Arthur.

Lancelot's expression conveyed both horror and incredulity, his rival's smug grin incensing him even further. 'With all due respect, sir,' he said, his voice shaking, 'you cannot be serious.'

'Had you remained in the British army,' continued Arthur, undeterred, 'you, Lance, would certainly have risen to the top. Had you, Gawain, continued to serve in the Royal Navy, I am equally confident that you would one day have become First Sea Lord.'

Lancelot shook his head pityingly, as if fearing for Arthur's sanity.

'In short,' said Arthur, 'you are both so supremely well qualified to lead our armed forces that I find it impossible to choose between you. I have therefore decided to ask you both to take part in a *tourney*.'

Both men looked blank.

'As you no doubt know,' explained Arthur, 'the old French word *tourney* became the word tournament, in other words a medieval joust, a sporting event in which two knights tried to knock each other off their horses with lances.'

'Horses!' echoed Gawain.

'Lances!' said Lancelot, scorn burning in his eyes.

'I propose a modern version of the medieval *tourney*,' explained Arthur.

'Excellent idea,' said Gawain, eager for a challenge.

Despite his show of indignation, Lancelot, too, was intrigued.

'Instead of horses and lances, I propose rowing, boxing and fencing,' said Arthur.

'Tame sports,' said Lancelot. 'Not exactly intellectually challenging.'

'What would you suggest, then?' said Gawain mischievously, 'Bridge? Chess? Draughts?'

'I see little point in prolonging this discussion,' said Lancelot. 'Whatever the nature of the contest, there is no doubt who the winner will be.'

'There I agree with you,' said Gawain.

News of the *tourney* generated enormous interest and excitement on the island. Bets were laid on the two men, most money on Gawain, considered a more approachable and less complex man than the aloof and introverted Lancelot. The majority approved the idea, though there were those who questioned whether such a competition was the right way to choose the Commander in Chief of Camelot's armed forces.

'Does winning a boat race or a boxing match qualify a man to command an army, a navy and an air force?' complained Leo Grant.

'There is more to a contest than winning.'

'Explain,' said Leo.

Arthur regarded his father-in-law with affection. 'Leo, my old friend, for you everything has to be rational and explicable. Not for me. There are times when we are all in the dark. And you know something? It's not such a bad place to be.'

'I like to see where I'm going,' said Leo.

'Not always possible,' said Arthur. 'We all want to believe we control our lives. But do we really? Are some things not best left to fate? I promise you, Leo, one way or another we shall find what we are looking for.'

Determined that the two men should compete without rancour, Arthur invited them to his apartment for dinner the day before the contest. Gawain was his usual genial self, Lancelot remote and taciturn. The more Guinevere saw of him the less she liked him, her antipathy heightened by the conviction that the feeling was mutual. The man treated her with indifference bordering on contempt, or so it seemed to her.

Arthur was disappointed and puzzled. He had hoped they

would be friends, the woman he so passionately loved and the young man he thought so highly of. Apparently it was not to be.

'Why don't you like Lancelot, Ginny?' he asked, when the two men had left.

'No special reason, darling. He bores me, that's all.'

Arthur sensed that it was not the whole story. 'I'd rather you were frank with me.'

'To be honest,' said Guinevere, 'I find the man insufferably vain. He struts around like a peacock showing off its tail, as if the whole world were there for no other reason than to admire him.'

'Admittedly he is a little self-obsessed,' acknowledged Arthur.

'And there's something weird about him.'

'What are you saying, Ginny?' said Arthur, looking concerned.

'I didn't mean that,' she said quickly, seeing the hurt in Arthur's eyes, and angry at having expressed herself so clumsily, 'I am not suggesting he's crazy or anything like that. But there's something odd going on inside that man's head, I'll swear there is.'

As for Lancelot, he made it abundantly clear to Lanky that he found her friend haughty and cold, describing her more than once as the Ice Maiden. Were it not for his love and respect for Arthur, he insisted, he would refuse to speak to her. In fact, so adamantly did he protest his absolute indifference to Guinevere, that Lanky wondered why he bothered to mention her at all.

But then, as everybody knew, Lancelot was a strange man.

Five

THE DAY OF THE boat race dawned overcast, threatening rain, but by midday a strong breeze had risen and blown the clouds away. Under the blue sky the sea was choppy, though not enough to deter the umpires; to the spectators' delight the race was on.

Arthur wished the two contestants well. 'I expect you to fight hard,' he said, his voice amplified to the watching crowds, 'but I also rely on you to uphold Camelot's high ideals. How the contest is fought is as important as who wins. May good fortune be with you both.'

Across the water the two rivals touched hands, neither, despite Arthur's exhortation, in the mood to give an inch to his opponent.

Almost every man and woman on the island – fans of either Lancelot or Gawain – were down on the shoreline or up on the clifftops shouting encouragement to their heroes, whilst the two men struggled to keep their tiny rowing boats in line with the starting posts to which they were tethered. The umpire, George Bedivere, bellowed his final instructions through a hand-held megaphone; 'You will start when I say go. The first man to complete a circuit of the island will be the winner. If neither of you reaches the finishing line, the race will be declared null and void and re-rowed tomorrow. Are you ready?'

Two nods.

'Go!'

The two competitors pulled away trailed by a small flotilla of boats, headed by the umpire's launch carrying Arthur and

Guinevere, George Bedivere – Arthur's old comrade in arms, Ian Duncan – Lancelot's close friend, Ban – Lancelot's father, and Guinevere's father, Leo Grant. For nearly a kilometre they were evenly matched, first one then the other drawing ahead, though never by more than a boat's length of clear water. The watching supporters cheered them on.

Then, slowly but surely, Gawain began to ease ahead, and after half a circuit of the island, was nearly twenty metres in the lead. With Lancelot struggling in the choppy sea, Gawain seemed certain to win the race, when suddenly, to the huge disappointment of his fans, disaster struck. In an effort to increase his lead, he rounded the island by Castle Rock too close to the shore and hit a patch of turbulent water. A wave struck his boat broadside on, overturning it. Struggling to stay afloat, he raised his arm as a signal that he was in trouble. In a few seconds the umpire's launch was alongside, and Arthur and George Bedivere pulled him from the water.

Rowing a course further out to sea, Lancelot rounded Castle Rock, punching the air in triumph as he did so. Unable to contain himself, Gawain exploded with anger at what he felt was unsporting behaviour. Shivering with cold, his wet hair clinging to his scalp like a flame red skullcap, he screamed his rage into the wind. Arthur knew better than to say anything, preferring to let his nephew rant the frustration out of his system.

Now that the outcome of the race was a foregone conclusion, the crowds began to drift away. And then it happened. A kilometre from the finishing line a wave capsized Lancelot's boat, and he was in the water. In the umpire's launch Gawain could barely restrain himself. Guinevere had no such scruples, shouting and waving her arms in delight.

As the umpire's launch drew alongside Lancelot, Arthur knelt by the gunwale and offered him his hand. 'No, thanks,' said Lancelot, 'I'll swim the rest of the course.'

Gawain said nothing. Lancelot's gesture was an act of derring-do, pointless but brave, one he could not help but admire.

'Water's pretty rough,' cautioned Leo Grant.

'Not a problem,' said Lancelot, rolling away in a slow, rhythmic crawl.

George Bedivere shrugged. 'I doubt he'll make it in this sea.'

'I wouldn't bet on it,' said Arthur.

Those few spectators still following the race had seen Lancelot overturn, though what came after was unclear. When they caught sight of his head bobbing in the water they waved and cheered from the cliffs and beaches, their cheers swelling and fading in the rising wind. Lancelot was swimming home, at least one kilometre to go, and in rough seas too! Why was he doing it? Sheer bloody-mindedness, or pride, or both, knowing Lancelot. Certainly he had nothing to gain. Sink or swim, he would have to row the race again tomorrow. But who cared! Not about winning but about character, this was the very stuff of drama, an audacious act that stirred their hearts. There was only one question now. Would he complete the course?

To their delight he did, and when finally he swam across the finishing line, he was given a hero's welcome. Hauled dripping and shivering into the umpire's launch, he was wrapped in blankets and congratulated in turn by Arthur, Ban, George, Ian Duncan and Leo Grant. Gawain, his anger quite forgotten, grabbed his rival's hand and shook it. 'Great stuff, Lance! Fantastic!' he kept repeating, genuinely impressed by Lancelot's gutsy swim.

Once ashore, the spectators who had followed in boats queued up to greet Lancelot. So cold and exhausted was he that for a few minutes he was unable to speak. When eventually he did, the impact of his words more than made up for the delay.

'I claim victory,' he announced.

Gawain's neck and face flared fiery red. 'You what!'

The two men squared up to each other, Gawain's head level with Lancelot's chest.

Arthur moved between them. 'Be calm, gentlemen.' He spoke

quietly. 'As I understand the rules, Lance, the race is void. It will be rowed again tomorrow.'

'With respect, sir,' said Lancelot, 'there is no need for that. I am the winner.'

'How can that be?'

'Correct me if I'm wrong,' said Lancelot, 'but before the race started did the umpire not say, "The first man to complete a circuit of the island will be the winner."?'

In the silence that followed, Arthur looked thoughtful, Gawain muttered angrily.

'Not the first *boat*,' said Lancelot, with heavy emphasis, 'the first *man*.' Looking around, he raised his voice. 'Does anyone here dispute that I was the first man to complete a circuit of the island?'

There was no response.

'But that's not how it was supposed to be,' protested Gawain. 'The race was about rowing, not swimming.' He lifted his arms in appeal, looking around for support.

'George,' said Arthur, 'you are the umpire. It's up to you.'

After a few moments reflection, George Bedivere made his decision: 'Lancelot is the winner!' he declared.

Six

CLIMBING INTO THE ring the master of ceremonies announced the main bout in the time-honoured manner. 'And now, lay*dees* and gentle*men*,' he intoned, 'the event you have all been waiting for – a contest of six, three minute rounds, between these two superb athletes – Gawain and Lancelot.'

There were cheers and applause as first Gawain, then Lancelot, ducked through the ropes and danced round the ring, waving to their supporters. Then came even louder cheers and counter cheers, as, to the especial delight of the ladies, they removed their robes, Gawain exposing scarlet shorts, Lancelot royal blue. Physically they presented a great contrast: Gawain short and thickset, with prominent pectorals and biceps; Lancelot, tall and lean, his muscles less conspicuous. Both men, as everyone knew, were extremely fit, both experienced boxers, Lancelot a university boxing blue, and Gawain a former navy middleweight champion. It promised to be an entertaining fight.

As the bell rang for round one Gawain caught Lancelot with two straight left jabs, followed by a wicked right hook that knocked him off balance. Dazed and confused, his legs buckling under him, it seemed he must surely go down, yet although he took severe punishment, he was still on his feet when the bell rang for the end of the round.

In the second round the match began to swing the other way. It was fighter against boxer, and the boxer was beginning to get the measure of his man. The second and third rounds were Lancelot's. Gawain was fast and aggressive, and his right hook was a potential match winner; Lancelot, however, was the more skilful boxer and had the advantage of a longer reach. Time and again, as Gawain rushed in, Lancelot caught him with left jabs, then danced away, teasing his opponent into wild swings that rarely made contact. Though he never looked like knocking Gawain out, he was beginning to make him look clumsy, the crowd applauding this exhibition of boxing skill, even though most of them were secretly hoping that Gawain would win.

Lanky was in awe of Lancelot, and thought him 'the dishiest man'. But if she was attracted to Lancelot, Gawain she found irresistible. Standing on her seat, she screamed encouragement, all the time blowing noisy kisses at him, much to the mortification of Guinevere. 'Do sit down! The whole world will know you fancy him.'

'What if they do?'

'Really, Lanky, you are too much,' said Guinevere, exasperated.

'Who do you support, Ginny?' asked Lanky, a glint of mischief in her eye.

'Why should I care who wins?' said Guinevere, her colour high, her breathing fast. Though she might feign indifference, there were some things one woman could not hide from another, especially one who knew her as well as Lanky.

The fourth round, too, was Lancelot's, the fifth shared. That made it three rounds to Lancelot and one to Gawain, with one round even. Only one round to go. Waiting in their corners for the sixth and final round, the two men listened to their trainers.

'Keep on jabbing and stay light on your feet,' urged Ian Duncan. 'You're odds on to win.'

'Odds on? I'm a certainty,' boasted Lancelot.

Gawain was in poor shape, his face bruised and swollen, his right eye rapidly closing, the cheek below it badly cut. Sponging his face tenderly, Gaheris, his younger brother, tried to stem the flow of blood. The big man adored everything about Gawain, his compact, sturdy frame, his red hair, his courage. If only the rules allowed it, he would have advanced into the ring himself, picked up Lancelot, lifted him high, whirled him round and tossed him into the crowd. The odds against Gawain winning were long, but one thing was certain, he would never give up, not till the final bell. Gaheris whispered deafeningly in Gawain's ear, 'Go for a knockout! One right hook and he's down!'

Everyone in the audience knew that if Lancelot were still standing at the end of the final round, he would win not just the boxing match, but the tournament. They cheered and stamped their feet, many of them, appreciating his fightback, shouting Lancelot! Lancelot! Lancelot! It was music to his ears. True, he had never courted popularity, had in fact disdained it, but he was human. This was a new experience, and he was loving it. Raising his arms high in a victory salute, he acknowledged the applause, so that when the bell rang for the final round he was distracted by the crowd's adulation, rising from his chair a fraction of a second too late. Charging across the ring like an angry bull, Gawain rocked his head back with a left jab and floored him with a savage right hook to the chin. Lancelot crumpled and fell. The referee stood over him and began to count.

'One! Two! Three!'

The crowd was stunned to silence.

'Four! Five! Six!'

Lancelot stirred . . .

'Seven! Eight!'

. . . pushed himself up from the canvas on one knee . . .

'Nine!'

. . . and fell back again.

'Ten!'

Arms wide, the referee signalled that the fight was over. The crowd erupted, cheering, stomping and waving their arms. Long after the boxers had left the hall, they were still chanting – first Gawain's name, then Lancelot's – with cheers and stamping of feet from the two rival camps. Though it might not have been the greatest boxing match anyone had seen, it was certainly the most exciting.

'I won fair and square,' said Gawain later in the changing room, 'though I admit I had a bit of luck.'

Lancelot sniffed. 'I made it easy for you.' Zipping up his holdall, he added, 'A mistake I shall not repeat.' And with that he stalked out.

'I confess I was wrong and you were right,' Leo told Arthur that evening. 'The contest has certainly brought out the best in those two young men.'

Arthur was delighted to have the blessing of his old mentor. 'Yes, it has, Leo. They have demonstrated all the qualities needed to be my Chief of Staff – except one.'

'What is that?'

'Chivalry.'

'An old concept, I would have thought.'

'No less relevant for being old,' said Arthur.

'You think chivalry is still relevant in the twenty-first century?'

'Most certainly I do.'

'When Lancelot swam to the finishing post, he was declared the winner in accordance with the letter of the law – certainly not the spirit. Was that chivalrous?'

'It was not,' said Arthur.

'And when Gawain knocked out Lancelot when his attention was distracted, was that chivalrous?'

'No.'

'There you are, then. Chivalry is dead. In this remorseless age of ours, Justice, Honour and Courtesy are worthy ideals, I grant you, but that's all they are. There's only one thing that counts.'

'And that is?'

'Winning.'

'I don't agree.'

'It's what Camelot has to do, isn't it?'

'Not at any cost,' said Arthur. 'We must keep faith with our ideals. If we forget what we are fighting for, we lose the moral right to fight.'

'Are you saying it is chivalry that distinguishes us from our enemies?'

Arthur considered his answer carefully. 'Animals are programmed to do what they do,' he said. 'They have no choice. We do. And one of the choices we have is to show compassion and consideration to our fellow men, even to our enemies – in other words, to be chivalrous.'

Leo was not persuaded. Being both man of action and man of conscience – a rare blend – was what made Arthur so special, and set him apart from men like Lancelot and Gawain. Yet conscience was a heavy burden to carry into battle, one that could ultimately weaken the arm that held the sword. Though he admired Arthur above all men, he pitied him too, observing in him a reluctant hero, a man of peace compelled by destiny to become a man of war.

Seven

THE HANGAR THAT housed Nimbles, Camelot's fighter aircraft, had been specially adapted for the fencing match. Five banked rows of seats each side of the hangar overlooked the white strip known as the piste on which the contestants were to fight.

Briefly the referee summarised the rules. 'As you will see, the fencer wears a mask to protect his face, a white jacket, and over it a silver-white metal mesh jacket, white shorts to below the knee, long white socks and soft shoes. On his back is a tiny radio that activates the light panel on the wall whenever there is a *hit* – that is when the tip of a foil makes contact with the opponent's metal jacket. To assist identification, one competitor's light is red, the other green. If there is a dispute, the referee's decision is final.'

As the time of the match drew near, the crowd became increasingly restless and excited, the noise amplified in the echoing expanse of the hangar. Above the din the referee shouted; 'The match will consist of three nine minute bouts, each bout divided into three sessions of three minutes each. The first contestant to make ten hits in a bout is the winner. If neither makes ten hits, then whoever has the greatest number of hits when time expires is the winner. If, at the end of the bout, there is an equal number of hits, the bout will be extended by one minute. Should that happen, I shall explain the rules that apply to the extension.'

To resounding cheers from their supporters, Lancelot and Gawain took up their starting positions, saluting each other with their foils.

'Ready?' asked the referee.

Two nods.

'Fence!'

The first to score ten hits was Gawain. It took him seven minutes, and in that time Lancelot scored only four. Of the two, Lancelot was the more elegant fencer, but Gawain was fierce and fast, most of his points being scored not in attack but in parry and riposte.

'First bout to Gawain!'

After a rest of fifteen minutes the second bout began. This one was much closer, and at the end of a tense struggle, Lancelot scraped home by ten hits to nine.

'One bout all!'

During the rest period the two men sipped water and listened attentively to the advice of their fencing masters.

'It seems a pity,' said Leo, leaning across to Arthur, 'that either one has to lose. There really is nothing to choose between them – as sportsmen or as men.'

'I agree,' said Arthur. 'But the fact is, there can only be one Chief of Staff.'

'Final bout,' announced the referee. The crowd fell silent.

'Ready?'

Two nods.

'Fence!'

The hits were confirmed with a brief explanation from the referee as red or green lights flashed on the electronic score board. 'Halt! A hit to Lancelot. Attack from the right on target. Fight on!' Engrossed in the fight, the crowd was hushed. 'Halt! A hit to Gawain. Attack from the front, parry septime and riposte. Fight on!' Then almost immediately, 'Halt! A hit to Gawain. Attack from the left on target, parry quatre and riposte. Fight on!'

It was a fascinating contrast in styles and temperament, almost as though their natural roles had been reversed, Lancelot now daringly aggressive, Gawain biding his time, waiting for his opponent to make a mistake. The first three minute session ended with a dazzling sequence of moves – Lancelot leaping into an audacious attack, Gawain's parry, Lancelot's riposte, counter parry by Gawain, counter riposte and hit! Gawain's point. Three hits to Gawain, two to Lancelot.

While the two fencers huddled with their fencing masters, the crowd stomped their feet, making such a din that even people sitting next to each other could barely make themselves heard.

The referee signalled the end of the brief rest period.

'Time!'

Silence.

'Ready?'

Two nods.

'Fence!'

When the second session ended, the score was Gawain, six hits, Lancelot four.

Two minutes into the third and last session of the final bout, the score was seven hits to Gawain, five to Lancelot. The noise was deafening, cheers and counter-cheers reverberating around the hall.

'Attack, disengage, counter-attack, riposte octave. Halt! A hit to Lancelot! Fight on! Attack from the right, parry quatre, riposte, counter-parry, counter-riposte, attack from the right, riposte septime. Halt! A hit to Gawain. Fight on!'

Thirty seconds to go. Eight hits to Gawain, six to Lancelot. The seconds ticked by. The crowd was silent again, so silent that they could hear the contestants' heavy breathing, the slap and squeal of soft-soled shoes on the piste, and the scrape of their foils as they clashed. Lancelot had abandoned all caution. With nothing to lose, he was constantly on the attack, the blade of his foil a blur of movement in the air.

'Halt! Hit to Lancelot! Fight on! Halt! Hit to Lancelot. Lancelot eight hits! Gawain eight hits! Time!'

There was not a sound in the great hangar, the crowd hardly

daring to stir in their seats.

Lancelot and Gawain removed their masks and wiped their foreheads with the back of their hands.

'Ladies and gentlemen, because the contestants are even at eight hits all,' said the referee, relishing the drama, 'the final bout will be extended by one minute.' There was a sudden flurry of excitement in the audience, and then, in response to the referee's admonishing hand, silence. 'I shall now toss a coin. Who will call?' Lancelot pointed at Gawain.

Gawain called, 'Heads!' as the coin spun in the air. The referee bent to pick it up. 'Heads it is,' he confirmed.

The crowd was chattering again. Once more the referee held up his hand for silence. His deep voice boomed round the big hangar. 'Gawain has won the toss. According to the rules of fencing he now has the advantage. The two contestants will fence for one minute. When the minute is up, if no hit has been scored, Gawain will be the winner. If there is a hit, or several hits, whichever contestant is ahead will be the winner. If both fencers score the same number of hits, the bout will be extended by a further minute.'

In the audience neighbour consulted neighbour, reminding each other that it was not just this session, not just this bout, not just this match, but the whole tournament that hung in the balance, and, as everyone knew, the winner would be Camelot's Chief of Staff.

The referee took up his position.

'Ready?'

Both men nodded.

'Fence!'

Lancelot immediately launched a fierce attack, driving Gawain back to the end of the piste and scoring with a lunge. To everyone's surprise the red light did not flash on the electronic screen. Lancelot flung his arms wide. 'I claim a hit!'

The referee nodded. 'A hit to Lancelot. Nine hits, Lancelot. Eight, Gawain. Fight on!'

Row after row of spectators sat still as statues. Forty seconds to go. Another frenzied attack from Lancelot. As Gawain retreated, the point of his foil touched his opponent's chest, and this time there was no green light on the wall screen. Gawain stuck out his jaw and looked at the referee.

'A hit to Gawain. Nine hits all. Fight on!'

Thirty seconds to go. Now Lancelot was more cautious, compelling Gawain to launch an attack. Lunge, riposte, attack from the left, parry quatre. Yet another attack. Gawain's blade was inches from Lancelot's chest, a swift disengage, a flick, and the point of his foil slid past his opponent's right arm as the tip of Gawain's blade appeared to make contact with Lancelot's chest. Yet again there was no green light on the wall screen. Gawain looked expectantly at the referee who shook his head.

'Time up! Nine all. Final session will recommence in one minute.'

There were a few subdued boos. Looking troubled, Arthur shifted in his seat. Lancelot removed his mask. 'It was a hit,' he said.

The referee looked dubious. 'Are you sure?'

Lancelot looked down his nose at the referee. 'It was a hit,' he repeated.

The referee hesitated. And then . . . 'A hit to Gawain!' A brief pause to milk the moment . . . 'Gawain is the winner! Ten hits to nine!'

The audience rose to its feet clapping and cheering, though whether for Lancelot or Gawain it was impossible to tell. As Arthur descended the stairs to the piste, the two contestants shuffled their feet and avoided each other's eyes.

'A good fight,' said Gawain gruffly.

'It was,' said Lancelot.

And then a strange thing happened; the crowd began to chant, 'Lancelot! Lancelot! Lancelot!' whilst Lancelot looked at the floor in embarrassment.

'What's all this about?' asked Lanky.

'They like what he did,' said Guinevere.

'Conceding the hit, you mean?'

'Yes.'

'But why?'

'I imagine they think it was chivalrous of him.'

Lanky was appalled. 'The hell with being chivalrous! Gawain won, didn't he? They should be cheering him, not Lancelot.'

A reproachful glare from Guinevere. 'Really, Lanky,' she said, 'sometimes you can be so insensitive.'

Lanky directed a searching look at her friend and held her peace.

As the chants of Lance-e-*lot*! Lanc-e-*lot*! Lanc-e-*lot*! continued, Gawain and Arthur were huddled in earnest conversation, and Lancelot, standing to one side, looked ill at ease. The crowd was silent, guessing that something unusual was happening.

'It's your decision, sir,' said Gawain. 'If you order me to do the job, I'll do it to the best of my ability. I have to be honest, though, I can live quite happily without it. All I ever wanted was to show that I'm as good a man as Lancelot, and I think I've done that. Frankly, I think he'd make a better Chief of Staff than me. Besides . . . ' – A rueful grin – 'he's taller and better-looking. He looks the part. I don't.'

Arthur observed the two young men: Gawain and Lancelot, Lancelot and Gawain. Little to choose between them: both intelligent, fearless and loyal, both dedicated to Camelot, both honest and chivalrous, as they had proved by their behaviour in the fencing match. Not an easy choice to make. Far from it. Yet, as he looked at them, he knew what his decision had to be. Gawain was right. Lancelot would make the better Commander in Chief. He did indeed look the part. It was not a matter of being tall or short, handsome or ugly. Lancelot had an air of purpose and conviction about him, and that unmistakable stamp of authority that distinguished him from other men, marking him out as a born leader.

'These last days,' said Arthur to Gawain, 'you have demonstrated that you are a superb athlete and a great competitor. But nothing you have achieved compares with what you are doing now.' Turning to Lancelot, he said, 'The job is yours, Lance – that is, if you want it.'

The truth was that Lancelot had never wanted anything as much. Choked with emotion, he was quite unable to speak. Words, though, were unnecessary, for Arthur understood very well what was going through his mind. Beaming, he laid his hands on the two men's shoulders. 'Friends,' he told the crowd, 'today there is no loser. These magnificent competitors are both winners – Gawain, who won the contest and surrendered the prize, and Lancelot, Camelot's Chief of Staff!'

Lancelot bowed his head, the knuckle of his index finger lightly brushing first the corner of one eye, then the other. Arthur, who missed nothing, noted the gesture and found it not at all surprising. Guinevere, who also saw it, was astonished and confused. Was Lancelot not an unfeeling and arrogant man? Of course he was! So what had it signified – that swift movement of the hand? Could it possibly have meant what it appeared to mean? Surely not. The very idea that such an insufferably conceited prig, such a monstrously vain and unfeeling creature could shed a tear at such a time – why, it was preposterous!

Or was it? Had she misjudged him? Could chronic shyness explain his distant and ungracious manner? Not, of course that it was of any consequence what she thought of Lancelot, nor he of her. Still, Arthur had such obvious affection for him and was so anxious for them to be friends that she felt under some pressure at least to make an effort. A chance meeting as Lancelot was leaving Arthur's observatory that same afternoon gave her the opportunity she was looking for. For an uncomfortable moment the two stood face to face, neither of them knowing what to say.

Finally, Guinevere blurted out, 'Congratulations on your appointment.'

'Thank you, ma'am.'

'And of course,' she added, after some hesitation, 'on your fine performance in the contest.'

Lancelot inclined his head in grateful acknowledgement.

Reflecting on it later, there must have been, Guinevere told herself, something about that mute response that encouraged her to offer one compliment too many. 'You were unlucky to lose.'

'The best man does not always win,' replied Lancelot with a condescending smile, frozen instantly on his face by Guinevere's icy response.

'True,' she said, 'though in this case he most certainly did.'

Eight

WHEN ARTHUR SUGGESTED that the time had come to talk to world leaders, there were some prominent members of the Round Table, notably Lancelot and Gawain, who disagreed with him.

'Why do we have to talk to anyone?' said Gawain.

'We don't need the world,' said Lancelot. 'The world needs us.'

'We may not need the world's military assistance,' said Arthur. 'What we do need, though, is its moral support. Our mission is about more than winning a war, it is about winning hearts and minds. It seems to me we have no choice; we must take the nations into our confidence and convince them of the justice of our cause.'

Arthur's view prevailed and preparations were begun. It would be impracticable and probably counter-productive, Arthur decided, to attempt to talk to every world leader. A shortlist was therefore drawn up of those who wielded global power and influence to a greater or lesser extent, and whose political agendas were very different: Russia, China, the US, Iran, France and the UK.

The first to appear on screen in Arthur's observatory was Winslow Marsden, the President of the United States. By nature sceptical, he was deeply suspicious of Arthur's motives. 'What exactly is in it for you guys?'

'It's not about money or territory or personal aggrandisement, if that's what you mean,' said Arthur.

'Then what is it about?'

'Defeating terrorism.'

'Terrorism is not a politically correct word these days.'

'I can live with that,' said Arthur.

There was a distant look in the President's eye. He was recalling many a verbal duel with Arthur. 'OK, so how do you define terrorist?'

'Terrorists,' said Arthur, 'are those who promote their cause by murdering and maiming innocent men, women and children, whose primary purpose is to create divisions between races, religions and nations. A worldwide, co-ordinated attempt to undermine social order constitutes terrorism, and those involved are terrorists.'

'I hear what you're saying, and I don't disagree with you,' said Winslow Marsden. 'I just don't see how you can help. I suggest you leave it to the big boys, Arthur.'

'The people have lost confidence in the big boys. They haven't done the job.'

'Not yet,' admitted Winslow Marsden, 'but we're getting there.'

'No, you're not,' said Arthur. 'With every year that passes, the terrorists are becoming more active. From time to time you win battles, but they are winning the war. The Islamists, for example, have access to plutonium, uranium, and all sorts of chemical and biological nasties. They have already used them. Not so long ago the Angels of Mercy tried to contaminate eight capital cities and murder countless innocents.'

'I haven't forgotten,' said the President grimly.

'If we don't act decisively now, it's only a matter of time before they decide to use nuclear weapons and inflict huge casualties and immeasurable economic and psychological damage on the world.'

'Even if you're right,' said Winslow Marsden, 'what can you bring to the table? You're talking to the President of the greatest power on earth.' He waved a dismissive hand. 'What can you do that we can't? You have neither the weapons nor the manpower.'

Arthur was too experienced and too wily to allow himself to be riled by the President. Calmly, he told him about Eclipse, the fastest, most advanced and powerful aircraft in the world, appearing and disappearing at will, capable of destroying enemy aircraft, warships and submarines at a range of a thousand kilometres, of transporting troops and their weapons within hours to any trouble spot on the globe, or, if the need should ever arise, with enough firepower to destroy an army or a city.

'So you and your buddies are going to save the world with one aircraft!' said the President with a mocking smile.

'And then there's Kraken,' continued Arthur undaunted. 'A massive surface and submarine craft, faster and more deadly than any vessel afloat or likely to be afloat for many years, with the same power and potential for destruction as Eclipse, plus some very special tricks of its own.'

'You scare me,' said the President.

'Nimbles, our fighter aircraft, are capable of flying in excess of Mach five,'

'Impossible. No human being could survive that kind of gravitational pressure.'

'That's why every pilot is a robot,' said Arthur.

A derisive snort. 'Of course he is,' said the President. 'And the navigator is Peter Pan.'

Without reacting, Arthur spoke briefly about Camelot's most devastating weapon. He was not trying to frighten the President, but it was vital he understood how deadly Excalibur was, and how far ahead of its time. 'Now let's talk energy,' he said.

'Be my guest,' said the President gloomily.

'In the late twentieth-century,' continued Arthur, 'the maximum energy achievable was one hundred Tesla per millisecond. Our energy source generates something in the region of eighty Giga Tesla.' A wry smile. 'I don't expect you to understand all this – I don't myself – but let's say that Tesla is equal to ten thousand units of magnetic induction. Giga is equivalent to ten to the power nine. What's more, we have succeeded in containing this enormous energy in the magnetic field. With it we bombard Space-Time and break it down. Experiments have been going all over the world for years – at Cern in Switzerland, and other places – but until now now no one has succeeded in producing sufficient energy to break down and reassemble matter. We have. We use the magnetic field as a giant battery to fuel our air, land and sea craft, and to power Excalibur. Eclipse and Kraken carry Excalibur, and every active carries an Excalibur portable.'

'I'm sorry,' said the President, 'but this has to be hooey.'

'You saw Excalibur in action in 2026 when we dealt with the Angels of Mercy,' Arthur reminded him.

The President chuckled. 'The disappearing buildings! Crap, Arthur! An illusion – a clever one, I'll give you that. The shrinks put it down to mass hysteria, didn't they? Whatever. One thing for sure – those buildings did not disappear. It never happened. '

'It happened, I assure you,' said Arthur. 'Excalibur can dematerialise matter in any form – buildings, weapons, air and sea craft, and yes, people. It has three modes – Demat, when matter is disassembled and Remat, when it is reassembled. The third mode is Elimat. It's the ultimate mode, when matter is permanently destroyed.'

'Do me a favour,' said Winslow Marsden, 'save your breath. I'm not impressed. I don't believe you have any fancy weapons. And even if you do, it's not going to disturb my slumbers. I'll tell you what is, though. The thought that a bunch of crazy vigilantes think they can run the world.'

Arthur, bitterly disappointed, had no more to say.

The President delivered a final warning. 'So here's how it's gonna be, Arthur. You will stay out of it. Understand? If you don't, me and some good friends of mine will hunt you down.' And with that, he cut the connection.

The President of Russia was as unimpressed as his US counterpart. 'My country is fighting terrorists since fifty years, and no one help us. Why now?'

'Sometime, somewhere, Mr. President,' said Arthur, 'someone has to make a stand. The real power is shifting from democratic countries to terror states. The free world is in decline. We are facing a global crisis.'

The President's face twisted in a caustic grin. 'Russia facing global crisis for a hundred years,' he said. 'Maybe more. You tell me – what has changed? And even if it has, what can you do about it? I regret, Mr. Arthur, but for me you are no one.'

'I understand your doubts,' said Arthur. 'We are, after all, only a small group of dedicated men and women, but I assure you . . . '

The President cut in. 'What means small group?'

Arthur hesitated. 'You mean soldiers?'

'What else?'

'Our active fighting force consists of a hundred and fifty soldiers,' said Arthur.

For a few moments the air waves were silent, then the President of Russia exploded into laughter. 'Hundred and fifty! Hundred and fifty!' he repeated incredulously. 'Very amusing, Mr. Arthur. Good! I like it! You make me laugh. President needs to laugh. You will save the world with hundred and fifty soldiers! Good! Excellent! Hundred and fifty!' And the Russian President threw back his head and shrieked with laughter until the tears rolled down his cheeks.

Arthur waited for him to calm down before making one last despairing effort. 'Believe me, Mr. President, we don't need huge armed forces. Our technology is much superior to yours. Our land, sea and air craft are many years ahead of their time. And our most powerful weapon . . . '

'Enough, Mr. Arthur, enough,' groaned the President. 'My belly hurts. I cannot laugh any more.' He wiped the tears from his face, all the time muttering and chuckling to himself in Russian. 'I think you well-meaning man, 'he said, hand to mouth, trying to smother mini eruptions of laughter. 'But serious – no. Not serious.'

'Let me finish.'

'Not serious.'

'Mr. President, I . . , '

Too late. The screen was blank. The President had gone.

The reaction of the President of France was just as negative. He, however, raised a different issue. 'Camelot is not a member of the United Nations. It is not even a recognised country. What right do you have to use military force against anyone?'

'The same right an individual has to defend himself if his life is threatened,' said Arthur. 'The same right a nation has. The civilised world must defend itself or die. It's as simple as that.'

The French President was not convinced. 'It is not simple at all. How are you justifying actions which are not sanctioned by the international community?'

'Our struggle is not against you, but against those who threaten the planet with chaos. I ask the free nations to accept that Camelot will only use its power justly.'

The President's eyebrows arched. 'And who, monsieur, decides what is just and what is not just?'

'We believe our cause is just,' said Arthur, 'because we are fighting not for ourselves, but for the good people of the world.'

'I assume that in this fight of yours you will consult world leaders before taking action?'

Arthur considered the artful question. 'Nothing will deter us from doing what has to be done.'

'You would take unilateral action unauthorised by the United Nations?'

Arthur hesitated. This was not going well. But he was not going to deceive anyone about Camelot's intentions. 'Whenever possible we will confer,' he said. 'But that will be our choice. The success of an operation and our own security may necessitate our acting without warning. Therefore we reserve the right to decide when to strike, where to strike, and whom to strike.'

Seeing the hostility in the French President's eyes, he knew he had lost him.

The Japanese Premier listened attentively and without interruption as Arthur first outlined Camelot's aims and ideals, then described its naval and air craft and its weapons. When Arthur had finished he had only one question: 'Do you believe that only force of arms can rid the world of terrorism?'

Arthur took his time before responding, and when he did, he spoke from the heart. 'Force can never be the only answer. It is a last resort when all other means have failed. Sadly, we have to admit that they have. To do nothing would be the very worst option. If we do not act now, it will be the wicked, not the meek, who will inherit the earth.'

The Japanese Premier nodded and smiled politely. But Arthur read in that smile what he was too courteous to say.

He had barely spoken when the President of Iran erupted angrily. Clearly he had been briefed about Camelot's intentions.

'Terrorists! Always terrorists! A meaningless word invented by the western nations to demonise the persecuted people of the world! The real terrorists are those who make war on nations whose natural resources they covet. Instead of talking nonsense, you should address the actual cause of tension in the world – the bullying of the smaller nations by the United States of America and their satellites.'

'We are dedicated to restoring order and harmony to the planet,' said Arthur mildly.

'Lies! You are a hypocrite! You are all hypocrites! You speak of order and harmony. I say you will plunge us all into global conflict!'

The Prime Minister of the United Kingdom had a strong suspicion that the island of Camelot was somewhere in the Atlantic, probably not that far from the UK. The thought made him extremely uneasy for all sorts of reasons, not least because, if he was right, any military action by or against Camelot might well spill over to the UK. 'The whole world is out there looking for you,' he said. 'And I don't just mean the terrorists. Sooner or later, someone will find you.'

Arthur explained that Camelot was permanently mantled.

'Meaning it cannot be seen?'

'More than that,' said Arthur. 'It cannot be detected. By mixing two optical beams we achieve electromagnetically induced transparency. A certain amount of heat is generated, but the infra red is dispersed so that the mantled object is undetectable, just as Kraken and all our aircraft are when they are mantled.'

'The island must be recorded on some chart.'

'Many islands have disappeared in volcanic eruptions,' said Arthur. 'That's what Camelot is believed to have done. No one looks for an island that no longer exists.'

'What if a ship ran into it?'

'If a ship were heading in our direction,' said Arthur, 'our sensors would pick it up many miles away, and we would manipulate the geo-magnetic fields. Confusing a compass is an excellent way of avoiding collisions.'

'And your communications?'

'Are secure.'

'How can you be so sure? No one can hide radio signals.'

'We don't use radio signals,' said Arthur.

'Some kind of electrical signals, then?'

'Not those either.'

The Prime Minister heaved a sigh of profound irritation. 'Stop playing games, Arthur. You have to communicate. So how do you do it?'

'We always knew the world would try to locate Camelot,'

said Arthur. 'Friends and enemies alike. So we had to find a new and totally secure method of communicating. That's what we did. We use gravitational waves – waves generated by Camelot's primary energy source – the same that powers our most powerful weapon – Excalibur. And to prevent anyone picking up vibrations, our communications, both internal and external, are decoded by Command Control, by Eclipse and Kraken, and by the miniature decoding devices every active carries.'

'You expect me to believe that load of rubbish?' demanded the UK Prime Minister rudely, cutting the connection and summoning the head of MI5 to Downing Street, confident that he would soon have Arthur where he wanted him.

'Did you trace it?'

'Did I trace what, Prime Minister?'

'Arthur's call, dammit! Did you trace it?'

The head of MI5 seemed surprised. 'I'm sorry, sir, I assumed it was cancelled.'

'Why would you assume that?'

'Because, PM, the whole of London was bristling with listening devices and we picked up nothing. We had satellites working on it too. There was no trace of any call.'

'You can be frank with me,' said the PM, flashing a spurious smile at his intelligence chief. 'Was there a cock-up?'

'We don't do cock-ups, Prime Minister.'

Pull the other one, it's got bells on, the PM was thinking, but decided not to say so. 'What's the explanation, then?'

'I'm afraid I don't have one.' At the door he turned. 'I have checked with the Americans, the Russians, the Chinese, the Japanese and the Iranians. They all spoke to Arthur, and none of them were able to trace or record their call.' A last few words slipped slyly round the door as it closed: 'If that's any consolation, sir.'

The Prime Minister thumped the desk with his fist. 'No, it bloody isn't!' he shouted angrily.

The last world leader to appear on Arthur's screen was the President of China. Because his English was limited, he was accompanied on screen by an interpreter.

'His excellency wishes to know how he can assist you.'

In the second and third decades of the 21st Century China's economy had grown fast, and the country was now the most prosperous on earth. Moreover, its huge army, navy and airforce, together with an enormous arsenal of nuclear weapons, made it, if not the greatest, then certainly the second greatest military power in the world.

'I ask the President to support Camelot in its war on terrorism,' said Arthur. 'Not with arms or weapons, but with words. For example, your support may be needed in the Security Council or the General Assembly.'

The Chinese President delivered a few, short sentences. Neither his expression nor the tone of his voice gave Arthur the slightest clue to his reaction. The interpreter nodded gravely as his master spoke.

'The President says China peaceful nation, and Chinese Government makes decisions in name of world peace.'

'Do you not consider global terrorism a threat to the security of China?' said Arthur.

The President's face remained impassive, but was there in his eyes the glimmer of a smile? The interpreter translated.

'Chinese people secure. We have Great Wall to protect us.'

'They refuse to co-operate because they don't take us seriously,' Arthur told Lancelot and Gawain.

The two young men were angry; they wanted to teach those world leaders a lesson. Lancelot suggested 'taking punitive action', as he called it, against the six powers.

Gawain ranted for a while, his face and the back of his neck bright red.

Arthur listened patiently, waiting for them to simmer down.

'Out of the question,' he said. 'We cannot turn on our friends.'

'Some friends,' said Gawain.

'We have to do something,' said Lancelot.

'I agree,' said Arthur.

'Then what do you suggest?' said Gawain.

For almost a minute Arthur stared into space, his eyes dreaming, and then a slow smile illuminated his face. 'The President of China made a little joke. He said the Chinese people were secure because they had the Great Wall to protect them.'

Lancelot saw nothing amusing in that. 'So?'

'So here's what we're going to do,' said Arthur.

Nine

A Flash of Excalibur

THE EARLY MORNING mist at the mouth of the Hudson river shrouded the Statue of Liberty. By 11 a.m. the mist was beginning to clear, unveiling first the huge granite pedestal, then slowly moving higher. As it did so, New Yorkers looking to catch their first morning glimpse of the statue itself, stared uncomprehendingly, closed their eyes, opened them, and stared again. As long as traces of mist still clung to the iconic structure, many convinced themselves that their eyes were deceiving them. But by twelve noon there was no longer any room for doubt. Something inexplicable had happened, and first a hundred, then a thousand, then a million, then a hundred million cell phones across the United States relayed the incredible story.

The Statue of Liberty had disappeared.

It was, it had to be, an ingenious trick devised by a master illusionist. Why, or how, it had been done, no one could explain. By midday, however, it had become clear that this was no illusion. The granite pedestal was there for everyone to see. The Statue of Liberty that had stood on the pedestal since 1886, was not. The disappearance of the most iconic statue in the United States of America, a symbol precious to a nation of immigrants, was reported by every newspaper, every TV channel , every radio station, not only in the US, but across the world. Who was responsible for this extraordinary theft? There was much speculation, the most popular theory being that the Russians were behind it.

At 1 p.m., New York time, a TV news channel in Chicago reported that the Statue of Liberty had been found. At first the report was not taken seriously, but in a matter of minutes current images of the statue were circulating on the internet. From the President down to the humblest US citizen the immediate reaction was naturally one of immense relief – shortly to be replaced by astonishment and outrage. For the Statue of Liberty was not in the United States. It was in Red Square, Moscow!

Within seconds, Winslow Marsden, the US President, was on the secure link to Moscow, ready to hurl abuse at his Russian counterpart. But before he could utter a word, the Secretary of State entered the Oval Office and placed a note on his desk. The President picked up the note, blinked, read it a second and again a third time, and banged down the phone, cutting off the Russian President.

'Will someone tell me what's going on?' he demanded.

'The Russian foreign minister has just been on,' said the Secretary of State. 'The statue of Lenin in October Square, Moscow, has been stolen.'

'So? Why is he calling us?'

'Because it's in New York.'

The President's eyes widened. 'What did you say?'

'It's in New York.'

'Lenin's statue?'

'Yes.'

'In New York?'

'Yes, sir.'

'Not possible.'

No response.

The President tried another approach. 'Let me get this straight.' He tried to assemble his confused thoughts. 'You say Lenin's statue is in New York?'

'That's correct, Mr. President.'

'Where in New York?'

'On the Ellis island pedestal – where the Statue of Liberty was, until it disappeared this morning.'

The President shielded his eyes with his hand. 'Tell me this is a joke,' he said.

The Secretary of State did not answer directly. Instead he picked up the remote and activated the wallscreen. There on screen was the statue of Lenin, a pigmy figure dwarfed by the pedestal of the Statue of Liberty. But Lenin none the less.

Billions of people across the world surfed the internet following these and the equally astonishing developments of the next twenty-four hours. First it was rumoured that the 1052 feet tall Eiffel Tower had disappeared, a rumour that was swiftly and categorically denied by an aide to the President at the Elysée Palace. Minutes later, the same aide was compelled to 'elaborate' on his denial, insisting that he had not misled anyone, and that it was correct to say that the Eiffel Tower had not actually disappeared. It had merely "changed its location". No longer in the centre of Paris, it had reappeared in Tehran, Iran. In its place now stood the 1427 feet high Milad Tower, the fourth highest tower in the world, which until today had stood in the centre of Tehran. How and why this exchange of monuments had come about was not clear, he admitted, but there was no cause for alarm; urgent investigations were being made, and announcements by both the President of France and the President of Iran were imminent.

In London, the sudden disruption of traffic in The Mall leading from Admiralty Arch to Buckingham Palace was thought to be some kind of political protest, until the news broke that the statue of Winston Churchill had disappeared from Parliament Square and reappeared in the centre of Tiananmen Square, Beijing. However, a swift forensic investigation of the massive jumble of masonry in The Mall revealed that what at first had appeared to come from a building site or a quarry, was in fact part of the Great Wall of China – a not inconsiderable part either – nearly thirty feet wide and almost as high. The British Government was concerned, but phlegmatic, the Chinese Government incensed, interpreting the spiriting away of a significant fragment of the Great Wall as a 'despicable act' in clear breach of international law, and the presence of the statue of the British Second World War leader in Tiananmen Square as a provocation, a crude attempt to promote insurrection against the people's government.

Less than twenty-four hours later a request appeared on a secure US website: the President wished to talk to Arthur. The necessary preparations were made, and Arthur, in the presence of Lancelot, Gawain, Leo Grant and senior advisers from the Round Table, opened the channel.

On screen, it was obvious that the President was angry. He was red-faced and breathing hard. 'Are you responsible for these idiotic tricks?'

'No,' said Arthur.

'Then who is?'

'You are, Mr. President.'

'What do you mean by that, for chrissake!'

'The last time we spoke, I gave you some indication of Camelot's power,' said Arthur. 'You didn't believe me. So I gave you a sample of what Excalibur can do. You left me no alternative.'

'I warn you, Arthur, don't mess with me.'

'You are in no position to make threats,' said Arthur. 'Any more of them, and I shall cut off all communication until you are ready to talk sensibly.'

Lancelot and Gawain grinned. They were enjoying themselves.

The President was an old campaigner. What's more, he knew whom he was dealing with. He gritted his teeth. 'What is it you want?'

'Respect,' said Arthur.

'That you have,' said Winslow Marsden, grudgingly.

'And I want you, Mr. President, to confirm unequivocally to your fellow world leaders your conviction that Camelot is fighting for the future of every man, woman and child on the planet who value peace – nothing more than that.' Arthur looked his old friend and adversary in the eye. 'Will you do that, Winslow? For all our sakes?'

'I will,' said Winslow Marsden, who knew he had little choice. 'Assuming of course that you . . . '

'All will be as before,' said Arthur.

In less than an hour, the Statue of Liberty stood on its pedestal once more, Lenin was back home in Moscow, the Eiffel Tower in Paris, the Milad Tower in Tehran, Winston Churchill presided over Parliament Square, and the breach in the Great Wall of China had been filled.

That same day, billions of people witnessed a remarkable phenomenon. In the sky above them a great sword appeared, its blade glowing so brightly that no one dared look at it longer than a split second. When the sun stood high in the heavens, the sword shone at its brightest. In the afternoon its light began to dim, and at the day's end when it sank below the horizon, the sword glowed blood red, fading at last with the dying light.

Ten

The Sea Lords

BARELY TWO WEEKS later the world was shocked by three major disasters at sea; the first, the mysterious disappearance of Ulysses Two, an American-owned container vessel, in mid-Atlantic. A brief distress call was received, a garbled message, not repeated. A search of the area revealed nothing, neither oil slick nor wreckage. No terror group claimed responsibility. An insurance fraud was suspected.

Three weeks after that, the Elysian Fields, a three-hundred-thousand ton American-owned tanker transporting crude oil from the Persian Gulf exploded in a ball of fire as it docked at an oil terminal in the Caribbean, with the loss of her entire crew and over fifty port workers. This second tragedy was believed to have been caused by a spark igniting a fuel tank, and was not thought to be linked to the disappearance of the Ulysses Two.

The third disaster occurred on the morning of July 31st when the Four Winds, a British passenger ferry, blew up in the English channel killing over two hundred people, including women and children. This time there could be no doubt. The explosion was no accident.

Within hours a message was posted on the internet.

We, the Sea Lords, acting in the name of Allah, have eliminated The Ulysses Two, the Elysian Fields and the Four Winds in response to the persecution of our brothers and sisters around the world. This time we have chosen the United States and Britain as our targets, but there will be others. In the name of hundreds of millions of our brethren, the victims of

persecution by Kafers and their allies in the Middle East, Asia, Africa, Europe, North and South America and South East Asia, we call on the imperialist powers to change their policies, or be prepared to suffer the consequences. Allahu Akbar!
Mujahid
The Sea Lords

The killing of so many innocents created worldwide revulsion. Though people had become accustomed to brutal acts of terror carried out by various groups of malcontents – Islamists, nationalists, neo-fascists and dissidents of all shades and convictions – the fact that there was another, as yet unknown, terror group, capable of such well-planned and co-ordinated murderous acts was deeply worrying. Who was Mujahid? The name was Arabic for fighter, and had obvious associations with the mujahedin in Afghanistan and elsewhere. The implication was clear – the Sea Lords were in some way associated with Al Qaeda.

With the usual exceptions, world leaders condemned the atrocities, vowing that the perpetrators would be hunted down and punished. Mossad believed that the group had links with Sadiq el Shaeb (the people's friend), the virulently anti-Western ruler of the Kingdom of the Euphrates, formerly Iraq; MI5 were convinced that Colombian drug cartels were involved; the KGB claimed to have evidence that the Sea Lords were one of many terrorist groups financed and armed by Muslim fundamentalists in three countries bordering on Russia; the CIA blamed the Iranians; the Iranians blamed Mossad and the CIA. The truth was that no one knew. The world's intelligence services were chasing shadows.

There was one question on everyone's mind; where and when would Mujahid strike next? The answer came all too soon. One week later Arthur was summoned urgently to Command Control.

At the heart of Command Control was Galaxy, a dimly lit

room, stacked to the ceiling with wall monitors, every terminal manned by aides of Techforce Ten, the ten supreme masters of cyberspace. Working in close harmony with these human wizards, the most sophisticated neural network of computers ever conceived, analysed a vast volume of data gathered round the clock by Camelot's eyes and ears: heat, light, sound and movement sensors in space, on land and sea, cameras circling the globe on static and orbiting satellites and UAV's.

In the centre of the room was a large semi-circular table, its computer monitor watched over by the presiding genius of Command Control, a plump, pasty-faced young man with shaven head and pink-tinted glasses.

'Welcome to the kingdom of the nerds,' said Agravaine, his face lighting up at the sight of his hero.

'What's up, Agro?'

'Someone has hijacked the US *Liberty*. It's one of the biggest ocean liners afloat.'

Arthur laid an affectionate hand on his nephew's shoulder and waited patiently as Agravaine's stubby, nail-bitten fingers, calloused by years of use and abuse, worried restlessly at the keyboard, searching for a lost image, challenging and harassing Techforce Ten: 'How can you lose an ocean liner for godsake!' Then, with a cry of triumph, 'Gotcha!' A bright light pulsed on the table screen as Techforce confirmed over Galaxy's speakers: *US Liberty relocated. Fourth largest liner afloat. Hundred and eighty thousand tons. Approximate number of passengers three thousand five hundred, crew approximately one thousand, seven hundred. Liner rounded Cape Horn August 1st. Present location – Indian Ocean. Destination – Sydney, Australia.*

He bounced excitedly on his stool. 'Listen to this, nuncle. We recorded it seven minutes ago.'

Over the control room's speakers a soft voice spoke in accented English.

'This is Mujahid. The US *Liberty*, its passengers and crew, are in the hands of the Sea Lords. The governments of the United

States of America and the European Commission are instructed to co-ordinate the payment of fifty billion United States dollars to accounts designated by us. In addition, three hundred and twelve heroes listed on our website, unjustly imprisoned for acts of so-called terrorism, are to be released immediately and flown by chartered aircraft to the destinations specified. Payment of the ransom and repatriation of the heroes is to be completed within forty-eight hours. I have set an exclusion zone of twenty kilometres around the US *Liberty*. Be sure that any breach of this zone, any rescue attempt or interference of any kind, will result in the immediate destruction of the US *Liberty* and everyone on board. Allahu Akbar!'

'That's it,' said Agravaine.

'I presume you have run a voice analysis?'

Agravaine nodded. 'It doesn't match any of our records. All we can say for sure is that the man is Middle-Eastern, possibly a native of Iran or the Kingdom of Euphrates.'

'Is this Mujahid on board the US *Liberty*?'

'No way of telling,' said Agravaine. 'In any case, the message was pre-recorded.'

'Can you trace the transmission?'

'We're working on it.' He did not sound hopeful.

Arthur prowled Galaxy. 'Any clues at all?'

'There is one thing,' said Agravaine. 'In the last two years the CIA have traced a number of multi-million dollar transfers to offshore banks they suspect of being fronts for the Sea Lords. When the companies making the transfers were questioned about it, they clammed up. Worse still, there's evidence that several governments are also paying off the Sea Lords.' He wiped doughnut icing sugar from his mouth and slurped a mouthful of coffee.

'Extortion,' said Arthur thoughtfully.

'Looks like it. But if it's just about money, why are they sinking ships? It doesn't make sense.'

'Terrorism is never just about money,' said Arthur. 'Money

is a means to an end.'

'Then what do they want?' asked Agravaine.

'World domination – assuming they are Islamists. They see all Muslims as victims of persecution by all non-Muslims. Their goal is a return of the Caliphate, the overthrow of secular Western democracies, and the establishment of Sharia law and the rule of mullahs on a global basis. For them and their converts – an increasing number of Muslims – this is a war to the death.'

'So you think this lot are Islamists?'

'Almost certainly,' said Arthur. 'And if they are, then we are fighting a merciless and cunning enemy. Their modus operandi is brutal but never random, their targets carefully selected, their message directed not just at America and Britain but at all those countries engaged in fighting Islamic terrorism. No one on the planet is safe. They have long term objectives and a plan of campaign, and that makes them very dangerous.'

The Great Hall's massive doors were closed by eight guardian robots, two to each double door, eight pairs of bulbous eyes winked, eight electronic voices confirmed in turn: *Doors shut and secured. Doors shut and secured. Doors shut and secured . . .*

On the table in front of Arthur lay the ceremonial sword, Excalibur, symbol of Camelot's power, signifying that the Round Table had been summoned to a council of war.

As Arthur signalled for silence, Mujahid's chilling message was played back over speakers installed at intervals around the hall.

Lancelot raised his hand. 'I propose we launch *Operation Sea Lord* without delay,' he urged.

Arthur consulted his nephew, Agravaine. 'Based on our intelligence, what are the chances of rescuing the hostages by force?'

'There are over five thousand passengers and crew on the US *Liberty*,' said Agravaine, 'most of them imprisoned on two lower decks. Obviously they are closely guarded by the terrorists, some of whom will be suicide bombers.'

'How many terrorists are there?' said Gawain.

'We estimate about fifty.'

'Can we use Excalibur to take them out?'

'Techforce Ten's analysis is that using Excalibur would be inappropriate – either in Demat and Remat, or in Elimat,' said Agravaine. 'There are simply too many targets, and the good guys and the bad guys are too close to each other.'

'Conventional weapons?'

'Same problem. We can't get near the ship without risking the hostages' lives. Techforce are picking up some chatter, and their reading is that the Sea Lords will blow it up if they are attacked. Some, if not all of them, are willing to die in the process.'

'Camelot cannot stand aside and do nothing,' said Lancelot. 'We have to rescue those people, whatever the risk.'

His words were greeted by stamping of feet and applause. Clearly he had the support of the Round Table. Arthur waited for members to calm down. 'The US and the other countries involved are hopeful they can persuade the Sea Lords to release the hostages,' he said. 'In the circumstances I suggest we await the outcome of their negotiations.'

Lancelot's frustration was shared by the majority of the Round Table. Was this not exactly the kind of crisis Camelot was created to deal with? Such was their respect for Arthur, however, that no one questioned his judgement, and it was agreed that no action would be taken until negotiations with the Sea Lords had either succeeded or broken down.

With so many passengers and crew, more than a dozen countries were involved, all of them participating in the negotiations. Every few hours Mujahid made and reneged on agreements, seeming to derive sadistic pleasure from tormenting the negotiators. When the deadline had expired and no agreement had been reached, five male and five female passengers were bound hand and foot and forced to kneel. One by one, in sight of the other hostages, they were slaughtered by a man thought to be Mujahid, who cut the women's throats, and beheaded the men slowly so that they died in agony, screaming to the end. These brutal executions were transmitted live across the globe by satellite cameras.

Within minutes Mujahid announced that he was extending the deadline by a further twelve hours, at the same time warning yet again that if his terms were not met in full, or if any attack were launched, the US *Liberty* would be destroyed, together with its passengers and crew. For the next few hours he continued to toy with the negotiators. Three hours before the expiration of the extended deadline the US President ordered his joint Chiefs of Staff to launch a rescue operation. It was the action of a desperate man, and it had tragic consequences.

Before a single ship, submarine or aircraft could get anywhere near the US *Liberty*, satellite cameras picked up a massive explosion in the Pacific. Minutes later, Mujahid's chillingly flat voice confirmed the horrifying news; the US *Liberty* had been blown up together with its passengers and crew. The blame, he said, rested entirely with the President of the United States who had, in bad faith, launched a military operation whilst negotiations were in progress.

Satellites and unmanned aircraft spotted wreckage floating in the sea; ships, submarines and aircraft rushed to the spot, and about two hundred survivors were picked up, many of them badly burned. The rest, passengers and crew, had perished – more than five thousand men, women and children – about half of them citizens of the United States, the rest from countries around the globe, amongst them, members of the European Union, Russia, South America, Japan, Korea, India, Pakistan and China. World leaders were unanimous in their condemnation of this cruel and senseless act, vowing to co-operate in hunting down and destroying whoever was responsible.

The world's leading military powers – China, Korea, the United States of America, the European Union, Russia, India and Pakistan – undertook to co-operate, their armed forces and intelligence services exchanging information on a round-the-clock basis. Satellites, ships, aircraft and unmanned vehicles scoured land and sea with one common goal – to find the terrorists, and either kill them or bring them to justice. Yet with all the sophisticated surveillance technology at their disposal, no one could find the Sea Lords. They had disappeared without trace.

Eleven

The Sea Lords

ARTHUR WAS ABOUT to leave for Command Control when the observatory door monitor crackled to life.

Name?

'Guinevere.'

In a nano-second her voice and iris were checked and approved.

Enter, Guinevere.

She put her arms round Arthur's neck and kissed him affectionately. 'Forgive me, darling, I know I shouldn't be disturbing you, but I've been hearing rumours. Is it true?'

'Camelot is at code red,' acknowledged Arthur. 'It's a party.'

Party. A macho word masking the truth, as if war really were a party, a night out with the boys.

'This one looks like being the biggest yet,' he said, an undertow of excitement in his voice.

'You won't be leading the actives, will you?' she asked anxiously.

'Afraid not.'

How like a man, she thought. How especially like Arthur. Not afraid to go to war, but afraid not to.

'Only wish I could. At thirty-four years old the Round Table tell me I'm too old to play soldiers,' said Arthur. 'Nonsense of course, but there'd be a palace revolution if I defied them, so I'm forced to leave the dangerous work to the youngsters.'

'I should think so too,' said Guinevere. 'You *are* Camelot. What if something were to happen to you?' She fiddled with her wedding ring. 'So, who . . . ?'

'Lancelot will be operational commander.'

'Lancelot?' Like a cloud passing the sun, a look of concern shadowed her face and was gone.

'No need to worry,' said Arthur, who had not missed that fleeting reaction, 'Lance can take care of himself.'

A toss of her long black hair. 'I assure you he's the last person I worry about.'

'All the same, darling, you might want to wish him luck. I'm sure he'd appreciate it if you called him.' Arthur cradled her hands in his and kissed them tenderly. 'I know I would.'

'If you wish it,' she said without enthusiasm.

'He'll be piloting Eclipse,' said Arthur. 'Great responsibility, and perhaps great danger too.'

Danger. For the first time in her life she was afraid. Almost everyone in the world lived with the threat of danger every day of their lives, especially in these demented times. Somehow, this was different though. With no thought of the consequences, she had exchanged the relative security of life in London for a life of danger, not just for the actives, but for Arthur, for her, for all of them. No longer could she take tranquillity and peace of mind for granted. Like a child she snuggled up to her husband for comfort, and he held her close.

Lancelot's A.D.C. buzzed him in his office in Command Control. 'The governor's wife would like a word with you, sir.'

Guinevere? What could she want? 'Put her on.'

For several seconds he waited on the line listening to her breathing.

'I just wanted to wish you luck,' she said at last.

'Good of you,' he murmured.

'Arthur . . . he, um . . . he thought . . . ' She ran out of words.

Message received and understood. She was comforting the troops, playing First Lady on hubby's orders. 'Thanks,' he said.

'Well then, goodbye . . . take care,' she said and cut the line.

In a matter of minutes the brief exchange was erased from

his mind; except for that final *take care*. For some reason those two words stuck.

As the sun set, Eclipse lifted off from the launch pad and Kraken slipped from its pen into the Atlantic ocean. Eclipse, captained by Lancelot, carried its standard complement of miniature unmanned space vehicles, surveillance, tracker and destroyer robots, together with two Scuttles and two troops of actives. Kraken, captained by Gawain, had a similar load of robots and UAV's, Sea Scuttles and actives, plus some high-tech equipment unique to Kraken. Supported by an umbrella of fixed and orbiting satellites and twenty roving UAV's, the two craft hunted for the Sea Lords.

After two days, they had found nothing.

Tuning in on Arthur's screen Agravaine looked tired and depressed. 'We have robots on standby, fixed satellites, roving satellites, UAV's, a thousand sensors – visual, aural, heat, light, movement, smell, you name it. If we had a sample of Mujahid's fart, we would have tracked him down by now, but we have nothing on him at all. And to top it all,' he moaned, 'Galaxy has run out of coffee and doughnuts.'

'Any hope of monitoring his communications?'

'Neural Network and Techforce Ten are keeping a twenty-four hour watch on the internet, and on radio, landline and cellphone communications. It's a mountain of input to handle, but we're doing our best.'

'How long will it take to locate him?'

'Sorry, nuncle, no can say. Mujahid knows when to strike and when to hide. Right now, he's hiding. How long for? There's no way of telling.'

'The Sea Lords must have a base somewhere,' said Arthur. 'Sooner or later we'll find them.'

Agravaine eased off his pink-tinted glasses, scratched his bald head five times on one side, five times on the other, and one more time on either side for luck. 'If they don't find us first,' he said, rubbing his tired eyes.

Arthur's eyes widened. 'What was that?'

'Did I say something wrong?'

'On the contrary,' said Arthur. And then, to Agravaine's surprise, his uncle said abruptly, 'Order Eclipse and Kraken back to Camelot.'

'But they're our only chance of finding the Sea Lords,' protested Agravaine.

'Do as I say.' It was a command.

Shaking his head gloomily, Agravaine thumped his keyboard. Arthur had obviously lost it. Who would have thought he would crack under pressure?

When the eight Guardian Robots had confirmed that the doors of the Great Hall were *shut and secured*, the hum of conversation died suddenly as Arthur began to speak.

'After discussions, the leaders of all the countries directly involved in this tragedy have reached a unanimous conclusion. From midnight tonight they will suspend the hunt for the Sea Lords for seven days.'

Incredulous looks greeted this statement. 'As a condition of that agreement,' continued Arthur, unruffled, 'I have undertaken that before the seven days are up, Camelot's armed forces will have located and destroyed the Sea Lords.'

Breaking the baffled silence, Leo Grant, the much respected Chief Justice of Camelot's High Court, Arthur's close friend, political mentor and father-in-law, expressed what almost every member of the Round Table was thinking. 'I am sorry, Arthur, but I fail to understand how you could possibly have given such an undertaking – especially now you have ordered Eclipse and Kraken back to base. What makes you so certain we shall find the Sea Lords?'

'I am not at all certain,' said Arthur. 'In fact I'm convinced we won't find them.'

Leo was now totally confused. 'Perhaps I am missing

something here,' he said, 'but if you are sure we won't find them, what is the point of looking for them?'

'No point at all,' said Arthur, the corners of his mouth twitching.

Suggestive glances were exchanged, harsh words muttered. Everyone was thinking the same thing; Arthur was making no sense. Had his mind been temporarily overwhelmed by the strain of the crisis and the harsh demands of decision-making?

'If we don't go looking for the Sea Lords,' rumbled George Bedivere, 'then how in hell do we find them?'

'We don't,' said Arthur. 'We let them find us.'

Twelve

The Sea Lords

IN THE SOUTH ATLANTIC the mv *Teal.com*, a cargo ship carrying gold bullion from South Africa to the Eastern Seaboard of the United States, drifted helplessly, its engines crippled by a fire the crew had fought for half a day before putting it out. A rescue ship was scheduled to reach Teal.com in a matter of hours to evacuate the vessel's crew and cargo, (said to be worth more than two billion US dollars at the current price of gold of approximately three thousand dollars an ounce), leaving a small team of specialists on board to attempt at least a partial repair of the ship's engines.

About two hours before the rescue ship's ETA, a gunboat raced to the scene, throttling back on a bed of white foam two hundred metres from the cargo ship. Minutes later a second gunboat pulled up half a kilometre away. Both boats flew the South African flag. A few hundred metres from the mv *Teal.com* a submarine's periscope pierced the surface of the sea.

Mujahid whistled under his breath. 'Can't make out the name.' He stood aside for his first mate. 'Take a look, Ahmed.'

'*Teal.com* – that's her,' said the first mate.

'Unusual name.'

'The owner's website?'

'Could be,' said Mujahid. 'She's flying a South African flag, but that means nothing. Call her up on the radio, ask if they want our help.'

Thirty seconds later. 'No reply.'

'Keep trying,' ordered Mujahid.

A full minute passed. 'Still no reply.'

A long look through the periscope. 'No sign of life. Where's the crew?'

'Could be working on the engines,' said Ahmed. 'Or just staying out of sight. You don't think they're afraid someone might steal their cargo?'

Mujahid acknowledged the witticism with a dry chuckle. 'Any more responses to the SOS?'

The first mate checked with the radio operator. 'Only the ship we heard, and she won't be here for a couple of hours. There's no danger to life, so no one's hurrying.'

Mujahid lowered the periscope. 'Get me Kassim.'

Ahmed handed him the radio phone. 'Kassim on the line, sir.'

'Kassim, there's someone on that ship,' said Mujahid. 'Try to raise them. Tell them we've brought a team of engineers to repair the ship's engines, that should do it. Ask for permission to board. Do it politely. Don't scare them. Clear?'

'Yes, sir.'

A few minutes later Kassim, captain of the gunboat nearest the mv *Teal.com*, was back on line. 'They're not responding.'

Mujahid was puzzled. 'You think they've abandoned ship?'

'And risk losing the ship and the cargo to the first comer?' said Ahmed. 'No, there has to be someone on board.'

Being defied made Mujahid fretful. 'Here's what you do, Kassim. Tell them if they don't respond immediately to our calls, they'll be boarded by armed men, and that any resistance will be met with force.'

'Very good, sir.'

Two minutes passed slowly. Kassim was on speaker. 'Still no response, sir.'

'Tell Mohammed to scramble the helicopter,' Mujahid told Ahmed. 'We'll take a closer look.'

As the two gunboats circled the mv *Teal.com*, the submarine surfaced and Mujahid stood in the open conning tower observing the cargo ship through binoculars. From the deck of the nearest gunboat a helicopter lifted off and hovered over the cargo ship. The pilot's voice crackled over the intercom. 'No sign of life.'

Mujahid called down to radio control: 'Check mv *Teal.com* in Lloyds' Shipping Register.'

Seconds later the reply came. 'Not listed, sir.'

Mujahid looked at his first mate. 'Odd, isn't it?'

'Could be a recent name change.'

Mujahid grunted. 'Check the *Teal.com* for signs of fire damage,' he told the helicopter pilot.

The helicopter banked, flew round the ship, banked again and did a second run twenty feet above the deck. 'No indication of fire damage,' reported the pilot.

Mujahid was growing increasingly uneasy. 'It doesn't make sense.'

'The fire was in the engine room,' the pilot pointed out. 'It might not have spread to the decks.'

Mujahid was not convinced. No response on the radio, no indication of fire damage, no sign of the crew. Even if they were scared, he would have thought they would at least make their presence known. Through his binoculars he searched the ship from stem to stern and back again. No sign of life, no movement at all apart from the slow rhythmic rock of the vessel in the wakes of the circling gunboats. He ordered the helicopter back to the gunboat.

Mid-afternoon. A low bank of cloud moved across the sun. The only sound was the lapping of the sea against the submarine's flanks. It was quiet, almost too quiet, thought Mujahid. He lifted his head like an animal sniffing the air for danger. An abandoned ship with a two billion dollar cargo of gold . . . was it too good to be true? Was he walking into a trap? But who was there to trap him? No one. Radar had picked up neither military aircraft nor ships of any kind anywhere in the vicinity. Yet again he checked with radio control. 'Position of rescue ship?'

'Approximately one hour, forty-five minutes away, sir.'

'Still no response from *Teal.com*?'

'Nothing, sir. Wait a minute. They're acknowledging our call! No, they're not, they're asking the rescue ship to speed up. They're saying it's an emergency.'

Mujahid punched the air in triumph. 'They've given themselves away. At least we know the crew is on that ship.'

'But what's the emergency?' said Ahmed.

Mujahid chuckled. He was beginning to enjoy himself. 'We are. They don't believe our story, which explains why they won't talk to us. They're scared.' He made a rapid assessment of the situation. The advantage of surprise was lost, but that was of little consequence. What could a defenceless cargo ship do against the mighty Sea Lords? At least now he knew what he was dealing with – not a trap – just a frightened crew. There was no time to lose. He intended to be well away with the gold bullion before the rescue ship arrived. He issued his orders briskly and clearly. The submarine's gun crew made ready. Through the loudhailer he issued a crisp ultimatum to the cargo ship. 'I want every member of your crew on deck with his hands raised. You have one minute.'

The seconds ticked by – a full minute – and not a single member of mv *Teal.com*'s crew had appeared. Either they were very brave or very foolish. Mujahid signalled the gun commander, and the submarine fired a salvo across the ship's bows. He waited for the echoes to die away. Still no reaction. 'They are dead men,' he muttered savagely, 'every one of them.'

The helicopter gunboat captained by Kassim stood off a few hundred metres from the mv *Teal.com* whilst the second gunboat captained by Mohammed picked up Mujahid from the submarine, edged cautiously forward and drew alongside the cargo ship. A dozen men armed with laser guns and carrying explosive charges boarded the mv *Teal.com* and searched the vessel, Mujahid remaining on deck, automatic weapon in hand. A few minutes later the men climbed back on deck. There was no one down below. The ship was deserted. If Mujahid was puzzled, his men, increasingly jittery, were beginning to ask questions he was unable to answer. If there was no one on board, who had sent the SOS messages? And who had spoken to the rescue ship barely five minutes ago? Scared looks and mutterings of a "ghost ship" angered Mujahid who ridiculed his men for being superstitious wimps – though even he had to admit to himself that it was a mystery. Where were the crew? They had to be on board the mv *Teal.com*. Where else could they be? He ordered his men to search the ship again.

One of the boarding party appeared on deck, followed by another and another, all of them shouting and beckoning to Mujahid to come below. What were they so excited about? Had they found the crew? No. Something much better. In a dark corner of the cargo hold they had stumbled on several wooden crates marked 'Product of South Africa'. Grinning triumphantly Mujahid rushed down the stairs after them.

'That one there. Open it!' Prized open with a jemmy, the lid fell back to reveal a white plastic sheet. Pulling back the cover with a flourish Mujahid revealed the contents – OUTSPAN ORANGES. For a moment or two his mind was blank, then, galvanised afresh, he scrabbled frenetically in the crate, hurling oranges in all directions, convinced that somewhere underneath them was the gold.

But there was no gold, at least not in that crate, only oranges, and yet more oranges. Lights flashed in front of Mujahid's eyes, shooting pains stabbed his head. Seeing his men standing idly by, not knowing what was expected of them, he startled them into action. 'Get back to work! Open all the crates!'

The lids of another four crates were jemmied off, and now there were oranges everywhere, splattered on the walls and trampled on the floor, until the hold and the men in it reeked of the smell of oranges. When the crates were empty, the men stood around, red-faced, resentful and baffled, looking accusingly at Mujahid. They did not like being tricked, nor did they expect their leader to fall for tricks, unless of course it was *he* who was tricking *them*.

He sensed danger. The look on his men's faces and the attitude of their bodies threatened violence. He was taking no chances. 'Everyone on deck,' he snapped. Accustomed to obeying orders and to fearsome punishments if they did not, the crew hesitated for only a few surly seconds before backing away and climbing on deck.

Though he was jittery, Mujahid was too clever to show it. Had he walked into a carefully laid trap? The gunboat sped him back to the submarine, leaving behind the twelve man boarding party to set the explosive charges below deck in preparation for scuttling the mv *Teal.com*, now rocking gently in a sea stirred by a moderate west wind. As he levelled his binoculars for one last look at the ship, something strange caught his attention.

The South African flag had been lowered and a new flag now flew from the mast, one he could not immediately identify as it flapped and rolled in the wind. Just for a second it unfurled and there it was; a hand drawing a sword from a stone. Mujahid frowned. Where had he seen that image before? Whose flag was it? He checked the name on the side of the ship's prow: the mv *Teal.com*. But even as he murmured the name aloud as if to reassure himself, the letters jumbled, rearranged themselves, and the ship's name was no longer the mv *Teal.com*. Mumbling fearfully, his hands trembling, Mujahid focused and refocused the binoculars. There was no doubt. The cargo ship's name was now the mv *Camelot*.

Camelot? . . . Camelot? . . . The name rang a bell . . . of course! The Sword in the Sky! **Arthur!** A sharp pang of fear knifed Mujahid's stomach. Sliding down the ladder he yelled 'Dive! Dive! Dive!' When the submarine was forty metres below the surface he ordered Mohammed, captain of the helicopter gunboat, to circle the cargo ship while the second gunboat stood by waiting to evacuate the twelve man boarding party. Not yet, though. That sudden change of name needed explaining.

More than an hour passed, and still no sign of life on the mv *Camelot*. The submarine inched cautiously up to periscope depth. 'Up periscope.' Mujahid studied every inch of the ship. No change there. The Sea Lords' boarding party seemed relaxed. Then suddenly the crew of the second gunboat were shouting and pointing. 'What are they getting excited about?' he asked Ahmed. 'I can't see anything. You take a look.'

Ahmed peered through the periscope. 'They're pointing at the gunboat. No, they're not – they're pointing at something in the water.'

Even as he spoke, the lookout on Kassim's gunboat spotted a streamlined shape heading towards him at speed and yelled a warning, realising at the last moment to his enormous relief that what he had feared might be a torpedo was in fact a whale. The great mammal stopped dead by the gunboat's stern, spouted and submerged. The captain was about to order full speed ahead when the whale resurfaced, this time barely a few metres from the gunboat's bow. With a quick burst of its starboard motor the boat swung to port to avoid it, but again, dead ahead, there was the whale. Two more swift evasive manoeuvres, and each time the whale moved to block the gunboat's path. It was a stand-off. Uncertain what to do, Kassim decided to await the whale's next manoeuvre.

Slowly, with majestic grace, the whale rolled three hundred and sixty degrees and swam away from the gunboat until it was two hundred metres off the port bow. Again it stopped, the upper third of its massive body above the surface of the ocean. Having more serious matters on his mind, Kassim was in no mood to play games with whales. This particular one was proving to be a nuisance. He gave the order to fire, but, even as he did so, the whale closed swiftly on the gunboat and the guns were useless. Where was it now? How could such a huge beast disappear so quickly?

'What happened to it?' he asked his first mate.

'Can't see it, sir.'

The boat started to rock violently. Kassim, the first mate, and the whole crew were thrown to the deck. In those petrifying moments they were helpless. There was nothing to be done but hold tight and pray that the whale would lose interest. Then, as abruptly as it started, the rocking stopped. Kassim staggered to the boat's rail, but there was nothing to be seen but the lowering clouds, the grey sea and the white crested waves tossed by the rising west wind.

And then, a hundred metres off the starboard bow, the whale heaved out of the ocean, uttered a strange, rumbling call and dived out of sight. What did it signify, that sound? Was it a warning to leave the area? Or a threat that it was about to attack again? Kassim was not waiting to find out.

'Fire at will!' he yelled.

Before the gunners could align their sights, the whale was racing towards the gunboat again, and this time it did not stop. A violent impact on the port side sent the boat heeling over at such an acute angle that its starboard rail dipped in the sea. Three of the crew were hurled overboard, the rest clung desperately to ropes and rails, muscles straining, gaping mouths screaming in terror. As the waves washed over the deck, it seemed that the gunboat must surely capsize. Then, slowly, it righted itself. The whale was nowhere to be seen. A full minute passed, the tension on board easing as the seconds ticked away. But just when it seemed that the whale had finally lost interest, it resurfaced fifty metres away and headed at speed for the gunboat. A second massive impact on the starboard side, and the boat was holed below the waterline.

'Abandon ship!' shouted Kassim.

The crew hesitated, fearful of the whale, but the choice was clear; either jump in the sea and take their chances, or risk being dragged to the seabed with the doomed gunboat. In seconds, captain and crew were swimming frantically towards the helicopter gunboat now speeding in their direction. A few hundred metres away the whale resurfaced. Treading water, captain and crew watched in horror as the huge mammal streaked towards the stricken vessel ramming it amidships. In seconds the gunboat had slipped below the surface leaving only wooden spars and a few lifebelts bobbing on the surface. The whale continued to circle, moving closer and closer to the survivors floundering in the water. As they cried out in terror it dived and resurfaced more than a hundred metres away. Once, twice, a third time it spouted, slapped the water with its huge tail and disappeared.

The helicopter gunboat picked up Kassim and fourteen survivors of the twenty-five man crew and circled the area at speed, weaving from side to side to present a more elusive target for the whale.

Having observed these extraordinary events through the periscope, Mujahid was convinced that technology, not nature, was responsible for the whale. He had walked into a trap and lost one of his gunboats and a number of his men. What were his options now?

The first was to fight his way out, inflicting as much damage on the enemy as possible. Yet how did you fight someone you could neither see nor hear? And how did you deal with technology as sophisticated as Camelot's? The second option was to get the hell out of it and live to fight another day. That had to be the option of preference; and if he were to make it back to base, there was no time to be lost. True, twelve of his men were still on the mv *Camelot* and sooner or later would be captured. Rescue, however, would involve considerable risk. The helicopter was too small to lift off twelve men. That meant at least two trips, and hovering over the cargo ship it would present an easy target. The only alternative would be for the gunboat to draw alongside mv *Camelot*, no doubt a speedier way to rescue the boarding party, but still a tempting target for the whale – or whatever else was out there.

He gave Ahmed the order: 'Tell Mohammed to return to base immediately.'

'What about the boarding party, sir? Shouldn't they pick them up first?'

Mujahid avoided his first mate's eyes. 'Do as I say.'

Through the periscope he watched the gunboat accelerating away leaving a double wake behind it. The two missiles struck it at precisely the same moment, one on the port, one on the starboard side. Rising several feet out of the water, boat and helicopter seemed to hang suspended in the air for a split second before exploding in a fireball. The steep walls of the gunboat's wake crumbled on the ocean, and an ominous cloud of dust and spray billowed high into the air.

Beneath the surface Mujahid's crew felt the impact of the explosion, the sound muffled by the ocean. When he told them what had happened, their faces remained impassive. Hard to tell what they were thinking, though he guessed from the looks they exchanged that they were losing confidence in him. Too many things were going wrong. He would have to be very careful.

What to do now? It would be foolish to put the submarine in danger searching for survivors of the helicopter gunboat's crew, or – whatever his first mate's scruples – taking off the boarding party from the mv *Camelot*. The only sensible course of action was to get the hell out of it. Or was it? A disturbing thought occurred to him. If, as seemed likely, his men on the mv *Camelot* were taken prisoner, would they not talk to save their skins? And if they did, Arthur would learn many things, including the location of the Sea Lords' base.

In Galaxy, at the heart of Command Control, Arthur and Agravaine pored over the big table monitor. Half a kilometre from mv *Camelot*, at a depth of forty-five metres, Kraken lay mantled. Ten thousand feet above, Eclipse circled, silent, invisible.

'Mujahid's position, Lance?'

'Moving in north-easterly direction. Shall I track him?'

'That's affirmative,' confirmed Arthur.

'Is he heading back to base?'

'It looks like it,' said Arthur. 'I'm relying on you, Lance. Watch him carefully, and keep the gravitational link open. Do you copy?'

'I copy,' said Lancelot.

'You think he might double back on his tracks and try to rescue the boarding party?' said Agravaine.

'It's possible,' said Arthur. 'Or he might feel it's too risky. Which reminds me, how long before the rescue ship arrives?'

Gawain responded from Kraken. 'Approximately thirty minutes sailing time from mv *Camelot*.'

'I want everything cleaned up before it gets there,' said Arthur. 'Recall the whale, launch Sea Scuttle and pick up the Sea Lords' boarding party. I doubt they'll give you any trouble, Gawain, but be prepared. You copy?'

'I copy,' said Gawain.

Gulping black coffee and wiping his brow, Agravaine fidgeted incessantly, shifting the position of the plastic cups and tissue boxes littering the centre table in an endlessly abortive effort to align them to his satisfaction.

Arthur checked on screen data every few seconds. Something was bothering him, though exactly what, he didn't know. 'Lance, let's have an update on Mujahid.'

'Now heading north-east at a depth of thirty metres . . . changing course frequently. You think he knows we're tracking him?'

'I don't see how,' said Agravaine. 'Evasive action is probably standard procedure.'

'Whatever you do,' said Arthur, 'don't lose him. He's tricky.'

On the table monitor Arthur and Agravaine watched the Sea Scuttle draw alongside the cargo ship. Three actives armed with portables climbed on board and fixed a rope ladder. One waited by the gunwale, the other two advanced on the Sea Lords cowering on deck not knowing whether they were about to be taken prisoner or slaughtered. As the actives herded them to the ship's side, down the ladder and into Sea Scuttle, Lancelot's agitated voice broke in from Eclipse: 'Contact lost! Mujahid loose!'

'Recall Sea Scuttle!' yelled Arthur.

The gravitational waves were silent . . . then a sudden shout of alarm from Gawain on Kraken. 'Torpedoes running!'

'Elimat! Elimat!' cried Arthur. Too late. Even as he shouted, the first torpedo hit mv *Camelot*, then a second and a third, and the cargo ship and the Sea Scuttle alongside it were enveloped in a ball of fire. Moments later the scene was obscured by a dust cloud of debris that swelled to a monstrous balloon and fanned out under the low canopy of cloud. Arthur's sombre voice raised Kraken: 'Gawain, pick up survivors.'

'I'm sorry, Arthur,' said Lancelot. 'I lost him. It's my fault.'

'It's no one's fault,' said Arthur. 'This is war. Relocate Mujahid. He'll run for home now.'

Tears welled in Agravaine's eyes. 'He even killed his own men. It doesn't make sense.'

'I'm afraid it does,' said Arthur. 'If they had fallen into our hands they would have talked, and that was a risk he was not prepared to take. For him the end justifies everything, including murdering his own. I've been a fool. What he did was entirely predictable. I should have foreseen it.'

Agravaine laid a hand on Arthur's arm. 'So should I, nuncle. And Lance shouldn't have let Mujahid give him the slip.'

True enough, thought Arthur, but he was Camelot's leader and that made him responsible for the deaths of all those men – his own three actives, and eleven Sea Lords. Had not Merlin taught him when he was a boy to imagine himself into the heads of birds and animals and people so that he could think like them, act like them, *be* them? It was a gift he had squandered. He would not do so again.

A second Sea Scuttle searched for survivors. Arthur and Agravaine waited anxiously for Gawain's report. In a few minutes it came. 'Eight bodies recovered – five Sea Lords, and our three actives.'

It was a bitter blow. Arthur knew the three men well, and he knew their families. No words of his could compensate them for the loss of sons and husbands.

'No survivors?'

'No, sir.'

For a long time he sat with head in hands. A voice whispered in his ear – Merlin's voice: 'The power is yours, Arthur.' It was what he needed to hear. There was work to be done. His doubts forgotten, he gave his orders: 'Leave the area, Gawain. Before you do, remove all floating oil and debris. It's essential to leave no clues. You copy?'

'I copy, sir.' A discreet cough. 'And then?'

'Join Eclipse in the hunt. Find Mujahid and bring him back.'

Gawain was happy. 'Yes, sir!'

Several minutes passed with no further communication from Eclipse, then Lancelot's voice was on speaker, calm but with an undercurrent of excitement. 'Relocated Mujahid heading north-east, depth fifty metres.'

'Keep tracking,' said Arthur. 'Remind you – our primary target remains the Sea Lords' base.'

When the rescue ship arrived a few minutes later, there was no cargo ship, no engines to repair, no crew to take off. A thorough search of the area revealed no oil slicks, no floating debris, nothing. The mv *Teal.com*, if ever there were such a vessel, had disappeared without trace. It was thought that either there had been some as yet unexplained disaster, or the SOS call had been a foolish and irresponsible hoax.

Thirteen

The Sea Lords

A S THE SUN SET, the Sea Lords' submarine rounded the Cape of Good Hope and headed into the Indian Ocean, all the time maintaining radio silence. On Command Control's big table monitor a mini-image of the submarine pulsed together with a constant stream of data transmitted by Eclipse and Kraken. From time to time the sub made minor adjustments to its course, speed and depth, and based on an analysis of these adjustments by Neural Network, the forecast of the submarine's destination was regularly updated. Though it was too early to be certain, it appeared to be on course for the east coast of Madagascar, its final destination either Pakistan, India, or the Persian Gulf, with the east coast of Africa a possibility that could not be excluded.

The sea lanes in the Indian Ocean were crowded with the usual complement of commercial shipping. There was also one passenger ship. When the sun rose the following morning, the two hundred and twenty thousand ton *Crystal Splendour*, largest ocean liner in the world, Chinese built, American owned, was approximately one thousand kilometres south of the Seychelles, heading south towards Capetown.

Shadowed by Kraken, Mujahid closed in. In less than an hour, submarine and liner would pass each other north of Mauritius. Would they pass without incident? Or did Mujahid have something else in mind? Kraken and Eclipse were on their highest state of alert. Tension mounted as submarine and liner moved closer, then relaxed, as the submarine, now at a depth of sixty metres, passed under the liner and continued north in the direction of the Arabian Sea.

A brief message from Gawain on speaker: 'Well, that's it. Either Mujahid isn't interested, or he doesn't know the liner is there.'

'He knows it's there,' said Agravaine. 'The sub's passive sonar would have picked up the sound of the liner's engines.'

'Which means he's anxious to return to base as soon as possible,' said Arthur.

As if in confirmation, Gawain reported from Kraken, 'Submarine now moving at over twenty knots.'

It was good news, though Arthur was taking no chances. 'Kraken and Eclipse, continue tracking Mujahid and remain on red alert,' he ordered.

Agravaine, hunched over his keyboard, was unusually quiet, and so focused, Arthur noticed, that he had left his latest cup of coffee untouched. His right leg, normally bouncing on the ball of his foot, was still. Even his pink-tinted lenses remained unwiped. Once, he spoke for several minutes to Gawain, then, briefly, to Kraken's robot controller.

'What are you up to?' asked Arthur, half lost in his own thoughts.

A casual response: 'Routine stuff.'

On edge a few minutes ago, Arthur began to relax.

It was an hour after sunrise, a clear bright morning with not a cloud in the sky. On the decks of the great liner early risers strolled or jogged or relaxed on deckchairs. A few hung over the ship's rails to watch a shoal of silver fish trailing the ship, no doubt hoping to be fed.

In spite of all the coffee he had drunk in the last twenty-four hours, Agravaine was having difficulty keeping his eyes open. Every minute or so his chin touched his chest and he was asleep on his stool, only to wake moments later with a start.

Arthur patted his shoulder. 'Get some rest, Agro.'

'I will.' Making no move.

'Now, Agro. You need some shut-eye. I'll cover.'

'OK, maybe I'll grab forty winks.' In seconds Agravaine was snoring loudly, flat on his back on a makeshift bunk-bed in a far corner of Galaxy. Arthur sat at the table monitor, he too struggling against sleep, eyes glazing over, head drooping. It had been a long and stressful vigil.

Galaxy's speakers blared: *Torpedoes running! Torpedoes running! Torpedoes running!*

Arthur jerked wide awake, Agravaine leaped from his bunk. The table monitor and several wall screens displayed the live action that followed. Two torpedoes sped through the water towards the liner's starboard flank. Passengers leaning over the ship's rails were the first to see them, some too terrified to cry out, others yelling a warning, though there was nothing anyone could do. It was too late for evasive action. The missiles were now less than two hundred metres from the liner and closing fast. In seconds they would hit it amidships.

No one on the liner who saw what happened would ever completely understand it. In the ocean there was a blinding flash of sunlight on silver as a shoal of fish darted from the liner's stern to its starboard side forming a shining shield of fish between the ship and the advancing missiles. Almost instantly, first one, then a second torpedo exploded harmlessly thirty metres from the liner. When the water subsided, the fish were nowhere to be seen.

Whatever the explanation for the extraordinary phenomenon they had just witnessed, it was clear to those who had seen it that somehow the fish had saved their lives, and in doing so had presumably lost their own. From the liner's rails the mesmerised passengers saw four steel barrels leap from the water, hang for a split second in the air and fall back into the sea. A moment's silence was followed in quick succession by four muffled explosions as four spouts of water erupted from the ocean and quickly subsided. Four circles of white foam spread wider and wider, merging into one big circle that slowly dispersed. 'Stun bombs dropped,' reported Gawain from Kraken. A few seconds later Techforce Ten reported: 'Submarine's engines stopped.'

'Any communication from Mujahid?' asked Arthur.

'He won't be able to communicate anything for a while, sir,' said Gawain. 'Nor will anyone else on board the sub. I doubt they can even move.'

Hundreds of passengers and crew rushed to the liner's rails. For a minute or two there was nothing to be seen but a few shreds of foam swirling on the water. Then a dark sinister shape broke the surface – the prow of a submarine, followed by the conning tower and finally the stern. An ungainly looking craft appeared from nowhere fifty metres away and manoeuvred alongside the submarine. Three men in dark blue uniforms with gold insignias on their chests jumped onto the deck, forced open the conning tower and disappeared into the submarine.

The first man to appear was unshaven, barrel-chested and muscular, wearing a black T-shirt and calf-length camouflage trousers.

'That's got to be him,' said Agravaine, hunched over the table screen, watching as the man was helped from the conning tower down to the listing submarine's deck by one of the actives. 'He's still groggy from the stun bombs.'

One by one, the submarine's crew, walking unsteadily, were transferred to Sea Scuttle. When the transfer was complete, Sea Scuttle moved slowly away, stopping at precisely the spot where it had first surfaced. As the water around it foamed and frothed, the craft slowly sank, until finally it disappeared.

Gawain was on screen again. 'Scuttle back in pen. Submarine's crew and Mujahid also on board,' he said, sounding like a man contented with life. 'Awaiting orders.'

Arthur beamed. 'Outstanding job, Gawain.'

'It wasn't me who saved the Crystal Splendour,' said Gawain.

'Come now,' said Arthur, 'don't be so modest.'

'It's a fact. The credit belongs to Agro. He told me to mobilise the silver fish as a precaution.'

Suddenly Arthur remembered. 'You spoke to Kraken, Agro,' he said, 'just before you took a nap. You said it was routine stuff.'

'So it was, nuncle,' said Agravaine.

'Far from it, Agro,' said Arthur. 'I salute you.'

'The man's a hero,' said Gawain.

Agravaine blushed crimson. Arthur had praised him. And Gawain too. And no doubt Lancelot, who always looked at him as though he were something dragged in by the cat – no doubt he too would hear about it. A wave of happiness and pride surged in his chest.

'Excalibur charged,' said Gawain. 'Permission to Elimat the submarine?'

Gawain was right. The submarine had to be destroyed. The question was how. Every second of the *Crystal Splendour* incident would in due course be transmitted to a global audience. Yet if they used Elimat to destroy the submarine, it would simply disappear, and people might not understand what had happened to it. 'No,' said Arthur, not Elimat. Let's give the world a show to remember.'

A few minutes later an enormous explosion lifted the submarine clean out of the water. As it blew apart in mid-air, a stream of liquid fire climbed the sky, revealing as it fell back a great sword, its blade glowing so brightly that no one dared look at it longer than a split second. When the sun stood high in the heavens, the sword shone at its brightest. In the afternoon its light began to dim, and at the day's end, as the sun sank below the horizon, the sword glowed blood red, fading with the dying light.

This extraordinary phenomenon was witnessed not just by the passengers and crew of the *Crystal Splendour*, but by billions of people across the globe. Some had cause to fear the sword, some believed it was an evil portent, most saw it as a sign of hope for the future, a pledge to the world that Camelot had both the will and the power to do what needed to be done to save mankind.

And the name on everyone's lips was Arthur.

Fourteen

The Sea Lords

AN HOUR AFTER the successful completion of Operation Sea Lord, the Prime Minister of the United Kingdom was on screen.

'My heartiest congratulations, Arthur. I don't have the full details yet, but I have seen all those amazing pictures on the internet. It seems you have destroyed the Sea Lords.'

'We have destroyed them as a fighting force,' said Arthur. 'We have not located and destroyed their home base.'

'Nevertheless, Britain is in your debt. The whole world is. On behalf of His Majesty's Government and the British people I offer you my sincere thanks. Is there anything we can do to help?'

'There is,' said Arthur promptly. 'We have taken a number of prisoners.'

'Prisoners?' The PM's nose convulsed, as though assaulted by a particularly offensive odour from a polluted drain.

'Fifty-two in all,' said Arthur, apparently oblivious to the PM's suffering. 'Including their leader, Mujahid.'

Guessing what was coming, the PM wished he had not so rashly offered his help.

'We shall be handing over about twenty prisoners to you, and the rest to the United States, including Mujahid. I am certain the President will be more than happy to put him on trial.'

The Prime Minister sighed. 'I imagine so. Though it does seem such a shameful waste of time and money,' A beam of a smile clicked on and off. 'Of course, no one actually *knows* that any of the terrorists survived, do they – apart from us, that is.' A sly look. 'What I'm suggesting,' the PM explained, in case Arthur had not grasped his message, 'is that you could – well – *deal* with them yourself, and no one would be the wiser.' A Prime Ministerial eyebrow cocked suggestively. 'Could you not?'

'We have only a very small prison in Camelot,' said Arthur.

'I had something else in mind,' said the PM, an insinuation accompanied by a grotesquely broad wink.

'You are suggesting that I murder the prisoners?'

The PM looked pained. 'Murder is not the word I would use. Murder is what terrorists commit.'

'All the more reason we should not sink to their level,' said Arthur. 'And why are you so reluctant to accept your share of prisoners? You would undoubtedly obtain useful intelligence from them which would help you in the fight against terrorism.'

'To tell you the truth, Arthur,' confessed the PM, 'we have more than enough intelligence already; a great deal more than we can handle.'

Arthur's blue eyes were cold. 'These men have murdered innocent British citizens. They have committed crimes against humanity. They must be brought to trial, and, if found guilty, punished.'

The PM's face betrayed his irritation. 'All very well for you to take that line, Arthur. Camelot is not a target, at least not yet,' he added ominously. 'The United Kingdom, on the other hand, is a target for a whole bunch of maniacs. If we convict and imprison these men we would face a wave of suicide bombings, hostage taking, and God knows what else.'

'No one said fighting terrorists was easy,' said Arthur. 'We have to hunt them down and kill or capture them. Those we take alive must be punished. If we fail to do that, they win, and we lose.'

'Very well,' said the Prime Minister wearily, 'send the bastards over and they'll go on trial and we'll do our best to keep them in jail. Of course . . . ' – he was a resourceful political animal who prided himself on his understanding of human nature – 'if your guests were to disappear, no questions asked . . . why then, my government would know how to express its appreciation.' An expansive gesture of his hands and an upward look suggested that the sky would be the limit.

Arthur's face was stony. 'Appreciation?'

'Honours would be showered on you.'

Arthur drew himself up proudly. 'I am President of the Round Table,' he said. 'I need no other honour.'

'Quite so,' murmured the PM, unperturbed. 'I totally understand. Totally,' he repeated with earnest emphasis. After all, what are titles and medals to a man like you? Trivial and shallow things – on the other hand –' his voice dropped discreetly 'you might perhaps be tempted by more tangible expressions of our nation's gratitude?'

'Thank you, Prime Minister,' said Arthur, 'but I'm not interested in tangibles.'

The PM's smile was resigned but melancholy. 'Such a shame,' he said.

The US President did not hesitate. 'Wheel them over, Arthur. About thirty, you say? Mujahid – he's the only one we really want, but I'll take the rest as well. We know how to deal with terrorists in the USA.'

'That's rather the point,' said Arthur. 'The world will want to see justice done.'

'Spare me the human rights lecture.'

'Even terrorists have rights.'

'You know something, Arthur,' said the President, 'I have a lot of respect for you, and I sure as hell admire what you're doing. But I regret to say that you are deceiving yourself. You want to be all things to all people – warrior and saint. I'm afraid that doesn't work. A saint is not supposed to get blood on his hands.'

Arthur had no answer to that. A distortion, yes, but close

enough to the truth to be disturbing.

'Let's be honest with each other,' said the President, 'Mujahid is dangerous. We both want him dead. Am I right?'

'It would certainly make life less complicated,' agreed Arthur.

'I gotta tell you, Arthur, if I were in your shoes – don't quote me or I'll call you a liar – I'd waste those Sea Lords of yours. You can say they died in battle, or resisting capture, or trying to escape. Fact is, you can say whatever you goddam well like, and who is going to know the difference?'

'So if we send you our prisoners, you will kill them? Is that what you're saying?'

The President was outraged. 'Kill them! We don't do things like that in the USA. Not any more, anyway. There'd be one hell of an outcry in the media. We'd be censured by the United Nations, the European Union and every crackpot liberal bleeding-heart do-gooder in the world! No, we have to watch our step these days, more's the pity. But not you, Arthur. What do you care what anyone says? You're accountable to no one. You're above the law, answerable only to God. Hell, man, I envy you.' The President slapped his desk. 'OK, send me the goddam prisoners, and we'll put them on trial. Just be sure you send me Mujahid. He's the pearl in the oyster.'

Long after the screen went blank Arthur was still mulling over the President's words. *Above the law. Accountable to no one.* Free to lie, free to kill. If that was how the world saw him, what hope was there for the future?

The Sea Lord prisoners were duly dispatched to the UK and the USA by Eclipse. Distrusting both leaders, Arthur decided to keep Mujahid under guard in Camelot until it was clear that the Sea Lord prisoners would indeed receive a fair trial. A message for Arthur was posted by the White House on a website whose complex of passwords was known only to Camelot's Command Control. *Copies received. Awaiting receipt of original.* Arthur replied. *Original will be dispatched when agreed conditions are met.* The same message was posted twice more, and each time met with the same response. The President was by now incandescent with rage. Arthur was unimpressed.

Meanwhile Command Control's surveillance revealed that many Sea Lord prisoners had simply disappeared. Some media sources suggested they were being held in secure camps in the US and in various eastern European countries. Others said they had been freed. Neither the White House nor Downing Street would comment, citing national security.

When, after several weeks, Arthur was compelled to accept that he had been duped, the Round Table was summoned and agreed unanimously that Mujahid was to be tried by Camelot's High Court for crimes against humanity. After a trial lasting two weeks, he was found guilty. A week later the three High Court judges passed sentence: Mujahid was to die.

Once more the Round Table met, this time to consider how the death sentence would be carried out. On this issue Gawain had a very basic view supported by a number of hawks. 'As long as we do it, what does it matter how it's done?' Nods of approval around the table made him more daring. 'Why don't we just Elimat him on camera and relay the images to the world?'

This suggestion was less well received and there was an embarrassed silence in the Great Hall.

'That's what terrorists do,' said Arthur. 'Most democracies have abolished the death sentence. Camelot retains it for acts of terror; all the more reason for demonstrating that Mujahid's trial was fair, and his execution humane and dignified.'

Most members of the Round Table agreed with Arthur. Several alternatives were debated. Mujahid could be Elimatted; he could be put to sleep by lethal injection; he could be painlessly killed by nano-organisms. It was Lancelot who came up with the solution that received the most support. 'I propose a military execution by firing squad.'

Arthur asked what seemed to many a strange question. 'Are we not putting the cart before the horse?'

A mystified silence was broken by George Bedivere. 'What cart? What horse?'

Arthur looked around the table at friends and colleagues. 'The question is not only how we do it, but who does it.'

Slowly Arthur's meaning became clear.

'Which of you agrees to carry out the sentence?'

Not a single member met Arthur's eye.

'Any volunteers?' said Arthur.

Big Gaheris's arm twitched, and then was still, as he became aware that everyone was looking at him. Folding his arms, he examined the table with great concentration.

'Why not draw lots?' Lancelot suggested. 'Whoever draws the short straw does the deed.'

George Bedivere asked shrewdly: 'If you drew the short straw, would you kill Mujahid?'

'I might ask you the same question,' retorted Lancelot.

'I asked you first,' said George.

The seconds ticked by. 'I don't know what I would do,' said Lancelot finally.

One unspoken thought was in everyone's head. Killing in battle was one thing, killing in cold blood quite another. No one, it seemed, had the stomach for it.

Every member was looking in Arthur's direction. Surely he would have the solution to their predicament. 'I have no answer,' he said. 'I suggest we adjourn to consider the matter, and meet again tomorrow.'

That night he tossed and turned on his bed, falling asleep shortly before dawn, dreaming, as he had so many times, of the knight in golden armour and his grim adversary. But in his dream the cruel eyes of the black knight were the eyes of Mujahid.

Fifteen

The Sea Lords

When he woke the following morning, Arthur knew what he had to do. Dressing in the plain dark blue uniform worn by every active, he strapped on his portable, making sure that it was set in Elimat mode.

Mujahid was held in Camelot's prison. Dismissing two alert robot guards and one sleepy active, Arthur identified himself by voice and iris to the wall sensor. As he opened the cell door, Mujahid looked at him with expressionless eyes. 'They tell me I'm to be executed.'

'The High Court has sentenced you to death, yes.'

Mujahid smirked. 'The High Court! On this tinpot little island! That's a joke.'

'You were given a fair trial,' said Arthur, 'which is a great deal more than you gave your victims.'

'Do what you want,' said Mujahid indifferently. 'I am not afraid to die for the cause.'

'What kind of cause is it,' said Arthur, 'that justifies murdering innocent men, women and children?'

'They deserved to die,' said Mujahid.

'No, they did not. But you do.'

Mujahid shrugged. 'There will be others to take my place,' he said.

Watching the man pour himself coffee from a flask, Arthur marvelled at how ordinary he looked. Men like him – hair cropped, unshaven, dressed in T-Shirts and baggy combat pants – were to be seen every day strolling along the King's Road, London, or Madison Avenue, New York. What distinguished this fanatic, this psychopathic killer from them? Nothing – nothing visible at least. There was no mark of Cain on his forehead, nothing in his demeanour that would suggest he was a mass murderer who took pleasure in blowing innocents to pieces and torturing people both mentally and physically. Indeed, looking at the Sea Lords' commander objectively, without knowing what he had done, Arthur would have guessed he was a doctor, a lawyer or a teacher; and somehow the very ordinariness of his appearance made what he actually was all the more horrifying.

Focusing his mind, he tried to look through those blank eyes and find a way into Mujahid's head as Merlin had taught him to do. But there was no way in. Behind the eyes was a steel door, and the door was firmly shut.

Mujahid yawned and stretched. 'When is my execution to be?'

'Very soon.'

'*How* soon is very soon?' Was that a glint of fear in his eyes? 'You mean now?'

'Yes.'

'*You* are going to kill me?'

'I have elected to carry out the High Court's sentence,' said Arthur.

Mujahid put down his cup of coffee. 'You are Camelot's leader, not its executioner.' A shake of the head. 'I don't believe it.'

'Nevertheless it is true,' said Arthur.

'No one else would do it, eh?' Mujahid saw from Arthur's reaction that he had hit the target. 'So Arthur Pendragon is forced to do his men's dirty work.'

'I don't ask my men to do anything I would not do myself,' said Arthur. He tapped the port at his belt. 'You are to be Elimatted. Painless and instantaneous. You will simply cease to exist.'

'Don't you think I deserve something better?'

'Better than the innocents you slaughtered?'

'In this world no one is innocent,' said Mujahid.

'I am not here for a philosophical debate,' said Arthur, his hand reaching for his portable, 'I am here to carry out the sentence of the High Court.'

'I have lived like a warrior,' said Mujahid. 'At least let me die like one.'

'What are you suggesting?' Arthur bit his tongue, sensing that with that question he had surrendered a measure of power to Mujahid.

Mujahid seized his chance. 'A fight to the death,' he said. 'Nothing high tech. Axes and knives. Man to man. You are a soldier, Arthur, not an executioner. If you kill me in cold blood, the memory will haunt you for the rest of your life.'

Arthur heard himself asking, 'What happens if you kill me?'

'In that unlikely event,' said Mujahid, 'I dare say your men will put me out of my misery.'

From the shadows came a soft whinnying . . . A black horse moved into the flickering light of flaming torches, on its back a knight clad from head to foot in black armour.

'I challenge you to a joust.'

'What do you say, Arthur?'

Arthur hesitated, not because he feared personal combat, but because he doubted it would solve anything. If he killed Mujahid, he would be criticised for bypassing the Round Table and recklessly endangering his own life. If Mujahid killed him . . . either way he would be the loser.

He shook his head. 'No.'

'Are you not afraid of being branded a coward?'

The world will know you are a coward.

Is that what the Round Table would think of him if he were to refuse to fight Mujahid? That he was a coward? He trusted not. Though human nature being what it was, some of them might have their doubts.

'I will not fight you.'

Mujahid fell to his knees. 'Then kill me now.'

Arthur drew the Excalibur port from its holster. 'Say your prayers.'

'I have said them. I am ready to die.'

'Then,' said Arthur, 'in the name of the Round Table, I hereby carry out the sentence pronounced by the High Court. May God absolve me from your death, and may He have mercy on your soul.' Pressing the barrel of the port to Mujahid's temple, his finger tightened on the trigger. But, as he was about to pull it, the deathbed confession of Uther, his father, reverberated in his head. *Godfrey Whittaker. I shot him. There was a bang and he dropped dead. The most amazing thing. That's all there is to a man's life. Bang. And it's over.*

Another hair's breadth of pressure with his finger and it would be finished. *Bang. And it's over.* In the heat of battle he had killed men. Not like this, though. Not in cold blood. That he had never done, and he could not do it now. Mujahid looked up and saw in Arthur's eyes what he was thinking. 'You have to fight me now,' he said.

At first light the following day the two men confronted each other on the cliffs above Castle Rock carrying axes and hunting knives in their belts. What Arthur did not know was that a patrolling robot had spotted him leaving his apartment before dawn, and that Lancelot and Gawain now lay concealed in the long grass a hundred metres away. After some discussion they decided not to intervene unless things were looking bad for Arthur. An ex-Special Forces man, Arthur knew how to handle himself, but, fit and experienced as he was, close combat was inevitably high risk, and Mujahid was fighting for his life, no doubt calculating that if he killed Arthur, he would have a chance, however small, of escaping from the island.

A nod from the two adversaries: they were ready to do battle. Circling each other warily, both men looked for an opening, Mujahid trying to distract his opponent with taunts – 'How will you explain this to the Round Table? Sorry you didn't Elimat me? – Arthur, his body perfectly balanced on the balls of his feet, conserving energy and breath, concentrating on his opponent's movements, waiting for the right moment to strike.

It was Mujahid, swaying from side to side, never taking his eyes off his opponent, who made the first move. Screaming dementedly he rushed at Arthur and swung his axe in a savage slice at his neck. Arthur jumped to one side, avoiding the sharp blade by inches. As the axe-head thumped the ground jolting Mujahid off balance Arthur brought his axe down with all his strength on his opponent's head. Fast as he moved, Mujahid moved faster, leaping to his left and dodging the blow.

As they circled each other, Mujahid shifted his axe constantly from his left to his right hand, trying to distract his opponent and catch him off guard. Arthur's axe, now pointing at Mujahid's head, now swaying from side to side, was always in his right hand. Both men launched simultaneous attacks, flailing their axes with such force that when they clashed sparks flew high in the air, the sound echoing along the clifftops. Suddenly the head of Arthur's axe flew off and he was standing there defenceless with only the shaft in his hand. So astonished was Mujahid that for an instant he was transfixed, and in that instant Arthur wrenched the axe from his enemy's hands and threw it over the cliffside. With a cry of rage Mujahid leaped at Arthur. Knives glinted in the rays of the rising sun, and in seconds both men were badly cut on arms and chests, their shirts stained with blood.

Raising himself on his forearms, Gawain whispered, 'I can't bear this any more. I'm stopping it.' Lancelot pushed him down. 'No. He'd never forgive us. Wait.'

Hoping to finish him off, Mujahid took another wild swing at Arthur. As he dodged the blow, Mujahid stumbled, his knife falling from his hand into the long grass. As Arthur stood over him, bloodstained hunting knife in hand, Mujahid raised his arms in surrender.

'You win,' he said, bowing his head.

Clasping the handle of his knife in both hands, Arthur raised it high.

'Do it, now,' hissed Gawain. 'Kill the bastard!'

'Give me a minute to make my peace with Allah,' said Mujahid meekly.

Arthur lowered the knife. 'You have one minute,' he said.

Gawain was nervous. 'What's happening? Why isn't he finishing him off?'

'Mujahid is praying,' said Lancelot.

As Arthur turned aside to grant his defeated opponent a last few moments of undisturbed prayer, Mujahid grabbed a rock he had spotted lying in the grass, leaped up and hit his opponent on the head with its jagged edge. Arthur fell back, stunned.

'Fool,' Mujahid muttered. 'Stupid fool.' Arthur stirred, his eyes opening and closing again.

Gawain and Lancelot raised their portables, and almost immediately lowered them. The port's positronic beam was less precise than a bullet. Even if the beam hit Mujahid, its residual power might seriously injure Arthur.

Seconds later Mujahid had dragged the semi-conscious Arthur to the cliff's edge, and now they had no choice. Yet again they aimed their ports. But before they could fire, the light of the rising sun was blocked out, as an eagle stooped in a near vertical dive, its deadly talons tearing at Mujahid's eyes. Crying out in pain, he clutched his face, blood spurting through his fingers. As Lancelot and Gawain watched in amazement, the eagle soared far out to sea, wheeled, and sped fast as an arrow directly at its prey. As the predator's talons ripped Mujahid's face a second time, he fell backwards over the cliff edge, screaming all the way down to the rocks below.

Recovering consciousness, Arthur rose unsteadily to his feet. Supporting him, Lancelot and Gawain searched the skies for the eagle, seeing nothing but a few clouds tinged with red by the rising sun. Suddenly it was hovering above Arthur, stroking the air serenely with its wings. Folding them, it landed on his shoulder. Reluctantly, the two men relaxed their hold on his arms, and backed uneasily away. For a full minute the eagle stood there, shifting its weight from one foot to the other, its head turning sharply this way and that, its yellow eyes peering angrily about, whilst Arthur, showing not a trace of fear, caressed its breast feathers. Then, with a flap of its great wings, the great bird rose a few feet in the air and circled Arthur three times, each time uttering a plaintive cry, "Kluee! Kluee! Kluee!" Banking left, right, and left again, it climbed steeply into the sky and disappeared.

Arthur's wounds, dressed in Camelot hospital, were fortunately superficial, and healed quickly. Like all the Round Table, Lancelot and Gawain were angry with him for risking his life, and wisely Arthur accepted their rebukes without attempting to justify himself, so that very soon, with no fuel to feed on, their anger cooled.

The story of the hand-to-hand combat and its dramatic climax spread round the island. Some remembered hearing that Arthur had been attacked by an eagle when he was a boy, hence the scar on his left cheek; though what the connection was – if any – they could not say. Obviously this could not have been the same eagle, and besides, far from attacking Arthur, it had saved his life. Some, amongst them Leo Grant, were convinced that the great bird's sudden appearance when Arthur's life was in danger was no accident, believing as they did that his relationship with all creation was special, a thing of wonder and mystery, beyond human understanding.

Whatever the truth, no one dared ask him for an explanation, nor did he ever volunteer one.

Sixteen

IT WAS WELL KNOWN in Camelot that Lancelot, Gawain and Agravaine had played key roles in the success of Operation Sea Lord. Revelling in his newly acquired celebrity status, Agravaine, self-esteem at a new high, swaggered round the island sporting a single diamond ear stud, and a T-shirt decorated with a pirate hanging from a yardarm. Gawain shrugged off adulation in his customary gruff fashion, as, to the surprise of many, did Lancelot.

His devoted friend, Ian Duncan, could not understand it. 'You were the captain of Eclipse. You deserve the lion's share of the credit.'

'If you must praise someone,' said Lancelot, 'praise Gawain for captaining Kraken so superbly, praise Merlin whose inventive genius created the silver fish, the whale, and all the other extraordinary weapons in Kraken's armoury, praise Arthur for his brilliant strategy, praise Agravaine for his cunning and foresight. But please, Ian, do not praise me. I don't deserve it, really I don't.'

Dumbfounded, Ian searched his friend's face for a clue, an indication that this might be nothing more than a strategic show of false modesty. Yet, looking into Lancelot's eyes, he was certain his reaction was genuine, and that this was no ploy to court popularity. Besides, Lancelot was too honest to play that sort of game. Had he experienced some kind of spiritual revelation that would account for his newfound humility? Conceivable, though hardly likely. What, then, had brought about this extraordinary transformation?

And then, one day, Lancelot dropped a casual remark that seemed to offer a clue: 'People think better of a man who does not praise his own achievements,' and on the face of it an innocuous statement few would disagree with. Coming from Lancelot, though, it made Ian sit up and take notice. Since when had Lancelot cared what people thought of him? How many times had he assured Ian that he found the price of popularity too high? Why, then, would such a man feel the need to impress anyone?

In the days following Operation Sea Lord, Lancelot and Guinevere encountered each other from time to time, necessitating the exchange of a few politely formal words. Whereas before the operation Guinevere avoided him like the plague, she now acknowledged to herself that she found his company endurable, albeit in small doses. Had this unapproachable and taciturn individual undergone some kind of personality change? Such things were not unheard of. If so, was this new improved version here to stay? Or was it nothing more than a momentary break in the sullen clouds that habitually overhung those haughty features?

Curiously enough, Lancelot was asking himself very similar questions about Guinevere. Why was his former sparring partner sparring no more? Where were the steely looks, the acerbic retorts, the needling insinuations? Had she declared a temporary truce? Or was it a genuine change of heart? And if it was, what sun had melted the ice maiden?

Ever romantic and ever watchful, Lanky was convinced she knew the answer. Something about Ginny was different; her eyes brighter and softer, her manner warmer. She had changed, not dramatically perhaps, yet enough to arouse her closest friend's suspicions. Ginny was interested in someone, and a good thing too, a girl needed a bit of excitement in her life. Though undoubtedly she had the most gorgeous hunk of a husband, Arthur was out playing war games much of the time, and Ginny could be excused for getting restless. Besides, a mild flirtation never hurt anyone.

For Lanky, the idea that some man had caught Ginny's eye added a new and intriguing dimension to life on the island. Who could Mr. X be? Camelot was a small place with relatively few eligible men. She was enthralled by the thrill and challenge of it all. One by one she eliminated the suspects, until finally there was no one left – no one, that is to say, except the one man Ginny loathed. So not by any stretch of the imagination could it be him.

More counting and recounting, more eliminating and re-eliminating. But if not him, then who? Oh, my God! Surely not! What a deliciously wicked thought! Well, there was only one way to find out. She would have to test the waters.

'Is it my imagination, or has Lancelot changed?' she asked Guinevere innocently.

'Who, darling?'

'Lancelot.'

A languid lift of the right eyebrow. 'What about him?'

'Has he changed, do you think?'

Guinevere could not have appeared more bored. 'In what way?'

'Don't you find him a lot friendlier these days? Rather endearing, actually.'

'Sorry, darling,' said Guinevere, 'who are we talking about again?'

Lanky suppressed a smile. 'Lancelot.'

'What about him?'

'He seems friendlier, wouldn't you say?'

'Friendlier to whom?'

Was Ginny reacting a touch testily? 'No one in particular.'

Guinevere stared abstractedly into the middle distance. 'How would I know?'

Lanky was by now convinced that she was on to something. Ginny's reaction was too studiedly indifferent to be genuine; she had to be hiding something. 'You haven't noticed that he's been behaving differently lately?'

Guinevere sighed. 'Really, darling, it's of no interest to me how Lancelot behaves.'

Lanky decided to have some sport. 'Do you ever wonder why such a divinely dishy man hasn't found himself a girlfriend?'

'I certainly do not. Why should I?'

'You don't think,' suggested Lanky provocatively, 'you don't think he might be gay?'

There was more than a touch of exasperation in Guinevere's voice. 'Why would you even ask me such a question?'

Lanky pouted an apology. 'Me and my big mouth, darling. I didn't mean to pry into your private life.'

The inference of those words provoked Guinevere, as they were intended to. 'My private life! What are you suggesting?'

'Nothing, darling. Nothing at all.'

Guinevere knew instinctively that the sensible thing to do would be to change the subject, except that she was too angry and too impetuous to be sensible. 'You are surely not insinuating that Lancelot and I are . . . ?' – she stopped in mid-sentence, aware that she had allowed herself to be trapped into an indiscretion.

'Are what, darling?' enquired Lanky, her expression infuriatingly coy.

Guinevere considered walking out on her friend, and decided against it; for that would only confirm her suspicions. Better to make light of her preposterous hints. She threw back her head and laughed what, in the trying circumstances, was the most convincingly scornful laugh she could produce. 'What an absurd idea. Me and Lancelot! Why, he is the very last person in the world I would ever be interested in, if . . . if I was ever . . . which,' she said quickly, 'I most certainly am not. How could I be when I have the best husband in the world?'

Lanky acted contrite, the two friends hugged, and Guinevere congratulated herself on her handling of what might have been an awkward business, little knowing that at that very moment

Lanky too was congratulating herself. She had her answer, no doubt about it, Ginny was soft on Lancelot. Well, good for her. It was high time she stopped being so goody-goody and had some fun. For that was all it could be, harmless fun. Lanky hugged herself in anticipation of exciting things to come. As it happened, she did not have long to wait.

The following day, she and Guinevere were in The Meeting Place, a combination of social club and coffee bar, popular with off-duty men and women, when Lancelot appeared in the doorway. The room was suddenly quiet. Lancelot, known to be the least sociable person in the world, was rarely seen here, and when he was, would invariably sit brooding alone in a dark corner munching a sandwich or sipping coffee and avoiding all eye contact. If he spoke to anyone, it would be to his father, Ban, or to Ian Duncan. What made his presence here today even more surprising was the fact he seemed to be focusing his attention on Guinevere and Lanky. For as everyone in Camelot knew, Lancelot and Guinevere shared a mutual antipathy, their encounters at best tense, at worst cantankerous. Not surprisingly, therefore, there were whispered comments and puzzled looks, some directed at Guinevere, some at Lancelot. Embarrassed, she shifted her chair so that she faced away from him.

'Why is he staring at me like that?' she hissed. As Lanky swung round to see who 'he' was, Guinevere grabbed her arm. 'Don't look! He'll think I'm encouraging him!'

Too late. At the perimeter of her vision she was aware that Lancelot was approaching, sensed that he was close, that he was standing by their table. A pulse throbbed in her neck.

'Good morning, ladies.' Lancelot's voice was jovial, the expression on his face positively pleasant. To Guinevere's horror, Lanky fluttered her eyelashes and patted her hair into place. For her, Lancelot was just the most handsome and romantic man in Camelot – after Arthur of course. And perhaps Gawain. And possibly Ian Duncan. 'Great to see you, Lance,' she said enticingly, as Guinevere cringed.

Since Lancelot was now standing in front of her she could hardly ignore him. 'I have to congratulate you,' she said, making it sound like an obligation. 'Arthur says we all owe you a great deal.'

'I was a mere cog in the wheel,' said Lancelot. 'Arthur is an inspirational leader. I am proud to serve him. We all are.'

So unexpectedly humble was this disarming response that both Guinevere and Lanky stared at Lancelot, not knowing what to say. Before either of them could think of anything, he made a slight bow, murmured his goodbyes and was gone.

'That was impressive,' said Lanky, nodding her head solemnly. 'So chivalrous, so modest.'

Guinevere could not but agree, if somewhat grudgingly. 'He behaved correctly,' she conceded.

Lanky was more generous 'He behaved like the gentleman he is,' she said, and could not resist adding, 'Whatever happened to Mr. Nose-in-the-Air?'

Guinevere's compressed lips and a lifting of her chin indicated that this particular discussion was at an end.

It was the first of several such "chance" encounters. For weeks, Guinevere refused even to consider what they signified, indeed if they signified anything at all, other than that she and Lancelot were now more at ease in each other's company. When unwelcome questions began to insinuate themselves into her head, she had her answer ready; Lancelot had become a friend, and that was all there was to it. No subconscious issues were allowed to break the surface of her conscious mind.

Despite which, as the days passed, she and Lancelot began to meet, sometimes in The Meeting Place, sometimes on an island walk, first fortuitously then by pre-arrangement, though an arrangement so delicately and casually contrived that it had all the appearance of being accidental. No one had the slightest reason to suspect that their interest in each other was anything more than social. Their conversation continued to be as innocent as it could possibly be, shy glances and occasional sighs conveying to themselves, if not to others, what words dared not.

From one day to the next Lancelot would disappear without warning, and she would learn that there had been a military operation – a *"party"*. To her own surprise and embarrassment she found herself worrying about him when he was away, and unable to conceal her delight when he returned. Excited and fearful, they were soon wandering happily in a magical no-man's-land, a blissfully uncommitted country bordering on love, enjoying the secret thrill of knowing, yet pretending not to know, acutely aware that it would take no more than a careless word to propel them both across that border, a step neither of them was ready to take.

Lancelot's peace of mind had always depended on everything in his life being neat and tidy; his clothes, his lists, his daily agenda, everything in its place, everything ready for use at the right time and for the appropriate occasion. His future was mapped, his course plotted, no deviations or distractions tolerated. His commitment was to Arthur and to Camelot, and he had no intention of betraying either.

For Guinevere, the matter was equally straightforward. She was a married woman. Besides, as she told herself, love 'of that sort' was not for her; by which she meant that she never had been, nor ever could be, passionately in love with anyone. Passion controlled, passion deceived, passion disrupted a woman's life, turning her into a silly, helpless fool. Arthur was her husband, lover and friend: her love for him was sensible, the kind of love that endured. So it was clear as a crystal ball that whatever she felt for Lancelot did not now, nor ever could, amount to love.

The more she saw of him, however, and the more confidences they shared, the cloudier that crystal ball became. She allowed her thoughts, if not her actions, to draw her into dangerous territory. Someone had once told her that you could always tell from a woman's eyes whether she was in love or not. Could that be true, she wondered. Waiting for Arthur one evening, she stood with lowered eyes before the mirror in their sitting room, not daring to look up, for fear of what she might see, until finally she plucked up the courage, and there in the eyes that looked back at her was a glow and an excitement she had never seen before. It was the first time she allowed herself to consider the possibility that she might be falling in love, something she neither expected nor wanted. What was worse, she had not the slightest idea how to deal with it.

Was it, she asked herself, possible to love two men? Her head said no, her heart, yes. Being Guinevere, her head triumphed; she was able to assure herself that whatever she felt for Lancelot was a fantasy, a thing without substance. Arthur was the reality, the man with whom she shared her bed and her life, the husband to whom she had vowed to be faithful. She was not like those heroines of nineteenth-century romantic novels, the sort of woman willing to sacrifice the world for a kiss.

Sensible was what she had always been: sensible was what she always would be.

Seventeen

As the weeks and months passed, Lanky began to doubt whether "harmless fun" was quite the way to describe whatever it was that Guinevere and Lancelot were involved in. Now and then she sat with them in The Meeting Place, usually with a group of friends, and though she was certain no one else noticed anything, she did. There was something about the way Ginny tried so hard not to look at Lancelot, and about the attentive way he listened when she was speaking, that, for her at least, gave the game away. There were no obvious clues, no girlish bursts of laughter, no tossing of hair or accidental brushing of hand against hand. You would have to know Ginny as well as Lanky did to suspect that these two people were interested in each other.

The time came when suspecting was not enough, she had to know. Over a glass of wine in her apartment one evening she abandoned caution. 'I know I have no right to ask you, and it's none of my business.'

'No it isn't,' said Guinevere, and regretted it immediately.

Lanky was jubilant, though she tried not to show it. That unconsidered retort amounted to an admission. 'What isn't?'

Guinevere was mortified at having given herself away. 'You invited me for a drink and a chat, not an interrogation.' Jumping up, she made for the door.

Lanky rushed after her. 'Please don't go,' she implored. 'I'm sorry, Ginny. I love you. I only want to help.'

Head down, Guinevere moved back into the room.

What was it about Ginny that so turned men on, Lanky asked

herself. Was it because she was beautiful, with that perfect oval face of hers, those luminous brown eyes and jet black hair? Or was there more to it? Of course there was. Ginny was a thoroughbred. She had that indefinable quality people called style. Lanky sighed enviously. If only men would look at her like the way they looked at Ginny. True, she had a gangly body, curly hair and protruding teeth, but she really wasn't all that bad, and what she lacked in beauty she more than compensated for in personality. And when she did find a man to love her – Gawain would do very nicely or perhaps Ian Duncan – she would love him like no man had ever been loved in the history of the world.

She decided to pretend that she knew. 'Why Lancelot?' Half expecting an angry denial, she was taken by surprise. There was no fight left in Ginny. She needed a friend, someone she could talk to.

'I don't know. It happened.'

Lanky's eyes bulged. 'You don't mean you already . . . ?'

Guinevere was close to tears. 'How can you think that of me?'

Lanky considered her friend anxiously. 'Is there something wrong between you and Arthur?'

Guinevere shook her head. 'Absolutely not. I love him.'

'I don't get it,' said Lanky. 'From where I'm sitting, you have everything – Arthur for a husband, first lady of Camelot, the world at your feet. What more could a girl want?'

Guinevere rocked back and forth on the sofa. 'Don't you think I've asked myself that question a hundred times?'

'So what's the problem?'

'Arthur puts me on a pedestal.'

'And Lancelot?'

Guinevere blushed. 'He treats me like a woman.'

'What is it you want?'

Guinevere's shoulders slumped. 'I don't know,' she said.

The observatory door panel stirred to life.

Name?

'Guinevere.'

The door clicked open.

She ran to Arthur. Her kiss was more intense than usual. He drew her to the sofa, sat her down beside him and put his arms round her. Guinevere rested her head on his shoulder and closed her eyes. It was like coming home. The love they had for each other was a warm and tender emotion, the sort of love that could only be shared with someone you admired, and above all understood.

'How much do you love me?' she asked like a child.

He spread his arms wide. 'My love for you is as big as the universe.'

'Be serious.'

'Ah, serious,' he said. 'If it's serious you want, Ginny, then, my darling, here it is.' He took her hand and kissed it gently. 'I love you so much that life without you would not make sense.'

Her spine tingled. He could not have put it better. It was exactly how she felt about him; life without Arthur would not make sense. That was why theirs was the ideal match. Whatever else love was, it had to make sense. But then, before she could stop herself, she was asking, 'Would you give up everything for me?'

'What is it, Ginny?' he asked, 'what's the matter?' It was never going to be easy, he had always known that. If life without Ginny would not make sense – and it wouldn't – then he ought to be sharing more of it with her. 'What's wrong?'

Did he suspect? No, how could he? She shook her head. 'Nothing's wrong, I'm fine.' With her fingers she traced the shallow wrinkles at the corners of his eyes, feeling closer to him than she had ever done before. Her love for Arthur was rock solid, founded on mutual respect and admiration, and, ironically enough, on trust. But then, that was the worst of it. It pained her not to be wholly honest with the man with whom she had shared everything . . . until now. Telling him the truth would be to risk losing him, and that would be unthinkable. Her marriage was central to her well-being, as necessary to her as the air she breathed. 'Being your wife isn't enough,' she said. 'Look at Lanky – she's in charge of nursing staff and liaising with doctors and surgeons. She would die of boredom if she didn't have something worthwhile to do. Most of the women here work. Why can't I?'

He looked thoughtful. 'I've been selfish, keeping you to myself. We shall have to find you a job.'

She tried to hide her disappointment. *We shall have to find you a job* sounded suspiciously like creating some feel-good, ego-boosting outlet for her frustrations.

Arthur was troubled, sensing her discomfort, and perhaps something more than discomfort – her pain? Was she mourning the fact that she could not have children? If so, her pain was his too. He would dearly have loved to have a son – a son like Lancelot. 'You are happy, aren't you, Ginny?'

Smiling reassuringly, she squeezed his hand. 'I count my blessings.' It was true. Counting them had become a daily ritual, a daily compulsion almost, as if she feared that if she did not, it would bring the avenging furies down on her.

She was happy, of course she was, or at least most of the time she was. There were good days and bad days. Wasn't that true of everyone's life? The good days came when the sun flared and the wind rose, parting sombre layers of cloud, when Camelot's white spheres and rectangles, its towers and turrets, its pillars and pyramids glowed magically in the sunlight, when the waves danced, and foam horses raced each other across the sea. The bad days were those monotonous, boring days, when heavy-bellied clouds hung low over the Atlantic, and her spirits were as overcast as the sky. On those days she felt trapped, missing the colour, the bustle, the sheer unexpectedness of the life she used to lead in London. It was then that she longed to have her life back; not that she wanted to be eating in celebrity restaurants, or sitting on charity committees, or shopping with chums. Not any more. She had changed. If she lived in London now, her life would be as different as she was. But whatever kind of life it would be, it would be *her* life. The life she was leading now was not hers; it was Arthur's.

'What kind of job?' she asked, bringing him back to the subject.

'The hospital badly needs an administrator,' he said. 'It would be a big responsibility. What do you think?'

For an instant she was afraid. 'I've never worked in a hospital.'

'You can learn.' Head on one side, eyebrows arched 'Deal?'

'I'll do it,' she said, and put her arms round him. 'Thank you.'

'For what?'

'For understanding. I'm not the easiest, am I.'

'Nor am I. That's what makes it interesting. You and I were destined for each other.'

'Prove it.'

Arthur tapped the computer's keyboard, and the monitor was suddenly alive with myriads of stars and washes of light. 'Galaxies,' he said. 'See there, and there, and there.'

She stood behind him, hands resting lovingly on his shoulders.

A few more taps, and the telescope moved in on the solar system, focusing on a single bright light.

'That's Venus,' he said. 'Now watch.' Around Venus a finger of light drew a heart, above it the name **Arthur,** below it the name **Guinevere.** Finally an arrow of light bisected the heart, linking the two names.

'There,' said Arthur. 'Our love is written in the stars.'

'You and your stars,' she said. 'What is it you see in them?'

'Apart from our love?'

'Apart from that,' she said, kissing the top of his head, noticing for the first time a few grey hairs streaking the gold.

'The starlight you and I are looking at now began its journey through space billions of years ago. In the little time we spend on earth the stars shed on us the light of all time and all knowledge. We can learn a great deal from them.'

Feeling a sudden surge of love, she slipped her arms round his neck. 'Like what?'

'They teach us inner harmony, they put us in touch with our intuition, our sense of destiny, our inner spiritual world. Discord and chaos are the enemies of all God's creation. Our planet's well-being, like that of the universe, depends on harmony. Camelot exists to restore that harmony to the world. That's why we are here, Ginny.'

Guinevere told herself that her husband was the wisest, the bravest, the most caring of men, and she the luckiest of women.

'Everything we are, or ever will be, is written in the stars,' said Arthur. 'When I look at them, I see the present and the past.'

'And the future? Can you see that too?'

'Would you want me to?'

Guinevere shivered, her mood darkening. 'No,' she said, 'no, I don't think I would.'

Eighteen

As LANCELOT LEFT The Meeting Place, there in Guinevere's lap was a nugget of paper. Not daring to touch it, she lingered over her coffee, looking furtively about to satisfy herself that no one had seen him put it there. There were no questioning glances or knowing looks, the friends at her table too busy talking to have noticed anything, and the room continuing to hum with mid-morning chatter. Casually she retrieved the note and slipped it in her bag.

Arthur was in Command Control. She had the apartment to herself. Her heart pounding, she unfolded the note.

I know it's wrong and I know I shouldn't say it but I think I've fallen in love with you. God knows, I've tried hard enough not to. I desperately need to talk to you. That at least you owe me. After all, it's you who have done this to me, you who have cast a spell on me. There's a triangular rock on the beach below NIWIS. 6 p.m. tonight. Please be there. If you are not, I shall pursue this no further.

She read it several times before putting it back in her bag. *I think I've fallen in love with you.* I think? What did he mean by that? Didn't he know? Either he *was* in love or he *wasn't*. It made him sound more like an uncertain teenager than a mature man. Retrieving the crumpled note from her bag, she smoothed it down and studied it yet again, this time with the most meticulous attention to every word, as though it were written in a code that had to be cracked in order to decipher its true meaning.

She mouthed silently, *God knows, I've tried hard enough*

not to. How presumptuous was that! Who asked him to fall in love with her? Not her, certainly. Was she not good enough for him? Was that it? Or did he think that falling in love was a sign of weakness in a man? Either way she was less than impressed. *That at least you owe me. After all, it's you who have done this to me.* More than presumptuous, downright impertinent! Was he implying that she had deliberately set her cap at him? She had done no such thing. Obviously he was not man enough to admit that it was he who had first . . . well…shown interest. And as for *You who have cast a spell on me*. Words failed her. What was he suggesting? That she was some kind of witch? How dare he! She was angry, as she had every right to be, didn't she? About to tear the note into small pieces, she thought better of it and stuffed it back in her bag.

Taking it out again almost immediately, she put it back, took it out, read it once more and put it back again. On the whole she was inclined to accept that Lancelot's message came from his heart, even if it was not as tactfully expressed as it might have been. It was typical of the man. She placed the bag at her side, laid her hand on it and caressed it gently. Her heart softened. Foolish though it might be, she could not help but pity him. *Please be there. If you are not, I shall pursue this no further.* At least he was not taking her for granted. Quite the contrary, in fact. He was not at all sure she would come.

On the other hand, she asked herself, why would a man so eager for her to keep a rendezvous, accept so readily that she might not? Why would he even consider the possibility? Should he not rather have *ordered* her to come? Or at the very least, begged and implored her? Whatever happened to the torments of love? To romance? To chivalry? Her hand strayed to her bosom. To passion? If she was not worthy of him, let him find someone who was. She would be a fool to allow her heart to rule her head. Wouldn't she? Of course she would!

But then again, she mused, he did give the impression of being very much in love. Goodness knows what he would do if she did not come to . . . where was it? Opening her bag she consulted the letter yet again. *A triangular rock on the beach below NIWIS.* She knew it well. Of course it was unthinkable, absolutely unthinkable . . . 6 p.m. he said.

It was 5.30 p.m., the autumn evening crisply cold, the sea troubled, the crests of the waves whipped to white spray by the wind. Slowly, Lancelot walked along the beach towards the triangular rock, taking care to stay close to the cliffs so that he would not be picked up by one of the island's surveillance cameras. Arriving there, he paced restlessly for several minutes, then sat on the rock, sifting sand through his fingers and trying to piece together the jigsaw of his fractured thoughts. Should he have written the letter? Would she come? And if she did, what then? What if she did not share his feelings? What if she did?

From time to time he glanced at his wristcom. With each passing minute he became more certain that she would not come, and began to regret having sent the note. It was foolish of him to have put something so fragile and so precious in writing. Even if, by some miracle, she had . . . some feeling for him, his note would most probably have scared her off. It needed a poet to express how he felt, and he was a plain soldier.

He was certain now; she was not coming. How could he ever have imagined that Arthur's wife . . . His peace of mind had gone. He had made a fool of himself. No doubt at this very moment she and Lanky were having a good laugh over his letter.

No, he refused to think so badly of her. Guinevere would never do that. She would more likely be furious with him for presuming to write the note at all. Either way, he regretted it. No, he didn't. He had to send it, had to let her know how he felt about her, had to know how she felt about him. Well, now he knew, and it hurt. It hurt like hell.

Standing on the shoreline, the tide lapped around his feet. He could feel the sea drawing him into its embrace. Somewhere out there was his mother. When he was a baby, she had drowned herself, and all these years later, the pain was still there in his father's eyes. She was not mad, he had assured him more than once, just mentally unstable – unstable enough, it seemed, to take her own life. It would be so easy to join her now. All he had to do was keep walking. She was calling him, 'Lancelot! Lancelot!' Closing his eyes, he took a step into the water.

Yet again he heard his name called. 'Lancelot!' This time it was closer, and the voice was coming not from the sea but from the shore. He looked round. Someone was walking along the beach towards him. Guinevere!

As she approached, he tried to read her expression, but her face was almost covered by a scarf. His heart hammered at his ribs. Pulling off her scarf, she shook loose her long black hair. Looking down at his wet shoes and trousers, she smiled. 'It's a bit chilly to go swimming, isn't it?'

He stood there looking sheepish. 'It's rough today, the sea,' he said, by way of explanation.

'It is.'

A small whirlpool of sand erupted in the wind. He sheltered her with his body, and as the wind dropped, pulled away sharply, embarrassed. 'I'm sorry.'

'No need to apologise. You were being a gentleman.'

'Thank you.'

Without a word they began to walk along the beach. Her hand brushed his, and suddenly, with not a word spoken, they were walking hand in hand. Joy welled up in Lancelot. Being in love was a new experience for him, as frightening as it was exhilarating. No words could express what he was feeling. They walked on, still not speaking, and with each step the sense of shared intimacy grew stronger, binding them closer. This could not be happening to her, Guinevere told herself.

'I thought you wouldn't come,' he said. Now that she was here, he was convinced it was meant to happen. No use trying to fight it.

She stopped and looked up at him, her gaze intense. 'I wasn't going to,' she said. 'I just couldn't stay away.'

'I love you.'

'I love you too.'

They kissed, drawing closer as the passion stirred. For a long time they clung to each other, until finally Guinevere gently disengaged herself.

'Come back with me,' he pleaded.

She shook her head, 'It wouldn't be right.'

Taking as long as he could, he tied her headscarf loosely at her neck.

'I'm on duty in a few minutes,' she said. 'I have to get back to the hospital.'

He watched her walk away along the beach. Once she stopped, looked back at him and walked on again. Lancelot was happier than he had ever been in his life, daring to believe that the woman he was in love with loved him too. But, as the first flood of happiness receded, other emotions were exposed – above all guilt. Where could this forbidden love lead? Would it not have been better to have looked and not touched? One thing was certain; now that they had declared their love for each other, things would never be the same again.

Nineteen

FROM TIME TO TIME Harold Pemberton received a call from his old friend, Ban. Though he never told him where he was calling from, he had a shrewd notion that Ban was on Camelot with his son, Lancelot. Their exchanges by gravitational link were invariably brief – Ban, the old soldier being economical with words – and about nothing special. This time, however, Harold had something very special indeed to tell his friend.

Ban needed time to take it in. 'Say again.'

'Galahad is Lancelot's son,' repeated Harold, picturing Ban's deadpan expression, and that barely perceptible wry twitch at the corner of his mouth.

'You sure?'

'Quite sure, Ban.'

'How do you know?'

'Helena told me.'

A long silence. 'Always hoped he and Helena would get together.'

'It seems they did,' said Harold dryly.

'Want me to tell him?'

'That's the idea.'

'Don't like to interfere.'

'For God's sake, Ban, we're talking about your grandson.'

'So we are.'

'Just do it,' said Harold, 'there's a good chap.'

'Right,' said Ban.

At first Lancelot did not want to believe it, though in his heart he knew it was true. Unable to think clearly, he left Command Control with a muttered excuse. For hours he wandered the island, his mind racing out of control. A son! Galahad his son! Helena the mother! Returning to his apartment he threw himself on a sofa and fell into a deep sleep. When he woke, his body seemed disconnected from his brain, his limbs refusing to obey its commands. His mind, though, was active and clear, alive with sounds and images from all those years ago. Returning from his overseas army posting he had rushed back to his love, Helena, only to be told she had a baby. It had been an enormous shock. Why had she said nothing about it before? Not a phone call, not even an e-mail. His first reaction had been that the baby could not be his, his second, to feel ashamed of himself for thinking such a thing, his third, to propose.

'We'll get married right away.'

'What if I were to tell you it isn't yours?'

At the time he had taken Helena's reply at its face value. What else was he supposed to do? Only now did he realise that she might have been testing him.

'Would you marry me if you were not the father?'

And how had he answered her? '*I would have to think about it . . .* '

He could see now how rejected she must have felt.

'*It's not your problem,*' she had said, ending the discussion.

The more he assured Guinevere that Helena no longer meant anything to him, the more aloof and cold she became. After much pleading, she agreed to meet him on the beach.

'I swear I never knew.'

'Why are you telling me this?'

'I'm still not certain he's my son. '

'But you slept with her.'

'Yes.'

'He's your son,' said Guinevere. 'Helena wouldn't lie.'

'I have to see her – you do understand that,' he said.

Her chin lifted in that proud gesture of hers that he knew so well. 'If you go, it's the end.'

'Don't do this,' he pleaded.

'It's either her or me.'

'It will always be you,' he said.

'Then don't go.'

'It's my duty to go,' said Lancelot.

'Duty!' Guinevere's eyes flashed scorn. 'That's just an excuse for doing what you want.'

'I'll be back very soon,' he promised.

An indifferent shrug. 'What do I care,' she said. 'Don't come back. Stay with Helena. You two deserve each other.'

Lancelot walked away with his head down. A hundred metres along the beach he rounded a protruding rock face and disappeared. She wanted to run after him, to cover his face with kisses and tell him she had not meant a word, that she loved him and always would. But her proud spirit held her back. Let him go. He had made his choice. And so had she. Never again, she vowed, would she make a fool of herself over a man.

Twenty

THE BELL RANG, and there at the door was Lancelot. In a daze, Helena ushered him into the sitting room and stood staring at him with wide eyes as if she had suddenly been confronted by an apparition.

'It's me,' he said, smiling.

She clapped her hands to her cheeks to hide her blushes. 'I'm sorry,' she said. 'Am I staring?'

He had promised himself not to rush in with questions. And yet, sitting here in this reassuringly familiar room so full of memories, he found it impossible to control his tongue. 'You never told me I was Galahad's father.'

'Are you sure you wanted to know?'

On the point of reacting angrily, he hesitated, honest enough to admit to himself that she might just have a point. 'I would have married you.'

'I know you would,' said Helena.

'Then why . . . ?'

'I had no intention of holding a gun to your head,' she said.

So that was it. It was her pride that had made her turn him away, that and the fact that she had sensed his reluctance to confront the truth. Sitting there now, trying to come to terms with those lost years, he asked himself a question – if he had known then that Galahad was his son, would he have stayed? Yes, of course he would. He would have done the right thing. Yes, but would the "right thing" have been the best thing to do? Would it have been right for her? Or him?

Helena had tried to convince herself that seeing Lancelot

again would somehow cure her, that they would be good friends and nothing more. It was nonsense, of course. Nothing had changed; she was more in love with him than ever. There could never be anyone else. Several men had asked her to marry them; good men, men who loved her and would care for her, all of them, though, with one fatal flaw; they were not Lancelot. Amazingly, it seemed that life had given her a second chance. This time, she told herself, she would seize it, though she would have to tread warily. If she tried to influence or pressurise him, however subtly, he would run, or even worse, stay with her and live to regret it. Once it had been her decision. Now it was his.

Tentatively she asked, knowing she ought not to, 'Is there anyone special in Camelot?'

A slight hesitation. 'I'm unattached,' he said, not comfortable with his answer.

Why wasn't he looking at her, she wondered.

'And you? Is there anyone?'

'No,' she said. No hesitation there. 'No one.'

He spread his hands as though asking a favour. 'Could I see him?'

'Of course.'

White blond, neatly brushed hair, a sturdy body, blue green eyes – Helena's colouring, not his. But his son, oh yes, most definitely his son. He held out his arms. The boy advanced hesitantly, step by step, wide-eyed and serious. Lancelot gestured to him to come and be hugged, but he stopped a pace away and looked at the ground.

'I'm your dad,' said Lancelot softly, marvelling at the strangeness of the words. Shyly the boy came to him and Lancelot enfolded him in his arms.

Helena watched from the door. 'What do you say?'

'Pleased to meet you, sir.'

Lancelot responded solemnly. 'And I am delighted to meet you, Galahad.'

It would take time, of course. The lad had grown up without a father. He would have to earn what once he could have taken for granted: his son's love. Over the course of the next few days he spent more and more time with him, enchanted and a little overawed by his composure and maturity. Extraordinarily self-possessed for an eight year old, Galahad was apparently never naughty. His vocabulary was far above average, and already he articulated his thoughts in perfect grammatical sentences, never in slang or clichés. It was therefore all the more astonishing to learn that his son had never been to school, having been educated at home by private tutors. Did he ever go to a movie or watch TV, he asked Helena? No, there was no TV in the house, and Galahad was not interested in movies. Did he play any sport? No, he was not a boy who enjoyed playing games. His favourite pursuit was reading. What did he read? The bible, mostly.

'Isn't that rather unusual for a boy of his age,' said Lancelot. 'Wouldn't he enjoy reading children's books? There are so many to choose from.'

Helena sounded resigned. 'Mother says the bible is the only book worth reading.'

Lancelot counted himself a religious man. He believed in God, and was committed to doing God's work. It disturbed him, nevertheless, to see a child carrying a bible with him wherever he went. He took his son to Battersea Park and tried to kick a football with him. Galahad humoured his father, but it was painfully obvious that the boy's heart was not in it. The playground? Galahad scorned it. 'Kids' stuff.' A movie? He preferred to stay at home and read the "Book", or, from time to time, play around with his computer. A board game? He was too old for board games. Too old at eight! Lancelot was rapidly running out of ideas. How was he ever to develop a father-son relationship with this solemnly precocious child?

He complained to Harold. 'He's not like a normal boy of his age. He seems to have no joy in him.'

'Francesca's doing,' said Harold Pemberton. 'She's taken him over – his timetable, his education, his mind. She'll make a priest of him if she gets her way, though if you ask me it's more to do with jealousy and possessiveness than love of God.'

Francesca, with ponderous tact, kept out of Lancelot's way during the day. In the evening, when the family sat down to dinner, potentially contentious issues were avoided, Francesca speaking only when spoken to, her manner towards Lancelot distant, but icily polite. It was clear to him that he made her uneasy, no doubt because she feared he would somehow contrive to take her beloved Galahad away from her. Harold remained his usual jovial self, embarrassing Lancelot and Helena and infuriating his wife, Francesca, by dropping heavy hints of a forthcoming "celebration", and, whenever conversation flagged, humming Mendelssohn's wedding march under his breath.

Accustomed to saying what he thought, and frustrated by this vacuous evening ritual, Lancelot broke the unspoken agreement restricting conversation to trivialities. 'What does Galahad do for exercise?' The question was directed at Francesca who was compelled to respond.

'He is a very active child.'

'What exactly are his activities?'

'Either I or his mother take him for a walk in the park every day.'

'A walk in the park is not sufficient exercise for a young lad,' said Lancelot, his dark eyes smouldering with disapproval. 'A normal boy his age needs to run around, play games, jump up and down.'

Francesca's lips tightened, the corners of her mouth drooped. 'Are you suggesting your son is not normal?'

'Not at all. I am suggesting that his upbringing is not normal.'

Francesca bridled. 'In what way?'

'He should be going to school,' said Lancelot. 'And not just because he's missing out on academic studies. He doesn't seem to have a single friend his own age.'

With grim deliberation Francesca folded her napkin, smoothing it down until the edges were knife sharp, all the time demonstrating by a barrage of resentful glances her disapproval of Lancelot. 'Galahad has his family. And he has God. What more does he need?'

This was too much for Lancelot. 'A great deal more. And I suggest you bear in mind that you are Galahad's grandmother. You are neither his mother nor his father.'

Francesca laid her napkin down, rose to her full height and launched her last verbal missile before walking out. 'And I suggest you bear in mind that, as an absentee father, you have forfeited any right you may have had to criticise Galahad's upbringing.'

The truth, as Lancelot acknowledged ruefully to himself, always hurt. Francesca was right. As an absentee father he had no right to interfere, not yet at least. If he were to stay and be a real father to Galahad and a husband to Helena, that would be different. Was that not what he should do? Was that not where his duty lay?

Yet what about his duty to Camelot? He had made Camelot his life's work and his mission. As Arthur's Chief of Staff he owed it to his leader not to desert him. And there was something else that drew him back to Camelot. Someone rather. A woman's hands reached out to him, her eyes filled with hurt and anger. And with love. What should he do? Stay or go? He was being torn apart. One way or another he would have to make a decision, and soon. If he stayed, he would be expected to marry Helena. He was fond of her, and no doubt they could make a happy life together. Galahad he loved, and the boy would surely grow to love him too. It would be wrong to leave him. He made up his mind; he would stay and be a father to his son, not an absentee father, but a real live presence, a father to kick a ball in Battersea Park with, a father to read him to sleep. And Helena? She needed a husband – no, that wasn't fair, she needed him. He went to bed determined to break the good news to her in the morning.

Yet in the morning the old doubts came flooding back. Camelot tugged at his heart. Had he not dedicated himself to Arthur? Had he not sworn to uphold the ideals of Camelot? How could he abandon all those good people who depended on him – Ian, Gawain, Agravaine and – what use to pretend – Guinevere. She was with him everywhere, every waking minute, her face, the smell of her hair, her voice, the touch of her hand. Guinevere or Helena? If he were honest with himself, the real choice was not between duty and duty, but between duty and love. Whichever he chose, there would be a price to pay.

'I'm staying,' he told Harold Pemberton.

Harold's hooded eyes showed mild surprise. 'Does Helena know?'

'Thought I'd run it by you first,' said Lancelot.

'I see.' Harold gnawed the inside of his lip. 'Are you asking for my advice, Lance?'

'Not exactly.'

'For my opinion, then?'

'Perhaps,' said Lancelot, on his guard.

'Very well, then, my opinion is that you are making a mistake.'

'I thought you wanted me to stay.'

'What I want is irrelevant.' said Harold. 'The question is – what do you want?'

'I want to stay.'

'Why?'

'Because it's the right thing to do.'

'You would not be the first man to do the right thing for the wrong reason.'

'Helena's happiness is all that matters.'

'How can she be happy if you are not?'

Lancelot brushed the question aside. 'And then there's Galahad. He needs me. I've been away too long.'

'You could visit him regularly.' said Harold. 'Now that you know you have a son, you can be a proper father to him.'

Though Harold Pemberton's pertinent comments hit home, they had not changed Lancelot's mind. He would do the chivalrous thing, and the sooner he told Helena, the better. Once he had committed himself there would be no turning back.

She had gone shopping, Francesca said. Wandering disconsolately into the hallway he found a parcel addressed to him in her neat handwriting. Inside was a navy blue heavy-knit sweater, and a note confirming that she had knitted it for him. He tried it on. It fitted perfectly. He was touched. Clearly it was a love token, the message it conveyed more powerful and more poignant than any words could have been.

Still wearing the sweater, he wandered back into the sitting room and waited for Helena to return, flipping a magazine here, a newspaper there, unable to concentrate. It was a chill winter's day, a fire burned in the grate. Suddenly he felt warm, then uncomfortably hot. The sweater he had thought fitted him perfectly was now constricting him, pulling under his arms and across his chest. Tearing it off he fell back on the sofa, head in hands, heart pounding, limbs trembling. He was trapped – trapped by the love of a woman he did not, and never could, love.

There was no need to say anything. She read in his eyes what he was going to tell her.

'Did you try it on?'

'It fits perfectly,' he said. 'It's a great sweater. Thank you.'

'When are you off?' She asked the question as casually as if he were going to the local for a beer.

'In a couple of days.'

Saying goodbye was always going to be difficult, though, in the event, less so than he had expected. Helena was very brave, which of course made him feel even guiltier.

'I'll miss you.' Her voice broke as she turned away. 'Gally

too,' she said over her shoulder. 'He's grown very fond of you.'

'I'll be back,' he assured her. 'As often as I can, I promise. And I'll call you and Gally regularly.'

The boy's eyes were big and serious, staring at Lancelot uncomprehendingly as he tried to explain why 'daddy has to say goodbye'. When Lancelot knelt, tears stinging his eyes, to hug his son, Galahad stood stiffly in his arms for a moment or two, then abruptly pushed him away and left the room without a backward look.

Twenty One

CONVINCED THAT Lancelot would never return to Camelot, Guinevere felt abandoned and abused. How could he have done this to her, first making her fall in love with him, and then deserting her? She had been happy enough with Arthur, had never dreamed of looking at another man.

What hurt even more was that her rival in love, Helena, had given Lancelot a son, something she would never be able to do for Arthur. It wasn't fair. Because Arthur had been so understanding, she had somehow convinced herself that it didn't matter, and it really hadn't until now. But now it did, it mattered a great deal. For days she scarcely ate or slept. Humiliated and angry, she told herself again and again that she didn't care whether Lancelot came back or not. Why should she? It was all over between them.

But when she heard that a Scuttle, piloted by Gawain, was on its way to fly Lancelot back to Camelot, she was unable to conceal her joy.

It seemed to Lanky that her friend's happiness was laced with triumph. Was it Lancelot's return she was celebrating, or was it the fact that he was coming back to her? If that was how she felt, she could hardly blame her, for it was confirmation that Lancelot loved her, wasn't it? Not even his own son and the mother of his child could keep him away. Lanky was happy for her friend, but troubled too. Ginny had lost her heart. Had she lost that famous sense of hers with it?

Lancelot returned to Camelot like a conquering hero. Not only Arthur, but everyone on the island was relieved to have the Chief of Staff back again. Yet even as he was being warmly embraced by his peers and followers, Lancelot was wondering why Guinevere was not there on the landing pad to greet him. Surely she knew it was neither duty nor his love for Arthur that had drawn him back to Camelot; it was her. There could be only one explanation for her absence; she had kept her word. *If you go, it's the end.*

The next day, his worst fears were confirmed. Early in the morning a note was delivered by Lanky who was clearly relishing her role in the drama. He tore the note open and read: *I'm sorry, but there's no future for us. Please forgive me if I ever did or said anything to make you think there could be.*

She had said she loved him, no ifs and buts about it. And she had said it not just with words but with her eyes, her hands, her lips. *If I ever did or said anything . . .* Of course she did! He read the note again. And again. And yet again. And the more he read it, the more confused he became. His eyes swam, his limbs twitched, the blood sang in his ears.

That night he dreamed that Arthur was standing by his bedside.

'You betrayed me.'

'No! I would never do that.'

'You made love to my wife.'

'It isn't true!' he cried.

Wide awake now, heart racing, he sat up sharply, peering fearfully about him. There was no one there. It was all in his imagination.

When he woke the next morning he had a high fever. Rolling out of bed, he staggered to Command Control and collapsed on the floor of his office where his PA found him minutes later. Rushed to Camelot's hospital he was taken to the intensive care unit. The doctors concentrated on rehydrating his body and bringing down his temperature. Though his condition was serious, there was no obvious reason for it, and they could make no diagnosis.

Arthur was deeply troubled. Lancelot's illness was as unexpected as it was puzzling. 'I can't seem to get any sense out of the doctors,' he told Guinevere. 'What can be wrong with him?'

Why, she wondered, would Arthur imagine she knew more than the doctors? 'Some kind of nervous breakdown?' she ventured.

'He has difficult decisions to make,' said Arthur, 'personal ones. And those are always the most stressful, aren't they? Helena and Galahad pulling him one way, Camelot the other.'

'I suppose so,' she murmured.

He looked out at Camelot's white buildings. 'Tell me, Ginny,' he said, turning away from the glare, 'what is your opinion? Is it love of Camelot or love of his family that is pulling Lancelot most strongly?'

She blinked nervously. Was she being consulted or cross-examined? 'I'm afraid I don't know.'

Arthur sat behind his desk and doodled on a notepad. 'Because if it's Camelot, then we must persuade him to stay with us, reassure him that we need him, that we can't do without him. He can easily be in regular touch with Helena and Galahad, and of course visit them from time to time.' Those piercing blue eyes of his seemed to illuminate the dark caverns of her mind. 'If, on the other hand, the pull of family is strongest, then for the sake of his peace of mind we must encourage him to leave, even though it would mean losing someone we all admire . . . and love.'

She did not know what to say.

'What do you think, Ginny? Camelot or London?'

'Why ask me?' she said, trying to keep her voice steady.

'I thought perhaps you might know how he feels about Helena.'

'How would I know that?'

An airy wave of the hand. 'Woman's intuition.'

'What about man's intuition?' she asked, to gain time.

He looked at her thoughtfully. 'My guess is that he really is in love with her. I believe he only came back out of a sense of duty to Camelot, and to me.'

She was silent.

'Of course, if he did decide to go back to her,' said Arthur, scribbling idly on his notepad, 'it would be a great loss for Camelot, and for me personally. I would miss him. I would miss him terribly.'

Guinevere was suddenly aware of her heart thumping against her ribs. Why was he telling her all this?

'And so would you, of course,' he added.

What did he mean by that? Fearing that the answer to the question was there in his eyes, she could not look at him.

For more than a week Lancelot's mind wandered. Nurses, their shifts organised by an ever attentive Lanky, watched over him night and day. Ban, Arthur, Gawain, Agravaine, Gaheris, Leo Grant, Ian Duncan, and the many actives who served under him, took turns sitting by his bedside trying to get through to him, though never succeeding. He talked incessantly in an incoherent gabble, sometimes whispering, sometimes shouting. From time to time he would push himself up on his bed and cry out as if he were a soul in torment, then fall back into a deep sleep.

Guinevere did not visit him, afraid that by word or look or gesture she might betray her true feelings. Ban sat at his bedside for hours on end, talking to him in characteristic staccato bursts of speech. Even he could not reach his son.

One morning the fever left him. He looked pale and gaunt and was very weak, but the worst was over. The doctors said he would soon be on his feet again. Arthur and Guinevere visited him together and sat on either side of his bed. Even as they came into the room he was already apologising to Arthur. 'I have let you down, sir. You will have my resignation on your desk this afternoon.'

'Nonsense,' said Arthur, 'you have been sick, so naturally you feel a bit down. Let's have no talk of resignation. We need you, Lance. We love you,' he added softly.

'I am not worthy of your love,' muttered Lancelot, and though he looked straight ahead as he spoke, Guinevere knew the words were directed as much to her as to Arthur.

When they said goodbye, Arthur patted Lancelot's shoulder self-consciously and Guinevere held his hand, squeezing it gently as Arthur waited by the door. Had she held Lancelot's hand a second too long, she wondered. If so, had Arthur noticed? Later she remembered with relief that he could not have seen anything because his back was turned. Her relief was short-lived. Why was it turned, she asked herself; for no good reason she could think of, or at least none she cared to acknowledge.

It was only the second note he had written her, and it begged her to come to his apartment that afternoon. Guinevere was in torment. It was impossible. If she went to him now, there would be no more wandering in that hinterland between flirtation and commitment, no more ambiguity, no turning back. She had tried to persuade herself that their love was a spiritual union of twin souls, not to be contaminated by physical passion. Yet what was the use of pretending? She was in love, passionately, distractedly in love with Lancelot, and he with her. She sent her reply via Lanky. Three words: *Will be there*. What else could she do?

Neither of them knew how it had happened, or cared. One minute they were swimming in calm waters, the next, swept out to sea by a tidal wave they were drowning, with no hope of rescue and no chance of swimming back to shore. Nothing could have been more unexpected, and nothing more inevitable. It was as if they had always been in love, as if they had known each other for a hundred lifetimes.

Against all good sense and reason, Guinevere had surrendered to passion. For once she had allowed her heart to rule her head, something she had sworn would never happen, and far from regretting it, she was blissfully happy. From that day, the memory of their love-making never left her. Wherever she was, whatever she was doing, whoever she was speaking to, she was still, in some secret part of her mind, in bed with Lancelot, kissing him, fondling him, shivering at the touch of his hands. It was exciting, but frightening too. Yet if anything troubled her it was not guilt, it was the fear that Arthur might find out. She would do anything not to hurt him; anything, that is, but give up Lancelot.

Lancelot's conscience, on the other hand, troubled him greatly. Since that day at Oxford when his prayers had brought Daniel Shalott back from the brink of death, he was convinced that his life had a special meaning and purpose, and that God had work for him to do. Not any more. Adultery was a sin, it contaminated his own image of what he was and what he aspired to be. He had done what he had so often criticised others for doing: he had lost control, and being out of control was frightening to a man accustomed to ordering every aspect of his life. Love was being out of control, love was chaos, love was a kind of madness.

And of all things, he feared madness.

Twenty Two

SINCE HE WAS NOT expecting visitors, Merlin was surprised when the doorbell of his cottage rang. At the door was a slightly built young man with a narrow face and dark eyes, about seventeen or eighteen years old.

'May I come in?'

'You are welcome,' said Merlin, ushering his visitor to a Windsor chair by the fireplace and taking the chair opposite.

'Do you know who I am?'

Images of the past – children playing, a country house, manicured lawns – drifted like spirits through Merlin's head.

'They tell me I am like my mother,' said Mordred, teasing Merlin's memory. 'Less like my father, apparently.'

Apparently. The word was obviously significant, and intended to be. Had his father died? Divorced? Left the country? Then suddenly he remembered . . . the blurred images were in focus, past and present merged. 'You are Mordred,' said Merlin, 'Lennox and Margot's son.'

'Partly right,' said Mordred with a wan smile.

Merlin made no comment, though he knew what Mordred meant, and why he was here.

'My dear mother tells me that her husband, Lennox Lotte, the man I always assumed was my father, is in fact no relation of mine.' Below Mordred's cheekbone a muscle twitched uncontrollably. 'It seems my real father is Arthur Pendragon. My mother had a brief fling with him at Oxford.' A keen look. 'But you knew that, didn't you?'

'Yes.'

'Why didn't you tell me?'

'Because I have seen neither you nor your family for many years,' said Merlin. 'Besides, it was for your mother to tell you, not me.'

'Or my father,' said Mordred.

'Arthur never knew he had a son,' said Merlin.

'You and Arthur go back a long way,' said Mordred insinuatingly.

'Yes, we do. Nevertheless it's the truth,'

'Is it?'A keen look. 'I imagine it is,' said Mordred. 'My mother said he wanted her to have an abortion, and she agreed – reluctantly – to have one. He must have thought she had taken care of his little foetus problem.'

Merlin said nothing.

'So it's thanks to my dear mother that I didn't end up a bloody pulp in some hospital trash can,' said Mordred. 'I suppose I should be grateful to her.' A bitter smile. 'I wonder why I'm not.'

Far from being grateful, she disgusted him, not just because she had committed adultery, but because of the man she had done it with. It had taken a while for the full significance of the adulterous coupling to dawn on him. Recalling that recent exchange with his mother, the hot bile rose in the back of his throat, souring his mouth.

'Igraine is your mother.'

'Yes.'

'And she was Arthur's mother too.'

'Yes.'

'So you had sex with your own brother!'

'My half-brother, darling. Don't exaggerate.'

'Only your half-brother! I do beg your pardon, mother. So it was only half incest.'

'You make it sound like something dirty. It wasn't like that at all.'

'How was it then? You mean you didn't fuck? What did you

do, then? Clink test tubes in the college bar?'

He and his brothers, Gawain, Agravaine, Gaheris and Gareth, had always known that their mother was chronically unfaithful. Lennox – either blissfully ignorant or burying his head in the sand – never once complained, nor ever seemed to waver in his love for her. Looking back now, it was clear they had all been complicit in their mother's extra-marital relationships, none of which, as it happened, greatly affected their lives. This one had, though. This one was different. It had given him life, at the same time creating in him the longing to be revenged on the very people who gave it to him.

'Tell me, mother, when you fucked him, did you know Arthur was your half-brother?'

Her reaction, he recalled, was first to howl indignantly, and then to break down in a torrent of tears that sent rivulets of mascara streaming down her face.

'How can you say such a thing? How cruel you are! Of course I didn't.' Wiping her face clean of make-up, she looked younger and curiously vulnerable. For an instant he had felt a pang of sympathy for her; and then he caught that slyly malicious look in her eye. *'But he knew! Oh yes, he knew alright. He told me later that screwing his sister was a huge turn-on.'*

Whether he believed her or not, the accusation left its mark. Never in his whole life had he hated anyone as much as he hated Arthur. It occurred to him to wonder whether his mother was manipulating him, using him as the instrument of her own revenge. Well then, if she was, so be it.

'If my father doesn't know he has a son,' said Mordred, forcing a cheerful smile, 'let me be the one to break the good news to him. I shall have found my real father, and he will have a son he never knew existed. A happy ending for both of us.'

Merlin was not so sure. Somehow he did not associate Mordred with happy endings.

'I intend to pay him a visit,' said Mordred. 'Gareth will be coming with me.'

Merlin knew how attached Margot's youngest son was to his mother, as was she to him, and wondered why he was leaving her. Was it because he wanted to join his brothers in Camelot, or had Mordred persuaded him to leave her out of spite?

'I shall need your help to get to Camelot,' said Mordred, trying to look and sound casual.

Which had to be the real reason for the unexpected visit. Mordred in Camelot? Merlin looked into the young man's heart, and what he saw there troubled him. Tempted to refuse, he decided he could not. Not even he could stop the wheel turning.

Twenty Three

GAWAIN, AGRAVAINE AND GAHERIS crowded eagerly round the new arrivals, greeting their younger brothers, Mordred and Gareth, with warm embraces. Waiting a few moments for the excitement to subside, Arthur came forward to welcome his two nephews. 'Let me get a good look at you,' he said, holding Gareth at arm's length. 'What brings you here?'

'I wasn't going to let Mordred leave me at home,' said Gareth.

Arthur chuckled. 'You've grown into a fine young man. How old are you now?'

'Sixteen, sir,' said Gareth, and then, observing Gawain's disapproving look, 'well, nearly sixteen. I want to be a member of the Round Table.'

'You don't think you're a bit young?' said Arthur, laughing.

'Not too young to do a man's work,' insisted Gareth.

'I like your spirit. We'll see about the Round Table in a couple of year's time.'

Gareth's mouth drooped.

'The years pass all too quickly,' said Arthur. 'Don't be in too much of a hurry.'

Next he clasped Mordred's hand, drew him close and hugged him. 'You are most welcome to Camelot, Mordred,' he said.

'It's an enormous privilege to be here, sir,' said Mordred.

'You are eighteen?'

'Yes, sir.'

'Then we shall make you a member of the Round Table.'

'Thank you, sir. A great honour,' murmured Mordred.

'And call me uncle,' said Arthur. 'All my other nephews do.'

Mordred hesitated. What an opportunity to embarrass his father here in the Great Hall of the Round Table in front of all his groupies. How satisfying it would be to gatecrash his party with the truth, the searing truth. God, it was tempting, indeed so tempting, it was almost impossible to resist...but no, it would not be right. Timing was everything. There would be better opportunities in the future. Arthur was strong now, a world hero. The time to strike would be when he was so weakened that one final blow would finish him off. 'Thank you, uncle,' said Mordred, his composed manner revealing nothing of the turmoil in his head. 'I should say,' he added, 'how much I admire what you are doing, and how honoured I feel to be given the chance to serve you.'

Touched by the warmth of Mordred's words, Arthur reached out and gently patted his cheek. 'You have left your parents and everything dear to you to join me, and I am grateful for that. From now on, let Camelot be your home.'

Taking Gareth and Mordred by the arm Arthur guided them through the hall to meet first Guinevere, then Lancelot, and in turn every member of the Round Table. When the introductions were almost completed, the two brothers having been separated by the crowd, an overweight man with pale eyes, thinning hair and a double chin, thrust out a hand at Mordred.

'Keir,' he said, and when Mordred looked blank, explained: 'Arthur's brother – actually his adoptive brother.' A grimace. 'Brother. Adoptive brother. Same difference. Eh, Arthur?'

Arthur murmured something indeterminate that might have indicated either agreement or disagreement.

'My parents took Arthur in when he was two weeks old. Very good to him, weren't they, Art? So we are no relation really – just good friends.'

Mordred had heard the story of Keir and Arthur from Margot. Jealous of Arthur, Keir envied everything about him; his success, his fame, his friends, above all the love that Keir's birth parents, Hector and Elizabeth, had lavished on their adopted son. As young men they had grown apart: Arthur first going to Oxford, then joining the army, and later embarking on a political career; Keir taking a succession of jobs in business, none of which lasted. Knowing he was out of work, Arthur had taken pity on him and offered him a post as an assistant controller in Camelot's transport unit.

'We need men like you,' said Keir, conveying an almost possessive interest in the new arrival. 'No doubt we shall be seeing a great deal of each other.' Wandering off, he left behind a thoughtful Mordred. Two things were obvious; the first that Keir was a born loser, the second that he hated Arthur. Nothing could be more damaging to your self-esteem than being dependent on another man's generosity, the more so when that man was the cuckoo in the nest, the usurper of your parents' affections. The time would come when Keir might prove a useful ally.

Arthur said goodbye. 'I have work to do, Mord. I leave you among friends.'

'Thank you, uncle, thank you for everything.' As Arthur was about to leave, Mordred remembered he had something more to say. 'Oh, I nearly forgot.'

'Yes?'

'My mother sends you her very special love.'

Arthur could hardly conceal his discomfort. 'She must have been sad to part with you and Gareth,' was all he could think of to say.

'She was, sir, indeed she was. Very sad. But happy for both of us, happy that we were leaving her to serve her beloved Arthur. She has a very soft spot for you, as I'm sure you know.'

Was it Arthur's imagination, or was there some disquieting innuendo in Mordred's words? But then, observing his nephew's steady and untroubled gaze, he thought he must have been mistaken, reflecting ruefully that sometimes a man's conscience played strange tricks on him, causing him to doubt the sincerity of others.

Both brothers made an excellent impression on Lancelot – Gareth for his boyish enthusiasm and engaging manner, Mordred for his modesty, even more so for his unreserved admiration for Camelot's Chief of Staff.

'It is an honour and a privilege to meet you, sir. I understand it was you who led the operation against those monstrous Sea Lords. The world is truly in your debt.'

Lancelot's gracious smile acknowledged the compliment. Clearly this young man was bright. He would make a point of looking out for him.

Guinevere found Gareth barely less enchanting than he found her. Young as he was, he could not disguise his instant infatuation for the most beautiful woman he had ever laid eyes on. Mordred she took to, though with less warmth, admiring his dark, saturnine looks, his intelligence and self-possession. Moreover she found his obvious interest in her flattering, if a shade intrusive, disturbing even. Why was that, she wondered. Was it the direct, uncompromising challenge of his stare? Or the fact that his eyes followed her round the hall long after she said goodbye to him?

As the members of the Round Table streamed out of the Great Hall and back to work, Lancelot caught up with Guinevere. Torn between his fear of compromising her and his overwhelming desire to be with her, speak to her, touch her, make love to her again, Lancelot was barely able to control his nervous energy, powered as it was by uneasiness and frustration.

Guinevere, too, was nervous, though for a different reason. Being ecstatically happy one moment and deeply troubled the next was not her notion of a happy life. Good sense told her she ought to end this dangerous affair now, or it would soon be too late; if it was not too late already.

Lancelot fought to control himself, nodding to friends and colleagues as he passed them, feigning indifference to the woman at his side. Was this what life would be like from now on? Subterfuge and yet more subterfuge? But then what if it was, he could not help himself. 'Tomorrow at the same place?' he said softly, looking straight ahead, his lips barely moving as he formed the words. Dissembling was for him a new experience, a despised but indispensable companion he would have to learn to live with.

'Tomorrow,' she whispered, longing to be in his arms again, and at the same time hating herself for being weak. It was all so demeaning to her pride and so damaging to her self-respect, both of which she had always valued. As they passed each other, a man walked quickly by, brushing against her and murmuring an apology. Turning, she saw that it was Mordred. He smiled and waved.

For some reason she hesitated before waving back.

Twenty Four

NIWIS

ABOVE THE ENTRANCE of a gleaming white spherical building, inscribed in letters so small that it could easily be missed, was a single, cryptic word – NIWIS. Everyone in Camelot knew its meaning: Nothing Is What It Seems.

The entrance panel buzzed, the door clicked open, and there, waiting for Arthur and Agravaine, was a mountain of a man. Everything about Ian Tichgame was big; his eyes, his belly, his hands, his voice, his laugh, his heart, his brain. So naturally he was Tich to everyone. It was rumoured that he had once been a magician and illusionist, and that Merlin had recognised his potential when he saw his act in a working man's club in Liverpool. What Merlin was doing there he had never explained, though nothing in his life ever happened by chance. It was Merlin and Tich who came up with the concept of NIWIS to explore the void between what was, and what appeared to be. At first Nothing Is What It Seems was simply an extension of the magician's art. It was Merlin who showed Tich that it could be much more than that; the creation by illusion of another world, a world in which reality is unreal, and unreality real, a world in which truths are lies, and lies, truths. Tich called it 'Disinformation'. Merlin preferred 'Virtual Unreality'.

Arthur greeted his friend warmly. 'What's on your mind, Tich?'

'Something that doesn't make sense. Two days ago Command Control launched a swarm of mini-satellites in low orbit over the Middle East. Some were tracked and destroyed, but a lot got through. Over a period of several hours maximum cover was achieved, and Techforce Ten has been processing a mass of data. The thing is, we're getting some strange feedback from two countries – the Kingdom of the Euphrates and the Democratic Arab Republic. I can call up a brief background history if you like.'

'Go ahead,' said Arthur.

Ian Tichgame worried his keyboard, and in seconds the text was on the monitor screen. Arthur studied it with interest.

In the year 2012, despite continued unrest, the last American troops were withdrawn from Iraq. Less than a year later the country was torn apart by civil war – Sunni against Shiite, with the Kurds caught in the middle. The United States had been badly burned invading Iraq in 2003 and was reluctant to intervene again. Whilst the United Nations dithered, order was quickly and brutally restored by Sadiq el Shaeb (the People's Friend), a man known to be close to the Islamist rulers of Iran. Under his leadership a group of the most powerful tribes took over the country, renaming it the Kingdom of the Euphrates, commonly known as the KOE, murdering those who dared oppose them, and imposing on a country worn out by killing, a regime even more brutal than that of Sadiq's great uncle, Saddam Hussein.

In 2014 a popular uprising led by Ibn Khalid, an American educated Saudi, and a personal friend of the US President, overthrew the extreme Islamists who had ruled the Democratic Arab Republic (formerly Saudi Arabia) since the coup that toppled the Royal Saudi House in 2012. Needless to say, the western world, and especially the United States, were delighted that the oil rich country was "back in the fold".

Since 2014 the DAR and its anti-Western neighbour, the KOE, have co-existed uneasily. There have been exchanges of insults, and, from time to time, border clashes. Foreign policy experts agree that as long as it does not heat up, this state of "no war no peace" between these two Middle East powers is good for the west, preserving the balance of power in the Middle East and taking the heat off Israel. It is well known that the United States supplies the Democratic Arab Republic with arms, technology and money, and is the largest buyer of the crude oil produced in that country.

By early August 2029, however, the mutual antagonism between the Democratic Arab Republic and the Kingdom of the Euphrates had become so acute that it threatened the stability of the whole region. Moreover the proliferation of nuclear weapons in the previous decade greatly increased the stakes in the Middle East. The missiles of both countries, mostly conventional, but some nuclear, were now targeting each other. The United Nations attempted to calm the situation, but its pleas were largely ignored. Moreover the USA's attention was distracted by a major terrorist incident in Jakarta, Indonesia, where Islamist suicide bombers breached the defences of a heavily guarded US military installation inflicting massive damage and many casualties.

'What exactly is bothering you?' asked Arthur.

Tich scratched his unshaven chin noisily with one massive finger. 'Sadiq and Khalid have been at each other's throat for years, we all know that, but recently things have been hotting up. In the last few days the world's media has reported a surge of activity on the border between the two countries; troops, tanks and armoured cars on the move. Yesterday, missiles with conventional warheads were fired, and both sides claim to have inflicted significant damage to the other's military installations, and a large number of casualties.'

None of this of course was news to Arthur. Command Control had kept him informed on a daily basis. 'I have spoken to the US President,' he said. 'He is putting huge pressure on both Sadiq and Khalid, threatening military action if they don't stop throwing missiles around. He sounds optimistic.'

'Now here's the thing,' said Tich. 'When you consider the

number of missiles launched by the DAR and the KOE, our surveillance shows surprisingly little damage, and no casualties.'

'Don't you think this whole exercise is just sabre rattling,' said Agravaine. 'Sadiq and Khalid have played this game countless times. It's a sideshow they put on to impress their friends and enemies. I don't think either of them really wants war. They know how serious the consequences would be.'

Tich's big fingers thumped the keyboard; on screen now was a magnified satellite image of KOE tanks, armoured cars, artillery and missile launchers – most of them damaged, many totally destroyed. A pause, and similar images, this time in the DAR, appeared on screen.

Agravaine was puzzled. 'I thought you said our surveillance showed hardly any damage.'

'That's exactly the point,' said Tich. 'None of what you are looking at is real. All those tanks, armoured cars and missile launchers are dummies.'

'It seems Sadiq and Khalid have learned a thing or two about the art of deception,' said Arthur.

'They certainly have,' said Tich. 'But who are they trying to deceive?'

'The USA?' suggested Agravaine.

'Khalid is America's friend,' said Arthur.

Tich shifted his big bulk left and right on his stool, releasing first one numb cheek, then the other, sighing with relief as the blood flowed slowly back to his buttocks. 'What if Khalid is only pretending to be America's friend?'

Now it was Arthur's turn to look puzzled. 'Why would he do that?'

Tich's hands looped and spiralled as if he were conjuring ideas out of the air. 'Let's imagine that the KOE and the DAR are not enemies, but allies . . . and that together they have hatched a master plan to take over the Middle East. To do that they would need to deal a mortal blow to the west, above all to America. Obviously the success of the plan would depend on surprise. What better way to achieve that than to start a phoney war, a war that is pure theatre, an illusion intended to deceive the real enemy.'

Arthur and Agravaine listened with growing astonishment.

'I believe the United States is in great danger,' said Tich.

A small mole of concern burrowed deep just above the bridge of Arthur's nose. 'In danger of what?'

'A first strike nuclear missile attack,' said Tich.

Twenty Five

NIWIS

THE FOUR DOUBLE DOORS of the Great Hall clanged shut, and the Guardian robots announced in their strident voices: *Doors shut and secured.*

When Tich had finished addressing its members, Arthur invited their comments. Lancelot was the first to speak. 'Does anyone seriously believe that Sadiq and Khalid would dare attack the greatest power on earth?'

'Sadiq is a psychopath, a power-hungry megalomaniac,' said Leo Grant. 'He wants to be the number one power in the Middle East. So far he has been frustrated in that ambition, largely by America. So yes, I do think it's conceivable that he may have decided to take them on. And a man like that would not even consider the possibility of failure.'

'What about Khalid?' said Gawain. 'They say he went to school with the President. I know for a fact that he's a personal friend of many prominent men in the US administration. Why would he turn against America? Sorry, Tich, it doesn't make sense.'

'Let's assume for a moment,' said Tich, 'that he isn't the friend of the west he pretends to be, and that he and Sadiq are allies. Those two working together would be a formidable power in the Middle East, one that would present a serious challenge to the West. With the advantage of surprise, the DAR and the KOE could in theory launch a nuclear strike against the United States. With a bit of luck they could destroy many US missile sites and military installations.'

Agravaine was not convinced. 'They would never catch

America by surprise in a million years. If Sadiq and Khalid tried to launch a missile attack, the Americans would know the second the missile motors started up. And even if, by some extraordinary mischance, they were taken by surprise, how many missiles would get through? Their anti-missile defence system is now fully functional. Besides, our surveillance confirms that the DAR and the KOE are not targeting the US. They are targeting each other, just as they have done for years.'

'They could re-target their missiles, couldn't they?' said Arthur.

'If they did,' said Gawain, 'the Americans would pick it up immediately.'

Tich looked thoughtful. 'Immediately? I wonder. Remember, someone has just destroyed their horizon radar in Indonesia. We all assumed that the aim of the terrorists was to destabilise the Far East. Supposing it wasn't? Supposing it was to make it more difficult for the Americans to get advance warning of a nuclear missile attack launched in the Middle East?'

There was an ominous silence whilst the Round Table absorbed the implications of Tich's question.

'The Americans still have hundreds of spy satellites,' Lancelot pointed out. 'Surely they would spot any unusual activity in and around missile sites? Long before their missile motors started up, the KOE and the DAR would be challenged for an explanation. If they couldn't give a satisfactory one damn quickly, the Americans would launch a pre-emptive strike. And that would be goodbye to the KOE and the DAR. They would be radioactive ash in minutes.'

Lancelot's argument seemed unanswerable. Even Tich conceded grudgingly, 'You could be right.'

The Round Table adjourned without reaching any conclusion. Command Control and NIWIS remained on red alert, keeping the Middle East under close observation. Arthur decided to warn the US President, though he might have saved himself the trouble.

'I'm sorry, Arthur, but this time you guys are chasing shadows. Khalid is a buddy of mine, and a great friend of the United States. I think you should know that only an hour ago I had a call from him asking for help. Sadiq is threatening the DAR with a nuclear attack. Khalid is worried. If the US doesn't do something, he'll be compelled to defend himself. He won't stand idly by while his country is threatened with destruction by a maniac.'

Two days later, in a diplomatic coup widely hailed as a triumph, the President brought Khalid and Sadiq to heel. A White House spokesman confirmed that in approximately forty-eight hours Ibn Khalid and Sadiq el Shaeb would fly to Washington, and from there to Camp David, for talks with the US President. It was generally acknowledged that the President's prompt and decisive action had averted the danger of a Middle East, possibly even a global, nuclear conflict.

When Command Control and NIWIS both reported a complete cessation of military activities in the DAR and the KOE, Gawain and Lancelot, backed by the majority of the Round Table, were convinced that the danger – if there had been any danger – had passed.

Arthur, nevertheless, was uneasy. At times like this he felt in need of his friend's wise counsel. He was sipping coffee in his kitchen, thinking not about the Middle East, but about the pink glow in Guinevere's cheeks and the new sparkle of excitement in her lovely eyes, when there, without warning, was Merlin's holographic head resting on a shelf between a tin of digestive biscuits and a bowl of sugar.

'You want to know about Khalid,' said the Magus. It was not a question.

Disconcerting though it was, Merlin's ability to read minds saved a great deal of time. Arthur shifted on his chair. 'Could you not manifest your whole body?'

A severe look. 'As I have told you before, full manifestations are tiring and usually quite unnecessary. It is, after all, my head you wish to consult, is it not?'

Arthur acknowledged with a smile that it was.

'You are wondering if Sadiq and Khalid are up to something,' continued Merlin.

'I am.'

'And yet you have the most advanced and sophisticated surveillance network on the planet.'

'It's as you always told me. Nothing is what it seems.'

As if to prove the point, the head glided from shelf to table where, disconcertingly, it came to a halt next to the mug of coffee, its big green eyes staring unblinkingly at Arthur. 'Mercury was only a few hours old when he stole the gods' cattle from Apollo,' said the head, apropos of nothing. 'Did I ever tell you that?'

'You might have done,' said Arthur. 'I can't remember.'

'You do know, of course,' said the head, looking sternly at Arthur, 'that Mercury is the patron of thieves?'

'I'm afraid not,' said Arthur, who found the proximity of the holographic head disturbing.

'Well, live and learn, he is,' said the head, retreating to its original position on the shelf between sugar and biscuits. 'He is also a chronic schemer.' Another penetrating look. 'Did you know that?'

'No,' said Arthur, 'I didn't.'

'Indeed?' Accompanied by steeply arched eyebrows, the word conveyed both astonishment and mild rebuke. 'Let me educate you, then,' said Merlin, as if Arthur were still his pupil at Glastonbury school. 'Mercury and Mars were the sons of Zeus, and Mercury loved playing tricks on his big oaf of a brother.'

'What has all this to do with Khalid?'

With a broad wink of a holographic eye, Merlin's head began to fade, and to Arthur's enormous frustration there was soon nothing on the shelf between the biscuit tin and the sugar bowl. The Magus had vanished, leaving behind him only his voice, and that too was fading fast. 'Mercury is the clue.'

Clue? What sort of clue? Why was the Magus being so infuriatingly obscure? Why couldn't he just say what he meant? When night came, Arthur fed the planetary codes into the telescope's computer and watched it track through the solar system, coming to rest at last on the planet Mercury; nothing especially distinguished about it, the second smallest of all the planets orbited the sun every eighty-eight days, and was barely visible to the naked eye.

So what did Merlin mean, *Mercury is the clue*?

Somewhere in the shadowy waters of Arthur's memory a thought glided, elusive as a fish.

Twenty Six

NIWIS

THROUGH THE AFTERNOON and evening, past midnight and on through the small hours of the next day until mid-morning, Ian Tichgame, Agravaine and Arthur debated, theorised and squabbled, venting their growing frustration. Sitting at his own terminal, saying nothing, but listening with great concentration to every word, was Mordred. At Arthur's request, Tich had taken him on as his assistant. 'My nephew is observant, and he's a good listener. I have a feeling he understands more than he says.' So far though, the young man had made no significant contribution to the business of NIWIS, and Tich was not overly impressed.

Agravaine raised two hands in mock surrender. 'I'm all thought out, nuncle. My head aches, my back is killing me, even my brain cells hurt.'

'Let's take a break,' said Tich. He was tired. Every part of his big body was tired, his arms, his legs, his shoulders, his belly, the wimples of fat round his neck – they were all tired. 'Let's look at it again in a couple of hours. Things could look different then.'

'In a couple of hours the world could be at war,' said Arthur. 'Let's look at it now.'

The bin at Agravaine's feet overflowed with soggy tissues. For the hundredth time he polished his pink-tinted spectacles fastidiously, deposited the used tissue in the bin, and, with compulsive care, realigned the tissue box until it was precisely parallel with his keyboard and equidistant from all the other tissue boxes. No one else, not Tich, not Mordred, not even

Arthur, understood that if that tissue box was not correctly aligned, the world would end.

For the umpteenth time Arthur repeated Merlin's words. 'Mercury and Mars were the sons of Zeus. Mercury loved playing tricks on his big oaf of a brother.'

Tich sighed. 'Let's give it one last try.'

'The clue is Mercury,' said Arthur. He tapped his keyboard, and **Mercury** pulsated on his monitor. 'What do we know about him?'

'He was the messenger of the gods,' droned Agravaine wearily.

'How does that help us?' asked Tich. Despite his exhaustion, there was the glint of adventure in his eye.

'I don't see how it does,' said Arthur. 'What else do we know?'

'We know Mercury was a thief,' said Tich.

'True,' said Arthur thoughtfully. 'He stole Apollo's cattle.'

'Who exactly was Apollo?' asked Agravaine.

'The sun god,' said Arthur.

More pondering. 'Wait a minute,' said Tich, his eyes seemingly focused on something far out in space. 'Apollo had to be an excellent guard for the gods to trust him with their cattle. Right?'

Agravaine was losing interest. 'So?'

'So how come Mercury was able to steal them?'

'Apollo was asleep,' suggested Arthur.

'The gods never sleep,' said Tich.

Agravaine yawned. 'Doesn't make sense,' he said. 'If he was awake, why didn't he see Mercury steal his cattle?'

A long, baffled silence was broken at last by Mordred sitting at his terminal. 'Perhaps he didn't know what he was looking at,' he murmured, his back to the three men.

'Are you suggesting he was awake and just wasn't looking,' said Tich.

Mordred hunched his shoulders in embarrassment. 'No,' he

said. 'He was looking. The thing is . . . ' Tailing off, he appeared to have lost heart.

'Go on, Mord,' prompted Arthur encouragingly, 'we're listening.'

Mordred swung round on his stool to face them. 'Apollo was looking alright,' he said, a glint of excitement in his eyes, 'but he only saw what Mercury wanted him to see. He didn't see what was there in front of his nose, because he was fooled by a master of deception. Isn't that what Merlin's clue was about?'

Tich stared wide-eyed at Mordred.

'I don't get it,' said Agravaine.

'Sadiq and Ibn both have their own call signs,' said Mordred. 'Right?'

'Right.'

'And Ibn's call sign is . . . ?' He left the question hanging.

Agravaine punched the air with his fist. 'Mercury!' he cried. 'Oh my god! His call sign is Mercury!'

'Mercury the schemer who plays tricks on Mars,' said Tich, a new respect in his eye as he looked at Mordred, 'Mercury the winged messenger whose messages no one trusts for fear they are lies and inventions.'

'So,' said Arthur slowly, 'Merlin is telling us Khalid is the arch deceiver.'

As the meeting broke up, Arthur put his arm round Mordred's shoulder. 'Congratulations, Mord. That was a brilliant insight of yours.'

'Pure luck,' said Mordred modestly.

Tich shook his head. 'That wasn't luck. You, young man, understand how truth can be manipulated, and that's a rare gift. You shall be my second-in-command. Together we shall develop the art of deception until it becomes a weapon as powerful as any in Camelot's armoury.'

Less than an hour after the meeting broke up, TV channels around the world showed first one, and then a second Titan – the largest commercial aircraft in the world – soaring into the blue sky above the Kingdom of the Euphrates and the Democratic Arab Republic, bound for Washington. Minutes later Arthur was on videolink to Tich and Agravaine to inform them that Techforce Ten in Command Control had just monitored two calls from the White House to the Titans wishing the two leaders God speed and expressing confidence that the historic Camp David meeting would be a fruitful one.

'Well, that's it,' said Agravaine, 'we were wrong.'

'It looks like it,' agreed Arthur, who had joined Agravaine in Galaxy. In rapid succession, he issued a number of orders. Eclipse, piloted by Lancelot, took off from the launch pad, and was soon heading west at top speed, its mission to stay mantled and track the two Titans on their flight to the US.

From Eclipse came the voice of the robot controller. 'Overhead Titans in ten minutes.'

Waiting for further news from Eclipse, Arthur pursued his train of thought. 'Do we have Sadiq and Khalid's signatures?'

Agravaine checked with Techforce Ten who confirmed they were analysing the available data. The "signatures" of world leaders, prominent politicians, army, navy and air force commanders, doctors, lawyers, businessmen, secret service agents, police and of course known terrorists, were stored in their thousands in Command Control's closely-guarded online storage depot. These "signatures", gathered over the years, mostly by satellites and robots, helped identify individuals by various means, including physical characteristics such as facial and body configuration, colour and shape of eyes, hair colour and texture, fingerprints, skin abnormalities like moles and scars, body temperature, smell, accents and voice. Not only physical clues, but behavioural patterns and gestures were analysed and stored. In a number of cases it had also been possible to obtain DNA profiles.

'We do,' confirmed Agravaine.

'And we can positively identify them?'

'All we have to do is programme a few holograph mini-satellites with their signatures.'

'Let's do it, then.'

'What's the point, nuncle? We already know they're on board the Titans.'

Arthur's expression gave nothing away. 'It will be a useful test for the holograph satellites,' he said.

Giving his uncle a strange look, Agravaine's fingers floated across the keyboard. He pointed at the monitor. 'Watch for circular red markers. A holograph satellite makes a pinging sound that becomes one steady signal when it locks on to its target.' The two men hung expectantly over the big table screen. Three red markers floated in and out of view making their pinging sounds, then another five, then nothing for thirty seconds, then another two. None of them was sending the lock-on signal. Agravaine gnawed at what was left of his nails.

'That's odd.' Agravaine frowned. 'All those satellites are within signal range of the Titans. We should have picked up Sadiq's and Khalid's signatures by now.'

More satellite images floated into view.

'Still no signal?'

'No,' said Agravaine. 'I don't understand it. Must be a satellite fault.'

'I dare say,' said Arthur. Picking up something odd in his voice, Agravaine looked at him sharply, but again his expression was inscrutable.

Now Lancelot was on speaker. 'We are mantled, overhead Titans at sixty thousand feet. Awaiting instructions.'

Arthur's hand hit the gravitational wave communicator. 'Scan both Titans, Lance.'

'What am I looking for, sir?'

'Anything that ought not to be there. Or anything that ought to be there and isn't.'

Lancelot was puzzled. 'Such as?'

'You'll know when you find it, or when you don't,' was the

laconic response.

Agravaine wiped the sweat from his bald head. 'What's this all about, nuncle?'

'When I know, I'll tell you.'

Which could hardly be less informative. Agravaine cursed under his breath, his admiration for Arthur sorely tested.

Minutes later, Arthur was on screen with the US President. ' I don't know where Khalid and Sadiq are, but one thing I do know – they are not on the Titans.'

'They were when I spoke to them a couple of hours ago,' said the President.

'How can you be certain of that?'

'I recognised their voices.' During the silence that followed, the US President was thinking hard. 'You don't think someone could have imitated them?'

'Perhaps,' said Arthur. 'Or maybe you really did speak to Sadiq and Khalid. But whoever you spoke to and wherever they were, they were not on the Titans.'

'I can't believe it,' said the President. 'Sadiq, I never trusted. But Khalid? For chrissake, Arthur, we went to school together. He and I are buddies from way back.'

'You're quite sure?'

'At my age you can't be sure of anything,' said the President glumly. 'Fact is, I can't afford to take risks. So let's say you are right, and those two are holed up somewhere else – who in God's name is on board those Titans?'

'Who, or what?' said Arthur.

On the screen Arthur watched the President's expression transform itself from confusion to horror. 'You don't think . . . ?'

'I don't want to speculate,' said Arthur. 'We have both aircraft under surveillance.'

The President was close to panic. 'They're planning to crash them on US targets,' he said, by now convinced that imminent catastrophe threatened. 'Filled with explosives they could kill a heck of a lot of people. This could be another 9/11 disaster.'

'I believe they may have other ideas,' said Arthur.

'Such as?'

Before Arthur could respond, Lancelot was on screen.

'Eclipse has just completed scanning the two Titans. First, we confirm that neither Sadiq nor Khalid are on board either aircraft. Second, both aircraft have been converted into missile launch pads and are carrying medium-range missiles armed with nuclear warheads. We can't be precise, but we think each Titan is carrying about eight missiles. Third, both craft are packed with high explosives and fissionable material, so aside from the missiles, the Titans themselves are deadly weapons.'

The President's face was grey. 'This can't be happening,' he said, his voice unsteady.

Lancelot continued relentlessly. 'Each Titan carries a crew of seven men. So it's a suicide mission. My guess is they'll launch the missiles at military complexes and missile sites across the USA, and then, if they haven't been destroyed, they'll crash both aircraft into pre-selected targets – quite possibly key civilian centres.' Having delivered his disturbing message, Lancelot faded from the screen.

'They'll never reach the USA,' declared the President, thumping his desk. 'We'll blow them out of the sky before they get there.' A moment's reflection, and he was having doubts. 'I hope to God we have enough time,' he muttered. Before Arthur could comment, the President broke off to consult his advisers. A minute later he was back on screen. 'The Senate is insisting on evidence before we shoot down two commercial aircraft.'

'The images we scanned from the Titans are on their way to your Space Defence Operations Centre,' said Arthur. 'They should be there by now.'

'Hold again,' said the President.

This time he was back on screen almost immediately. 'Space Centre has the data, and I have the Senate's go-ahead. This is it, Arthur. We have five fighters in the air.'

'How long before they reach the targets?'

'Approximately fifteen minutes. Pray God they get there in time.'

'Why not use heat-seeking missiles to shoot down the Titans?'

'If they see missiles coming at them, the Titans might launch their nuclear missiles. It's a close call, but my Defence Chiefs have opted for fighter aircraft. They believe they'll have surprise on their side. Either way there's a risk.'

'I can take the risk out of the equation,' said Arthur.

'How?'

'Eclipse is overhead the Titans. Let me order her to Elimat them.'

The President hesitated. 'It's tempting, but I can't let you do that,' he said. 'Letting Camelot do the job for us would be like admitting to the terrorists that the USA can't defend itself.'

Arthur did not argue the point. America's prestige as the greatest power on earth was at stake. Yet as time ran out and the two aircraft lumbered through the air toward the US Eastern Seaboard, it was obvious that the President was taking a big chance. Millions of people were in danger. The connection was cut, the two men agreeing to consult again shortly.

The US fighters were now ten minutes from their target, the Titans twenty minutes from the east coast of the USA.

'We have visual, Lance,' said Agravaine. 'Give me sound.'

Mini-images of two fat-bellied Titans were on the table monitor, the piercing high-pitched whine of their engines shrill in Galaxy's speakers. Then, like a bass counterpoint, came Lancelot's deep voice: 'Transmitting visuals of Titan's interior. Minimal activity, as you see.'

The seconds ticked by. Techforce Ten gave an update. *Fighters nine minutes from target, Titans nineteen minutes from US coast.* From Eclipse, Lancelot continued to report on the activity, or lack of it, in the Titans' cabins: 'No significant movement. Everyone seems to be waiting. Missile launch believed imminent. Exact timing uncertain.'

And again from Techforce: *Fighters seven minutes from*

target, Titans seventeen minutes from US coast. Each successive Techforce update heightened the tension in the control room. Arthur studied the pictures transmitted from the interior of the Titans, searching for possible clues to the timing of the missile launch. Agravaine, too nervous to look, circled the dimly-lit Galaxy, helped himself to some coffee from the dispenser and hopping back on his stool, resumed his frenzied realigning of tissue boxes and plastic cups to the left and right of him.

Once more from Techforce: *Fighters five minutes from target, Titans fifteen minutes . . .*

Lancelot cut in. 'Lead Titan braking. Speed dropping sharply.'

Agravaine wiped the sweat from his bald head. Crouched over the table monitor, Arthur muttered, 'The wings! Look at the wings!' In the wings of both Titans four portholes had opened.

From Techforce came the news they were all dreading: '*Missile motors start-up! Missile motors start-up!*'

Twenty Seven

NIWIS

HIGH ABOVE THE OCEAN the Titans floated like great birds, their wings quivering in the turbulence created by the opened portholes.

From Techforce: *Fighters four minutes from target, Titans fourteen minutes from US coast.*

'Excalibur fully charged,' reported Lancelot, conveying by his tone of voice his extreme disapproval of the high-risk waiting game they were playing. Why had Arthur not ordered him to take out the Titans? If the US fighters arrived too late, the consequences would be unthinkable.

'Stand by, Lance,' said Arthur. The President was on screen and came straight to the point. 'NASA is picking up infra-red signals from the Titans. The missile motors are running,' he said, 'but I guess you knew that already.'

'Yes,' said Arthur.

'My experts assure me it will be at least another four minutes before the Titans are able to launch their missiles. By that time our fighters will have taken them out.'

'I hope your experts know what they're talking about,' said Arthur.

'That makes two of us,' said the President.

From Techforce: *Fighters two minutes from target, Titans twelve minutes from US coast.*

The strain showed on everyone's face. Agravaine in Galaxy and Tich in NIWIS were both thinking the same thing. Had Arthur left it too late? Agravaine's fingers hovered uncertainly over the keyboard, but there was nothing to feed into his computer, nothing to transmit, nothing to be done but wait.

From Techforce: *Fighters one minute from target, Titans eleven minutes from US coast.*

From the lead fighter, relayed by Techforce, came the signal confirming that all five fighter aircraft were locked on to their targets. Five seconds later the dispassionate voice of the pilot was on speaker: 'Missiles launched . . . twenty seconds to impact.' Then silence.

As Agravaine hammered the keyboard, Galaxy's wall monitors displayed ten missiles homing in on their targets. Over the speakers Techforce relayed the final countdown . . . *seventeen, sixteen, fifteen, fourteen* . . . Agravaine bounced nervously on his stool, Arthur sat motionless, eyes bright . . . *Ten, nine, eight, seven, six, five, four, three* . . . On the count of *two* came Lancelot's frenzied shout: 'Titan missiles launching!'

As the US missiles hit their targets the two aircraft disintegrated, the dramatic images captured on the big table screen and on the banks of monitors lining the control room walls. Two flowers of fire bloomed in the blue sky, merging instantly into one massive fireball that was itself obliterated by a billowing mass of dust and smoke. A split second later, from the centre of the seething maelstrom, the boom of two near-simultaneous explosions reverberated in Galaxy. As if protesting at this affront to their kingdom, the Atlantic winds shrieked and howled their fury, tearing apart the dust cloud and scattering it to the four corners of the globe.

The unspoken thought was on everyone's mind. In those last dying seconds before they were destroyed, had the Titans launched their nuclear missiles? Arthur was the first to react. 'Calling Eclipse.' No answer.

Once more he tried. 'Lance, do you copy?'

The gravitational waves were silent. 'Lancelot, do you copy?'

After what seemed an interminable delay came the response. 'I copy.'

'Were Titans' missiles launched? I repeat – were Titans'

missiles launched?'

'That's a negative,' said Lancelot. 'Missiles were not, repeat not launched,'

The tension in the control room eased. Agravaine slumped on his stool, Arthur breathed an audible sigh of relief. 'Missiles were destroyed when the Titans blew up,' confirmed Lancelot, who sounded less than pleased. 'Another second,' he could not resist adding, 'and it would have been a very different story.'

As Eclipse, still mantled, hovered at sixty thousand feet, Techforce analysed the incoming data: *Prevailing wind east-north-east, dust clouds have re-formed into one main cloud mass one thousand metres high, three thousand metres wide . . . now moving towards US east coast . . .*

Agravaine handed Arthur the calculation. Based on current wind speed and direction the cloud would reach the east coast in half an hour. Data from a mini-satellite sent into the cloud by Eclipse revealed that it was filled with millions of fragments and dust particles all contaminated by radiation from the destroyed nuclear warheads and fissionable material on board the Titans.

Though the President was exultant that his fighters had destroyed the Titans and their deadly payload, he too had received disturbing data from the dust cloud. 'Frankly, Arthur, this whole business is turning into a major disaster for the United States. We're being made to look like fools. We'll just have to handle it the best way we can, but I'm gonna make damned sure nothing like this ever happens again.'

'How will you do that?' asked Arthur.

'Nuke the bastards,' said the President harshly.

It was what Arthur had feared. 'No,' he said, 'that's not the answer. It could start a world nuclear war, and it would kill thousands, perhaps hundreds of thousands of people.'

The President shrugged. 'I didn't make the world the way it is,' he said. 'From time to time I ask myself who's guilty and who's innocent. And you know what? There's no answer to that question. Of course I worry about taking civilian lives. If I could kill Sadiq and Khalid with one surgical strike and no collateral damage, don't you think I would? Unfortunately that's not how it works. And remember, Arthur, I have to think about all those American lives we could be saving by destroying those goddam bastards. If those Titans had launched their missiles, millions of Americans would have died. As it is, the contamination from the dust cloud could affect the whole eastern seaboard of the United States.'

'Nuking the DOR and the KOE won't make the dust cloud go away.'

'I can't do anything about the dust cloud,' said the President.

'No, but I can,' said Arthur.

'What are you saying?'

'Eclipse can Elimat the dust cloud.'

'I don't get it.'

'Just take my word for it,' said Arthur. 'Eclipse can take care of the dust cloud.' He waited a few seconds for the words to sink in. 'I'll do it on one condition.'

The President had an aversion to conditions – unless he was the one making them. 'What's that?'

'You take no action of any kind against the KOE and the DAR for twenty-four hours. Let Camelot take care of them.'

'With nuclear weapons?'

'I told you before,' said Arthur, 'we don't have nuclear weapons. No, we shall try and capture Sadiq and Khalid and hand them over to you. If that proves impossible . . . we shall kill them.'

Impressed by Arthur's calm confidence, the President was tempted. 'And their missile sites and military bases?'

'Will be destroyed,' said Arthur.

The President meditated for a few moments. 'You do understand,' he said, 'that if you fail in either of those objectives, the United States will be free to take whatever action it chooses when the deadline expires?'

'I do.'

Under normal circumstances, the President would not contemplate making such a deal with any world leader. These were, however, clearly not normal circumstances, nor was Arthur a normal world leader. What's more, he was right. If the US launched a nuclear strike, hundreds of thousands, perhaps millions of people in the KOE and the DAR would surely die, and many more would be contaminated by radiation. Moreover, now that so many nations possessed at least some nuclear capability, the consequence could well be a nuclear attack on the USA, or even global war. The deal Arthur was offering might be a long shot, but it was the only deal on offer.

'You got it,' said the President.

Seconds after the order was given, Eclipse directed a positronic beam at the dust cloud that was now only twenty minutes from the east coast of the United States. In less than a second the cloud had vaporised, and with it all trace of radioactive contamination. As Arthur knew, the Americans would now be searching for the dust cloud, checking by every available means, including satellites, meteorological balloons, radar, and ships and aircraft in the area. When the President appeared on screen again, the expression on his face was one of grudging admiration. 'The United States is in your debt, Arthur. I gotta hand it to you guys, you know your business.'

Arthur acknowledged the compliment with a nod and a smile.

The President consulted his watch. 'It is now seven p.m. here in Washington,' he said. 'You have until seven p.m. Eastern Seaboard time tomorrow evening – midnight British time.'

With that the screen blanked.

Agravaine had bad news for Arthur: 'We can't find either Sadiq or Khalid. They've done a runner. Obviously they know their plot has failed, and they'll be expecting the Americans to hit them hard.'

'We'll find them,' said Arthur and called up Eclipse.

'Lance, your estimated time of arrival KOE and DAR?'

After a few seconds came the answer. 'ETA in one hour, four minutes.'

'Make your way there immediately and open channels when you arrive. Programme all mini-robots on board Eclipse to release micro-tracking devices and organisms. You copy?'

'I copy, sir.'

His fingers flying, Agravaine tapped out Arthur's orders to Techforce Ten. On Galaxy's wall screens and on the big central monitor a hundred orbiting and static satellites and UAV's focused their attention on the KOE and the DAR, sending back swarms of data. So far, though, none of them had located either Khalid or Sadiq.

Precisely one hour, four minutes later, Lancelot was on speaker. 'Eclipse overhead Middle East.'

'Excellent, Lance. Programmed mini-robots are to be dropped on targets Techforce Ten has given you: mostly palaces, military bases and missile sites. We need urgent feedback on the whereabouts of Khalid or Sadiq. Also on the activities of their generals and close advisors.'

Meanwhile, controlled by Agravaine, a team of computer hackers specialising in code breaking had already broken into a number of key KOE and DAR sites controlling missiles, air and sea transport, communications, oil terminals and military operations. The first breakthrough came just before 2 a.m.. A small group of circular red markers floated onto the big table monitor when suddenly one of them began transmitting the continuous lock-on signal. Sadiq had been located holed up in the command post of a missile site in the western desert of the KOE.

Arthur needed to be sure. 'Are Techforce certain it's Sadiq?'

Agravaine rapped the keyboard, and in seconds Sadiq's face was on the table screen. Arthur was considering his next move when a second satellite locked on to Khalid in a military base in the south of the DAR.

'We have located Sadiq and Khalid,' Arthur told Lancelot. 'Techforce are transmitting the co-ordinates. I want you to take them prisoner using Demat and Remat.'

'We have a temporary problem, sir,' said Lancelot. 'Our batteries are too low to operate Demat and Remat. We don't even have sufficient power to remain mantled. It looks as though we suffered some system damage when the Titans exploded. Robot Controller is confident we can fix it, but it may take a while.'

'How long?' said Arthur.

'A few hours. Maybe more,' admitted Lancelot reluctantly. 'After that we'll need another ten hours to recharge to full Excalibur power.'

'Only ten?'

'Well, say fifteen, but I'm confident . . . '

Arthur needed to hear no more. 'Return to base, Lance.'

Lancelot was mortified. 'I must protest, sir.'

Arthur was in no mood to argue. 'Your protest noted. Return to base.' There was no point in a crippled Eclipse remaining in a hostile zone. It could play no further part in this operation.

The deadline was now twenty-one and a half hours away. With no Eclipse, and Kraken too far away to reach the target area in time, it seemed there was nothing more to be done. Pleading for more time would be a wasted effort; the President would refuse to extend the deadline. Camelot's failure to perform would make the US military more hawkish. For the first time since 1945 the United States would almost certainly launch a nuclear attack.

Agravaine's fingers twitched impotently on the keyboard. Over the speakers Tich's voice boomed. 'What kind of surveillance satellites do the KOE and the DAR operate?'

'They don't have surveillance satellites,' said Agravaine.

'Why not?'

'They're too expensive, and they're quite difficult to launch and maintain.'

'Then how come they know what's going on in the world?' asked Tich.

'They send up anchored balloons packed with cameras and sensors,' explained Agravaine. 'They're relatively primitive, but effective enough for most purposes.'

At first there was no reaction from Tich. And then: 'Could I ask you, sir, and you Agravaine, to step across to NIWIS? I have something to show you.'

With Mordred looking over his shoulder, and flanked by Arthur and Agravaine, Tich eased his bulk carefully onto a stool, rested his hands on his belly and puffed out his bulbous cheeks. In front of him was the NIWIS command computer from which flowed a stream of instructions implementing what Tich termed 'my tricks'. In the rooms adjoining the control room were the 'conjurers' – all cyberspace travellers and masters of the black art of deception.

On Tich's face was that distant look Arthur and Agravaine had seen many times before. The big man was thinking illusion. 'Balloons are good,' he said in his dark chocolate voice. 'Now if they had satellites, it would be difficult, perhaps impossible. Since it's balloons, I think we can do it.'

'Do what?' asked Agravaine, piqued at being kept in the dark.

'Fool them,' said Tich, 'fool them into seeing things . . . like this.' Using the keyboard he drew a dove on his screen. When he snapped his fingers, the dove flew out of the screen straight at Agravaine's head. Agravaine ducked, and the dove disappeared.

'Fine, Tich,' said Agravaine, 'we all know you're a magician. You create illusions. I may not know how you do it, but I still know they're illusions.'

'Then why did you duck?' asked Tich, to which Agravaine had no answer.

Arthur was intrigued. 'What's on your mind, Tich?'

'We are going to plant a Trojan Horse in their midst,' said Tich. 'It will not be there, but we'll convince them that it is.'

As he spoke NIWIS' control room speakers boomed an alarming message: *Red Alert! Red Alert! Missile launch on screen! Missile launch on screen!*

On the wall monitors was a satellite map of the Middle East over which was superimposed wave after wave of missiles soaring into the sky in a north easterly direction. As the missiles were tracked by satellites the monitor data counter indicated their precise speed and direction. *Target Camelot! Target Camelot! Three minutes to impact!* The countdown began: *Two fifty-nine, two fifty-eight, two fifty-seven . . .*

Agravaine, his hands shaking, tried vainly to realign cups and tissue boxes, Arthur was strangely relaxed, Tich inscrutable, Mordred brooding.

Two forty-five, two forty-four, two forty-three . . .

'For God's sake, what are we waiting for?' said Agravaine, 'let's take those missiles out before we're all toast.'

'What do you say, Tich?' said Arthur coolly, 'shall we take them out?'

In the circumstances it seemed to Agravaine an absurd question. Why was Arthur consulting Tich when it was crystal clear what had to be done?

'It's your call,' said Tich.

Agravaine stared uncomprehendingly at Tich, then back at the flight of missiles heading ever nearer Camelot, then at Arthur, then back again at Tich. In less than two minutes the missiles would be on them, and no one was doing a damn thing about it. And still the ominous countdown continued . . . *one-fifty two, one fifty-one, one fifty, one forty-nine . . .* 'Will someone tell me what the hell is going on?' he demanded.

End of missile strike simulation! boomed the speakers. *End of missile strike simulation! End of missile strike simulation! End of missile . . .*

The control room was deathly silent. Agravaine slumped over

his keyboard, his face drained of blood. 'You rotten bastard,' he said, 'why didn't you warn us it was a simulation?' Mordred was grinning. 'Not funny,' said Agravaine.

'The object,' said Tich, 'was to see if you were fooled. You were.'

'There is no shame in being deceived,' said Arthur. 'Tich made his point.'

'What point exactly?' said Agravaine irritably.

'The point,' said Arthur, 'that throughout history wars have been won and lost by deception. Tich has reminded us that deceiving the enemy can be the best way to defeat him.' He clapped Agravaine on the back. 'Let's go, Agro. It's nearly four a.m. – twenty hours to the deadline. We have work to do.'

As their hovercraft sped back to Command Control, Arthur was thinking what the Magus had once told him . *It's not a man's weakness you use to destroy him. It's his strength.* Sadiq had the power to destroy Khalid. Khalid had the power to destroy Sadiq. Yet how did that help Camelot? It was unthinkable that two such close allies would turn on each other.

Twenty Eight

NIWIS

ARTHUR GLANCED at the control room clock: 19.06 hrs. – less than five hours to the deadline, and there was still much to do. A nod to Agravaine, and within seconds the connection was made. If Sadiq was surprised, he did not show it. 'Mr. Pendragon, what a pleasure. You have a message from the President?'

Arthur recognised this as a not so subtle jibe, intended to convey that he took his orders direct from the President of the USA.

'The message is my own,' said Arthur. 'I bring you a warning, Sadiq.'

Sadiq frowned. 'I am not impressed by threats.'

'I said a warning, not a threat,' said Arthur.

'And the warning is?'

'That you and your country are in mortal danger.'

'Let the Americans send their missiles,' said Sadiq. 'We shall know how to respond.'

'There will be a missile strike,' said Arthur, 'but it is not from America that it will come.'

Sadiq's dark eyes gleamed. 'Who else would dare attack the KOE?'

Arthur waited for a few seconds, prolonging the suspense. 'The man who plotted with you to attack the greatest power on earth,' he said, 'the man who pretends to be your ally.'

Sadiq's face registered first incredulity, then amusement. 'You are not speaking of my brother, Ibn Khalid?'

'I am.'

'You are trying to trick me. He is my friend.' Despite Sadiq's protestations, there was uncertainty in his voice.

'Khalid's friendship is a tradeable commodity. He has made a deal,' said Arthur, who perfectly understood the paranoid nature of his adversary. Trusting no one, not even those closest to him, Sadiq el Shaeb's only commitment was to self-interest. His suspicions were judge, jury and executioner, as many enemies, as well as loyal friends and family members, had learned to their cost.

'A deal? With whom?'

'With the President of the United States, his old school friend and comrade.'

'Why would he do that?'

'To save his own skin, and to avoid an American missile strike on his country, Khalid has agreed to launch a pre-emptive strike against you,' said Arthur. 'As you know, his missiles are still locked on KOE targets, as are yours on his. That was a vital part of your joint plan to deceive the USA, wasn't it? It would be relatively easy for him to destroy your missile sites and military bases, not forgetting you, of course, Sadiq. You too would be destroyed. Politically it would be a master stroke, an ideal solution for the US President. Sadiq would be punished for his aggression, and not by his enemy, the United States, but by his friend and brother.'

Crazy as at first it sounded, the story was beginning to make sense to Sadiq. 'And the Democratic Arab Republic?'

'Will become an American satellite, sanitised in accordance with the democratic principles of the west. No doubt American troops will be stationed there for a number of years to ensure its good behaviour.'

Sadiq pondered. 'And Ibn Khalid goes unpunished for daring to attack the United States? Impossible.'

'Ibn Khalid will publicly beg forgiveness for his treacherous attack, and pledge his loyalty to the West. No doubt he will be tried, probably by the International Court of Justice, and serve a short prison sentence. He will then be quietly released, given a new identity and allowed to lose himself in some sympathetic country on a nauseatingly fat income.'

Sadiq's face gave nothing away. 'Why are you telling me all this?'

'What you and Khalid did was wrong,' said Arthur, 'but I also think it's wrong that you should be made the scapegoat. The deal Khalid and the President have made will send a confusing message to the world. I find it immoral.'

'Immoral,' repeated Sadiq, rolling the word round his mouth as though submitting it to a taste test. Though the concept was entirely foreign to him, he was nevertheless able to relate to the theoretical proposition that Arthur believed in morality, and that therefore his story might just conceivably be true. 'Give me proof,' he said.

When he said that, Arthur knew that the job of convincing him was more than half done. 'You shall have it,' he said. 'Meanwhile, I advise you to be on the alert.'

The control room clock showed 19.30 hrs. – four and a half hours to the deadline.

When he was Prime Minister of the Federation, Arthur met Ibn Khalid two or three times. Had anyone suggested then that one day warm-hearted, dependable Khalid would launch a nuclear attack on the United States, Arthur would have laughed in their face. Clearly though, Khalid was as devious and ruthless as his friend, Sadiq.

At 20.00 hrs. Arthur was on a secure channel to Khalid via gravitational waves. 'Good evening, sir. I am Arthur Pendragon. I hope I am not disrupting your schedule.'

'You are welcome at any time,' said Khalid courteously.

'I'll come straight to the point,' said Arthur. 'Sadiq is not the friend you think he is.'

'I never thought he was my friend,' said Khalid. 'On the contrary, we are enemies.'

'You were once enemies,' said Arthur, 'until common interests made you friends. Together you plotted a nuclear attack on the USA. It was your missiles and his which were on those Titans.'

Ibn Khalid thrust out his lips, expressing his disdain. 'I know nothing of any missiles, Mr Pendragon. What I do know is that the Americans launched an unprovoked attack on the Titans and shot them down with much loss of innocent life.'

'You were supposed to be on board one of those Titans on your way to talk peace with Sadiq and the President,' said Arthur. 'Instead, you were hiding out in your own country. What's more, you still are. How do you explain that?'

'Why should I explain anything to you?'

It was obvious there was no point in prolonging the argument, and besides, time was short. 'The purpose of my call is to tell you that Sadiq has made a deal with the President of the United States.'

'What nonsense is this?'

'Sadiq,' continued Arthur undeterred, 'has agreed to make a dramatic policy shift. The Kingdom of the Euphrates will become a staunch ally of the west, and in return will receive much needed economic aid. He has also confessed that you and he loaded the Titans with nuclear missiles, and that you planned a strike on American targets.'

'Why would Sadiq confess such rubbish? And why would he make a deal with the United States?'

'To save his life,' said Arthur, 'something he seems to value highly. Frankly he had no choice. If he did not co-operate, the United States was ready to turn his country to ash, and him with it. As part of the deal he is to be tried by the International Court of Justice and sentenced to a short term of imprisonment. After that he'll be released and offered a new identity and a life of luxury. He will have lost his power, but he'll live. It seems the idea of living appeals to him, now that the Titans have blown up in his face.'

'These are children's stories.' Though Khalid's reaction was contemptuous, his eyes hinted at his unease.

'What's more,' said Arthur, 'Sadiq has agreed to use his nuclear arsenal to destroy military targets in the Democratic Arab Republic: missile sites, military bases and so on. Obviously he knows where they all are. He's been targeting them for years.'

Distrustful by nature, Khalid suspected that Arthur's story, far-fetched as it sounded, might just have an element of truth to it. Concerned, but not yet convinced, he asked a crucial question: 'The President of the United States could order the destruction of my country in a matter of minutes,' he said. 'Why does he need Sadiq to do his dirty work for him?'

'I'll tell you why,' said Arthur. 'The President is afraid of provoking a global nuclear war. Attacking either the KOE or the DAR with nuclear missiles would risk doing just that. The US has taken a lot of stick in the last thirty years for throwing its weight around, and it doesn't want to be seen as the world's bully boy. The American people would react badly to any military action by their government involving civilian casualties. An important condition of the deal is that Sadiq has undertaken not to target civilians.' Arthur paused for effect. 'Unless of course you classify yourself as a civilian,' he said, provocatively.

Ibn Khalid winced. 'Are you suggesting . . . ?'

'That you are part of the deal, Ibn? Indeed I am. There's a missile in the KOE with your name on it.'

Incredible though his story seemed, Pendragon was making sense. Ibn Khalid knew Sadiq of old. He had been a treacherous enemy. No doubt he could be a treacherous friend.

'Why are you telling me all this?'

'I have served as a soldier in the KOE,' said Arthur. 'I saw terrible things there. Sadiq massacred thousands of his fellow countrymen. I know him for what he is, a tyrant and a murderer. Murderers deserve to be punished for their crimes.'

Almost ready to believe Arthur, Khalid would need more than words to be totally convinced. 'I shall need proof,' he said.

'You shall have it,' said Arthur. 'Meanwhile I recommend you watch your screens carefully.'

As the connection was cut, the hands of the control room clock stood at 20.30 hrs. – three and a half hours to the deadline.

Arthur opened the line to Tich. 'Targets primed,' he said. 'How long do you need?'

Tich's reaction was disturbingly vague. 'About three hours or so.'

'You have two hours maximum. The deadline expires at midnight.'

Ian Tichgame blew his cheeks into giant balloons. 'I'll get back to you,' he said.

Whilst Agravaine busied himself at his keyboard, Arthur closed his eyes and, as Merlin had taught him to do when he was a boy, emptied his mind of all tension and discordant thoughts, replacing it with the harmonious sounds of nature, of breezes sifting through trees, of the rush of the sea, of the evening song of the blackbird – God's song, as Merlin called it.

Moments later, with spirits revived and head cleared, he was focused again on what had to be done. Agravaine flicked specks of dust from his trousers until he was satisfied that there were the same number of specks on each leg. 'You think they'll fall for it, nuncle?'

'There'll be deaths, Agro, many deaths,' said Arthur.

'And many more will live who would have died,' said Agravaine.

Agravaine was right, of course. Small comfort, all the same.

Arthur consulted the control room clock and was startled to see the time: 22.50 hrs. One hour, ten minutes to go. Where was Tich?

Less than a minute later, Ian Tichgame's rotund face reappeared on one of the wall screens, and over the speakers Techforce Ten confirmed . . . *Ten seconds to Trojan Horse*. The big table monitor divided, images of the KOE and DAR missile sites pixelated on both sides. *Ten, nine, eight, seven, six, five, four, three, two, one . . .*

'Trojan Horse is 'go'!' boomed Tich's voice over Galaxy's speakers, and then immediately from Techforce Ten: *DAR missile* **start-up** *simulation active! DAR missile* **start-up** *simulation active.*

In the command bunker that served as the control room for KOE's missiles sites Sadiq jumped nervously as the hooters blared a raucous warning. 'What the hell is that noise?'

Scared by what he was hearing and seeing, and no less scared of his master's temper, Sadiq's aide mumbled, 'The DAR missile motors.'

'I can't hear you. Turn off those damned hooters!' The hooters fell silent. 'What are you saying, idiot?'

'The DAR missile motors, sir!' The aide was still shouting even though the hooters had been switched off.

'What about them, fool!'

'They've started up!'

'Liar!' yelled Sadiq, raising his hand to strike the man.

The aide flinched. 'Look sir, look!' There on screen was the evidence. The DAR missile motors were running. Sadiq fought back a surge of panic. 'Who are they targeting?'

'Us, sir! They're targeting us!'

Fear wrenched Sadiq's stomach. This couldn't be, this wasn't happening. His men were looking at him in bewilderment. Reminding himself that they depended on him, and he on them, he drew himself up, looking proud and confident, remembering who he was. 'Check surveillance sensors.' In a few seconds the puzzled aide reported. 'I don't understand it. The balloon sensors are picking up no unusual activity.'

That was odd, very odd. The sensors had never failed them before. 'A system fault?' Sadiq suggested, praying that it was, yet knowing there was too much at stake to rely on guesswork.

The aide was too scared to say either yes or no. 'It could be, sir.'

'How long to launch time?'

'Just over two minutes, sir.'

There could be only one explanation: Arthur had spoken the truth. Khalid had made a deal with the Americans. The panicky voice of his aide pressured him. 'Two minutes to launch, sir.'

In Galaxy, Techforce Ten reported the next phase of Trojan Horse: *KOE missile* **start-up** *simulation active! KOE missile* **start-up** *simulation active.*

In his command bunker, Ibn Khalid stared transfixed at the monitor that showed Sadiq's missile motors firing. So Pendragon was right. First Khalid's hands, then his whole body began to shake with rage and fear. Sadiq had sold out to the American pigs.

A strange message scrolled across the command monitor: 'Sensors do not confirm missile start-up.'

How could that be? 'Can we rely on the sensors?' he asked his deputy.

'They have never been wrong before, but . . . '

Right or wrong, there was no time to check. Safer, much safer, to believe the evidence of his own eyes.

'Permission to start missile motors, sir?'

Khalid thrashed the air wildly with his arms as though to drive off an unwelcome thought; but he could not dismiss so easily the fearsome prospect of war with his neighbour, of missile strikes and counter strikes, of warring armies and devastated cities.

The deputy was trembling with fear. 'What do I do, sir?'

He was being pushed where he did not want to go. But what option did he have? 'Start missile motors,' he said, his voice so low that his deputy wavered uncertainly, and Khalid was forced to repeat the order. 'Start missile motors!' This time he yelled the words.

In the KOE command bunker Sadiq's face was grim. He was about to order the launch of nuclear missiles against a neighbour and former friend. It was unthinkable, his worst nightmare. He looked at his deputy, a man in the prime of life, as were all the other technicians and soldiers who worked in the bunker. He knew exactly what they were thinking; they were all going to die.

'Start missile motors!' he ordered.

In Galaxy, Techforce Ten reported the penultimate phase of Trojan Horse: *KOE and DAR missile* **launch** *simulations active . . . KOE and DAR missile* **launch** *simulations active . . .*

In his bunker, Ibn Khalid was having second thoughts. The start-up could be aborted. There was still time, precious time, time to talk, time to make one last effort to keep the peace. 'Get me Sadiq,' he ordered. Even as the connection was made, his terrified deputy pointed a shaking finger at the monitor. From the KOE sites six missiles were rising slowly into the sky, their slim bodies flashing in the sun. Over the bunker's speakers a panic-stricken voice cried, 'KOE Missiles flying! KOE Missiles flying!'

Khalid grabbed the phone. 'You crazy bastard!' he yelled, 'you launched your missiles?'

'I never did. I swear it!'

'You lie, you dog!' screamed Khalid.

'DAR missiles flying!' cried a frightened voice over the bunker's speakers. Sadiq and his men shrank back in horror as on their monitor screens six DAR missiles rose from their launch sites.

'Khalid, you treacherous pig,' sneered Sadiq, 'you are the one who launched his missiles.'

Khalid clasped his hands. 'For the sake of peace,' he pleaded, 'for the sake of our beloved brothers and countrymen, let us talk.'

'It is too late for talking,' said Sadiq. 'We are all going to die.

It is the will of Allah.'

'There is still time to destroy our missiles,' said Khalid.

Sadiq hesitated. 'I will do so, but only if you destroy your missiles first.'

Khalid knew from long experience that Sadiq's word was worth little. One day he was your friend, the next your enemy. If it was Allah's will that he should die, he would make sure Sadiq died with him. 'Let us destroy our missiles at precisely the same time,' he suggested.

'Pig! Liar! Traitor! Satan's dog!' Sadiq screamed his rage and frustration and broke the connection.

In the silence Ibn Khalid's aide asked, 'What are your orders, sir?'

'Shoot down the KOE missiles,' he said in desperation.

'We don't have the weapons to do that.' The aide looked at the bunker clock. 'I need a decision, sir. It is less than one minute to impact. If we don't fire our missiles now, they will be destroyed on the pads.'

They would not, could not save themselves, they would simply lose the power to retaliate in kind. Mutual destruction. Was there no alternative? 'Give me options,' pleaded Khalid. 'I will make a decision if you give me options.'

His voice shaking, the aide answered: 'There are no options, sir.'

Khalid lifted his shoulders and let them drop in a gesture of surrender. 'Launch missiles,' he said, his voice hoarse.

'Missile launch in ten seconds,' his deputy confirmed, his face ashen. The countdown began . . . *ten, nine, eight, seven, six* . . .

Sadiq paced his bunker, his aide following him with his eyes. Suddenly he stopped pacing and confronted the frightened man. 'Are you afraid to die?' The man cowered. 'Forgive me, sir.' To his astonishment Sadiq patted him on the shoulder, a compassionate gesture, the first he had ever known his master make. It crossed his mind that for the first and last time he and his ruler shared a common fate. They were both about to die. Sadiq stared mesmerised at the monitor, murmuring, 'Do not be afraid. We must all die when Allah wills it.' The aide bowed low, kissing his master's hand, and Sadiq patted his head consolingly. 'Launch missiles,' he said, and fell to his knees in prayer.

'Missile launch in ten seconds,' said the aide. The countdown began . . . *ten, nine, eight, seven, six* . . .

As Arthur and Agravaine crouched over Galaxy's big table monitor, Techforce Ten relayed the sombre news: *Missile motors firing in KOE . . . missile motors firing in DAR . . . ten seconds to launch in KOE . . . ten seconds to launch in DAR . . .* ' And seconds later . . . '**Missiles airborne!**'

At 23.58 hrs., two minutes before the deadline Arthur had agreed with the US President, the missiles struck the KOE and the DAR within seconds of each other. Minutes later a shocked world learnt that there had been an exchange of missiles – at least some armed with nuclear warheads – between the Democratic Arab Republic and the Kingdom of the Euphrates. Within an hour the world's media reported the dramatic news: Sadiq el Shaeb, ruler of the Kingdom of the Euphrates, and Ibn Khalid, ruler of the Democratic Arab Republic, had both been killed, and their countries' missile sites obliterated. It was also thought that significant damage had been inflicted on both countries' key military bases and installations. There was much speculation about the sudden upsurge of violence. Some journalists, especially in the Arab media, claimed that it was the work of the United States of America, some suggested it was the Iranians, others blamed Israel.

The US President was ecstatic. With one master stroke Arthur had cut off the heads and removed the teeth and claws of two of America's most dangerous enemies. The aborted missile attack on the United States had been avenged without the USA being drawn into a nuclear conflict. The President had only one niggle: Arthur refused to explain how Camelot had persuaded Sadiq and Khalid to attack each other. All he would say was that one Ian Tichgame deserved the credit. The name meant nothing either to the White House or the War Department. A young cryptologist pointed out that the name Ian Tichgame was an anagram for The Magician, an interesting observation that was, however, thought to have no special significance.

On the day following these extraordinary events in the Middle East, millions of people across the two hemispheres of the planet witnessed an amazing phenomenon. As the sun rose, a light blazed, a light as powerful as a hundred lightning flashes, and there in the sky hung a great sword, its blade glowing so brightly that no one dared look at it for more than a second or two. As the sun rose higher in the heavens, the sword shone brighter still. In the afternoon its light began to dim, and at the day's end, as the sun sank below the horizon, the sword glowed blood red, fading finally with the dying light. It was not the first time that the world had seen the Sword in the Sky, and there were few people across the globe who did not recognise its significance.

Both the KOE and the DAR suffered widespread destruction, chiefly, though not exclusively, to military installations. There were also several thousand casualties, some of them civilian. The United States and the European Union collaborated in organising a rehabilitation programme, injecting many billions of dollars and euros to build hospitals, restore public services and reconstruct damaged civilian property, partly from humanitarian motives, partly in the hope that the two countries would embrace democracy and a pro-western foreign policy. In less than a year, however, the DAR and the KOE were in a state of anarchy, the majority of their citizens longing for another dictator to seize power and restore order.

In Camelot, the success of *Operation NIWIS*, and its

disappointing aftermath, widened the gap between hawks and doves. The doves were unhappy, arguing that Camelot should not have been involved in a nuclear conflict. The hawks questioned what had been gained by tricking the KOE and the DAR into attacking each other. As an example to others, they argued, and to demonstrate its power, Camelot should have attacked both countries with Excalibur.

The disputes at the Round Table troubled Arthur, as did the battle he fought with his conscience. With the passing of the years there were more questions and fewer answers. The image of the headless black knight haunted his dreams. Would good ever overcome evil? Did he have the power to change the world? And even if he did, what gave him the *right* to change it? Plagued by doubts, he walked the dark corridors of despair, questioning the destiny that Merlin said he was born to fulfil.

Twenty Nine

A SILVER BENTLEY – a present to Margot from Adrian Pellinore, her latest lover – drew up outside her house. From the first floor window of his study, her husband, Lennox Lotte, watched as the uniformed driver held the car door open for his beloved wife. Stepping in, she waved up at him through the rear window, and lowered the blind. For Lennox it was like the fall of the curtain at the end of the play. Slowly the Bentley crunched down the driveway, turned into the road and disappeared. When the sound of the engine had faded, he walked across the room to his desk and opened the top right hand drawer.

The sudden death of Lennox Lotte came as a shock to everyone who knew him, not least to his sons. It was Mordred who broke the news to Gawain.

'No, it can't be.'

'I'm afraid it is.'

'How did you hear?'

'The internet.'

Gawain was unable to take it in. His father was in his mid-fifties and had always enjoyed good health. 'Was it a heart attack?'

'It doesn't say.' Mordred handed him the print-out.

Gawain read the words aloud. *Lennox Lotte, a well-known investment banker, died yesterday at his house in Sussex. It has been rumoured in the city in recent months that Lotte Enterprises was experiencing financial difficulties.*

'Nothing more?'

'Not that I could find.'

'Do the others know?'

'I rather hoped you'd . . . '

'Of course.' As the oldest brother, Gawain was the one they all relied on. Calling Agravaine, Gaheris and Gareth to his apartment he told them what had happened. Agravaine stared at him in dismay, Gaheris hugged himself, groaning fiercely, and Gareth looked uncomprehendingly from brother to brother, hoping that one of them could explain what to him was inexplicable.

'We must talk to mumsy,' said Agravaine.

Gawain nodded. 'I booked a line.'

When the link opened and Margot was on screen, Agravaine, who adored his mother, spoke – or tried to speak – first. 'Mumsy,' he said, 'mumsy . . . ' But then he broke down.

'Mother,' said Gawain, 'we are all so sorry.'

'I'm in a state, darlings. Such a shock, you know. I never dreamed . . . ' Tears filled her eyes.

'Of course you didn't, mother,' said Gawain soothingly, waiting for her to calm herself. 'What actually happened?'

Her hand to her bosom, Margot said faintly, 'Your father shot himself.'

The brothers looked at each other in horror. For a long time the gravitational waves were silent. 'In the name of God, why?' asked Gawain finally.

'I have no idea.'

'On the internet it said there were problems with the business. Was that it?'

Margot pouted. 'All I know is that lately your father was behaving very strangely. For one thing, he never stopped complaining about my credit card bills, said I shopped too much. What's wrong with shopping? Everyone knows you meet the nicest people in shops. What did he expect me to do to relieve the monotony? Sit on charity committees? Deliver meals on wheels, for godsake!'

'Of course not, mumsy,' said Agravaine.

'And then he started criticising my friends.'

The blood rose in Agravaine's face. 'What sort of friends, mumsy?'

'You know what I mean, darling. He was accusing me of . . . '

'Accusing you of having affairs, was he, mother?' said Mordred, who, like all the brothers, had grown up with his mother's peccadillos, 'instead of looking the other way, like he always used to.'

'That is *so* unfair!' Margot's face puckered, a solitary tear rolled down her cheek. 'Why are you picking on me?' she wailed.

Agravaine rounded on Mordred and Gawain. 'Stop picking on mumsy,' he snapped. 'She's upset.'

'Mumsy's upset,' said Gaheris, nodding vigorously.

'A girl's allowed to have friends, isn't she?' said Margot. 'Elaine is gone. Morgan is mad. You all deserted me. I'm lonely,' she moaned, 'so desperately lonely.' Taking care not to damage her make-up, she absorbed a tear with the edge of a tissue. 'Anyway, what right did he have to be jealous? Tell me that. A man of his age.' Her voice dropped. 'He'd become impossible to live with,' she said, nodding her head jerkily like a mechanical doll, as if to reassure herself that everything in her world was alright.

Since childhood, Mordred, like all the brothers, had seen his mother leave the family house "for good" on at least a dozen occasions, although, knowing which side her bread was buttered, she had always come back. This time, he surmised, it might have been different. Then, Lennox was rich. Now, apparently, he had lost everything.

'Did you walk out on him, mother?' he asked bluntly.

Margot was indignant. 'Of course I didn't. Why would you even suggest such a thing?'

'Perhaps I misunderstood you,' said Mordred. 'Didn't you

say he was impossible to live with?'

'Flinging my words in my face,' she muttered.

'So naturally I thought . . . '

'Naturally you thought the worst of me, like you always do, Mord.' The corners of Margot's mouth drooped sulkily. 'Where did you learn to be so cruel?'

'From you, mother,' said Mordred.

'You are heartless!' cried Margot. 'To accuse your mother of . . . of I don't know what, when you can see how much I'm suffering.' Covering her face with her hands, she heaved tumultuous sobs that alternated with long, shuddering intakes of breath.

Mordred waited for the storm to subside. 'No one's accusing you of anything, mother. We simply want to know why father took his own life.'

Margot's hands shook, though whether from rage or nerves was impossible to tell. 'Isn't it obvious?' she said. Her voice was strangled, trapped deep in her throat. 'He lost all his money. Why else would he kill himself?'

The brothers looked at each other.

'Why indeed?' said Mordred.

Thirty

THE FAMILY GATHERED round the open grave: Margot and her five sons – Gawain, Agravaine, Gaheris, Mordred and Gareth – Igraine, Arthur's mother, in her mid-sixties still fresh-complexioned and beautiful; Arthur and Guinevere, hand in hand, and Margot's sister, mad Morgan, released for a few hours from a secure psychiatric ward under the supervision of two male nurses, dressed, inappropriately for a funeral, in white uniforms.

Behind them were a number of friends and business associates, including a man in his fifties whom Agravaine did not recognise. 'That man over there – the short, chubby one. Who's he?'

'Adrian Pellinore,' said Mordred.

'What's he doing here?'

For a while Mordred did not answer, his attention apparently distracted by a crow pecking at the freshly dug earth piled round the open grave. 'I believe he's mother's friend.'

Agravaine knew from experience that Mordred always chose his words carefully. Not a friend of his mother he had said, but *mother's friend.*

'You mean they're lovers,' he said, his expression betraying his distaste.

Mordred flicked idly through his Book of Common Prayer. 'Did I say that?'

No, but he implied it, didn't he? Agravaine suffered a massive heave of jealousy that surged from his stomach to his throat. He worshipped his mother, had always been closer to her than the other brothers, rather too close, his father would often say, too touchy-feely to be altogether healthy.

The clouds parted briefly, allowing a shaft of sunlight to penetrate the overcast sky before closing in again. *I am the resurrection and the life . . .*

The vicar invited those mourners who wished to do so to pick up a spade and throw earth on the coffin. His unemotional, sing-song delivery made the timeless words sound curiously bland: *Man that is born of woman hath but a short time to live . . . In the midst of life we are in death . . .* Spadefuls of earth thudded onto the coffin until it was covered . . . *we therefore commit his body to the ground; earth to earth, ashes to ashes, dust to dust . . .*

Before anyone could stop her, Margot jumped into the open grave. Sprawling face down on the coffin she clasped it in her arms and began to wail loudly. As Agravaine leaped after her, prised his mother from the coffin and hauled her out of the grave, Mordred whispered in Gawain's ear, 'That's the closest she's been to Lennox for years.' Brushing off the earth and smoothing down his mother's dress, Agravaine – who had overheard the sardonic comment – darted venomous looks at Mordred.

The funeral service over, Arthur and Guinevere said their farewells and left for their rendezvous with the Scuttle for the flight back to Camelot, taking the youngest son, Gareth, with them. Margot, family and friends, went back to Brackett Hall for drinks.

In an hour the crowd had thinned out, only a few close friends and family remaining. Igraine, Margot's mother, had left, and Morgan, her sister, was dragged off by her minders, protesting shrilly. A great deal of wine and spirits had been consumed. Agravaine and Gaheris, having nothing better to do, concentrated on getting drunk, Agravaine on red wine, Gaheris – less discriminating in matters of alcohol – on gin, vodka and whisky. Mordred nursed the same glass of white wine he was handed when he arrived at the reception.

Whilst drinking, Agravaine followed his mother with his eyes. She made no pretence of mourning. On the contrary, she seemed in good spirits, chatting animatedly to friends and family alike. Now and then she exchanged words with Adrian Pellinore, nothing in either his or her manner suggesting anything other than a friendly relationship. The fact was, nevertheless, that he was still in the house long after most people had left, and that disturbed Agravaine.

'Why is that poncey little man still here?' he asked Mordred.

'I told you,' said Mordred. 'He's mother's friend.'

With a shaking hand, Agravaine poured himself a glass of wine, in the process spilling a few drops on the carpet. The slight accident did not escape Mordred's watchful eye.

'Wassort of friend?'

'If you don't mind my saying so, Agro,' said Mordred, 'you've had quite enough to drink.'

Agravaine scowled. 'None of your damn business.'

Gaheris appeared, clutching a glass and a bottle of vodka.

Mordred considered his two brothers. Drunk they were not; not yet. Well on the way, though.

'Wassort of friend?' demanded Agravaine again.

'Who we talking about?' said Gaheris.

'Smellymore,' said Agravaine, cackling at his jest.

'Who?'

'Adrian Pellinore,' said Mordred.

'Want me to smash his face in?' enquired Gaheris, holding up a huge fist.

'Look,' said Mordred hastily, 'why don't we go somewhere else? I'm bored with this party.' He consulted his wristcom. 'We still have a few hours before Scuttle takes off.'

Agravaine was in stubborn mood. 'Wanna stay here.'

'Wanna stay here,' said Gaheris.

Mordred nodded. Here might not be a bad place to be. But not in the house. Things might get out of hand before their time, and then all would be lost.

'Alright,' he said, 'why don't we stock up with booze and adjourn to the summer house – have ourselves our own private party.'

Agravaine brightened. 'Good idea,' he said.

'Good idea,' said Gaheris.

In the next hour, Agravaine drank another bottle of red wine, and Gaheris a bottle and a half of vodka. Mordred pretended to drink Scotch, disposing of glass after glass in a flower pot behind his chair. The summer house was a hundred metres from the house. The sound of laughter and conversation drifted across the lawn, growing fainter as the sun went down.

Mordred prided himself on his ability to plan for all eventualities. Even he, though, could never have contrived a situation as promising as this. He took a sip of whisky – his first ever – and leaned back in his chair enjoying the warm glow in his stomach. 'We should talk,' he said, flinching as Agravaine belched loudly.

'Washit you wanna talk about?'

Mordred took his second sip of Scotch. 'Truth,' he said. 'Unless there's something else you would rather talk about.'

Agravaine swayed onto the lawn, measured a slow, deliberate circle round a flower bed, waved his glass of wine in the air spilling most of it, and made his way back to the summer house, pausing with one leg in the air as he struggled to regain his balance. Collapsed in his chair again, he regarded Mordred with suspicious eyes.

'Wadja mean?'

'It's a game.' said Mordred. 'I call it "truth gatecrashing the party".'

Closing first one eye, then the other, Agravaine leaned back his head and, with some difficulty, lined up the neck of the wine bottle with his mouth. 'Lesh play.' he said.

'Would you like me to start?' said Mordred. Interpreting

silence as consent, he said, 'Adrian Pellinore knows our mother – I mean, of course, that he knows her in the biblical sense,' he explained with a malicious grin.

Agravaine sat up sharply, choking on his wine.

'Wash bibli . . . bibli . . . ?' asked Gaheris.

'It means he fucks her,' said Mordred.

Gaheris whimpered, Agravaine, red-faced, coughed and spluttered.

'I've been hearing some naughty things about our mother,' said Mordred. 'Apparently she fell madly in love with Adrian Pellinore's wallet. So she's been having it off with him for months. And then one day she discovered that Adrian had a son – a pretty boy. So she screwed him too. Must have been quite a turn on, fucking father and son – presumably not at the same time – though come to think of it, I wouldn't put it past her.'

Agravaine covered his face with his hands, tears squeezing through clenched fingers. 'Poor mumsy,' he groaned, over and over again. Gaheris rocked back and forth, whining like an animal in pain. Mordred clasped his hands behind his head and surveyed his brothers. 'How do you like the truth game so far?' he enquired amiably.

Agravaine mumbled something unintelligible.

'You want to stop playing?'

Agravaine uncovered his tear-stained face. 'No,' he said, and immediately covered it again.

Mordred continued. 'Some of Lennox's good friends found out, and being good friends, they told him the truth. That's what good friends are for, isn't it?'

Gaheris was grunting in a menacing way that made Mordred extremely nervous. Most of the time the gentlest and most accomodating of men, his brother had, as Mordred knew, a temper from hell, and when he lost it, his rages could be fearsome, and dangerous to anyone near him. Recognising the warning signs, he eased himself out of his chair and wandered round the summer house, ready to make a run for it in case of need.

'Bastards!' said Agravaine, though whether he meant the good friends, or the Pellinores was not clear.

'Bastards,' agreed Gaheris.

Concluding that his brothers' anger was now redirected to its proper target, Mordred sidled back to his chair. 'As we all know, mother had her . . . ' – An indulgent smile – 'shall we say indiscretions? And father always knew about them. But this was something else. Having a wife who plays away is one thing, having your friends know all about it is a humiliation too far, I'd say. Wouldn't you?'

Gaheris, who had forgotten why he was angry, peered, fascinated, at his tumbler of vodka, as the transparent liquid turned gold in the rays of the setting sun. Agravaine rushed onto the lawn and threw up.

'Oh, for godsake,' said Mordred, turning his head away in disgust.

'Poor Agro sick,' said Gaheris.

Agravaine wandered back to the summer house wiping vomit from his mouth with the back of his hand. 'I'll murder the bastards,' he said.

Mordred's lips writhed. 'Do what you like,' he said. 'Just don't throw up again.'

Gaheris was more sympathetic. Putting his arms round Agravaine's shoulders he demonstrated his concern for his brother. 'Murder them for you, Agro,' he suggested. 'D'you like me to?'

Agro was too ill to answer.

Mordred prepared to turn the screw tighter. Truth, the gatecrasher at this particular party, was creating havoc, just as he hoped it would. 'I totally understand why you hate Pellinore so much – why you want to kill him. Still, best not take the law into your own hands – though when you think how he used our mother . . . ' – He bowed his head, as if overcome with grief and shame – 'he deserves everything he gets.' From under his brows he observed the reaction to his provocative words. 'Mind you, fair's fair – wasn't it mother who led him on, just like she always leads men on? Wasn't it mother who shamed our father?'

'No one gonna hurt her,' said Agravaine.

Gaheris growled and shook his head. 'No one hurt her.'

'Did I say anything about hurting her?' Mordred's face was a caricature of outrage. 'What do you take me for? Hurt my own mother! As God is my witness . . . ' He broke off, waving his hands rapidly in front of his face as if to scatter all murderous thoughts.

The three men sat without speaking. The house was quiet now. In the twilight a blackbird sang. Far off, another blackbird answered its call. Mordred stood and stretched. 'Shall we say our goodbyes?'

It seemed that all the guests had left. Margot was nowhere to be seen. Arm in arm, supporting each other, Agravaine and Gaheris lurched down the corridor to the sitting room where the lights were still on, chairs and tables littered with discarded glasses and bottles. Mordred threw himself on a sofa and watched his two brothers scavenge their way through the room.

Gaheris wolfed the remains of a plate of sandwiches, then, to his delight, found a half-full bottle of gin which he gulped down. Agravaine drained the dregs of every wine glass and bottle he could find and collapsed on the floor by the sofa, hugging an empty bottle. Gaheris joined him.

'Where's mumsy?' said Agravaine.

'In bed, I expect,' said Mordred.

'Say goodnight,' said Agravaine, trying to get up.

'I wouldn't recommend it.'

'Why not?'

Mordred gazed at the ceiling and said nothing.

Using the empty bottle as leverage and panting with the

effort, Agravaine thrust himself into a sitting position, his nose almost touching Mordred's.

'Why not?'

Tapping his temple with his forefinger, Mordred gave a grotesque wink. 'Who knows if she's alone?'

Screaming his rage, Agravaine hurled the empty wine bottle across the room, smashing the bottle and several glasses.

From upstairs a man's voice called, 'Who's there?' A door opened.

The three men froze, staring at each other.

'Come back to bed, darling.' A woman's voice: their mother's. 'There's no one there. They've all gone home.' A door closed. Faint footsteps . . . silence.

For a full minute neither Agravaine nor Gaheris moved. Then without a word Gaheris picked up an empty vodka bottle.

The stairs from the hall led to the first floor landing and Margot's bedroom. Agravaine sat on the top step, Gaheris listened at the bedroom door. At first there was no sound, then their mother was sighing and moaning by turns. Elbows on knees, Agravaine rocked back and forth, covering his ears with his hands.

'Poor mumsy,' said Gaheris.

Mordred called up the stairs, 'I'll be off, then. Need some fresh air.'

No answer.

'Look, I know exactly how you feel. You have every reason to be angry – more than angry.'

Still no response.

'See you at the rendezvous in . . . ' – looking at his wristcom – 'an hour and a quarter. No hurry, you have time to kill.'

The front door slammed.

Margot's sighs grew higher-pitched and more insistent. A man grunted, hoarse grunts like a baboon's. Carefully, inch by inch, Gaheris turned the handle, eased open the door and moved silently into the room. On the bed Margot lay naked, legs wide apart, her moaning frantic now, turning to loud cries of ecstasy. On top of her Adrian Pellinore's white buttocks pumped faster and faster as he reached his climax. Gaheris stood by the bed, raised the vodka bottle high and brought it down with all his strength on Adrian Pellinore just as he rolled off Margot. The bottle struck Margot's head with massive force.

Agravaine rushed into the bedroom and knelt by the bed. 'What have you done! What have you done!' he cried. 'Mumsy,' he pleaded, 'talk to me, mumsy, talk to me.' Margot lay still, eyes closed. 'I love you, mumsy. Talk to me.' As he patted her face, blood oozed from the splintered skull. He looked at his bloodstained hand in horror. 'You killed mumsy!' he screamed. 'You killed her! You killed her!'

'I never did,' said Gaheris.

'You killed her, you mad dog!'

'I'm not mad,' said Gaheris, biting his knuckles anxiously. 'I'm not.' The trauma of the killing had sobered him, as it had Agravaine. Both men were in shock.

Agravaine clasped Margot in his arms. 'Wake up, mumsy,' he whispered, 'please wake up.' Laying his head on her breast he began to sob, deep-throated sobs that shook his whole body. 'You killed mumsy,' he said, 'you killed my mumsy.'

Gaheris looked blankly at his brother. 'Did I?' he said, his brows drawn down as if he were trying to recall something that happened a long time ago. 'Anyway, it wasn't my fault. It was him, it was his fault. It was him I was trying to hit.'

At the same instant they both became aware of Adrian Pellinore cowering naked and trembling in the far corner of the room. Rounding the bed, Gaheris stood over the terrified man. 'Don't hurt me,' he pleaded, 'please don't hurt me.' Gaheris's lips curled contemptuously, Agravaine, blubbering, stood by his brother. Adrian Pellinore, his hands clasped protectively over his head, curled into a ball. 'Don't hurt me,' he begged, 'let me go. I won't say a word, I swear I won't, I swear to God. On my son's life, I won't breathe a word to anyone. I'm a rich man,' he babbled, 'I'll give you anything you want – a million, two million, three million. Just don't hurt me, please don't hurt me.' Jumping up, he made a despairing run for his life, but before he could reach the door, Gaheris's huge fist felled him with a terrible blow to the head. As he lay in the foetal position groaning with pain, the two brothers kicked him again and again – in the kidneys, the ribs, the head. In seconds the groaning stopped, Adrian Pellinore's eyes turned back in their sockets, his body convulsed once, twice, three times, and lay still.

At fifteen minutes past midnight the night sky was overcast. A thin drizzle of rain fell on the waiting Scuttle. Mordred touched his earlobe once and spoke. 'No sign of them yet. How long have we got?'

'We're two hours behind schedule,' said the pilot. 'If we stay much longer we risk being spotted. Remember, we are not mantled on the ground.'

'Let's give them another five minutes.'

A herd of deer sheltered close by under an oak tree. Mordred clapped his hands. The females jumped and ran, the stag stood his ground, looking in his direction, then he too ran off.

'Smart fellow,' said Mordred under his breath. 'Knows who his enemies are.'

Shadows moved. Mordred drew his port. 'Who's there?'

'Gaheris.'

'Agravaine.'

The Scuttle took off. Several minutes passed before anyone said a word.

Mordred broke the strained silence. 'How was mother?'

Agravaine and Gaheris exchanged glances.

The hairs tingled on the back of Mordred's neck. 'What have you done?' he said.

'Nothing,' said Agravaine, avoiding his brother's eyes.

'What happened, Agro?'

'Nothing,' said Agravaine sullenly.

Mordred stared at Gaheris. 'What's that on your face?'

'It's dirt,' said Agravaine.

Mordred swiped Gaheris's cheek with the ball of his thumb. 'That's not dirt,' he said, 'it's blood.'

Agravaine pointed a trembling finger at Gaheris. 'He did it.'

Gaheris cowered. 'I d-didn't mean to! I d-didn't mean to,' he stammered.

'What didn't you mean to do?' said Mordred.

Shame-faced, Agravaine told him. When he had finished, Mordred said nothing, nor by his expression did he offer the smallest clue to what he was thinking.

Thirty One

THE INSTANT THE Scuttle touched down, Mordred rushed the two brothers to his apartment. For a few moments he paced the room, stopping now and then to confront them with a reproachful look and a shake of the head. Finally he spoke: 'Murder. Two murders. My own brothers, murderers. It's appalling. Unbelievable.'

'We're all in this together,' insisted Agravaine.

Mordred raised an eyebrow. 'Remind me again – was it you or me who killed our mother?'

A resentful look from Agravaine. 'You put us up to it.'

'Put us up to it,' said Gaheris.

'That is a wicked lie,' said Mordred. 'As God is my witness, I did my best to restrain you.'

'You dropped hints,' said Agravaine.

'Dropped hints,' said Gaheris.

'Who was it said they wanted to murder the Pellinores?' asked Mordred.

'Who was it said they deserved everything they got?' countered Agravaine.

An indifferent shrug. 'Did I say that? I really don't remember. I do quite distinctly remember warning you not to take the law into your own hands.'

Agravaine began to tremble.

Gaheris looked from one to the other. 'Is anything wrong, Mord?'

'Wrong!' Mordred cupped a hand round his ear. 'Did you just say what I think you said? Is anything wrong! Wrong! You have just murdered our mother and her lover, two perfectly innocent people, and you ask me if anything is wrong!'

Gaheris flinched, and turned his head away, not because he felt ashamed, but because he was afraid of Mordred. 'Is it?'

'For God's sake, Mord,' said Agravaine in a low voice, 'help us.'

Whilst Mordred kept them in suspense, his two brothers watched him with eager eyes, like two dogs awaiting their master's command. 'Very well,' he said at last, 'I will do what I can for you. You are, when all is said and done, my flesh and blood. A word of advice, though – don't try and pin the blame on me. Just admit what you did. A bit of remorse would not be out of place.'

'We are sorry for what we did,' said Agravaine immediately.

'We are very sorry,' said Gaheris.

'Well, that's a start,' said Mordred.

'What will happen to us?' said Agravaine.

Mordred considered the question. 'Perhaps I shouldn't be asking you this,' he said, 'but did you wipe Gaheris's fingerprints off that bottle of – whatever it was?'

'Vodka,' said Gaheris. 'It had a blue label and foreign writing,' he added helpfully. 'It was Polish,' said Agravaine.

Mordred raised his eyes to heaven. 'I am not interested in the damned label, or where it came from. All I want to know is – did you wipe the bottle?'

'I think so,' said Agravaine, 'but we didn't think of cleaning up in the sitting room. We were in a panic.'

'No matter,' said Mordred, 'there'll be hundreds of fingerprints all over the place. Hordes of people went back to the house for drinks after the funeral.'

Agravaine clenched his hands to stop them trembling. 'What do we do, Mord?' he said, 'what do we do?'

In a way Mordred felt sorry for Agro and Gaheris. Still, murder was murder. True, he had fired up their furnace, but they had done the deed, not him. Yet he felt not a scrap of remorse. Why should he? Adrian Pellinore deserved to die. A pity about mother, though, that had come as a bit of a shock. How did he feel about it? In two minds. His relationship with his mother had been messy to put it mildly; love and hate in equal measure.

Which way now? Tell Arthur? If he knew that his nephews had committed murder, what would he do? He would have no option but to hand them over to the High Council or the British police, demonstrating that even his own family was not above the law, confirming his exalted status as the guardian of justice, and cementing his hold on the Round Table. So, nothing to be gained by telling Arthur.

He gave it some more thought. Should he keep silent? How would that serve his purpose? It would not. Having lit the fire, he must tend it, ensure that it never went out.

'Agravaine and Gaheris have something to tell you, Gawain,' said Mordred. 'They need your help.'

The two brothers exchanged scared looks and said nothing, each willing the other to pluck up the courage to confess. Yet neither of them could find the words. What words were there to describe what they had done? How to explain killing your own mother? Confessing to Mordred was one thing, confessing to Gawain something else. He was their elder brother, and of all men, the one they most respected.

Gawain considered his brothers with shrewd eyes. 'You have done something bad, haven't you?'

Neither of them dared answer the question. It was left to Mordred to describe what they had done. As he did so, Gawain's face displayed alternately shock and disbelief, the blood rushing to his face, the veins bulging in his temples. Agravaine wept and Gaheris squirmed, both of them fearing that Gawain would turn on them and knock them senseless. But when the story was told, he sat at his computer staring at it transfixed, as if hoping that somewhere in the boundless regions of cyberspace lay the explanation for what, here, in the real world, made no sense at all. When finally he spoke, there was no anger and no recrimination. 'Is it true?' he demanded. 'Did you kill our mother and Adrian Pellinore?' Agravaine and Gaheris hung their heads and said nothing.

Mordred went first to Agravaine and then to Gaheris, took their hands, and gripped them in both of his, as if he were trying to charge their weakness with his strength. Gawain was moved by the gesture.

'What's done is done,' said Mordred. 'You must tell Gawain the truth.'

'I killed mother,' mumbled Gaheris. 'I didn't mean to, Gawain, really I didn't. It was an accident.'

'We killed Adrian Pellinore,' said Agravaine in a low voice. 'We lost control of ourselves.'

'I punched him in the head, and we kicked him in the kidneys,' said Gaheris, 'and in the chest too, didn't we, Agro?'

Gawain regarded his two brothers with stern eyes. 'You have committed murder,' he said, 'and you must pay the penalty. If the British police issue warrants for your arrest, you will be handed over to them. If they do not, you will be tried by the High Council. Either way, you will be brought to justice. Now go back to your rooms and wait there until you hear from me.'

Agravaine and Gaheris slunk away.

'I checked the internet,' said Mordred when they had gone. 'They have found the bodies, but so far the police have no particular suspects.'

'It makes no difference,' said Gawain, 'they have confessed to the murders.'

'Only to us,' said Mordred.

'So?'

Mordred chose his words carefully. 'Gawain, you are the man I have always looked up to.'

'Thank you, Mord,' said Gawain, 'I appreciate that.'

'And I know,' continued Mordred, 'how much importance

you attach to family loyalty.'

'We are talking about murder.'

Mordred opened his hands in a gesture of appeal. 'Isn't the future of Camelot more important than anything? Anything,' he repeated with solemn emphasis.

'Yes, but . . . '

'Think of the trouble and distress this will cause Arthur. Does he really need to know?'

'I can't keep Arthur in the dark,' said Gawain. 'It's unthinkable.'

'Is it?' said Mordred. 'What good will it do if we tell him? There would have to be a trial. What if Agravaine and Gaheris were acquitted, would they leave the court without a stain on their character? I doubt it. Some would say the trial was fixed. And if they were convicted of murder, what then? Who would trust the family any more? Who would trust Arthur? I'm telling you, Gawain, whatever the outcome, a trial would turn brother against brother, friend against friend, comrade against comrade. Some would support us, some would say we were all tarred with the same brush as Gaheris and Agravaine – killers at heart. And if they didn't say it, they would think it.'

'It wouldn't be like that,' said Gawain, though he suspected it might well be.

'No?' said Mordred. 'Well let me tell you, there are those here in Camelot who are already losing faith in our mission, people who think we are just a bunch of vigilantes. Already the vultures are up in the trees. A case like this would bring them down, and they would tear us to pieces.'

Mordred had sown a seed of doubt in Gawain's mind. 'Is there an alternative?'

'Let's at least wait until we hear what the British police have to say. If they issue arrest warrants for Agro and Gaheris, we shall have to hand them over. If they don't . . . ' A lift of the shoulders. 'Why not let sleeping dogs lie?'

Gawain had some sympathy with Mordred's point of view.

Undoubtedly the revelation that Agravaine and Gaheris had committed these terrible murders would be highly damaging to Arthur, indeed to the whole family. Yet what Mordred was proposing was equally unpalatable. To conceal the truth – would that not be to betray the very principles on which Camelot was founded?

'Let me get this straight. You are suggesting that we cover up murder?'

'Gawain, my dear brother,' said Mordred, 'I am suggesting we do what is best for Arthur and for Camelot. Let's look at the facts. How can we be sure it was murder? Were Agravaine and Gaheris truly responsible for what happened? Was it not rather a cruel accident of fate? Gaheris is not a full deck of cards as we know, hardly responsible for his actions. Is he to blame? Or are we? Should we not have looked after him better? As for Agravaine, he has always been – shall we say – *attached* to mother, something which, by the way, she encouraged. He was maddened by jealousy. And a madman cannot be convicted of murder.'

'So what is your conclusion?'

'Men die every day, and women too,' said Mordred, 'some deservedly, some not. We are dealing here with killings carried out by two mentally unstable individuals, killings, moreover, that were to a great extent provoked by our mother, and by the callous way she betrayed her husband over the years. I hate to say it . . . ' Mordred's voice dropped to a dramatic whisper, 'but in many ways mother was responsible for her own death.' Had he gone too far?

Gawain was shocked. 'That is a terrible thing to say.'

'Believe me,' said Mordred, 'it breaks my heart to say it.'

'Even if it were true,' said Gawain, 'it is not for us to make that judgement. It is for the courts to decide whether our brothers are guilty.'

'At the very worst,' said Mordred, 'this is a crime of passion. They would probably both walk free.'

'I respect your opinion, Mord, but it changes nothing,' said Gawain. 'It's my duty to report this matter to Arthur.'

'Your *duty?*'

'Yes.'

'I am puzzled,' said Mordred, withdrawing to his second line of defence, 'why you, a man of principle and integrity, feel it your duty to report this crime of passion when . . . when there are other crimes . . . ' His eyes slid away from Gawain's hostile stare.

'What crimes? What are you talking about?'

Mordred's face was a theatre of conflicting emotions. 'I spoke too hastily. Forget what I said.'

Gawain's jaw set firm. 'Explain.'

'I would prefer not to.'

Gawain was fast losing patience with his brother. 'I insist you explain what you just said.'

'Do you not consider adultery a crime of passion?' said Mordred in a rush of words which he appeared instantly to regret. 'Forgive me, I should not have said that. I beg you, Gawain, please don't be angry with me. It's just that there are times when an honest man feels compelled to speak his mind.'

From the window of his apartment Gawain looked out at Camelot. A few hundred metres to the east was Command Control, dazzlingly white in the afternoon sun. Command Control. He had always believed that a man could control his actions, his thoughts even. It seemed he was wrong. With all the technology and weapons and brains in the world, what could anyone control? Nothing. Control was an illusion. 'I believe you may be referring to certain mischievous and unfounded rumours,' he said.

'I do hope you are right,' said Mordred, 'and that they are unfounded. Because there are those who might be tempted to – um – communicate their suspicions to Arthur.'

Gawain felt the hairs rise on his spine. 'Spread malicious gossip? Why would anyone do such a contemptible thing?'

'They might feel it was their duty to do so,' said Mordred, directing a sly look at Gawain.

'Duty? To what?'

'To the truth,' said Mordred.

Gritting his teeth, Gawain could barely control his anger. 'Are you saying that *you* could be the one to report these filthy stories to Arthur?'

Eyes wide with indignation, Mordred stepped back a pace. '*Me!*' Another backward step. '*Me!*' And yet another . . . '*Me report them!*'

'Perhaps I misunderstood you,' said Gawain, impressed by the fervour of his brother's outrage.

'I swear to you,' said Mordred, 'that I would never betray my family,' adding in a faltering voice, 'and I must say you disappoint me, brother. I thought you had more faith in me. This is where being honest gets you – being slandered by your own. I should have known better than to speak the truth.'

'I apologise.' said Gawain, genuinely contrite. 'Then who do you think would do such a thing?'

'I prefer not to name names,' said Mordred. 'In any case you can rely on me to persuade them not to do anything foolish.'

Gawain regarded his young brother with some astonishment. The introspective, solitary child he remembered had grown into a young man of strong character, with the integrity to go with it. 'Forgive me, Mordred, I misjudged you. For a moment there, I thought you were – well – gunning for uncle.'

'Uncle?' For a moment Mordred was caught off guard. 'Far from it,' he said. 'I love my uncle.' A glint of mischief flashed in his eyes and was gone. 'I couldn't love him more if he were my own father.'

'Arthur *is* Camelot,' said Gawain earnestly. 'We need him. Without him we are lost. We must never do anything to harm him. If he knew about . . . about Lancelot and Guinevere, it would break his heart.'

'It would indeed,' said Mordred. 'Which is exactly why I

suggest we say nothing about it.' A sly look. 'And for the same reason – though only with your consent, of course – we should say nothing about our brothers' confession.' He held out his arms.

As the two brothers embraced, Gawain was feeling unaccountably ill-at-ease.

Two days later the British police announced at a press conference that the late Lennox Lotte had been heavily in debt when he committed suicide, and that his wife had disowned his debts. In their view, therefore, it was likely that Margot Lotte had been murdered by a paid hit man. As for the unfortunate Mr. Pellinore, he had simply been in the wrong place at the wrong time.

Mordred was content to bide his time. By his contriving, truth had gatecrashed the party, and brought down Agravaine and Gaheris. One day it would do the same for Lancelot, Gawain and the rest of them. And Arthur. Oh, yes, above all, Arthur. What fools they were, the lot of them! Let them brandish their swords and strut their ramparts. He would lay siege to their citadels as Joshua once did. And when he sounded the trumpet, the walls would come tumbling down!

Thirty Two

CAMELOT WAS A small island, and despite Gawain and Mordred's pact, disturbing stories circulated that Arthur found hard to ignore. At first, like most people in Camelot, he was certain that neither Agravaine nor Gaheris had anything to do with the murders. Later, talking to Mordred and Gawain, he was less sure. Gawain, normally forthcoming, appeared defensive as if he were hiding something, and Mordred simply claimed that he knew nothing. Summoning Agravaine and Gaheris, he hoped they would convince him of their innocence, but in that hope he was disappointed, their protestations of innocence a touch too vehement for his liking, and their accounts of their movements after the funeral inconsistent.

Leo Grant, man of law, and George Bedivere, man of action, each had their point of view. In order to try and settle their differences, they requested a joint meeting with their leader.

'I say clear the air of these poisonous rumours, Arthur,' said George. 'Arrest Agravaine and Gaheris and summon them before the Round Table.'

'On what grounds?'

'Suspicion of murder.'

'Without evidence there is no case to answer,' objected Leo.

George thumped the arm of his chair with his steel right hand. 'These stories need to be investigated.'

'You cannot charge a man without evidence,' insisted Leo. 'It would make a mockery of justice.'

'Then I say the hell with justice!' said George. 'What legal evidence did we have against the Sea Lords before we took them out? None that I know of. And what about Sadiq and Khalid? I don't remember anyone reading them their rights.'

'Whether there is due process or not,' said Arthur, 'justice must be seen to be done, and if not justice that is strictly in accordance with the letter of the law, then at least justice that is morally defensible. That is crucial, and that is what distinguishes us from vigilantes. If we abandon the aims and ideals of Camelot, we lose our moral authority. If we lose that, we lose the war against the terrorists.'

'I agree with Arthur,' said Leo. 'How do we know Gaheris and Agravaine committed this terrible crime? We don't. Neither we nor the British police have any evidence against them. All we have is rumours, and you can't prosecute people on the basis of rumours.'

'Then we are agreed?' said Arthur. 'We do not arrest Agravaine and Gaheris.'

A quick nod from Leo and a reluctant growl of assent from George Bedivere.

In his heart of hearts, though, Arthur knew it was not the end of the story. Until the truth was established, the murder of Margot Lotte and Adrian Pellinore would remain an indelible stain on the integrity and reputation of Camelot.

Mordred was frustrated. Things were not proceeding according to plan. Those whom he had marked out as potential allies appeared to have no stomach for the fight. Determined though he was to bring Arthur down, he knew he could not do it alone. Moreover it was not in his nature to lead from the front. Let others have that dubious honour and assume the risks that went with it. As a child he had observed his older brothers from dark hiding places, sheltering behind chairs and tables, a habit that had not altered when he became an adult; except that now, instead of tables and chairs, he sheltered behind people, manipulating others to do his work for him. He needed an ally to front the palace revolution he was planning.

Keir had at least one qualification for such a role. He was, as Mordred knew, jealous of Arthur, jealous of his many friends and admirers, jealous of his standing and reputation in Camelot and the world.

'How long have you been in Camelot?' he asked him.

'A few years,' said Keir. 'Why?'

'No special reason,' said Mordred. 'It's just that in all that time you have never been offered a position of authority, and I can't help wondering why.' Keir reddened, sensing an implied criticism. 'I mean,' Mordred clarified hastily, 'why your obvious talents appear to have gone unnoticed.' Keir relaxed, reassured by the comment. Cautiously, Mordred developed his argument. 'I know it's none of my business, and who am I to find fault with my elders and betters? but I do find it odd that you have been overlooked for so long. And I can assure you,' he added for good measure, 'that I am not the only one who thinks it strange.'

Mordred's words had struck a chord. He was right, Keir was thinking. Arthur had never given him the recognition he deserved.

'There are those who feel,' went on Mordred, observing with satisfaction that his words were prodding the slumbering beast awake, 'that Arthur needs to be guided, and that you are just the man to do it.'

It was obvious to Keir that Mordred had a high regard for him, and that he saw him participating in secret and vital discussions, offering his advice, making suggestions that might affect the very future of the world, earning the respect and admiration of his peers.

Mordred expanded on his theme. 'There are so many key positions up for grabs. Let's face it, even I have been given something to do – only Tich's assistant in NIWIS, but at least it's something. You deserve better than some obscure job in transport, Keir, a great deal better. You're a top man. You should be Head of Command Control, or Commander of

Robots, or perhaps running Medical Services.'

Keir received the accolade cautiously, like a dog nosing an exotic titbit. It was tempting, if a shade too rich for him. Sitting at the councils of the great was one thing, having to make decisions was something else. Vulnerable to flattery, he had, nevertheless, like many vain men, a more realistic perception of his own abilities than he conveyed to the world.

'It troubles me,' said Mordred, 'that men of quality like you with so much to offer, are ignored, when lesser talents – and dare I say it, less honourable men – are rewarded.'

Keir was intrigued. 'Such as?'

'Please don't ask me that question,' said Mordred. 'As everyone in Camelot knows, I am a plain, straightforward sort of man. With me what you see is what you get. I am not one to stab people in the back, or spread rumours.' With a sharp glance at the target of his machinations, he added, 'There is already far too much tittle-tattle in Camelot as it is.'

'There are certainly some pretty unpleasant rumours floating round the island,' agreed Keir.

Mordred raised his hands as if to fend off evil spirits. 'I don't listen to gossip.'

'Have you not heard them?'

'I told you, I never listen to rumours,' said Mordred, 'never.' He looked away and quickly back again at Keir. 'What rumours?'

'About the murders.'

'Loyalty,' said Mordred unexpectedly, 'is the most precious and wonderful thing – especially loyalty to friends and family.'

For a moment Keir was confused, wondering what loyalty had to do with rumours.

Mordred's voice was low and intense. 'But, important as loyalty is, it must never be used as an excuse for concealing the truth.'

Keir's eyes brightened. 'So it *is* true!'

'What is?' said Mordred.

'That Agravaine and Gaheris killed your mother and her boyfriend!'

'In heaven's name,' said Mordred, 'what makes you say such a terrible thing?'

Keir smiled, congratulating himself on his cleverness, 'That comment of yours about loyalty to friends and family. It gave the game away.'

'I am too gullible in these matters,' said Mordred, clapping an admonishing hand to his forehead. 'Promise me you'll keep it to yourself.'

Keir's eyes flickered. 'I swear I won't breathe a word to anyone,' he said.

If the skill of dissembling were measured on a scale of one to ten, Mordred was thinking, Keir would barely make a two. 'What grieves me more than anything,' he said, 'is the thought that Arthur might be covering up wicked deeds out of a misguided sense of loyalty. Believe me,' he said, his eyes shining fervently, 'I am the most loyal of his followers. But there are some things even more important than loyalty. These rumours raise vital issues.'

'What sort of issues?'

'Issues that affect our right to call ourselves a democracy,' said Mordred, 'issues that cast doubt on our enduring commitment to the ideals of justice and honour. Arthur is powerful, perhaps too powerful. As someone once said, *power tends to corrupt and absolute power corrupts absolutely.*'

It was easy to tell from Keir's expression that he was not displeased with what he was hearing. The moment had come, thought Mordred, to put him to the test.

'Someone should do something about it,' he said, making it sound like an invitation.

Keir's pulse quickened. 'About what?'

'About double standards in Camelot. About the fact that murder is covered up, that good men are cast aside and bad ones flourish.' He laid a hand on Keir's shoulder. 'Some might say it was time for change.'

'What can I do?' Keir's dubious tone suggested he had little faith in his ability to change anything.

'Has it ever occurred to you that perhaps you too have a destiny, like everyone says Arthur has?'

'Me? A destiny?'

Mordred rubbed his hands together in a way that conveyed both humility and apprehension. 'May I speak frankly?'

'Please.'

'Someone should deliver Arthur a warning, a friendly warning, of course, nothing excessive, but firm, you understand, firm enough to ensure that the message gets through.' Mordred opened his arms to Keir as if he were offering him the keys of the kingdom. 'What better man to do it than his own brother?'

Keir flinched and drew back, a wary look in his eyes, and Mordred knew instantly that he had picked the wrong man. Keir hated his brother, but he feared him too; he would never openly oppose him. When Mordred's rebels laid siege to the palace, he would not be in the vanguard urging them on, he would be at the back of the crowd.

Unless of course Arthur was lying on the ground mortally wounded, in which case, thought Mordred disdainfully, Keir would be the one to finish him off.

Thirty Three

WORKING OUT IN Camelot's gymnasium, Lancelot shared his concerns with George Bedivere. 'George, you know Arthur as well as anyone. Why isn't he doing anything about Agravaine and Gaheris?'

George sweated and groaned as he lifted the barbell with huge weights on either end. Lancelot watched fascinated. George, they said, had lost his hand fighting insurgents in the Middle East. Not a man to let a minor handicap like a steel hand frustrate him, he had the machine shop fit a claw-like contraption that snapped onto his steel hand and locked around the barbell.

'Because there's no evidence against them.' Grunting, he heaved the barbell high. 'Not yet, anyway.'

'Then why doesn't he order an investigation?'

George lowered the barbell to the ground and unsnapped the gadget. His first loyalty was to Arthur. What Arthur said to him in private was just that – private. 'If I were you, Lance, I would leave it to Arthur. He's a wise man. Don't ask me how he got to be so wise. Maybe because he listens a lot more than he talks.'

Lancelot attacked the step machine savagely. 'Arthur is under pressure. I should hate to see him crack.'

With his left hand George lifted a massive dumb-bell and held it high. 'This will crack before he does,' he said, dropping the weight with a crash to emphasise his point. 'And just because he's not acting now doesn't mean he won't when the time is right.' Removing his peaked cap, he wiped his balding head and bulldog neck, and put the cap back on. His end of work-out ritual complete, he pulled on his tracksuit bottom, stumped across the gym's wooden floor and opened the door. Without turning his head, he said quietly, as if he were talking to himself, 'Don't kid yourself, Lance, there's nothing in Camelot that Arthur doesn't know about.' And he was gone, leaving the gym door swinging.

Slowly Lancelot eased himself off the step machine. *Don't kid yourself.* Why would he kid himself? And about what? He didn't like the sound of that, didn't like it at all. *Nothing in Camelot that Arthur doesn't know about.* Was George talking about the murders, or was he talking about Guinevere?

How often had they agreed to end the affair. Fantasy, of course. They were inextricably linked; hearts, minds and bodies. There were times when he was certain that Arthur suspected something: a look in his eye perhaps, or an uncharacteristic stumble of words. Ginny was convinced he knew nothing. Was that what she truly believed? Or was it what she needed to believe?

For a while he sat in his apartment thinking of the last time he made love to Ginny – and the next. Though his conscience troubled him from time to time, he tried not to see his ongoing affair as an act of betrayal. Rather it was his fate, something over which he had no control. Most other things in his life he had managed to control; not this. It was meant to be, and there was little point in soul-searching when there was nothing he could do about it. What made it more difficult was not being able to share his secret with anyone but the person who shared his guilt. The need to unburden himself was overwhelming.

In the House of Prayer Arthur was kneeling, head bowed. Lancelot took a seat a few rows behind. He had never seen Arthur in the act of prayer before, and wondered whom he was praying to, and for what. For a time he waited, hoping he would notice him. But he did not. Ginny always said that Arthur had one happy and one sad eye. Was that true? Or did he have one ear open and one closed, so that with his good ear he heard what he wanted to hear, turning his deaf ear to all the rest? No, that couldn't be true either. If he knew, he would do something about it, and in a way he wished he would; at least it would end this torment of uncertainty, this void of unknowing.

As Arthur walked back down the aisle of the House of Prayer, he stopped and looked at Lancelot. Impossible to tell by his expression what he was thinking. It was as though his mind had disappeared into some remote corner of his being. Lancelot's heart beat fast as he waited for the axe to fall. Arthur's face was suddenly alive with recognition. 'Lance! Good to see you!' he exclaimed, and then, face drained of expression once more, passed by without another word.

Lancelot sank to his knees, his whole body trembling, as it did every time he went into battle; though no one else in the world knew that. Composing himself, he walked slowly to the exit. As he stepped outside, he stopped, shielding his eyes, blinded by the light of the midday sun.

Thirty Four

THE COTTAGE DOOR was opened by a beautiful young woman with brown eyes and long black hair.

'I'm Nimue.'

'Arthur,' he said, extending his hand. She took it gravely. So this was Nimue, the mysterious young woman who had stolen the great man's heart. Never would he forget the sight of the Magus trotting along the beach behind her. It had made him angry, and perhaps a little jealous too.

They sat in high-backed Windsor armchairs opposite each other. 'Merlin's playing with his computers,' she said. Her English was fluent, with just the merest hint of an accent. What was it? Spanish? South American? 'He'll be down shortly. Can I get you anything?'

'Thank you, no.'

He looked directly at her, trying to tease out a comment, but she did not speak. No doubt she suspected he was here to check up on her – which was partly true – and was trying to protect herself. For a long time neither of them said anything. Both his body and his spirit felt the weight of silence. There were many kinds of silences, he was thinking; relaxed, comforting, guarded, threatening. At first this was a guarded silence, transforming itself by degrees to a threatening one. Nimue sat demurely, hands in lap, showing no sign of being under strain. What was this power she had over the Magus? Was it love? So why had Merlin fallen for her? Because she was beautiful? Because she was so much younger than he was? She would be – what? – in her late twenties or early thirties, and Merlin well into his sixties.

He began to feel claustrophobic, and then to sense an ominous presence in the room, as if some creature were trying to draw him into its embrace to be inspected, as a spider inspects a fly before sucking its blood. He was imagining things, he told himself. She was a perfectly harmless and very attractive woman with olive skin, high cheek bones, almond eyes and white teeth. Yet strikingly beautiful as she was, there was something about her that made his spine tingle.

'You miss Merlin?' she asked suddenly, smoothing the tights on one leg. She had wonderful legs.

'I do, yes,' he admitted.

'You would like him to come to Camelot?'

'I came to see an old friend.'

He knew by her expression that she did not believe him. 'It's for him to decide. I won't stand in his way.'

He did not respond.

'I only want what's best for him,' she said, and looked as though she meant it.

He felt himself believing her, being drawn to her, wanting her to befriend him. She really was the most fascinating creature, possessing that seductively elusive quality that drew a man to a woman and held him in her thrall.

Then she was gone, and Merlin was in the room, smiling that special smile that lit up his face whenever he saw Arthur again. Virgil hopped onto Arthur's shoulder and gently nibbled his ear, whilst the Magus sat upright in his chair and focused his green eyes on his protégé in a benign but inquisitive stare.

'Nimue is very beautiful,' said Arthur.

'Were you under her spell just now?'

'I believe I was.'

Merlin chuckled. 'I've taught her a thing or two.'

'What exactly have you taught her?' Arthur could not resist asking.

Merlin looked sheepish. Virgil inflated his feathers, uttered a harsh shriek and flew back to his master's shoulder. 'Some of my secrets,' said Merlin. Seeing the concerned look on Arthur's face, he added quickly, 'Not all of them, of course. Not the secrets of Camelot, I promise you.'

One day, Arthur was thinking, when Merlin was old, Nimue might trick him and rob him of his powers. What then? 'Why Nimue?' he asked.

'You are thinking I am stupid to throw away my power for the love of a woman.'

Arthur nodded. Useless to deny it when the Magus could read his mind.

For a while Merlin was silent, stroking Virgil's breast feathers. 'Perhaps I am stupid. But what can I do? When I look at Nimue, I hear the sirens singing those sweet melodies that they say lure passing sailors to their deaths. And you know something, Arthur? I really don't care.' A mischievous look. 'We are both in denial.'

'What are you denying, Merlin?'

'That Nimue does not love me,' said Merlin sadly, 'that she has something else on her mind – something she does not share with me.'

'And me?'

'How is Guinevere?' enquired Merlin pleasantly.

His fingers straying to the scar on his left cheek, Arthur looked away, unable to face those challenging green orbs. What was Merlin hinting? That Guinevere, like Nimue, had something on her mind she did not share? Trying vainly to dismiss thoughts too painful to be confronted, his mood darkened.

'You are troubled, Arthur,' said Merlin.

'I am having doubts, yes.'

'About what?'

'About myself. About what we do.'

'Why now? *Operation Sea Lord* and *NIWIS* were triumphs.'

'We win battles,' said Arthur, 'but what about the war? Will we ever win that? Things change for a time, and then . . . ' A despairing shrug. 'nothing really changes. And the cost to us and the world in human lives and misery is so high. I can't help wondering if the price is worth it.'

'Let me tell you a story,' said Merlin after a while. 'A true story.' He leaned back in his chair, the glow in his eyes dimming as his mind retreated into his head.

'Once, years ago, I too was having doubts. It was the winter of the year the Master of Camelot died, and it was cold as cold could be. I went to a remote island in the Hebrides to meditate. There, by chance, or so I thought at the time, I met a sculptor who carved life-like figures of animals, birds and sea creatures; wolves and rabbits, foxes and polar bears, dolphins, seals, sharks, whales and porpoises, sunfish and turtles, penguins and gulls, cormorants, guillemots and kittiwakes, eagles, herons and kites – all of them so perfectly sculpted that it seemed as if the birds were ready to fly away, the animals to pad off across the ice, and the sea creatures to slip into the ocean.'

Engrossed, Arthur leaned forward in his chair, even though he had no idea what all this had to do with him.

'And you know the most extraordinary thing about those figures?' said Merlin. 'They were carved in ice! Every year when winter came, the sculptor fashioned them with hammer and chisel. When they were done, he lived with his family of ice creatures, cherishing and loving them until the spring came and they melted in the sun, water streaming down their bodies and faces as if they were weeping at their own fate. At first I found that strange; inexplicable, in fact. Why did the sculptor not work in stone or marble? Why did he sculpt in ice, knowing his creations could not last?'

A long silence. Arthur hardly dared breathe for fear of disturbing the Magus.

'And then it came to me. That sculptor *deliberately chose to work in ice.* In his own humble way, like every creator, he was mimicking the greatest Creator of all. Life is transient, Arthur. Nothing lasts. We are born, we live a brief moment and we die.

All God's creatures melt in the sun. But though life is finite, the process of creation is without end. That is why, every year when winter returns, the sculptor gathers his ice family around him again, reaffirming his faith in the circle of life.'

Arthur was moved. Tears stung his eyes.

'You and I have every reason in the world to share that sculptor's faith,' said Merlin, 'for we both know that death is not an end, or we would not be here.'

For a while there was no sound in the room but the ponderous ticking of the longcase clock in the corner, and a few subdued squawks from Virgil catching a mouse in his sleep. 'I know you are right, Magus,' said Arthur, 'and I understand why you are telling me this. Still, I can't help but mourn the many victims of terror who have died so cruelly and needlessly. And the pain is all the greater, because in a way I feel responsible for their deaths.'

'That is part of the burden you must bear,' said Merlin. 'The road you have chosen is hard and lonely.'

Arthur smiled sadly. 'If only I had known how lonely.'

'You have stolen the fire,' said Merlin. 'As I told you long ago, the pain of loneliness is the vengeance of the gods. It is the price you must pay.' His green eyes glowed tenderly. 'Remember, I am always with you.'

'Is that a farewell?' said Arthur.

'I don't know,' said Merlin, 'but I fear it might be.'

Thirty Five

MORDRED WAS PUZZLED and frustrated. Was everyone in Camelot deaf, blind and dumb? Didn't they know that Lancelot and Guinevere were lovers? So why was no one doing anything about it? Didn't they care? Was it downright stupidity? Or a conspiracy of silence to protect Arthur? Well aware that the prolonged affair could bring down Lancelot, and perhaps Arthur too, he was uncertain how to exploit it to his best advantage. One option would be to denounce the two lovers at the next session of the Round Table, a high risk strategy that could well rebound on him.

Not a man to take unnecessary risks, he preferred to let someone else get their hands dirty. Keir had been found wanting. Who else could do the job? There was Ian Duncan, Lancelot's close friend. It was possible he already knew about the affair, and then again he might not. There were still many who didn't. How would he react if he discovered that the idol he worshipped had the proverbial feet of clay?

He dropped in on him. 'Some time ago I heard something that shocked me deeply. I've been keeping it to myself, but it's driving me crazy, and I don't know what to do.'

'How can I help?' asked Ian, concerned.

'Let me first assure you,' said Mordred, 'that I despise gossips. It's just that sometimes . . . ' He hesitated, seeming lost for the right words to express his predicament. 'The fact is I am desperate. I can't keep quiet any longer. I simply have to confide in someone I can trust. And I would trust you with my life.'

Ian Duncan, extrovert and uncomplicated, was touched.

'Thank you, Mord.'

Mordred put on a convincing show of a man struggling with his conscience. 'If only it was not so hard to talk about,' he said.

'Whatever it is, it's obviously preying on your mind,' said Ian. 'Best get it off your chest.'

'They say the ancient Greeks executed messengers who brought bad news.'

Ian grinned. 'You have my solemn promise that I won't execute you,' he said.

'It's about Lancelot,' said Mordred.

'What's he been up to?'

'About him and Guinevere, I mean.'

Ian stiffened. 'What are you saying, Mordred?'

'I'm not saying anything,' said Mordred, lifting his hands in pious protestation. 'It's the gossips – they're the ones saying those wicked things.'

'What things?' said Ian, his face pale as a death mask.

'Dear God, I wish I had never started this,' muttered Mordred, chin cupped in hands, fingertips gouging his cheeks. 'Forget I said anything, Ian. Please forget it.'

Ian ignored him. 'What things?' he asked again.

'That . . . that Lancelot is . . . that he's . . . ' Mordred's voice dropped 'God help me,' he muttered.

'That Lancelot is what, Mordred?'

'Close to Guinevere.'

'Are you suggesting they are having an affair?'

'The gossips are spreading poison. What do we do, Ian? Tell me.'

'Do?' Ian shook his head as if to clear it. 'I don't know,' he said, 'I really don't know.'

For a week Ian tried to dismiss the thought from his mind, but it refused to go away, stalking his days and nights. Who could be spreading this monstrous lie? For a lie it must be.

Yet what if it were true? Not that he had any right to sit in judgement. His own record was nothing to be proud of; many women, numerous affairs, most recently with Lanky. Knowing that her feelings for him were far stronger than his for her, he should have ended the affair long ago, or better still, never started it. The shameful truth was, that where women were concerned, his own sexual gratification was paramount, and if a woman got hurt in the process, he would not lose sleep over it. No, he had no right to judge anyone, let alone Lancelot.

Though if there were any truth in the rumour, someone ought to do something about it. Could there be? Was it possible that his high-minded friend, so critical of others, could be so dishonourable in his own life? Men should practice what they preached. What if Lancelot really was playing around with Arthur's wife? The more he thought about it, the more outraged he became. Lancelot and Guinevere? Could his dearest friend be so two-faced? Hard to credit. One way or another, he needed to be sure. He consulted Gawain, an honest man, a man you could depend on; Arthur's friend, and Lancelot's too, despite their rivalry.

'Have you heard the rumours?'

Protecting Arthur and his good name was an absolute priority for Gawain. 'Mordred could have got it wrong,' he said, avoiding a direct response.

'Is that likely?'

'I don't know, and I really don't care,' said Gawain. 'What I do know is that it's none of my business. Or anyone's but Lancelot's and Guinevere's. And Arthur's. What right do we have to interfere? People's sex lives are not my concern. Nor should they be yours.'

'The issue is not people's sex lives,' said Ian. 'The issue is truth.'

'Better to leave what you call truth unspoken,' said Gawain, 'than let it destroy everything we are working to achieve.'

There was a time when Ian would have endorsed that

philosophy. Not now, though, and not when Lancelot was involved. 'Truth is what Camelot is founded on,' he said. 'It's what we have all taken an oath to uphold. Without truth we are nothing.'

Gawain had heard enough. 'No one appointed you Minister of Morals, Ian,' he said peevishly, 'and anyway, as I understand it, we are talking about rumours and gossip, not truth. The best thing you can do for all our sakes is to forget what Mordred told you.'

Try as he might, Ian could not take that advice. What should he do? Go straight to Arthur? No, that would be unfair. The very least he owed Lancelot was the chance to defend himself.

As he stammered and stuttered out the rumour, Lancelot regarded his friend with disdain.

'Do you deny it?'

For a moment it was the old haughty Lancelot. 'How dare you interrogate me?' Then, seeing how wretched Ian looked, his voice softened. 'I thought you were my friend.'

'I am, as you well know, Lance, which makes this all the more painful.'

'What do you want me to tell you?'

'The truth.'

He considered lying; it would be the prudent thing to do. But lying was for lesser men. He was too honest and too proud to lie. 'Is it so important to know the truth?'

That was enough for Ian. 'So it *is* true,' he said.

Lancelot looked away. 'I wish it were not.'

'But why, Lance, why?'

Lancelot lifted his arms, and let them drop to his side. 'It happened, that's all. I wasn't looking for trouble, it came looking for me.'

Some things were more important than friendship. 'You must end it, Lance, and end it now,' urged Ian. 'You owe it to Arthur, and to Camelot. You owe it to yourself. It's a matter of principle, I don't need to tell you that.'

'There was a time when I would have died rather than betray my principles,' said Lancelot. 'Now I would die rather than lose Guinevere.'

Ian had never known what it was to be in love, had even doubted that such a thing existed. Now, looking at Lancelot, he had to admit that he was wrong.

'So what do you intend to do about it?' asked Lancelot. 'Will you look the other way? Will you do that for me?'

Ian hesitated. Hard to resist the appeal. He could scarcely remember a world in which Lancelot had not been his best friend. No man had ever been closer to his heart. Yet now it appeared that Lancelot was not the man he thought he was. 'I'm sorry,' he said, 'truly sorry, Lance. I need your assurance that you will give her up. If you don't give me that assurance, I shall go to Arthur.'

'A long time ago you saved my life,' said Lancelot. 'You should have let me die.'

'You were not meant to die,' said Ian. 'You have a divine mission, Lance.'

'You believe that?'

'Yes, I do.'

'I need time, Ian, time to think.'

Ian hesitated, touched by his friend's distress. 'We'll speak about this again,' he said.

Either way he was damned. Confess to Arthur, or end the affair. Both were unthinkable, yet nothing else would do, not now that he had confessed to Ian. After a sleepless night, he appeared in Guinevere's apartment without warning, unshaven, eyes wild.

'What's wrong?'

He blurted it out. 'Ian Duncan knows everything. I don't know how he found out. People are talking.'

Guinevere responded with that characteristically proud tilt

of the chin. 'Let them talk.'

Lancelot threw himself into an armchair. 'We shall have to cool it for a while. If we don't, he'll go to Arthur.'

'He would never do that.'

'I'm afraid he would.'

Guinevere directed a withering look at Lancelot. 'This is not about Ian, is it?'

'What do you mean?'

'It's about you,' she said. 'You've been looking for an excuse to end it, and now you've found one.'

'That's not true, Ginny,' he protested, 'I love you. I'll never give you up.'

'Make up your mind. You just said you wanted to cool it.'

'I'm suggesting we keep our heads down for a few weeks, that's all.'

'A few weeks? Or months? Or years?'

'You're being unreasonable.'

'Perhaps I am, but at least I'm being honest.' She was close to tears. 'You say you love me, but how much is your love worth if you scamper away like a scared rabbit at the first sign of trouble?'

Too angry and too emotional to argue any more, Lancelot left, head down, feeling thoroughly wretched. Guinevere wept for a minute or two, dried her eyes, washed her face and thought of calling Lanky. No, she decided, this was something she would have to deal with herself. No one could help her. The first question she asked herself was a simple one. Could she imagine a world without Lance? The answer was no. The second question was more problematic. Was Lancelot as committed to her as she was to him? She wanted to believe he was, yet, at this moment, she doubted it. His love for Arthur was curiously untouched by the fact that he was sleeping with his wife. That in itself was infuriating, reminding her constantly that she would always be excluded from that masculine brotherhood of men who talked and laughed and drank together, and were friends in a way they could never be friends with women.

Consumed by an irrational desire to possess her lover, she burned with those emotions she had once scorned: passion and jealousy. Why did she have to share Lancelot with anyone or anything? She had convinced herself that it was possible to love two men, albeit in different ways. Now she was in danger of losing them both.

Thirty Six

Bad Boy

I N COMMAND CONTROL, Arthur and Agravaine stared at the disquieting message on the central computer monitor.

Doctor Giraud and his team of doctors and nurses are in the hands of the Cambodian People's Government. They will be released when I receive the money and military equipment I need to fight the illegal and corrupt regime in Phnom Penh. As an indication of the seriousness of my intentions one nurse has already been executed and the video of her beheading released. If my demands are met in full, there will be no more needless deaths. If they are not, one nurse or doctor will be executed every week until they are.
Bad Boy

'Short, sharp and cruel,' said Agravaine with a shiver.

'What do we know about Dr. Giraud?'

'He's a member of One Planet, the international relief organisation,' said Agravaine.

'Didn't he develop a vaccine that he claimed was a cure for AIDS?'

'He did,' said Agravaine, 'but then several major pharmaceutical companies lobbied governments, and the testing programme was suspended.'

'I remember,' said Arthur. 'They said the vaccine was unstable and would never work.'

'Right,' said Agravaine. 'I've downloaded a couple of articles from leading medical journals published at the time. They strongly support the pharmaceutical companies, and more or less suggest that Dr. Giraud is a charlatan.'

'What happened to him?'

Agravaine tapped his keyboard. 'These are news releases from last year. He disappeared for a time, and then reappeared briefly in a remote forest region in the north of Cambodia.'

Arthur meditated. 'Hasn't Cambodia lost millions of people to AIDS?'

'Yes,' said Agravaine. 'No doubt that's why he chose to go and work there.' His fingers roamed the keyboard. 'Now look at this. A few weeks ago several TV channels in Cambodia reported that AIDS has been all but eradicated in the area where the doctor's team is working. The news didn't receive much publicity. The pharmaceutical companies kept quiet.'

'No doubt they had their reasons,' said Arthur.

'And then the French government stepped in. They asked Doctor Giraud to come back to France, and promised him unlimited financial backing to produce the vaccine. Giraud agreed. A few days later he and his team were seized on their way to Phnom Penh airport.'

'What do we know about *Bad Boy*?'

'Very little,' said Agravaine, 'except that he leads one of several rebel groups fighting the central government. He's tough and resourceful, and he has a reputation for brutality.'

For two weeks nothing further was heard from the rebel leader; and then, on day fifteen following *Bad Boy's* ultimatum, a video of Dr. Giraud was sent to a TV station in Paris. The rebels were deadly serious, he said. Two more nurses had been executed in the last two weeks. Only five nurses and three doctors still survived. The situation was desperate. He pleaded with world leaders, and the French government in particular, to accept the rebels' terms for the release of his team and himself, not just for their sakes, but for the sake of millions of people around the world suffering the ravages of AIDS.

Following secret negotiations between the French government and the rebel leader, a deal for the release of the One Planet team was agreed. The exact terms were not revealed, but were thought to involve a ransom in excess of three billion dollars, and an unspecified quantity of automatic weapons, mortars and hand-held missile launchers. Camelot's Neural Network was able to monitor the exchanges during these negotiations and obtain *Bad Boy's* voice signature.

Less than an hour after the agreement was announced, it was vetoed by the Cambodian government, claiming they had not been consulted by their French counterparts. There would be no further negotiations, and the rebels would be caught and brought to justice. Since there was little hope of rescuing the hostages, world leaders pleaded with the Cambodian President. In view of the exceptional circumstances, would he not accept *Bad Boy's* terms? A day passed whilst the world awaited his response. Finally it came. There would be no deal.

It was stalemate. The countries whose nationals had been taken hostage were compelled to await developments, leaving any action to the Cambodian government, even though the Cambodian army was no nearer to locating the rebels than it had been when the hostages were first taken.

At a meeting of the Round Table summoned to discuss the problem, some members were eager to rescue the hostages, some were less enthusiastic, feeling that it should be left to the Cambodian government, supported, it was hoped, by the international community. Arthur urged immediate action, pointing out that *Bad Boy* had nothing to lose by executing all the remaining doctors and nurses, with the possible exception of Dr. Giraud himself. It was finally agreed that Camelot would attempt to rescue Dr. Giraud and as many of his team as possible. No warning and no ultimatum were to be given, since *Bad Boy* was unlikely to be persuaded by threats.

In view of the difficult terrain in the mountainous north of Cambodia where huge tracts of land were covered by dense forest, it was decided that this would have to be a ground-based operation. When the rebels were located, a troop of actives would be dropped as close to their camp as possible. Because the hostages were being held in a confined space, it was considered too risky to use Excalibur portables.

In view of the special nature of the rescue mission, the competition to participate was fierce. Lancelot was besieged by officers, all making a forceful case to command the nine man ground force. As Chief of Staff, Lancelot was excluded from leading the actives himself, and would, as in previous operations, be piloting Eclipse. One by one he considered the qualifications of the volunteers, and one by one, eliminated them until he was left with three names: George Bedivere, Gawain and Ian Duncan. The leading contender had to be Gawain, George Bedivere being a little too old, and Ian Duncan relatively inexperienced. 'You know very well,' Gawain told Lancelot, 'that apart from Arthur, you and I have more experience in ground ops. than anyone in Camelot. You can't do it. That leaves me.'

Gawain was right, of course; he was the natural choice to lead the mission. Yet for some reason Lancelot hesitated. 'I'll let you have my decision in the morning,' he said.

The door panel buzzed, the speaker crackled.
Name?
'Lancelot.'
In a nano-second the computer had matched voice and iris with its records.
Enter, Lancelot.
Guinevere ran to him, her eyes anxious. 'Is something wrong?'
'I just wanted to talk.'
Now she was angry. 'You are always telling me not to take risks. It's madness to come here without any warning. Someone might have seen you.'

'I was careful.'

'Arthur could have been here.'

'I checked. He's in Command Control.' He wanted to kiss her, but she was on edge, the look in her eyes hardly inviting.

'What is it?'

'You know about *Operation Bad Boy*?'

'Yes. Why?'

'I have to appoint the commander of the rescue team. I wanted to know what you thought.'

Strange, she thought. Since when did Lancelot consult her about military matters?

He chose his words carefully. 'Gawain is the leading contender. The problem is, this is likely to be a dangerous mission – very dangerous – and he's my deputy, one of our key men.'

She understood immediately. 'So if anything happened to him . . . '

'It would be a huge loss,' said Lancelot, 'and a big blow to morale.'

'You have someone else in mind?'

'There's a short list.'

'Who is on it?'

'George Bedivere.'

'Anyone else?'

He looked at his hands. 'Ian Duncan.'

A long pause. 'I'm sure he would do an excellent job,' she said finally.

'Yes, he would.'

'That's settled, then.'

At the door they said an awkward goodbye, the unspoken thought between them; they could be sending Ian to his death.

Ian was surprised and delighted to be offered the command.

'You do understand, Ian,' said Lancelot, 'that this is not an order, it's an offer.'

'I accept the offer with thanks,' said Ian.

Lancelot hesitated, considering how best to put it. 'I presume you know that it's likely to be a highly dangerous mission?'

'Trying to scare me?'

'I just want you to be clear that the decision is yours,' he said, half hoping that Ian would back off. 'If you prefer not to do the job, no one will know I asked you, so no one will know you turned me down.'

'I'd be crazy to do that. It's the chance of a lifetime.'

'You are quite certain?'

'Absolutely.'

The two men shook hands. 'That – um – that matter we were discussing,' said Lancelot. 'Can we forget it?'

Ian shifted awkwardly on his feet and said nothing.

'Put it on the back burner, then?'

'For the time being,' said Ian.

When Eclipse lifted off with Lancelot at the controls, Ian Duncan took his troop through the various contingencies that might arise when they were on the ground. In two hours they were hovering, mantled, over the mountains and forests of northern Cambodia. Satellite sensors were launched, some static, others circling the area. It was not known how sophisticated the enemy technology was, but in order to confuse any potential surveillance from ground or air, Lancelot switched Eclipse to satellite mode, and began to send out weather reports to throw the enemy off the scent.

A day passed, then a second and a third, and still the rebel camp had not been located. In Camelot Command Control, Agravaine and Arthur, perched on their stools, worked at the Galaxy table monitor.

From Eclipse came worrying news. 'We're running low on power, sir,' reported Lancelot.

Agravaine had updated the calculations with Neural Network and Techforce a hundred times over the last three days. 'Eclipse must leave in two hours, or they may not be able to make it back to Camelot,' he told Arthur.

'Permission to unmantle Eclipse,' said Lancelot.

Unmantled, Eclipse would consume far less power, and would probably be able to remain in the target area another twenty-four hours.

Agravaine weighed their limited options. Unmantled, Eclipse would be vulnerable to ground-to-air missiles, the more so since she was designed for speed and was therefore only lightly armoured. On the other hand, she was hovering at fifty thousand feet, well out of range of most missiles.

'Do the rebels have ground-to-air missiles?' asked Arthur.

'Months ago they shot down a government helicopter,' said Agravaine, 'so there's circumstantial evidence that they probably do.'

'What about long range missiles?'

Agravaine winced as his raw fingertips hit the keys, asking the question. 'Neural Network is ninety per cent sure they do not have long range missiles.'

Ninety per cent. A one in ten chance of losing Lancelot and Ian Duncan and his troop, together with Eclipse. A ten per cent risk could not be dismissed. 'The only risk-free option we have,' concluded Arthur, 'is for Eclipse to return to base, recharge, and head back to Cambodia.' He drummed his fingers on the desk. 'How long would that take?'

Agravaine was prepared for that question. 'Including recharging time here, approximately twenty-two hours.' He could see that his uncle was struggling to make the right decision. 'If you ask me, nuncle,' he said, 'we have no choice. We can't afford to take risks with Eclipse.'

'What are the chances of locating the rebels' position in the next twenty-two hours?' said Arthur.

Agravaine grimaced. 'I'd say low to zero.'

Arthur made his decision. 'Open the gravitational link, Agro.'

The link crackled. 'Eclipse online.'

'Return to base, Lancelot,' said Arthur. 'You are to remain mantled. You will recharge in Camelot and take up your present position again as soon as possible. We estimate that will be twenty-two hours from now.'

'If we abandon these poor people, they'll all be murdered,' said Lancelot. 'Don't ask me to leave, sir.'

Arthur reconsidered his options, and concluded that the primary object of the mission was to rescue Dr. Giraud, and that everything else was secondary, even the possible death of more hostages. Though Lancelot was the operational commander, the overall strategic decisions were not his, but Arthur's. He could not allow his Commander-in-Chief to overrule him. 'There is no question of abandoning the One Planet team,' he said. 'The fact is, there is no reasonable prospect of locating the rebels in the next twenty-four hours. Eclipse will be back long before then.'

'I know they're in the area we're patrolling,' said Lancelot. 'Just give me a few hours to find them.'

'I'm sorry, Lance,' said Arthur, 'it's too risky. My order stands. You are to return to Camelot immediately. Do you copy?'

No response.

'Do you copy, Lance?'

Silence.

'Lancelot, do you copy?'

Still no response.

Arthur glanced at Agravaine. 'Is there a problem with the link?'

'Link functioning normally.' Seconds later Agravaine was bouncing on his stool and pointing at the table screen. Instead of a pulsating bleep on the screen, there was now a perfect miniature image of Eclipse. 'He's unmantled Eclipse, nuncle!'

'What the hell does he think he's doing? Come in Lancelot!'

Yet again, there was no response.

As Arthur was considering how to handle this latest development, Agravaine pointed excitedly at Eclipse's image on the table screen. 'Eclipse heading south-west, losing height rapidly!'

'Is there a problem?'

Agravaine attacked the keyboard and consulted the screen. 'No apparent problem on board Eclipse. All systems go.'

'It's a controlled dive,' said Arthur.

From Galaxy's speakers came the countdown as Eclipse plunged to earth: *Forty thousand . . . thirty-six thousand . . . thirty-two thousand . . .*

Panic rose in Agravaine's throat. 'What do we do, nuncle?'

'Get Lancelot on line.'

Agravaine's legs joggled furiously on his stool. 'Lancelot, do you copy? Come in Lancelot. Lancelot, do you copy?'

The link was silent.

Agravaine nursed his raw fingertips. 'Eclipse still losing height rapidly.'

Twenty-five thousand . . . twenty thousand . . . Fifteen thousand . . .

Arthur and Agravaine were both thinking the same thing. With every second that passed, the chances of Eclipse being hit by a ground-to–air missile were increasing dramatically.

Ten thousand . . .

Over the speakers from Techforce came the news they were dreading. ***Ground-to-air missiles launched! Ground-to-air missiles launched!*** On the big table screen six tiny bleeps rose swiftly from the rebel position towards Eclipse, and over the speakers the countdown to impact began: *Impact in fifteen seconds . . . fourteen . . . thirteen . . . twelve . . . eleven . . . ten . . . nine . . . eight . . .*

Thirty Seven

Bad Boy

WITHIN FIVE SECONDS of the missile launch, Eclipse's pro-active sensors had calculated their precise speed and distance and programmed Eclipse's interceptor missiles. In five seconds they were launched, and three seconds later all six incoming missiles were destroyed.

Arthur, lips set in a grim line, stared at the table screen and the wall monitors in disbelief. Six white puffs of smoke told him what he needed to know; the immediate danger had passed. With approximately two seconds to spare, Eclipse had destroyed the incoming ground-to-air missiles. There, on a dozen screens, was the proof. The puffs of smoke had quickly disappeared, but Eclipse was still on screen unmantled, hovering over the rebel position at barely a thousand feet.

Agravaine screamed into the gravitational link. 'For godsake, Lance, mantle! They'll shoot you down! Mantle!'

The two men watched transfixed as full-sized mother and six baby robots floated down from Eclipse by parachute. Virtually simultaneously Eclipse seemed to stand on its tail as it took off in the steepest of climbs, reaching fifty thousand feet in a matter of seconds. The image of the cigar-shaped aircraft was on all screens, then suddenly was only a pulsating bleep. Eclipse had mantled.

The gravitational link was live again. Lancelot's triumphant voice reported, 'Enemy position located. Robots launched. Scuttle standing by for launching.'

Relieved though Arthur was, he was also furious. This, however, was neither the time nor the place to chastise his Chief of Staff. That would have to wait until he was back in Camelot.

'Launch Scuttle,' he ordered. 'We will direct ground operations from Command Control.'

'Very good, sir.' Lancelot sounded almost humble. 'Request permission to continue monitoring operation.'

'Permission denied,' said Arthur, in no mood to argue. 'When Scuttle is launched you will return to base immediately, recharge and await further orders. Do you copy?'

'I copy, sir,' confirmed Lancelot, and the link was cut.

For a few moments Arthur said nothing. Agravaine was on edge, having good reason to be wary of his uncle these days. 'He disobeyed my orders,' said Arthur. 'There is no excuse for that.'

'No, nuncle,' said Agravaine, 'there isn't. But we both know why he did it. He took Eclipse down to draw the enemy's fire. And they fell for it. When they fired their missiles, they gave their position away. Pretty damned smart, eh?'

'Pretty damned reckless,' said Arthur. 'He risked Eclipse, he risked his own life and the lives of Ian Duncan and all the actives on board. What's more he risked compromising not just this operation, but future operations. If Eclipse had suffered significant damage it would have been a serious blow to Camelot.'

For a long time neither man spoke. Agravaine fiddled absently with his keyboard, from time to time sneaking a wary glance at his uncle, fearful what he might say or do. Arthur's blue eyes were cold and steely, his jaw jutting aggressively, his lips set firm. It was obvious that Lancelot's insubordination had both angered and disturbed him.

And then, to Agravaine's astonishment and relief, Arthur's sombre expression dissolved in a slow grin. 'You know what, Agro,' he said, 'you are right. It *was* pretty damned smart.'

In Eclipse's control room Lancelot gave Ian his final briefing. 'Scuttle will drop you ten kilometres north of the rebels' camp.

The co-ordinates of the clearing you will land in have been fed into your troop's computers, so you don't have to worry about finding your way. After you land you'll get feedback from mother robot. Let's hope mother and six landed safely and weren't spotted.'

'Mother and six?'

Lancelot explained. 'Merlin created the robots. The first prototype robot he called mother. Later he assembled a batch of small robots from the parts he discarded in making her. He always thought of them as mother's babies. Indeed I'm told he actually planted that idea in the mother's computer.'

Ian liked that. 'So they're special,' he said.

'Indeed they are. Merlin would be devastated if anything happened to them. So would Arthur.'

'Then,' said Ian, 'I'll see to it that they come back in one piece.'

A gruff response from Lancelot. 'Make sure you do too.'

The two men took their seats, Lancelot at the controls of Eclipse, Ian in Scuttle's belly with his nine man troop. At Scuttle's controls was the robo-pilot who would command Scuttle from now until the end of the Operation. Over the intercom Lancelot wound up his briefing. 'When you land, I'll be on my way back to Camelot. I'll be overhead again in twenty-two hours. Robo-pilot is programmed to guard Scuttle whilst the rescue mission is underway, and to destroy it if there is any risk of it falling into enemy hands.'

'Understood.'

'You know what your objective is.'

'To rescue the hostages.'

'Dr. Giraud is the number one priority. You understand what I'm saying?'

'I do.'

'Good luck, then.'

Ian's heartbeat quickened. This was it. Taking his time, he walked up and down Scuttle's fuselage cracking jokes and wishing his men good luck. This kind of social interaction was what Ian did best. His men liked him, knowing he was one of them, a dependable man with a no-nonsense approach to life. Reacting to his cheerful face and self-assured manner, they put aside their fears and concentrated their minds in anticipation of the battle to come. They were a hundred per cent focused now, strapping on the back-packs with built-in engines known as seven-league boots. What were they thinking, Ian wondered; the same as he was, presumably. Would the seven-league-boots get them down in one piece? Would the robots do their work? Would they be able to rescue the hostages alive? Would Scuttle be there to fly them back to Eclipse? And the all-consuming question in every man's mind. Would they be going home alive?

The countdown to launch began. In ten seconds Scuttle dropped down from Eclipse, its engines firing immediately, to the great relief of everyone on board. Watching on their screens, Arthur and Agravaine cheered. Over the speakers came an answering cheer from Techforce Ten.

At fifteen hundred feet the curved doors of Scuttle's belly opened, and one by one, Ian Duncan and his men jumped with the seven-league boots strapped to their backs. When they were clear of Scuttle the robo-pilot put the aircraft down on the designated landing site and went into guard mode. Belching fire, the great vault of stars above, and the dark forbidding mass of forest below, the seven-league boots propelled the ten men over the trees and down to a small clearing about a kilometre from the rebel camp.

Thirty Eight

Bad Boy

LANDING WITHOUT MISHAP, the nine actives and their commander stowed their back packs, prepared their weapons, strapped on their night vision screens and set off on foot in the direction of the rebel camp. Wearing virtual reality head packs fed with the latest updates on *Bad Boy* and his men, they could identify and target an enemy far away by means of thermal imaging sensors that operated effectively day or night in any kind of weather. At 2.30 a.m., after hours of stealthy progress through the forest, the troop halted, taking up positions less than a hundred metres from the rebel camp.

A text message from mother robot unscrolled on Ian's headset. *Mother and babies in position.* They were well hidden. Even with the benefit of night vision goggles and sound and heat sensors, it took him several minutes to locate them. *Identify targets and positions* he texted back. Within seconds he and his men had the response on their screens. *Two large tents at two hundred and ten metres – tent* **One** *at two o'clock, tent* **Two** *at nine o'clock. Inside tent* **One** *thirty humans. Inside tent* **Two** *forty-two humans. A smaller tent – tent* **Three** *– at one hundred and sixteen metres and six o'clock, contains fifteen humans – eleven male, four female. Unverified assumption: first two tents contain rebel soldiers, smaller tent contains as yet unknown number of hostages plus guards. Closer scrutiny recommended. Eight guards on patrol. Two static machine gun emplacements north and south of camp perimeter. Also in camp area, two helicopters, five armoured cars, ten trucks, one munitions depot.*

The text went on to describe in detail the rebels' weapons, including automatic rifles, hand-held missiles and a variety of bombs and grenades, also the precise location of the two machine gun emplacements, the munitions dump, phone mast and radio transmitter. There was no indication of *Bad Boy*'s location.

Ian exchanged views with his men.

'Before we make our move, we must know exactly where the hostages are.'

'What if they've separated them?' asked one of the actives.

'We'll handle it,' said Ian. Though he sounded confident, no one was fooled. If the hostages were not all in one tent, the risk of casualties, both for actives and hostages, would inevitably be greater. They discussed options.

The first would be to use missiles. Both mother robot and the six babies could be instructed to target the enemy with "artful dodgers", highly accurate at a range of thirty metres. Destroying the guards this way would be the safest option for the hostages and also for the actives who would not then be involved in close combat. Realistically, though, it might be difficult, if not impossible, to get close enough to the enemy. As commander in the field, Ian was responsible for making all tactical decisions, including, as a last resort, any that might involve the death of one or more of the hostages. Understandably, calculated risks might have to be taken, though not with Dr. Giraud's life. Ian's orders were clear, whatever the cost, the doctor was to be rescued alive. For that reason alone, mini-missiles looked like a non-starter.

The second option would be to use microscopic soft weapons. Whilst full size destroyer robots had the capacity to eliminate the enemy, they could also flood them with micro-organisms that would confuse, or put them to sleep. The problem with this technique was that there could be a delay of several seconds, perhaps more, before the micro-organisms took effect – enough time for the guards to kill the hostages.

That left only one viable option. Ian outlined the plan to his men. 'I'm instructing mother to send in the babies to carry out a detailed survey of the smaller tent. Each baby robot carries a micro-holographic image of every member of the One Planet team, including Dr. Giraud. If they can get close enough, I'm hoping they'll be able to identify the hostages. Once we've done that, we'll have to see exactly how they are guarded. Hopefully we can attack before dawn. If not, we'll lie up and attack this time tomorrow.'

Directed by Ian's robo-computer, mother robot ordered her six babies to record and transmit the image of every man and woman in the rebel encampment. A short delay, and the babies, each no more than six centimetres tall and eight centimetres wide, were on the move, scurrying noiselessly through the forest, taking advantage of every scrap of cover it offered. In order to obtain the best results, they would position themselves thirty metres from the tent under surveillance. Though the babies were tiny, the risk of discovery was always there. If they were seen or heard by the rebels, the ground force would lose the advantage of surprise.

Minutes later, eight hostages – three doctors, four surviving nurses and Dr. Giraud – all, to Ian's relief, in the smallest tent – had been identified by the baby robots, their features matched with images carried in their data banks. Another minute, and Ian raised a clenched fist. 'He's in there with them!' *Bad Boy* had been located in the smaller tent with the hostages.

In less than three hours it would be dawn. A daylight attack would be infinitely more hazardous. Moving forward with infinite caution Ian and his troop laid up a hundred metres from the camp and consolidated their position. By means of thermal imaging they concluded that every rebel guarding the hostages was armed with an automatic weapon and a belt carrying small bombs or hand grenades. A tunnelling accelerometer able to detect acoustic waves confirmed the exact position in the tent of the eight hostages, their seven guards and *Bad Boy*, their leader.

He went into a huddle with his troop, weighing the pros and cons of immediate action. Clearly an assault, either now or later, would involve putting the lives of the hostages at risk. Hopefully they would have the advantage of surprise, and the rebels would be panicked in the first seconds of the attack. The question was – could they take out the rebels fast enough to guarantee that none of the One Planet team would be killed or wounded? Probably not. What about Dr. Giraud, their primary objective? How would *Bad Boy* react to an attack? Would he kill the doctor? A majority of the troop thought he would. Ian disagreed. 'Dr. Giraud represents *Bad Boy's* only chance of extracting a ransom from the world community, and quite probably his only hope of escaping death. Without Dr. Giraud he is doomed. In any event, I don't see what is to be gained by delaying our attack. Every minute that passes increases the risk of our being detected.'

Ian's view carried the day. An hour before dawn mother robot sent in her six babies to encircle the smallest tent in which *Bad Boy* and Dr. Giraud were sleeping, their task to report back any sign of movement indicating that the guards were alerted. A few minutes later the confirmation came through from mother robot. *Babies in position. No unusual activity reported.*

Whilst the actives moved closer to the rebel camp, taking care not to alert the patrolling guards, mother robot disabled the two helicopters, the five armoured cars and the ten trucks with a barrage of micro-organisms that decomposed tyres and infected fuel. In the munitions depot one of the actives planted bombs ready to be detonated when the ground attack was launched, another disabled the phone mast and another jammed the radio transmitter. Their mission successfully accomplished, they rejoined the troop. Still apparently unaware what was happening, the rebels slept on, their transport disabled, their communications cut, their ammunition dump ready to blow.

Less than thirty minutes to dawn . . . Ian held up his right arm. They were ready to go. With wristcoms synchronised, ten second hands moved as one. In five minutes precisely the troop would launch the attack.

In Galaxy two men waited for news, Arthur outwardly calm, Agravaine fidgety, his nerves sparking like a shorting electrical circuit. Over the gravitational link came the all-important message: *Five minutes to launch.*

Ahead of him, only metres from the camp, Ian could just make out the dark shape of mother robot, her camouflaged metallic body glinted for a second in the starlight. To his surprise her flashing "eyes" indicated that she was transmitting. His robo-computer recorded *message sent to babies*, but nothing else. No message was recorded on his headset. Odd that, he thought. How could mother robot send messages to the babies without his direct instructions? That should not be possible. And why was the message not showing on his screen? Must be a malfunction; hopefully nothing serious. For the time being he dismissed the query from his head, having more important things to worry about.

He began the final countdown. 'Ten, nine, eight, seven, six, five, four, three, two, one, zero!'

An ear-splitting bang, and the ground shook as the munitions dump exploded. For an instant the actives stared at the dazzling pyrotechnic display, then advanced, firing their automatic weapons as more than fifty rebels rushed out of the two larger tents. In seconds three actives were dead and more than forty rebels killed or wounded, the rest fleeing panic-stricken into the forest. As Ian and his men stormed the hostage tent the seven guards inside opened fire. In seconds five guards were dead, the remaining two severely wounded. Three actives, two nurses and a doctor were also killed. Two doctors and two nurses were unharmed.

The fire fight was over, but where was *Bad Boy?* And where was Dr. Giraud? A thorough search of the camp revealed nothing. Ian's heart sank. He could try to follow *Bad Boy* into the forest, but what was the use? Which way had he gone? The only one who had any chance of finding them was mother robot, and she too had disappeared. He tried to raise her, but she did not answer. His robo-computer showed him that his message had been received by her. That meant her computer was functioning normally. Why had she not responded? Again it was odd, very odd, almost as if she were developing a mind of her own, though that of course was impossible.

'Come in, mother,' he repeated again and again. 'Come in, mother. Come in, mother.' Still no response. 'Please come in, mother. Ian Duncan, Operation commander here.' What was he saying? Why was he talking to her as if she were human? He was getting desperate. Without mother robot's help, there little chance of rescuing Dr. Giraud.

Suddenly there was a text message on his headset: *Bad Boy and Dr. Giraud static half a kilometre due west your position.*

Leaving the six surviving actives in the camp to guard prisoners, Ian rushed into the forest heading west, moving as fast as he could through the huge trees and dense undergrowth, all the time following mother robot's directions. A warning message flashed on his headset, but before he could stop himself he was in a clearing. On the far side of it was *Bad Boy*, and Dr. Giraud standing close to him. From his expression it was obvious that he thought his last hour had come. Near Ian was mother robot, and at her feet, barely visible, the six baby robots.

Bad Boy was in high spirits. 'That was quite a show you boys put on just now. Pity it was all wasted effort.'

Ian's attention was caught by the pouched belt round Dr. Giraud's waist. 'That's right,' said *Bad Boy*, 'a very special belt.' He patted the pocket of his camouflage jacket. 'And here is the detonator. Not too much explosive. Just enough to blow our friend the doctor to pieces, not enough to harm me. Or you, for that matter, as long as you keep your distance.'

As Ian's fingers inched towards the trigger of his automatic weapon, *Bad Boy*'s hand moved to his jacket pocket again. 'Want to see which of us is the fastest draw, Mr. Duncan?' Ian let his hand fall to his side. 'No? Very sensible. Drop your weapon, please. Now!'

Ian's rifle fell to the ground and *Bad Boy* picked it up. Amid the debris of branches and leaves that covered the clearing he could see the tiny robot babies inching forward, presumably trying to get close enough to fire their "artful dodger" mini-missiles at *Bad Boy*. Who had given them the order? If he saw them, they were done for. Ian could only pray he wouldn't.

But he did. His face contorted with rage, *Bad Boy* opened fire with Ian's automatic rifle and kept on firing. When he stopped, the charred remains of six tiny robots were strewn across the clearing. The eyes of mother robot flashed, and from the gap in her head that mimicked a mouth came a dry, rasping sound, the only warning of the mini-missile that drilled a neat hole in the centre of *Bad Boy*'s forehead.

Ian stared in astonishment, first at the lifeless figure of *Bad Boy*, then at mother robot standing silent and motionless at the clearing's edge. He checked his headset; there was no record of any order given or received, no record of any transmission from his robo-computer. It confirmed what he already knew; that he had not given mother robot the order to fire at *Bad Boy*. Since there was no guarantee that she would kill him with her first shot, he would have judged the risk to Dr. Giraud far too great. But if *he* had not given the order, then *who had*? Incredible as it seemed, there was no one else who could have done. He tried to push away the insistent thought nagging at his brain; the thought that, defying all logic, what he had just witnessed had all the appearance of a mother's revenge for the killing of her babies. Inconceivable, of course. Ordering mother robot to follow him, he received the correct acknowledgment and breathed a half-sigh of relief. For a moment he had thought the unthinkable, when obviously the truth was that a robot malfunction had been rewarded with a most fortunate outcome. What tricks imagination played in the heat of battle!

Trailed at a distance by mother robot, Ian supported the weakened Dr. Giraud back to the rebel camp. Yet even in his hour of triumph, Ian was sad – sad for the actives and hostages who had died in the battle, sad for those hostages brutally executed, sad for the mini-robots whose existence had been so cruelly terminated, and sad for the mother who had lost her babies. Like all actives who had trained with robots, Ian had developed an enormous respect for them, being constantly impressed by their skills, and not least by their humanity, or rather by the illusion of humanity. For illusion was all it possibly could be.

With Lancelot at the controls, Eclipse was on its way back, its ETA five hours from now. Dr. Giraud was carefully relieved of his explosive belt, and he and the surviving members of his team given food and water. The Scuttle robo-pilot was alerted, and directed to land in the rebel camp.

Ian, his task complete, wandered round the camp, relaxed, and in the mood for talking, whilst the surviving doctors and nurses of the Planet One team did what they could for the wounded rebels. As a nurse bandaged his head, one of them pulled a knife from his loose robes and cut her throat. Ian hurled himself at the rebel, the knife flashed and he staggered back. A furious active whirled round and killed the man with a shot to the head. Slowly Ian sank to his knees and rolled over on his back. The doctors rushed over and knelt by him, one taking his pulse, the other examining the terrible knife wound that sliced him open from chest to stomach.

Even as Eclipse, with Scuttle in its belly, sped back to Camelot, the Cambodian government was being given the co-ordinates of the rebel camp so that they could pick up the wounded and track down those rebels who had fled into the forest. The world waited anxiously for news of Dr. Giraud. For twenty-four hours nothing was heard, and then, wandering under the Arc de Triomphe in Paris, looking bewildered, (he remembered nothing of his rescue) but in good health, was Dr. Giraud. It was an enthralling mystery. Who, the media asked, was responsible for rescuing him? The French? The Chinese? The Russians? The Americans? The British?

The mystery was soon solved. For when the sun rose the next morning, a light blazed in the sky, a light as powerful as a hundred lightning flashes, first above France, and then – as the planet revolved and dawn broke around the globe – in every country in the world. The higher the sun climbed, the brighter the sword shone. In the afternoon its light began to dim, and at the day's end, with the setting of the sun, it glowed blood red, fading from view with the dying light.

Thirty Nine

THE DAY AFTER THE mysterious reappearance of Dr. Giraud in Paris, Cambodia submitted to the United Nations a formal protest against what it described as "foreign mercenaries" waging war on Cambodia's sovereign territory. But foreign mercenaries or not, the Cambodian government, without lifting a finger, had been handed victory over the rebels, and the world presented with a cure for the most virulent disease known to mankind.

Although *Operation Bad Boy* had been a notable victory, acknowledged as a triumph by nations across the globe, the mood in Camelot was far from triumphal. Whilst the rescue mission had been successful, the human cost had been considerable. Five actives had been killed, and two seriously wounded, and the commander of the operation, Ian Duncan, lay in Intensive Care in a deep coma. In a desperate effort to save his life, doctors were growing a replacement heart and lungs from his own stem cells banked for such an emergency, a procedure that would take time, something Ian did not have.

Meanwhile at the Round Table, questions were being asked, questions embarrassing for Lancelot, and for Arthur too.

'Why was an inexperienced officer asked to lead such a dangerous operation?'

'Was the Chief of Staff not aware that there were a number of other officers better qualified for the job?'

'Whose decision was this? Was it the Chief of Staff's? Or was Arthur consulted?'

No one was more critical of Lancelot than he himself,

though he tried to take comfort from the fact that he had given Ian the opportunity to pull out, and that Ian had been happy to lead the mission. But however he twisted and turned and doubled in his tracks, he always arrived back at the same place; as supreme commander he, and he alone, was responsible. Had he, he asked himself, appointed the man best qualified to lead *Operation Bad Boy*? Or had he tried to silence his best friend?

It was several days before he was able to meet Guinevere in his apartment; there were too many prying eyes to allow them to take the slightest risk. For a full minute the two lovers held each other, their troubles momentarily forgotten.

'How is Ian?' She lit a cigarette. He had never known her smoke before.

'Not good.' She was mortified when he added, 'If he dies, it will be God's punishment.'

Hurt and angry, Guinevere lashed out with words calculated to provoke. 'I would interpret Ian's death as a sign of God's favour, not as a punishment.'

Lancelot was dismayed. 'I know you too well to believe you mean that.'

'Then perhaps you don't know me as well as you think you do,' she said, her eyes cold.

'Ian is my best friend.'

'Your best friend would destroy us if we gave him half a chance.'

'Perhaps, but to wish him dead . . . '

They stood there, confronting each other, the anger surging, and then as quickly draining away. 'Don't you know,' she said, tears welling in her eyes, 'that our love is the only thing that matters to me. I would do anything to protect it. Anything.' Fiercely possessive, she clung to him. 'I would die for you.'

'And I for you.'

Guinevere apart, there was no one Lancelot could turn to. His closest friend and confidant was in a coma, Gawain was avoiding him, Agravaine and Gaheris were not interested in his problems, Lanky, who until now, had been his only female friend, had, by her reproachful looks, made it clear that she held him responsible for what had happened to Ian. Who else could he confide in? No one. No one but Arthur. If only he could be honest with him.

In the event, it was not a decision he had to make. Arthur sent for him. 'Thought you might need someone to talk to,' he said, in his direct fashion.

Those understanding words coming from a man who had every reason to hate him were almost more than Lancelot could endure. The volcanic emotion he had been suppressing for days erupted, and tears streamed down his face. He and Arthur embraced, separating swiftly in embarrassment, unaccustomed to such open displays of affection.

'You have nothing to blame yourself for, Lance.'

'If Ian should die . . . '

'If he dies,' said Arthur, 'he will have died in a great cause.'

Arthur surely did not know about Ginny and him. If he did, how could he talk to him like this, like a son, a well-loved son? No one could be that forgiving. And yet . . . what was it George had said? *Don't kid yourself, Lance, there's nothing in Camelot that Arthur doesn't know about.*

Another week went by, and Ian still lay in a coma. The doctors were losing hope. Unable to sleep, Lancelot dressed and made his way to the hospital. Lanky was sitting by Ian's bed holding his hand. When she saw Lancelot, she left without a word or a glance in his direction.

It was three-thirty in the morning, the night nurse dozed at her desk, the beeping of the heart monitor the only sound in the Intensive Care ward. Lancelot pulled up a chair and sat by Ian's bed. Resting his chin on clasped hands, he closed his eyes and prayed. *We must pray for a miracle* was what the neurosurgeon had said when Daniel Shalott was lying in a coma all those years ago. And God had granted it. He believed then, and still wanted to believe, that God had chosen him as His instrument.

'Give me a sign, Lord. Give me a sign that you forgive me. Save Ian's life as you saved Daniel Shalott's.' The heart monitor beeped, and Ian, the friend he had so cruelly betrayed, slept on in the shadows. 'Do what you want with me, Lord,' whispered Lancelot. 'Only save his life, I beg you.'

Back in his apartment he collapsed on his bed, and in seconds was in a deep sleep. An hour later he opened his eyes. The phone was beeping. It was the sister on duty. 'I'm so sorry, sir . . . '

He was devastated by Ian's death, even more by Guinevere's reaction to it. Instead of consoling him for the loss of his friend, she scolded him.

'What's happened to you? You used to be your own man. Not any more. You've sold out.'

'Who have I sold out to?'

A disdainful look. 'To God! You asked God for a present, a neat little gift-wrapped miracle. And God said no, you've had one present already, I'm not giving you any more. That's it, isn't it? All that praying wasn't for Ian, was it? It was for you. You wanted God to confirm your miracle ranking, that's all. And you're miffed because he didn't.'

'God has punished me,' said Lancelot. 'I shall have to live with my conscience until the day I die.'

The colour rose in Guinevere's cheeks. 'Damn you, Lance! Damn you and damn your arrogance! If there really is a God, I'd say he had more important things to worry about than your bloody conscience.'

Expecting him to fight back, she was surprised when all he said was, 'You are right. Why should God bother about me? I am nothing.'

As swiftly as it flared, her anger died. Impulsively she seized his hand and kissed it. As they held each other she tried to take comfort from his repeated assurances. 'I love you, I'll always love you. What happened to Ian hasn't changed anything.'

But it had. In her despair she convinced herself that Lancelot had abandoned her, not for a woman but for God. *God has punished me.* How self-centred was that! Instead of trying to make her happy, he was worrying about his relationship with the Deity. Helena, she could handle, Galahad, even. But God – now that was something else.

Forty

To retain his sanity, he needed somehow to relieve himself of the burden of guilt – if not for the death of his friend, then for the affair he was having with Arthur's wife. He desperately needed forgiveness, and only one man could give him that.

The door panel buzzed, the speaker crackled.

Name?

'Lancelot.'

In a nano-second the computer had matched voice and iris with its records.

Enter Lancelot.

He had prepared his speech and could hardly wait to unburden himself. As it happened, he was frustrated by Arthur who was in talkative mood. At first he spoke about the stars and the universe, though Lancelot paid little attention, his mind rehearsing his confession down to the last syllable. Then came a word that was out of place, a word that was neither about stars nor universe . . . *obligations* . . . Obligations? Where did that come from?

'Obligations can be difficult things to deal with,' Arthur was saying. 'Because of obligations we find ourselves in places we don't necessarily want to be. I understand that, I understand it very well. There's no one I depend on more than you, no one I would rather have by my side in these difficult times. It's not that I want you to go, Lance, you mustn't think that.'

Go? What did he mean? Go where?

'At least give it a try.'

Give what a try? What had he missed? 'Sir,' he began

haltingly, 'I have something to tell you. Something I . . . ' It was no use. He couldn't go on. He could barely remember what it was he had wanted to say. In the silence Arthur gestured at an armchair and Lancelot fell into it gratefully.

'Let me tell you something, Lance,' said Arthur, sitting opposite him. 'You could be my son.'

Lancelot looked surprised. 'What I mean is,' explained Arthur, 'I think of you as a son. You are the son I never had. There was a time,' he said wistfully, his eyes focused on another time and place, 'when I might have had a son. But that's another story . . . ' He raised his hands and let them fall despairingly on the arms of his chair 'one I regret very much.'

What son might Arthur have had? And why was he telling him now? He was puzzled.

'So Lance,' said Arthur jovially, 'since you are the son I never had, I feel I have the right to offer you some fatherly advice.'

'Advice?' Lancelot was more confused than ever.

'You are unhappy, I can see that. If I read you correctly, your conscience is troubling you.'

So that was it. He knew.

'But it's my belief that if you had known Galahad was your son, you would have married Helena. Am I right?'

How was that relevant? 'I'm sorry?'

'Would you have married Helena if you had known Galahad was your son?'

'I imagine so,' said Lancelot cautiously.

Arthur nodded. 'I am convinced you would.' He leaned forward in his chair. 'So my advice is this; leave Camelot, go back to England, and be a husband to Helena and a father to Galahad.'

Was Arthur banishing him from Camelot? Was that it? What else? He wanted to see the back of him. Why? *Because he knew!* Knew about him and Guinevere. All this nonsense about Helena was a smokescreen. For Arthur it would be a neat solution, one that would silence the gossips.

'Stay there as long as you like. When you have sorted things out, come back to Camelot with Helena and Galahad. For good, Lance,' said Arthur, 'for good.' Those dazzling blue eyes seemed to read Lancelot's every thought. 'For your good,' he said, 'for your wife's good, for your son's good, for Camelot's good.' As he got to his feet, signalling that the meeting was at an end, Arthur said softly, as if it were an afterthought, 'For my good too,' leaving Lancelot wondering what he meant by that.

In a daze, he said goodbye and left. When he had gone, Arthur toyed with the keyboard of his computer, his thoughts closer to earth than heaven. If only he had had a son like Lancelot. If only Margot had not aborted their love child. Not that he could blame her. Without his support, what else could she have done? At the time she was married, he an eighteen year old student. It could so easily have been different, though. He could see it all as if it were happening now. Margot had left, and he was sitting at the table not knowing what to do . . . bustling waiters noisily clearing the tea-time debris . . . he jumping up and rushing out of the Café Royal into Regent Street, calling after her . . . she, nowhere to be seen, lost in the crowd. He had sat at the table a minute too long, had thought one thought too many, had left it too late. And that decision, or indecision, had haunted him all these years, and would haunt him for ever.

'I'm still not certain if he knows or not,' said Lancelot.

'He knows,' said Guinevere.

'Why do you say that?'

'Because I know Arthur,' said Guinevere. 'He's wise and he's forgiving. But make no mistake, Lance, anything that threatens him, threatens Camelot too. And Camelot is more important to him than anything else. More important than you.' A wistful look. 'More important than me.'

'What do I do?'

If he had expected her to plead with him to stay, he was disappointed. 'Do as he says.'

'It was only his advice.'

'No it wasn't,' she said, 'it was an order.'

His reaction was almost petulant. 'You want me to go.'

'You know that isn't true,' she said. 'It's simply that it's probably the best thing to do. After Arthur, your first duty is to your family. You must go to them.'

His *duty*! Could this be the same woman who had scorned him when, not so long ago, he had spoken of his duty to visit his family? What had transformed her? Why was she now allowing him – no, urging him – to leave Camelot? Why was this passionate, possessive woman not begging him to stay? Had her love cooled? Was that it? Though if it had, why had she not told him so? Ginny usually had no difficulty speaking her mind. A pang of fear . . . was there someone else? He tried to block out the unworthy thought. Nevertheless, in the days and nights that followed, it continued to knock gently but persistently at his door.

Lanky, too, had difficulty understanding Ginny. 'Why did you let him go?'

'Because he needs his space,' said Guinevere. 'Everyone does. I could have made him stay, of course I could, but if I had, the day would have come when he resented me for doing it. His decisions have to be his, not mine. Else what sort of man would he be? Not one who could love me, that's for sure. Perhaps not one that I could love. No, Lanky, if I had put my foot down, it would never have been the same between us.'

Lanky was impressed. Guinevere was not ruled entirely by her heart after all. When the volcano blew its top, sensible Ginny had somehow survived the eruption. Passion and sense. What a devastating combination!

What Lanky did not know was how much concealing her true feelings had cost Guinevere in mental turmoil and lost sleep. Had she done the right thing, she asked herself. Or had she been a fool? Had she bound Lancelot to her with invisible tendrils of love? Or had she cut for ever the bonds that tied them?

Forty One

FROM UNDER DROOPING lids Harold Pemberton's shrewd eyes considered Lancelot. 'Why have you come this time?'

Good question. How to answer it? Because Arthur ordered him to? Because he felt guilty for rejecting Helena, and abandoning his son? Because he was racked by divided loyalties? Because he wanted to settle down with his family? 'I like to keep in touch,' was all he said.

Only Harold could sip a whisky and soda and look profoundly sceptical at the same time. 'A handful of visits over the years is not what I call keeping in touch.'

An apologetic shrug. 'Time passes so quickly.'

'Galahad misses having a father. Not that he would admit it.'

'How is he?'

Harold refilled his glass. 'Fine.' A few seconds contemplation, and he changed his mind. 'No, dammit, he's not fine. That bloody woman has got her claws even deeper into him.'

That bloody woman being, presumably, Harold's wife, the devout Francesca.

'He's under his granny's thumb, still carries a bible around everywhere. Knows the whole thing by heart – New and Old Testaments.' Harold Pemberton downed his drink in one ferocious gulp. 'My own Grandson! Used to be such a great kid. I worshipped him. Now look at him. Sixteen going on sixty! Hardly speaks to me any more. Thinks I'm a godless sinner – which of course I am, but what's it to him? That woman has taken over his mind, turned him into a religious freak. Praying and reading the good book is about all he does. Next thing you know she'll incarcerate him in some monastery. Get him away from here, Lance, grab him before the priests do. It may be too late, but it's worth a try. Take him back to Camelot with you and make a man of him.'

Though Harold's outburst came as a shock to Lancelot, it clarified his thinking and firmed his resolve. For Helena he felt goodwill, and would do anything he could for her, short of taking her back to Camelot. That he could not do; there was only one woman in his life. Galahad, though, was an altogether different matter.

Each time she saw Lancelot again, Helena was forced to acknowledge to herself that she had driven away the only man she had ever loved. One evening she told him the story of the Snow Queen who fell in love with a handsome young man and turned his heart to ice so that he would stay with her for ever, and of how he lived under her spell, until one day the girl he loved found him, and shed tears over him, and melted his heart.

It was her way of telling him that she loved him. The little tale of the Snow Queen moved Lancelot more than any declaration of love could have done. Listening to it, he almost persuaded himself that he was that young man, and that Helena had found him and shed tears over him and melted his heart. If at that moment she had asked him to, he would have stayed.

But she did not. Knowing him as she did, she knew he could never be Battersea man, never commute to the office every day, or kick a ball in the park with Galahad at weekends. Lancelot was not born to be a husband and father, so what would be the point of dragging him up the aisle? It was guilt, not love, that had brought him back to her, and a bad conscience was no basis for a good marriage.

It took several days for her to pluck up the courage to say what in her heart she knew she had to say: 'This life is not for you.'

About to protest, he thought better of it. She deserved the

truth. 'No,' he admitted, 'it isn't.'

'Come and see me as often as you can.' A brave smile. 'Don't worry, Lance, I shall be fine.'

He was grateful for that. 'And Galahad?'

'All he does, all he has ever done, is study the scriptures and pray.' Her voice broke. 'Oh, Lance,' – tears shone in her eyes – 'he scarcely notices me any more.'

'That can't be true.'

'I'm afraid it is. Mother has taken him over. He needs to get away from her. He needs a life.' She brushed a thread of cotton from Lancelot's shoulder. 'He needs a father.'

'Would you let me take him back to Camelot?'

A long pause. 'He would come and see me?'

'Yes.'

'Often?'

'Yes.'

'And you?'

'As often as I can,' he said.

'And if he doesn't like Camelot?'

'I'll bring him back, I promise you.'

'Don't ask him to fight,' she said. 'He won't kill, Lance, whatever the cause.'

'I shall never ask him to harm a fellow human being,' he promised.

Helena sighed and straightened her shoulders, her decision made. 'Then as far as I am concerned he is free to go. If you can convince him, I won't stand in his way.'

At first he tiptoed round the subject, fearing to scare Galahad off. Would he like to spend more time with his father, do things together, as fathers and sons ought to do? A change of scenery, perhaps, just for a while? Camelot, for example?

It was a sufficiently startling suggestion to make Galahad put down his bible. After some thought, he asked, 'Why did you go to Camelot?'

'To serve Arthur.'

'You kill people?'

'Sometimes, yes.'

'What is God's sixth commandment?'

'*Thou shalt not kill.*'

'But you disobey Him.'

'I do what I believe is right,' said Lancelot.

They were at least communicating, though it was hard to reach a teenager whose entire view of life was shaped by what he read in the bible.

'I doubt that Camelot is the place for me.'

'What is wrong with it?'

'You wage war,' said Galahad. 'War is wrong. Killing is wrong.'

He did not much care for the words, but how he admired the way they were spoken! His son had a mind of his own, and the courage to match it. He was proud of him.

Francesca opposed Galahad's leaving, and said so in her customary uncompromising fashion: 'No one will ever take him away from me. God will not permit it.'

Had it ended there, the story might have been different, but she made the mistake of overplaying her hand. Afraid of losing Galahad, she tried to convince him that his father and mother were trying to separate him from the only person in the world who cared about him. 'I am the one in this house who has your best interests at heart, my darling, the only one who truly loves you,' she insisted tearfully, embracing her grandson so tightly he could hardly breathe.

Though Galahad loved his grandmother, his love for her was by no means exclusive. He loved his mother, and even – though he might not have shown it recently – that incorrigible old sinner, his grandfather, who had confessed more than once to breaking the seventh commandment – *Thou shalt not commit adultery* .

The truth was that the only exclusive commitment Galahad

was prepared to make was to God. No one owned him, not his grandmother, not his mother, not granddad, not anyone. Asserting that she was the only one who cared about him was a mistake. It wasn't true, and he knew it. His mother loved him, and her love, unlike gran's, was unselfish. Or why would she be encouraging him to make his own decision? One thing had become clear; it was time for him to get out of the house. God's ways were mysterious; He had not yet revealed how He expected Galahad to serve Him.

He decided to take a chance. If God did not approve of his going to Camelot, He would find a way of telling him. He went to his father and told him he was willing to give Camelot a try. 'That is if you still want me.'

There was nothing Lancelot wanted more.

When Galahad told Francesca he was leaving home to go to Camelot with his father, she covered her ears and ran out of the room weeping. Running up the stairs screaming all the way she locked herself in her bedroom and vowed never to come out. Galahad tried to talk to her through the door, but she drowned out his pleas with shrieking and sobbing.

Overjoyed that, as he put it, his grandson had at last been "given the chance to lead a man's life", Harold was nevertheless saddened at the prospect of being parted from him. Embracing Galahad roughly, he was moved and astonished to feel an answering pressure. He would have been even more astonished had he known that, after their last goodbye, Galahad went to his room and wept as he packed a suitcase. In a sudden rush of feeling he had never before experienced, he remembered how he used to sit on his granddad's knee, pulling the loose skin under his chin, stroking the veins on the back of his hand.

'*Why are your veins swollen, granddad?*'
'*Because I'm getting old, boy.*'
'*You'll never be old, granddad.*'
'*Wish it were true.*'
'*Why are they blue?*'

'*Blue blood, Gally. I'm descended from kings. That means you are too.*'

'*Am I really?*'

'*You most certainly are, your majesty.*'

Hugging his mother goodbye, Galahad was ready to change his mind, but she pushed him out of the door. 'See you soon,' she said, and blew a kiss.

When he and Lancelot had gone, Helena and her father sat silently at the kitchen table, Harold studying the veins on the back of his hands, Helena thinking of Lancelot.

Forty Two

TOO SHY TO BE INTRODUCED to the Round Table, Galahad was taken by his father straight to Arthur's apartment where Arthur, Guinevere, and a few close friends and aides waited to greet him.

'It is a pleasure and an honour to welcome Lancelot's son,' said Arthur, holding his arms wide, inviting Galahad to accept his embrace. Galahad clutched his bible and looked at the floor.

Lancelot felt obliged to explain. 'He's a bit overwhelmed by all this attention. He means no offence.'

'None taken,' said Arthur. Expecting to see a young replica of Lancelot, he looked in vain for some family resemblance. No son could have resembled his father less; Lancelot, tall and slender with dark hair and brown eyes, Galahad short and stocky with white blonde hair and blue eyes. Yet different in appearance though they were, there was something about the teenager that reminded Arthur irresistibly of Lance, something they had in common that distinguished them from other men; an aura of remoteness, of not being involved with those around them.

Whilst Arthur made the introductions, Guinevere hung back. For her it was painful to have to confront Lancelot's past in the shape of his son, the tangible expression of his relationship with Helena. And then Arthur was introducing them: 'Darling, this is Galahad.' As their eyes met and they shook hands, the gauche sixteen year old and the sophisticated woman of the world, Galahad was her slave, ready to die for her. Never in his short life had he seen such a beautiful woman. Spellbound, he could not stop gazing at her. Guinevere's colour was high, her eyes shining. She found this intensely serious, rather timid young man, charming, and his undisguised admiration flattering.

'How happy you must be, Lance, to have your son with you in Camelot,' said Arthur. 'I know he will make his father proud – as proud as he must be of his father.'

The next day Mordred visited Camelot's library, borrowed a book he had never opened before, and for a few days studied it with great attention. When he felt sufficiently prepared, he invited Galahad to his room for tea.

The door panel buzzed, the speaker crackled.

Name?

'Galahad.'

In a nano-second the computer matched voice and iris with its records.

Enter, Galahad.

Mordred jumped up from the sofa. 'Come in, come in,' he said eagerly. 'Welcome.'

A respectful bow of the head. 'Thank you, sir.'

'Please! No need to call me sir. Mordred is my name. Or Mord, when you get to know me better.'

Sipping his tea, Galahad looked round the small bedsit, observing how functional it was. There was not a photograph, not a painting or drawing, not a single decorative object to express the occupant's taste; only exposed light bulbs, a bed, a sofa, two uncomfortable wooden chairs and curtainless windows.

'Uncluttered is what I call it,' said Mordred, following his visitor's eyes.

'Oh, but I d-didn't m-mean to . . . ' stammered Galahad.

'Not everyone's cup of tea, I know. Some people like flowered curtains, oodles of bric-a-brac. Frankly, I find all that sort of thing distracting. I need my undivided concentration for what I do in my spare time,' said Mordred, leaving a void of silence that Galahad felt compelled to fill.

'And what is that?'

'I read books,' said Mordred, who had scarcely read a book in his life. 'Well, actually, one book in particular,' he murmured, looking as ashamed as if he had just confessed to a mortal sin. With a self-conscious twitch of the hand he indicated a book lying next to him on the arm of the sofa. 'That one,' he murmured.

The book had a plain cover. As Mordred opened it, a look of wonder spread across Galahad's face. 'The Bible!'

'I dare say it seems strange to you,' said Mordred, 'but the Old and New Testament tell me all I need to know about this life. And the life to come,' he added, kissing the bible in a pious gesture.

'Not strange at all,' said Galahad. 'I read the bible too.'

Mordred's eyes dilated. 'You read the bible!'

'Every day,' Galahad assured him.

'Astounding! Simply astounding!' said Mordred, as though he could scarcely believe his ears. 'Well, well, well. How extraordinary that we should meet like this. What are the chances of you and I meeting? A million to one, I should imagine. So few people read the good book these days.'

Galahad nodded in solemn agreement. 'That's because most of them dedicate their lives to material things.'

'How true,' said Mordred,' how very true. And then, seizing the opportunity to demonstrate his biblical credentials, '*Man doth not live by bread only,*' he observed, raising his eyes heavenward, '*but by every word that proceedeth out of the mouth of the Lord . . .* '

'Amen,' said Galahad.

Mordred extended his hand. 'I can see that you and I will be good friends,' he said. 'Would you care to sit and study the bible with me now and then?'

'An excellent idea,' said Galahad.

One day, thought Mordred, Galahad could prove useful,

more than useful. Calm and unflappable, he seemed detached from the emotions that afflicted other men's souls. Yet beneath that placid surface, he suspected, was a very different person, a compulsively driven young man who set himself the very highest standards, and was intolerant of the failings of others. Didn't they say still waters ran deep? Unless he was very much mistaken, these particular still waters, untroubled though they appeared to be, would begin to seethe and boil when a few drops of poison were administered.

Forty Three

Rain clouds hung low over the Atlantic, the surging sea thrashing the shoreline, scattering cascades of white foam. As Arthur jogged along the beach towards Castle Point he heard a voice calling his name. He stopped to listen. There it was again: 'Arthur! Arthur!' Through the mist he saw Mordred stumbling along the beach, and waited for him to catch up. 'Looking for me, Mord?'

'No,' said Mordred, his chest heaving, 'a fortuitous encounter. I was taking a stroll.'

Never once had Arthur seen his nephew walking on the beach, nor indeed anywhere else for that matter, his invariable means of locomotion being not legs but hovercart. 'I know you're not a jogger,' he said. 'Care to walk with me to Castle Point?'

'With pleasure.'

The two men moved on in silence, each absorbed in his own thoughts. When Arthur was a boy and Merlin's pupil, the Magus had taught him how to imagine himself into other people's heads. Though Mordred guarded his thoughts, Arthur saw enough of them to know that his nephew had something important to say, and that this meeting was no accident.

As if in confirmation, Mordred said, 'As it happens, I do have a couple of things to share with you.' He darted a sidelong look at Arthur. 'In confidence.'

They walked at a brisk pace, Mordred's breathing growing more and more laboured. 'Mind if we . . . ' he panted 'take time out?'

'We're nearly there,' said Arthur, pointing.

Castle Point was high up on the cliffs, almost directly above them. On the beach below the ruined castle was a flat rock.

'How are you enjoying NIWIS?' he asked, sitting on the rock and beckoning Mordred to join him.

'Tremendously,' said Mordred. 'Tich is a great teacher.'

'He tells me you are doing a fine job. It's obvious you have a special aptitude for the work,' said Arthur, who found it remarkable that a young man as honest and transparent as Mordred should have such a talent for deception.

'Thank you, sir.'

An awkward pause followed. Mordred had something to say, yet for some reason appeared to have a problem saying it. Arthur liked him and appreciated his dedication and intelligence, even if his manner was more that of a respectful employee than a close family member.

'What is it you want to talk to me about?' he asked, surmising that Mordred might have promotion in mind, or was perhaps seeking some personal advice, now that his father was dead.

'Delicate matters,' said Mordred, tossing a small lump of rock in the air and catching it. 'For a long time now,' he began haltingly, 'there have been – you know – stories.'

'Stories?' prompted Arthur.

'About Agravaine and Gaheris.'

Arthur tensed, suddenly apprehensive. 'What sort of stories?'

'Stories that link them to those terrible murders.' Reaching back his arm and grunting with the exertion, Mordred threw the lump of rock into the sea. 'Slanderous stories. You must have heard them.'

'I have,' said Arthur, 'and I don't believe a word of them. There is no evidence whatever that your brothers were involved.'

'You cannot imagine how relieved I am to hear you say that,' said Mordred. 'Still, you know how it is – people talk.'

'What do they say?'

'Oh you know, that there ought to be a trial to clear the air

– that sort of thing – rather than . . . '

'Rather than what?'

'Rather than covering things up,' murmured Mordred.

'Covering things up!' Arthur was unable to conceal his indignation. 'That is not what happened, I assure you. There was no cover-up. The reason your brothers were not put on trial was simply – I repeat – that there was not a scrap of evidence against them.'

Mordred hunched over his knees. 'I should have kept my mouth shut,' he mumbled.

'Not at all,' said Arthur. 'You are doing what you perceive to be your duty.' In a gesture of affection he laid his hand on Mordred's shoulder. 'I hope you feel better for speaking your mind,' he said.

'Oh I do,' said Mordred, throwing Arthur a grateful look.

Arthur consulted his wristcom. 'You said there were a couple of things on your mind. Was there something else?'

'I have already said too much for one day.'

'Come now, Mord,' said Arthur, 'say what you have to say. It's all in the family. You are my nephew, after all.'

An odd look came over Mordred's face. 'Well, that's rather the point,' he said.

'How do you mean?'

'I am not.'

Arthur's brow crinkled. 'Not what?'

'Not your nephew,' said Mordred.

Was this one of those mind games they were always thinking up in NIWIS? Very well then, he would play.

'You are not my nephew?'

'No.'

'Who are you, then?'

Mordred picked up a handful of sand, sifted it through his fingers and rubbed his hands together in a washing motion until he had cleansed them of the very last grain. 'I am your son,' he said at last.

Arthur stared blankly out to sea. There are moments in a man's life, he was thinking, when, without warning, everything changes. 'My son?'

'Yes,' said Mordred.

'How can that be?'

'It just is.'

'How do you know?'

'My mother told me.'

His mother? . . . his mother . . . And then in a flash it came to him. 'You mean Margot?'

Mordred nodded. 'It's quite simple, really,' he said. 'She told me that you and her . . . that you had a one night stand at the Commem. Ball at Oxford. And she was pregnant and you wanted to have the baby aborted, and she agreed, and then decided not to. Apparently she never told you that she changed her mind.'

'No,' said Arthur, 'she didn't.'

Mordred spread his arms. 'So here I am,' he said cheerfully, 'your long-lost son.' From under his brows he peered at Arthur. 'You don't seem very happy, father,' he said. 'You look like you've seen a ghost. But then of course in a way you have,' he concluded with a grin.

'You – my son,' said Arthur, his head knowing that it must be true, his heart unwilling to accept it.

'I imagine it comes as a bit of a shock.'

An understatement. 'Why have you kept silent all this time?'

'I'm truly sorry, father,' said Mordred. 'I should have told you ages ago, but I just couldn't bring myself to do it. I thought that knowing I was your son might embarrass you, that it might even create problems with the Round Table. Naturally that was the last thing I wanted to do. I love and respect you too much for that. Why did I change my mind?' He shrugged. 'I couldn't live with the lie any longer. I needed to unburden myself – tell you the truth.'

It all made perfect sense. He had never thought to ask when

Mordred was born, because he had always assumed he was Lennox's child. Why had Margot never told him he had a son? Presumably because she didn't want to break up her marriage to go and live with a penniless student. In any case, she had made it plain she didn't love him, never had, never would.

Mordred nudged his father's arm playfully with his elbow. 'No hard feelings?'

'On the contrary.'

The two men walked quickly back along the beach.

'All these years it has been on my conscience,' said Arthur. 'Agreeing to an abortion, I mean. I want you to know that.'

'Happens every day, I shouldn't wonder,' said Mordred. 'Dad tries to have his baby done away with, and mum saves it.' Arthur winced. 'Oh God, I'm sorry. How tactless of me . . . that was a terrible thing to say.'

'True, nevertheless,' said Arthur.

Struggling to keep up, Mordred tripped on a rock and fell. As he tried to stand, his left leg buckled under him. 'My ankle,' he groaned, his face distorted with pain, 'I've twisted it.'

Let me help you,' said Arthur, taking Mordred's arm and pulling him to his feet. The wind rose, whirling the beach into mini-tornados of sand. Thunder rolled menacingly, heralding the long-threatened storm. If only he had run after her, if only he had stopped her, he would have told her he had changed his mind . . . that he didn't want an abortion. Wouldn't he?

Supported by Arthur, Mordred limped along the shore, alternately grinning and grimacing with pain. 'A couple of old crocks we are, father,' he said, 'me with my ankle, and you with your conscience.'

At the door Mordred was challenged by the security sensor. *Name?*

'Pendragon. Mordred Pendragon.'

Name not recognised. Entry refused.

A sardonic grin. 'Talk to my father,' said Mordred.

The two men sipped coffee.

'I can only say again how sorry I am to have caused you a problem.' He sounded genuinely penitent.

'Problem! No, indeed. You have made me a happy man, Mord. I always wanted a son. Now I have one.'

'Back from the dead, eh?'

Arthur swallowed hard. Some things were best left unsaid. 'I can only thank God that you are alive.'

Mordred mentally doffed his cap to Arthur. He was making the best of a bad job. 'Good for you, father,' he said. 'No use crying over spilt milk – or spilt sperm for that matter.' A broad wink. 'Will you tell the Round Table?'

'Of course.'

'When?'

'Tomorrow.'

Mordred puffed out his chest proudly. 'I want the world to know that Arthur Pendragon is my father,' he said. And in his heart of hearts he meant it.

The world turned, Arthur was thinking. History had a way of repeating itself. His own father, Uther, had given him up for adoption when he was a baby. Mordred must surely be asking much the same questions Arthur asked himself when he was a young man. What had he done to deserve his father's rejection? Was there something wrong with his father? Or was there something wrong with him?

All these years he had robbed Mordred of his real father, and – were it not for Margot – would have robbed him of his life. It was a heavy burden of guilt he would have to live with. Only one thing could lighten it; earning the love of his new-found son.

Forty Four

THE UNPRECEDENTED summoning of the Round Table for no apparent reason intrigued every man and woman on Camelot. The fact that no one seemed to know what it was about was in itself puzzling, and for some alarming. Everyone had a theory, no one had the answer. Their curiosity aroused, members took their seats more than an hour before the meeting was due to start, in their excitement provoking arguments and counter-arguments, theories and counter-theories, none of them even close to the mark. When finally the four double doors were closed, the hall fell silent as every head turned towards Arthur.

'As most of you know,' he began, his fingers brushing the scar on his cheek, 'my darling wife Guinevere and I have not been granted the blessing of children. However . . . ' Arthur paused, not for effect but because he could hardly trust himself to speak, 'when I was a young man, I met a girl and fell in love. We had a brief affair and parted. As a result of that affair, she gave birth to a baby boy.'

If it were possible for the Great Hall to be even more hushed than it was before Arthur began speaking, then it had to be now. If, at this moment, a mouse had run across the flagstones, its footfall would have been clearly heard by every member. Astonishment imprinted on their faces, their eyes fixed on Arthur, they hardly dared breathe, fearing to miss a single syllable of his speech; for clearly this was a speech, a formal statement carefully prepared.

'She never told me about it,' said Arthur, 'and so, for all these years I never knew I had a son. Until now.' His eyes sought out

Mordred, seated on the other side of the Round Table. 'That son is Mordred.'

A few seconds stunned silence...then suddenly everyone was talking at once. Leo Grant, Arthur's father-in-law, though shocked by the revelation, was the first to offer his congratulations. 'I believe I speak for the Round Table when I wish you great joy in your son.' He gestured in Mordred's direction. 'And you, Mordred, in your father.'

Gawain, Agravaine, Gaheris and Gareth exchanged troubled looks. Gawain raised his hand.

'Yes, Gawain?'

'This girl you mentioned, uncle . . . who is she?'

It was the question Arthur feared he would be asked, and found impossible to answer. What could he say? That he had not known who she was? That didn't alter the fact that he had slept with his half-sister, their mother. How to justify that? Impossible. To confess the truth would undoubtedly end his relationship with the Lennox brothers, and almost certainly damage his reputation and standing in Camelot. On the other hand, lying would be wrong and also foolish, because Mordred might well contradict him.

In his moment of indecision he found himself looking at his son who, unknown to him, had already concluded he had nothing to gain by revealing who his mother was. That he was the child of an incestuous relationship was not something Mordred cared to share with the world. 'Apart from my father and I,' he said, 'that is a secret known only to those dear departed souls who took me in. Out of respect for my beloved mother,' he said, in a clear, firm voice, 'my father and I wish to preserve her anonymity. I believe that is our right.' He looked round the table, as if challenging anyone to object. No one did.

Arthur breathed a sigh of relief. Mordred's statement, hinting as it did that Margot and Lennox adopted him, had saved him further embarrassment. It had also put him in his son's debt.

Crossing the hall, he bent and whispered in his ear, 'Thank you for that.'

Seizing Arthur's hand, Mordred raised it high, shook it triumphantly, as though inviting applause for the victor, and to the accompaniment of cheers, led him out of the Great Hall, demonstrating not only his affection for his father, but a degree of proprietorial interest.

Forty Five

THOUGH ARTHUR TRIED hard to get closer to his son, Mordred's response was unexpectedly cool. Invitations to dinner were either refused or postponed on flimsy excuses, calls remained unanswered. The truth was that "outing" his father had neither satisfied Mordred's thirst for revenge, nor diminished his hatred of him. So far so good, but more, much more, remained to be done.

'You and I will be partners in a great enterprise,' he told Galahad.

It excited and flattered Galahad that someone as important as Mordred could think of him as a partner. 'What kind of enterprise?'

Mordred spread his arms as if he were embracing the whole sinful world. 'The purification of Camelot,' he said.

Galahad was mystified. 'My father has spoken to me many times of Camelot's ideals – love, honour, justice – and of how every man and woman on the island has sworn to live by them.'

'If everyone in Camelot lived by such noble ideals,' observed Mordred, 'Camelot would not need purifying.'

Galahad's blue eyes were troubled.

Mordred leaned forward on the sofa, his forehead furrowed, as if he were debating some difficult issue with himself. 'I imagine you and your father are close.'

'He tells me everything,' said Galahad.

'Does he?'

Something about the tone of Mordred's voice made Galahad shift uncomfortably in his chair. 'Is there some doubt in your mind?' he asked.

Nothing could have been more innocent than Mordred's expression. 'No doubt, I assure you, none whatsoever. Or, at any rate,' – A tactical pause to ensure he still commanded Galahad's full attention – 'none you need concern yourself with.'

Galahad drew himself up proudly. 'I am not a child,' he said. 'If there is something I ought to know about my father, I insist you tell me.'

Mordred's tormented eyes conveyed the impression of a man engaged in a struggle with his conscience. 'It is not for me to utter a single word against your father whom I love and respect as much as any man I know. If it were not for . . . ' Abruptly, he stopped.

'If it were not for what?' insisted Galahad.

Mordred fingered his bible. 'If it were not for the seventh commandment,' he said in a low voice.

Galahad's eyes widened. 'You are surely not accusing my father of . . . ?' He broke off, unable to articulate the word.

'Adultery?' Mordred lifted his shoulders in a resigned shrug, mute acknowledgment that it was, when all was said and done, a degenerate world.

'I refuse to believe that he . . . that he . . . ' Galahad clasped his bible to his chest for comfort.

'My poor Galahad,' said Mordred, 'I never meant to hurt you. If it were not for Arthur being so cruelly deceived . . . ' He stood looking out of the window at a Nimble lifting off the launch pad, visible for a few brief seconds before mantling. Now you see it, now you don't, he was thinking, much like the games he played.

Arthur cruelly deceived! Did that mean? . . . No. Impossible. Surely that beautiful, gracious, *honest* lady would never betray her husband. 'Are you saying – are you telling me that my father and Guinevere are . . . ' Galahad's head lifted, his chest heaved, his mouth gaped as he gulped air. 'Tell me it isn't true.'

Keeping Galahad under observation whilst he did so, Mordred poured himself a coffee, deliberating over every detail of the ritual: first the coffee, then the milk, then, after much hesitation, the sugar, and finally, the slow, measured stirring that preceded the first sip. At last he spoke: 'How I wish I could,' he said.

'Why are you telling me this?'

'Because you have a right to know,' said Mordred. 'Frankly, I had not intended to mention it so soon. I was going to wait a few weeks. And then it just came out. But then that's the way with truth, isn't it? *Truth will out.* Isn't that what they say?'

'Does anyone else in Camelot know?'

'An interesting question,' said Mordred. He sipped his coffee again, and, after careful reflection, added more sugar. 'It reminds me of the story of King Midas. Apollo was angry with the king, so he gave him a pair of ass's ears, and Midas was so ashamed that he hid them under a cap. Only his hairdresser knew his secret, and he was too scared to reveal it. The problem was that he couldn't keep it entirely to himself, so he dug a hole in the riverbank and whispered into it: *King Midas has ass's ears!* As luck would have it, a reed sprouted from the bank and whispered the secret to everyone who passed.'

'You mean everyone knows!'

'Some do. Not everyone.'

'Why don't they tell Arthur?'

'Good question. Let's say they prefer to let sleeping dogs lie.' A sardonic grin. 'And bitches, too.'

Galahad jumped up. 'I don't. I'm going to tell him.'

An impulsive reaction that alarmed Mordred. Things were moving too fast. Those still waters were still no longer, they were seething. He had administered too large a dose of poison. Too much, too soon. 'No,' he said, 'better not.' For his plan to work, he needed time and careful preparation. Galahad was a pawn in a complex game. If he blundered in to Arthur now, the consequences could be disastrous. 'Arthur won't believe you, and you will be accused of spreading false rumours.'

Galahad was indignant. 'But they aren't false. You say my father and Guinevere are . . . '

'Like rabbits,' said Mordred.

Galahad shuddered.

'Unfortunately,' Mordred cautioned him, 'we have no definite proof.'

'How do we get it?' said Galahad, gripping his bible so tightly that the tips of his fingers were white.

Mordred's tongue moistened his lips. 'Catch them in the act.'

Galahad blushed. The thought of those naked, entwined bodies was shameful, disgusting, too horrible to contemplate. 'Are you saying, Mordred – are you saying that they . . . that they actually . . . ?'

'Fuck?' suggested Mordred helpfully.

Galahad nodded, his face crimson.

Mordred laid his hand on his bible. 'I swear they do,' he said, looking him in the eye.

No words could express Galahad's revulsion. His father and that woman! He had seen the way she was with Arthur, her loving looks, the way she held his hand, the whispered confidences. And it was all a masquerade! Behind that lovely face was a deceitful, treacherous woman, no better than a whore! Worse! Whores sold their sexual favours honestly, they did not deceive men, lie to them, tell them they loved them.

The rest of the day he spent lying on his bed and running to the bathroom to throw up. That night he slept fitfully and woke feeling tired and confused. Though he had promised Mordred not to say anything to Arthur, he spent most of the next morning praying to God for guidance. What was he to do? Tell Arthur? Or keep silent? He found himself wishing Mordred had not taken him into his confidence. For there were some things it was better not to know.

Forty Six

THE MORE HE THOUGHT about it, the less sure of himself he became. What if Mordred were wrong? He had admitted there was no actual proof, and a man ought not to be accused, let alone condemned, on the basis of rumours. The question was, how to separate rumour from fact? Who would know the truth? Who could be relied upon to tell it? Only one man that he could think of – his father. He would confront him, ask him in plain English: was he having an affair with Guinevere – yes or no? His father would say no, and that would be the end of it. Setting aside all doubts, he made an appointment to see Lancelot, steeling himself for what inevitably would be a traumatic confrontation.

Sensing immediately that something was troubling his son, Lancelot experienced a father's concern, a new, and not entirely unpleasant, sensation. 'What's wrong?'

Galahad held his bible tight, focusing his gaze a few inches to the left of his father's head. 'I have a question to ask you.'

Lancelot knew instinctively what the question was going to be.

'There are people who say – who say that you are . . . having an affair with . . . ' – He could not speak the name – 'with Arthur's wife. Is it true?'

If Galahad knew, who else did? Arthur? Had he known all along? If so, this was surely the end; he would be banished from Camelot. And Guinevere? What would happen to her?

'Is it?'

It took all Lancelot's courage to answer truthfully. 'Yes.'

Galahad swayed on his feet.

'I never meant to fall in love with her,' said Lancelot. 'I tried hard not to.'

Galahad's voice trembled. 'It was you who persuaded me to come to Camelot, father. You spoke of your dreams for the future, and you invited me to share them with you. You made me swear an oath pledging my allegiance to Arthur and to the ideals of Camelot – honour, justice and love.'

Lancelot bowed his head, every word his son spoke stabbing his heart.

Galahad levelled an accusing finger at his father. 'You are a hypocrite. You have broken your oath and betrayed your leader. What's more, you lied to my mother.'

'That I never did,' said Lancelot.

'You deserted her when I was a baby. And what was your excuse? That you had a mission. What mission was that, father – screwing Arthur's wife?' Excited and appalled by his own daring, Galahad's chest heaved.

Lancelot groaned. 'Enough, Galahad, enough,' he pleaded, 'have pity on me.' It was astonishing and unnerving to witness this normally placid and compliant young man transformed into an avenging angel. He wanted to protest, to fight back, to challenge his right to talk to his father like this, to ask for – no, to *demand* his respect. Instead, he was begging for mercy. 'Try to understand,' he said, knowing it was no use. Galahad, of all people, would never understand. Looking into his son's eyes, he saw a man uncontaminated by the vices that corrupted other men. He saw a pure and honest man, and he owed it to him to be honest in return.

'All my life I dreamed of being God's servant,' he said. 'My love for Guinevere changed that. I shall never see the promised land. But you, my son, you will.' Placing the palms of his hands together, he rested his forehead on them as though he were praying. 'There is nothing left for me but to ask your forgiveness.'

'It is not for me to forgive,' said Galahad. 'Only God can do that.'

Galahad's path should now have been clear. Yet, to his surprise, it was not. Something prevented him from doing the right thing. His mind clouded by sleepless nights, he decided to consult Gawain.

'Galahad,' said Gawain, 'what are you? Sixteen? Seventeen? What do you know about love?'

'I know a lot,' said Galahad.

'Really?' Gawain's tongue probed his cheek. 'When was the last time you had sex?'

Galahad flushed. 'I – I have learned from books.'

'What have you learned?'

Galahad was determined not to be bullied. 'I know what sin is,' he said defiantly, 'and that's what we are talking about. 'The bible says *Thou shalt not commit adultery.*'

'The bible also says *Honour thy father and thy mother.*'

'My father has broken God's law.'

'If it is God's law he has broken,' said Gawain, 'let God punish him.'

'God works in mysterious ways,' said Galahad.

'Through you? Is that what you mean?' said Gawain with a disdainful look. 'So you are God's emissary, are you?'

'His servant.'

'Only his servant, eh?' Gawain's eyes glinted. 'Then how dare you presume to speak in His name.'

'Because He tells me to,' said Galahad, hugging his bible.

'Does he indeed?' Gawain's eyebrows arched provocatively. 'Then do me a favour, Galahad, next time you speak to God, ask Him how He rates humility in his servants – especially the teenage variety.'

Galahad squirmed. 'You are mocking me.'

Gawain did not deny it. 'Let me ask you something. Does it ever occur to you that you might be wrong? Wrong about

296

God, wrong about your father, wrong about a lot of things? Apparently not. But then you are young, and the young always think they know everything.'

'If I thought I knew everything,' said Galahad, 'I would not be asking you for advice.'

'Is that what you are doing?'

'Yes.'

'Then here it is. Do nothing.'

'What will that achieve?'

'What will you achieve by running to Arthur?' demanded Gawain. 'If you expose your father and Guinevere, the one who will be most damaged is Arthur himself.'

'How so?'

'Because he will be compelled to take action against Lancelot, and that could lead to virtual civil war in Camelot. Some will support Arthur, others Lancelot. You will set father against son, brother against brother, friend against friend. The only winners will be our enemies. The losers will be the good people we are trying to help. Is that what you want?'

'Not for all the world.'

'Then can I count on you to keep these rumours to yourself?'

Galahad folded his lips primly. 'I shall pray for God's guidance,' he said.

Forty Seven

THINGS WERE HAPPENING that Arthur could not understand. In his early forties, a man was supposed to be in command of his life, not feeling weary and disillusioned. God knows, though, he had reason enough to feel this way. He had lost brave comrades, many innocents had died, the Round Table was increasingly riven by dissension between the doves and the hawks, and there were still as many terrorists and terror groups, still as many preachers of hate and violence, still as many brutal dictators, still as many drug barons, and, most shameful of all, still as many countries making secret, self-serving deals with the enemy – for money, for trade, for power.

The old doubts were returning. From another time and another place a conversation with Merlin on Glastonbury Tor came back to him.

The world had gone mad. The king tried to bring it back to its senses, and restore meaning to people's lives. He wanted to give them courage and hope for the future. But to do that he first had to impose order on chaos.

How do you mean, impose?

You are right to question that word. He questioned it too. The thought of using force troubled him. But after much heart searching he decided that if mankind was to be saved, he had no other choice.

Was it true? Was there really no other choice?

If he summoned his old friend, he would come, knowing that he needed him. Yet Arthur was a proud man, too proud to ask for help. He would battle on without the Magus. But when he entered the observatory a few days later, Virgil, his eyes shuttered, was perched on the monitor screen, and Merlin, in one of his rare full-length manifestations, lay asleep in an armchair, mouth gaping, snoring like a rhinoceros. Greeting Arthur with a loud hoo-hoo, Virgil fluffed up his feathers till his body was a huge puffball, and Merlin woke with a startled grunt.

'Sometimes,' said Arthur gloomily, 'I wonder whether the price we pay is too high.'

'No struggle is without cost,' said Merlin. 'Be strong, Arthur. The good people of the world depend on you. You are the only hope for their future and their children's future. It is your destiny to save them.'

'Forgive me, Magus, but I have only your word for that.'

The green orbs glowed with a tender light. 'When you were seven years old, you and your adoptive father and brother, Hector and Keir, went to Devon for the weekend. Do you remember what happened?'

Arthur's memory drifted back. 'They were attacked by an eagle.'

'You *thought* it was attacking them. And what did you do?'

'I ran away. Keir said I was a coward.'

'He was wrong, wasn't he? You were trying to save your family.'

Arthur said nothing.

'Hector and Keir ran along the cliffside in a panic, and *you deliberately ran inland shouting at the top of your voice*. Why did you do that?'

No answer.

'To distract the eagle and make it follow you,' said Merlin. 'Which it did.'

Again Arthur was silent.

'And when it dived on you, what did you do?' Merlin left a pause, though he knew Arthur would not answer him. 'You stood there calmly, waiting for the end. Even though you were expecting the eagle to tear you to pieces at any second, you didn't cry out, you didn't move – at least not until its talons were inches from your face. And then you flinched.'

Arthur nodded silently.

'And because you flinched, because you lost faith, the eagle punished you by scratching you, leaving that tiny scar on your cheek.'

Unconsciously, Arthur's hand moved to his left cheek.

'You remember what the eagle did next?'

Arthur nodded. 'Yes.'

'It stood on your shoulder for a long time, as if it knew and trusted you, both of which, of course, it did. After a while it took off, circled you three times, each time crying its strange cry, then flew away.' Merlin reached out and lightly touched the scar on Arthur's face. 'That scar is not a badge of shame, Arthur. It is there to remind you that you are flawed, as every human being is, but it is also there to remind you that you are one with all of God's creation. You have been chosen. And because you have been chosen, the creatures of the wild pay homage to you and protect you, just as the eagle did when you fought Mujahid.'

For a long time there was silence in the room, both men occupied with their own thoughts. Arthur started up his computer, and for a time concentrated on the screen. 'See that spiral there, Merlin – that's a galaxy formed only a couple of billion years after the Big Bang. Imagine! What we are looking at on this screen happened eleven billion years ago! What was our solar system then?'

Even Merlin could not answer that.

'No more than a swirling mass of gas, I would guess,' said Arthur, responding to his own question, 'and then, as things cooled down over billions of years, clumps of material coalesced into rocks and finally clusters. And one of the smallest of those clusters is the planet we live on.' He swivelled on his stool to face Merlin. 'What is planet Earth in the whole scheme of things? Insignificant. In terms of size, almost nothing. You could fit over a million earths inside the sun. And some of those stars out there are thousands, perhaps billions of times bigger than the sun!'

'It puts our problems into perspective, doesn't it?' said Merlin.

An unexpected question: 'How old are you, Magus?'

Merlin's green eyes blinked. 'This time around? Pushing seventy.'

As Arthur shut down the computer, the universe died on the screen. 'I would never have guessed it,' he said.

Merlin turned happily to Arthur like a sunflower to the sun. 'I held you two weeks after you were born. Now look at you,' he said, his eyes full of pride.

'A man changes with the years,' reflected Arthur. ' It's not that you don't care any more. It certainly isn't that you don't hurt. Your bones still break, your veins still bleed, and your heart, Merlin, your heart aches as much as ever it did. Pain is still pain.'

'Forgive me for being blunt,' said Merlin, 'but you might hurt less if you were honest with yourself. And with Guinevere.'

'Being honest,' said Arthur, 'could be the end of my marriage.'

'It would be like cutting out a cancerous growth.'

'It would be like cutting out my heart,' said Arthur.

Where were his friends now when he needed them? Whom could he confide in? Not in Guinevere, however much he loved her. Nor in Lancelot. Nor in his son, Mordred. There was wise Leo Grant of course, but how could he tell Guinevere's father that his daughter was . . . not what he thought she was. There was loyal and ever-devoted George Bedivere. If Arthur told him the truth, George, bless him, would probably go and thump Lancelot with his steel hand. Unless of course he already knew. Now there was a thought. Did George know? Did they all know? Were they keeping quiet about it to avoid rocking the boat? Were they talking behind his back, judging him, pitying him . . . were they mocking him?

There was only one man to whom he could open his heart; Keir, his adoptive brother. Never in his whole life had he needed a brother more, someone he could trust. Keir would be his friend, and he would not be alone any longer. Was he clutching at straws? Well, that's what drowning men did, wasn't it?

He invited Keir round and sat him down with a glass of wine. 'Family becomes more important as you grow older.'

Keir's response was short and brutal. 'We are not family.'

Determined not to lose patience, 'You and I are brothers,' said Arthur. 'Not blood brothers, but what does that matter? We have a common history, the same background, the same home, the same parents. It was our world, Keir, yours and mine, we grew up together, we played together, we went to school together, we fished together. Remember how we used to fish by Ponterlally bridge?'

'You dreamed. I caught the fish,' said Keir ungraciously.

Arthur grinned. 'And I always came home with an empty basket.'

Keir remembered only too well. He was always so proud of his full basket of fish, and his father would hug him, though never as affectionately as he hugged Arthur for having an empty one. Keir never understood that. It hurt then, and it still did.

'All those things we shared make us brothers, don't they?'

'We were never brothers,' said Keir, 'and we never will be. You were adopted. Hector and Elizabeth are my parents, not yours.'

'We were brought up as brothers,' said Arthur. 'Surely that takes precedence over genes and chromosomes? ' He held out his hand in one last despairing plea for acceptance, and Keir turned and walked away, leaving Arthur wondering what he could ever do to make his brother love him.

Forty Eight

TORN BETWEEN THE TWO men in her life, and refusing to contemplate giving up either of them, Guinevere now lived in fear, certain that if Arthur ever discovered that she and Lancelot were lovers, he would have no choice but to banish them from Camelot. Galahad, once her favourite, was now the object of her scorn. What right did he have to judge his father? 'That sanctimonious little creep snaps his fingers, and you come running. It's pathetic.'

Lancelot's protestations of love did little to ease her troubled mind, not least because she suspected that he regarded his love for her as a weakness, something not to celebrate but to be ashamed of. If he truly loved her, would he have run back to Helena? Would he have brought back his son? Would he allow himself to be dictated to by him?

Comparing the two men in her life, she found herself appreciating Arthur more than ever. What a truly exceptional man he was. In all these years he had not uttered a single word in anger, had never been anything but caring and loving. There could only be one conclusion; either he knew nothing, or he said nothing because he loved her so much; a thought that moved her to tears.

For a few weeks they enjoyed a second honeymoon in which Arthur's unquestioning love aroused in Guinevere a combination of passion and tenderness that, until now, she had only experienced with Lancelot. Before long, however, they had, without being aware of it, slipped into the old easy-going routine, their relationship becoming what it had been before;

loving and companionable. It ought to have been enough. Yet the more she tried to persuade herself that Arthur was everything a woman could possibly desire in a man, the more she found herself thinking of Lancelot.

He, meanwhile, felt hurt and betrayed. By a cruel twist of fate it was at this stressful time that a brief coded signal was received by Command Control asking him to call Harold Pemberton urgently. Having set up the gravitational link, Lancelot stared at the communicator, his fingers refusing to do what he needed them to do. What could Harold want? At last he forced himself to dial the link digits and press the communicator button.

'Harold?'

'I'm sorry, Lance, it's bad news.'

'What is it?'

'It's Helena.' The pause was so long that Lancelot thought the link had been cut. 'I'm afraid she's dead.'

Not possible. His brain refused to accept it. 'Helena.'

'Yes.'

For a long time he could neither think nor speak. Then . . . 'Helena,' he repeated blankly.

'I'm afraid so.'

'What happened?'

'She's been depressed,' said Harold, 'not eating properly, taking anti-depressants and sleeping pills. She was seeing a therapist, and we thought she was perking up. It seems she took an overdose. Last night she went into a coma, and this morning she had a massive haemorrhage.'

'An overdose?'

'It was an accident.'

'I'm so sorry, Harold,' He searched desperately for words of comfort, but there were none, or at least none that were not trite and banal.

Severing the link, he sat staring at the wall, trying not to think, above all not to feel. After a while he roused himself. Galahad. He must tell him before someone else did.

Galahad's reaction was at first subdued, then frenzied, his rage directed at his father. 'You did this! It's your fault! You killed my mother!' Lancelot tried to reason with him, but Galahad would have none of it. 'You made me leave her! I should never have listened to you.' He began to beat his father with his fists on the chest and face, and Lancelot made no effort to defend himself. Worn out at last, Galahad threw himself into a chair and burst into tears. Staggering to the bathroom, Lancelot dabbed his bruised face with a towel soaked in water, muttering over and over again, 'God forgive me, God forgive me,' and thinking all the time that though God might, Galahad never would.

For days Lancelot neither ate nor slept. Never leaving his apartment, he refused to see anyone. Most of the time he sat staring into space, his body periodically galvanised by mini-eruptions of shivering. When these quakes subsided he would nod his head knowingly and mutter to himself. Even more worrying to his friends, he began to have hallucinations, holding long conversations with his mother, pleading with her to explain what he had done to make her abandon him, begging her to forgive him, as if he were responsible for her death.

'You killed yourself, mother . . . Ban told me you did . . . It was because of me, wasn't it? . . . It must have been, or you would never have left me.'

Visiting him one evening, Gawain found Lancelot marching about his apartment in a trance-like state, drilling himself, just as he once did when he was a young captain in the British army.

'You're a disgrace, Lancelot! A disgrace to the Army! Get those arms up! Left, left, left right, left! You're on a charge of murder, captain! About turn! Swing those arms! Eyes right, d'you hear! You're on a charge of adultery, captain! Left, left, left right, left! You're on a charge of murder and adultery, you horrible creature!'

The harangue continued for nearly an hour before Lancelot collapsed on his bed, closed his eyes and slept. In the morning he remembered nothing. For a week his mind wandered; then one day he was himself again, unsteady on his feet but coherent. He asked to see his son, meaning to tell him how sorry he was, to confess he felt responsible for Helena's death, and to throw himself on his mercy. To his surprise it was Galahad who apologised.

'I should not have blamed you for mother's death. It was my decision to leave her, not yours.'

Shared guilt, and the knowledge that they depended on each other's support to become whole again, led to a partial reconciliation between father and son. What prevented it from being complete was the knowledge that his father was having an affair with Arthur's wife, something Galahad could not understand, certainly not condone.

The next morning Gawain found Lancelot sitting at his computer in Command Control.

'You OK?'

'Why wouldn't I be?'

'You need a break, Lance.'

'I need you to stop fussing.'

'A couple of weeks, that's all.'

'So you can steal my job? Forget it. I'm still your boss.'

Grinning broadly, Gawain made for the door. 'Welcome back,' he said.

'Once, a long time ago, I saved a life,' said Lancelot, apropos of nothing.

'I heard.'

'I thought God had granted me a miracle.' His fingers toyed with the keyboard. 'It wasn't a miracle of course, it was a freak of nature.'

'Stop tormenting yourself,' said Gawain.

'So you see,' said Lancelot, 'I am not the man I thought I was.'

'I don't know about that,' said Gawain. 'What I do know is that you are greatly loved and respected for what you are, and for the things you have achieved.'

'Like murder and adultery.'

'If you are talking about Helena,' said Gawain, 'you are most definitely not a murderer, Lance. You were not responsible for her death. As for being an adulterer . . . ' – he drummed his fingers on the door jamb – 'it's in your hands.'

Yes, it was in his hands. Or it was until he saw Guinevere again, smiling at him with those entrancing eyes of hers. In an instant, all his good intentions were forgotten. Soon they were meeting as often as before, their love-making more passionate than ever, animated now by a kind of defiant desperation and a sense of foreboding about the future.

Forty Nine

The Hand of God

A T 6 P.M. Eastern Seaboard time the lights in New York went out. It was unusual, though not that unusual. Whilst there was concern and anger at whichever incompetent authority was responsible, there was no panic. Power outages happened every few years, some of them lasting many hours, and so, tough New Yorkers, accustomed to dealing with crises, blamed everyone they could think of, from the Mayor to the President, and tried to go about their business as usual.

The fact was, however, that a major electrical failure that was merely inconvenient for some, was frightening and potentially dangerous for others. A million people were trapped in subway trains with no air conditioning and no way of knowing how long they would be sitting there, many more in skyscraper elevators. In a matter of minutes, every cab in the city was taken, public transport had slowed to a halt in streets jammed with automobiles, and hundreds of thousands of commuters roamed the canyons of Manhattan aimlessly, growing increasingly frustrated and anxious. Mobile communications were disrupted by a huge overload, and fire, police and ambulance services either did not receive emergency calls, or, in jammed Manhattan streets, were unable to respond to them.

Fortunately the outage did not last long. Sixty minutes later, at exactly 7 p.m., the lights went on again. In the twenty-four hours that followed, the numerous federal and state agencies involved sought to play down the "interruption" as it was generally referred to, though no one explained what had caused it. By the third day following the event, it was accepted by both media and public that the power outage had demonstrated the resilience and guts of the American public, and the success of the administration's contingency plans for dealing with such emergencies. Backup generators had taken over swiftly in all key services. Communications, whilst certainly affected, had not broken down, and there were few reports of panic amongst members of the public.

In Command Control, Agravaine sat with Arthur, Gawain and Lancelot at Galaxy's big table monitor.

'Was it an accident?' Arthur wanted to know.

'It's possible,' said Agravaine.

That wasn't good enough for Gawain. 'Was it, or wasn't it?'

'The Americans are saying it was,' said Agravaine. 'Obviously they don't want to scare people for no reason.'

'If it wasn't an accident,' said Lancelot, 'then what was it?'

Agravaine meandered across the dimly lit room and poured himself a coffee at the machine. 'It might have been – I'm not saying it was, mind you – it might have been hackers.'

'They would have to be very superior hackers, wouldn't they?' said Arthur.

Agravaine nodded. 'They broke into some of the best defended sites on the planet.' There was a hint of admiration in his voice, as of one master saluting another.

'Any idea who it could be?' asked Gawain.

Lancelot squirmed as Agravaine slurped his coffee noisily. 'Techforce Ten and Neural Network are on the case. So are the Americans, though they won't admit it. They're worried, whatever the President says.'

'What are the chances of tracking them down?' asked Arthur.

'Not great,' said Agravaine. 'These guys are pros. They know what they're doing.'

'We must face the fact that we could be dealing with terrorists,' said Arthur. 'Cyber terrorists.'

A week later, at precisely 6 p.m., the lights went out again in New York. In a repetition of the same scenario as the previous week the power failure lasted exactly sixty minutes. This time, however, there was widespread panic, and the disruption was far greater than it had been the previous week.

When the lights went on again at 7 p.m., a message was posted on the internet:–

The power outages in New York were only a taste of what is to come. Experience has shown us that you will not listen to reason. Therefore we shall not attempt to reason with you. We shall attack your so-called civilisation which worships not Allah but material things. We shall destroy your economies, your cities, your degenerate way of life. And in their place we shall build God's Empire on earth. Allahu Akbar!
Ronin
The Hand of God

If the threat was genuine, then it was likely that it came from one of a number of fanatical Islamist groups: Al Qaeda, or one of its fundamentalist offshoots. There was no indication which group was involved, nor could the message be traced. Whoever was behind it had the protection of cyberspace. No demands were made, a fact that in itself created much speculation in the world's media.

Some commentators claimed it was an encouraging sign, an indication that hackers, not terrorists, were behind the power outings and the internet message. Hackers, they reasoned, were less likely to make demands than terrorists. Others were less optimistic. No threats meant that no deal was being offered, which implied that further incidents, perhaps far more serious ones, were to be expected. Despite the President's assurance that whoever was responsible would be found and punished, the mood in the United States, was sceptical, people having long since lost faith in the promises of politicians.

Arthur asked Agravaine to address the Round Table. 'We are all familiar with the Internet,' he began. 'It allows us to travel electronically anywhere in the world through computerised gateways. With one tap on our keyboards we can span the planet in a second, and with a bit of ingenuity and a few simple commands we can access computers anywhere we choose. Cyberspace has been described as the world's nervous system. Every developed country functions by means of electronic links to web servers and control systems, and as a result, every country on the internet is globally interdependent. The world's economy runs on cyber space which makes it incredibly efficient. It also makes it extremely vulnerable. Inflict damage on the system and you can deal a body blow to a nation. Or to the world.'

By now he had the complete attention of the Round Table. On a huge screen at the end of the Great Hall appeared an apparently random network of boxes. 'As you see,' he continued, 'all these boxes are linked, each of them representing a vital function of pretty much every developed country in the world. Some of them – for example telecommunications – are globally linked.' One by one he identified each box with a remote-controlled laser beam. 'Electrical power supplies, natural gas lines and gas-powered electric systems, hydro-electric plants and water supplies, water treatment plants, air traffic control, road and rail transport, telecommunications, oil and chemical refineries, nuclear power plants, communication networks, stock markets, commodity exchanges, financial institutions, hospitals, emergency services, and last, but certainly not least, the command and control systems of all military sites relating to everything from intelligence agencies to nuclear hardware.'

When every box had been signposted, he paused and looked round the hall. Rows of expectant faces were turned towards him. No one moved, there was not a sound. It was understood that no questions would be asked until he had finished his presentation. A beam of sunlight breaking through the clouds lanced through a window directly onto his tinted glasses, casting pink lozenges of light on the stone floor, on the Round Table and on Arthur. The effect was magical and at the same time ominous, as though it were a warning of things to come, of things beyond the control even of Camelot. Agravaine removed his spectacles and wiped them compulsively before putting them on again.

'By means of viruses or worms,' he continued, 'often contained in apparently innocent programmes, it is theoretically possible to access and severely damage, or put out of action, any of those boxes on the screen. The people who try to do this – until now, it must be said, with limited success – are called hackers. In the last decade their expertise has grown exponentially. So, it should be said, have the defences designed to protect us against their intrusion. We have learned a great deal about the techniques hackers use, and we have information technology to protect our systems, but . . . there is no such thing as total protection, and there probably never will be. It's like an arms race. As defences become more sophisticated, so do hackers.'

Time passed, Agravaine was still talking, and the mood in the Great Hall grew more despondent by the minute. 'There have been isolated cyber attacks which have caused disruption and resulted in some casualties. In every case, standby or emergency services and equipment such as generators have been successfully used to limit the effects of the attack. But until now no attack has targeted a country's infrastructure on a massive scale, involving, for example, what are now termed "botnets" – computers hijacked by clandestine viruses. A co-ordinated attack on the systems in these boxes could paralyse a country, or several countries, for a significant period of time. That in itself would be serious enough. Even more serious, any cyber attack might well be accompanied by a physical attack, or by a series of physical attacks – suicide bombers, car bombs, missiles, 'dirty' bombs, biological weapons, poisons etc. – the aim, maximum loss of life and also maximum psychological impact.

'As for the choice of targets, the possibilities are endless; oil terminals, ports, ships, town centres, government institutions, important buildings, airports, aircraft, nuclear power stations, and so on.' Agravaine surveyed the hall. 'I could go on, but I think you have the general idea.'

Leo Grant raised his hand. 'All very interesting, Agravaine,' he said, 'but if you'll forgive me for saying so, there is something missing in your talk.' A dry smile. 'You have succeeded in scaring the Round Table – not an easy thing to do. But here's what I want to know. How do we track down these cyber-terrorists, assuming they are terrorists, so we can deal with them?'

Leo's contribution broke the ice. Members banged the table in approval. Agravaine wiped the sweat from his shining bald head. 'I'm sorry, but there's no simple answer to that question.'

Leo Grant was not to be fobbed off. 'Are you saying it can't be done?'

Arthur intervened. 'Like most things man has discovered or invented, the internet is our servant and our master, a blessing and a curse. No use disguising the fact that it can be a potent weapon in the hands of evil men. If it turns out that the men we are dealing with are terrorists, you have my word that we shall track them down.'

Arthur's optimistic words sounded to most members more like morale boosting than a realistic appraisal of the situation. Meanwhile, crucial questions remained unanswered. Was the message from Ronin a hoax? Could the power failures in New York have been accidental? Was some misguided hacker or group of hackers behind it?

Or was there a more sinister explanation?

Fifty

The Hand of God

A WEEK AFTER THE SECOND power outage, at exactly 6 p.m. Eastern Seaboard time, vital internet control systems in the USA, Canada, Russia, India, Pakistan, China, Japan, Korea, Australia, and every member of the European Union, were simultaneously targeted by computer viruses. In the skies, Air Traffic Control systems had difficulty making contact with pilots; communication was sporadic – in most cases non-existent. Because many TV and radio networks had shut down, it was difficult for ordinary citizens to follow the developing global crisis. Camelot's orbiting and static satellites and UAV's beamed back a huge amount of data, instantly broken down by Neural Network and processed by Techforce Ten. In Galaxy, columns of constantly updated information scrolled down the banks of wall screens.

Estimate globally several thousand commercial aircraft grounded, many compelled *at short notice to land at nearest airport . . . multiple air crash over Beijing... runway collision at London's Heathrow . . . aircraft crashes at Kennedy airport . . . believe ran out of fuel . . .*

Arthur and Agravaine sat grim-faced at the big central monitor, trying to absorb the mounting toll of disasters.

Rail crash in France . . . signal failures lead to head-on rail crashes in India . . . thousands feared dead . . . Power failures raise concerns over safety of nuclear power stations in Russia . . .

The scale of the attack, and the fact that it was so well co-ordinated, created widespread panic. In Moscow and New York, in Washington, London, Paris and Berlin, in Tokyo,

Beijing, Delhi and Karachi, millions fled homes and offices. Major roads out of cities were jammed with traffic, cars and public transport unable to move.

Global disruption generated fear, and in its wake violence. In almost every city centre angry crowds gathered in the streets, crowds that swiftly became mobs. Tempers frayed, fights broke out, government buildings were besieged and in some cases attacked. Shots were fired and firebombs hurled at the Kremlin in Moscow, the White House in Washington, the Houses of Parliament in London, and the Elysée Palace in Paris.

And with every hour that passed, the news became worse.

Latest estimate of global casualties exceeds one hundred thousand and mounting . . . Latest Techforce summary . . . Electricity failures and the severing of oil and gas supplies have affected transport, communications, hospitals and emergency services and heating systems throughout the world . . . in the USA, Canada, Iceland, Sweden, Denmark, Norway and Sweden people are dying of hypothermia – mostly the elderly and the very young.

Fresh water supplies were cut or contaminated in many countries. Fire, police and ambulance services functioned at fifty per cent efficiency or less. Because many surgeons, doctors and nurses had fled to take care of their families, the sick and injured fortunate enough to reach hospitals often remained untreated. Throughout the world major banks and stock markets, shops, stores, supermarkets, restaurants, factories and warehouses closed their doors. It seemed that the terrorists' threat to destroy the economy of the free world was not an idle one.

As Neural Network and Techforce Ten hunted cyberspace for the terrorists, Kraken, under Gawain's command, slipped into the Atlantic. Seconds later, Eclipse, captained by Lancelot, lifted off from the launch pad, its silver cigar shape briefly dazzling in the afternoon sun, vanishing as it mantled.

Agravaine summarised the situation for Arthur. 'Eclipse is

covering the northern hemisphere, Kraken the south. They both have a full complement of actives, Scuttles and robots, and are fully charged with Excalibur. If in the next few hours they have no luck, we'll begin dropping surveillance robots in suspect areas of the Middle East.'

On the big table monitor there was now a map of the world. The tiny images of the two great battle craft moved slowly across the screen, doubling and redoubling their tracks, Eclipse heading north, Kraken south. Over the speaker came the voice of Techforce Ten's controller. 'US President on screen.'

His eyes red and swollen, his cheeks sagging, the President had not slept for several nights. 'We're getting nowhere fast. What about you?'

'Nothing to report,' said Arthur.

'The cost in lives and destruction of property is already mega. If we don't find the bastards responsible soon, they'll do lasting damage to the world's economy. The whole goddam system – computers, servers, routers, switches, fibre optic cables – is close to meltdown. Who the fuck invented the internet anyway?'

Arthur suppressed a smile. 'The United States is where it all started.'

'You don't say,' said the President. 'Well, if that's true, we've paid a heavy price for it. These power outages are bringing the country to its knees.'

'Do you have any idea who is behind all this?' asked Arthur.

'It's gotta be some Iran-backed terror group. And I tell you, Arthur,' said the President, lowering his voice to a conspiratorial whisper, 'one way or another we're going to have to deal with them.'

'Meaning?'

'You know damned well what I mean.'

Yet again, it seemed, the US President was considering the nuclear option.

'Where's the evidence that Iran is behind this?'

'Who needs fucking evidence!' the President screamed, his

face bright red. 'You know as well as I do they're the ones pulling the strings.'

'Launching a nuclear attack would be playing into the hands of the terrorists. It's probably exactly what they want you to do.'

The President's bloodshot eyes glinted with anger. 'Don't give me that psychological bullshit, Arthur. This time the Islamists have gone too far. They've got their heel on our jugular, they're humiliating the greatest nation on earth. How much more can we take?' For a few seconds the President was distracted by a TV news report. 'Get this, Arthur. Just about every supermarket in the country is shut. Supplies aren't getting through – no food, not even bottled water. I just see that in a downtown Washington mall two guys were fighting over a carton of chicken legs, and one of them drew a knife and stabbed the other through the heart.' A despondent shake of the head. 'In the name of God, Arthur, what have we come to? Americans killing each other for chicken legs! Those evil bastards are pushing us back into the dark ages. I won't let them get away with it.'

'Attacking Iran is not the answer.'

'The finger's pointing at them. They set this whole thing up.'

'You do know,' said Arthur, 'that this Ronin is just as likely to be sitting in an internet cafe in Manhattan as in Tehran?'

The President's patience was stretched to the limit. 'Jesus, Arthur, what do you want me to do?' he said. 'I can't nuke New York, and I sure as hell won't sit on my hands. What about you? Where do you stand in all this? You are the one who always wants action. What's changed?'

'Nothing,' said Arthur. 'I'm still for action. My record shows that. But reasonable, focused action.'

The President threw up his hands. 'What in heaven's name do we do?' To Arthur he sounded desperate.

'Find the terrorists.'

'And if we don't?'

'We'll talk again.'

The President shook his head. 'No more talking,' he said. 'We've been talking to maniacs like these for years, and where has it got us? Nowhere. You hear me, Arthur. I'm President of the most powerful nation on earth, and I say the time for talking is over.'

Early the following morning, Arthur and Agravaine were still monitoring incoming data when the speakers crackled and a message from Techforce Ten brought both men to their feet.

White House bombed! . . . White House bombed! . . .

Seconds passed, and there on the big table monitor was a horrifying sight. The White House was a smouldering ruin. Over it, dark and menacing, hung a cloud of ash and dust. Two dazed survivors staggered out of the remains of the building and collapsed on the lawns now strewn with burning debris. In the distance a siren wailed, then another and another. Arthur and Agravaine stared at the devastation in disbelief.

During the course of the next hour, confused and contradictory reports reached them from the few US TV and radio stations still operating. Based on these, and the more accurate data from Techforce, they were able to assemble the facts.

At 2 a.m. Eastern Seaboard time a powerful missile had hit the White House killing almost everyone inside, including the President and his wife. A handful of badly injured people had already been taken to hospital. Rescue teams were searching for survivors.

By the following morning the attention of the media was focusing on the missile itself, whether it was long, medium or short range, and whether it had been launched from a ship, or an aircraft, or from land. Every security service was on high alert. Forensic teams worked feverishly at the impact site. An official announcement was awaited hourly.

At 11 a.m. an embarrassed Defence Department spokesman announced that the White House had been struck not by a foreign missile but by a US missile launched from a missile site in the south of the United States. Newscasters and military experts on the few T.V. channels still broadcasting speculated endlessly. First reaction was that an unplanned missile launch had been an accident waiting to happen, the surprise being, not that it had happened, but that it hadn't happened before.

Later in the day the same Defence Department official revealed at a press conference that the missile strike was not an accident, but was thought to be 'linked to the activities of cyber-terrorists'. The implications were frightening, even more frightening than the chaos and devastation the terrorists had already caused. Either they had succeeded in breaking into a well-guarded US military installation, or they had somehow deceived the computer network that controlled it into launching a missile targeted on the White House. The most probable explanation was that rogue software had infected the commercial operating system at source, when the circuit boards were assembled.

As a result, the United States and many other countries subjected military suppliers of everything, from highly sophisticated weaponry and software down to nuts and bolts, to the most ruthless and exhaustive scrutiny. The search for scapegoats created endless suspects. It was even suggested that treachery on a massive scale was involved, and that some rogue elements in the military had knowingly purchased an infected back-up system. There was no evidence to support this, or any other theory, nothing that could be proved, nothing except for the alarming fact that vital military networks had been compromised. Both media and public were asking what guarantees there were that the same thing could not happen again. Who would be the next target? How many more missiles would be launched?

What the military and security services knew, and the general public did not, was that in a number of countries military networks were linked, so that one rogue command could fire hundreds of missiles simultaneously, some of them locked on to overseas targets. If that were to happen, the consequences were horrifyingly predictable. There was little doubt that any country under attack would respond in kind, leading inevitably to world nuclear war.

As America mourned its dead, Arvin Wingrove, the Vice-President, was sworn in as President and immediately broadcast to the nation, making it clear that his first priority was to decide how best to respond to the murderous and unprovoked attack on the White House. 'America will not be intimidated by terrorists. They have hurt us, that I will not deny. They have murdered our President and our First Lady, and with them many other fine men and women. But they have not broken our spirit. No one will ever do that. In the past this great country of ours has played a leading role in defeating tyranny. We shall do so again. I give my solemn word to the American people that we shall hunt these terrorists down and mete out swift justice. And we will do it in our own time and in our own way.'

For all the President's brave words, neither the Americans, nor anyone else, knew who the terrorists were, nor where they were. Despite which, the world was fighting back as best it could. Every hour that passed, progress was being made in strengthening cyber defences, rebuilding destroyed and damaged systems and eradicating software viruses.

At 12 noon Eastern Seaboard time the following day, the cyber-terrorists posted a second message:

What you have suffered until now are no more than minor inconveniences. We assure you that the worst is yet to come. When two days have passed by Eastern Seaboard time we shall demonstrate our power in a way that our most arrogant enemy will never forget. You shall know what it is to shed bitter tears. And your tears will engulf you. Allahu Akbar!
Ronin
The Hand of God

The chilling threat in this second message both worried and confused world leaders. Almost as frightening as the threat itself was the absence of any conditions – still no demands for money or for the release of prisoners. Without negotiations there was little hope of tracking down the terrorists. The outlook could hardly be worse. The terrorists, whoever they were, were still out there, and no one had the slightest idea what the next target would be. Only one thing was certain; in the next forty-eight hours *The Hand of God* would strike again.

Fifty One

The Hand of God

IN GALAXY the debate continued through the evening and night, into the small hours of the morning. Where would the next major strike be? Arthur, Agravaine, Ian Tichgame and Mordred all had their own ideas. Yet by noon, Eastern Seaboard time, twenty-four hours before the deadline expired, they were still no nearer to finding a solution.

Agravaine and Tich agreed that the most likely potential targets were airports, railway stations, subway systems, nuclear power stations, and heavily populated city centres.

'Somehow I don't think they'll go for obvious targets,' said Mordred. 'They'll pick a spectacular site, yes, but not one that's likely to be heavily defended.'

'For example?' said Tich.

'I don't know,' said Mordred.

The task of strengthening the world's cyber defences continued. Agravaine was growing more and more agitated. Little progress had been made, even though every country under attack was co-operating as never before in the huge task of cleansing cyber-space of viruses and worms, and attempting to repair and reactivate essential control systems. As a temporary measure many of these systems had been isolated from the network. Thousands of firewall logs were trawled through to establish what messages and instructions were being sent and received, in many cases blocking the relevant IP addresses. Such tactics were criticised as locking the barn door after the horse had bolted, but lessons, politicians claimed, had been learned. If a similar attack were launched in the future it would be unlikely to meet with the same success; which did not alter the fact that *The Hand of God* had won an impressive victory, disrupting and scaring the world.

Agravaine polished his pink-tinted spectacles with great concentration. 'We've tracked down hundreds of hackers, some of them using pretty sophisticated techniques. But they are either criminals stealing user names, passwords, bank account details – that kind of thing – or teenage hackers creating chaos for fun.'

Arthur scrolled down the list of names. 'None of them are our terrorists?'

'Not as far as we can see. Let's hope Eclipse or Kraken come up with something soon.'

'They've launched land surveillance robots and orbiting satellites,' said Arthur. 'It's guesswork, though. They don't know where to look, or who they are looking for.'

Agravaine eased himself off his stool and walked stiffly across the room for yet another cup of coffee.

'You should get some sleep, Agro.'

'I can't sleep, nuncle – not until we've found the bastards.' He stretched and yawned. '*The Hand of God*,' he said disdainfully. 'These murderers claim they speak and act in the name of God. What kind of God condones the murder of innocent people? It's sick, sick, sick.'

Tich spoke up. 'Shouldn't we be looking for a zombie?'

Agravaine's stubby fingers ranged his keyboard. The mini-images of Eclipse and Kraken floated in and out of view, hunting land, air and sea for elusive demons, and finding none.

Arthur waited vainly for an explanation. 'Will someone tell me what a zombie is?'

'A zombie,' said Agravaine, 'is a machine that has been corrupted, usually by the introduction of software containing some kind of virus.'

'There was a time,' said Tich, 'when it was relatively easy to corrupt an internet-connected machine remotely. These days it's much more difficult; there have been many improvements in online security. A machine is more likely to be corrupted by someone posing as a friend selling the user an infected programme.'

'The software contains a Trojan Horse,' said Agravaine, 'one that allows it to attack other internet sites.'

'Once the computer is compromised,' explained Tich, 'it has no will of its own, it just does what it's told. The computer operator doesn't know it, but his computer has become a zombie ready to take orders.'

'Do they go on to attack other internet sites?' asked Arthur.

'They might,' said Tich, 'or they might simply prime the computer with a hidden code that they can activate at a later date.'

'How do you locate a computer zombie out of the billions of computers in the world?' asked Arthur.

Tich smiled, his big eyes squeezed by his ample cheeks. 'Which is easier?' he asked, 'to compromise a hundred machines? Or to compromise one?'

'To compromise one, I presume,' said Arthur.

'Correct,' said Tich. 'It saves time and effort, and there's less chance of being discovered.'

'But if you were a terrorist,' said Arthur, 'wouldn't you want to compromise as many computers as possible? The more machines you infiltrate, the more sites you can attack.'

'Unless you infiltrate a group,' suggested Mordred.

For several seconds Galaxy was silent, whilst Tich nodded approval, and Arthur and Agravaine digested the comment.

'What sort of group?' said Agravaine.

'Any group with world-wide connections,' said Mordred. 'It would have to be relatively innocent, or why would a terrorist choose to infiltrate it? And it would need to have a great many contacts on the internet.'

'OK,' said Arthur, 'we're running out of time. Let's work on the assumption that we are looking for a zombie. That still leaves a hell of a lot of groups to investigate.'

'It would make it easier if we had a clue to start with,' agreed Agravaine. 'Meanwhile the best way to track down the zombie or zombies is to look in the logs on the servers that have been attacked, and their associated firewalls. By combining the logs from a lot of different servers, we might be able to spot the machines that are in regular communication. Then we'll narrow down those groups to a list of probable suspects.'

Agravaine checked Techforce Ten's latest analysis of internet messages, talking out loud as he did. 'Neural Network absorbs millions of messages every day, and Techforce sifts through them and updates their analysis every few minutes. He pointed at the central monitor. Now that's interesting. See that e-mail there? It's reproducing itself all over the internet. What's more, according to Techforce, it only appears on machines that have been attacked by the cyber-terrorists.'

'What's the message?' asked Tich, joining them at the central computer.

'*Have met Ronin.* '

Tich peered at it, scowled and shook his head. Whatever he had in mind, he seemed disappointed.

'Is that the whole message?' asked Mordred.

'Yes,' said Agravaine.

'No signature?'

Agravaine's fingers danced, and Mordred read the full message aloud: *Have met Ronin, Steven.* Peering at the screen, his clever eyes alert as a fox's, he was suddenly smiling broadly. 'D'you get it?'

Agravaine's shoulders lifted helplessly as Arthur studied the words with a puzzled frown.

'It's an anagram,' said Mordred.

Tich's enormous face ruptured into cracks, fissures, gullies, mountains, ravines and crevasses. 'Hats off to Mord,' he said. 'The man's a genius!'

Agravaine's brows contracted. Suddenly the light dawned,

and he too was smiling.

'Will someone tell me what you are talking about,' said Arthur, feeling very much out of it.

Mordred obliged. '*Have met Ronin, Steven* is an anagram for *Save the Environment*.'

'It means,' said Agravaine, miffed that he had not broken the code himself, 'that the terrorists may have infiltrated an environmental group with worldwide connections. As yet we have no means of knowing which group, but it certainly reduces our list of suspects.'

'We have to look for a well-known environmental group led by a man whose first name is Steven,' said Tich. 'If I'm right, they'll have offices, or at least computers, all over the world.'

'And every one of them is now a zombie, infected by cyber-terrorists,' said Agravaine, his fingers already tapping instructions to Techforce Ten.

Every green/environmental group in the world was swiftly investigated. In less than an hour Techforce had come up with six possibilities, rapidly reduced to three, then two, then one: an environmental organisation with hundreds of machines all over the world. The group's name: *The World is Ours*, its leader, Steven Adams.

By 7 p.m. Eastern Seaboard time that evening, Neural Network had penetrated the Group's computers in their head office in London. Agravaine explained the process. 'We have infiltrated their computers with our own monitoring programme, hooked into their operating systems and are intercepting all traffic. In other words we have introduced our own Trojan Horse. When we know for sure that this is the group whose network is infected, we can start tracking the terrorists.'

'One question,' said Arthur. 'Does Ronin exist? Or is it just a code name?'

For a second or two Agravaine's stubby fingers rested on the keyboard, then darted into action again. 'He exists all right.

We're checking him out. Either he's the leader of *The Hand of God*, or he's a key member of it.'

'I still don't understand how he managed to infiltrate the environmentalists' sites.'

'My guess,' said Tich, 'is that Steven needed to upgrade the group's security. Many of their so-called 'green' activities are either borderline or downright illegal, and he probably suspected he was being monitored by security services. The chances are that he consulted a cyber expert who introduced him to Ronin. Ronin told Steven about a programme tailor-made to erect a solid wall against intrusion. Steven fell for it, bought the programme and installed it. From that day, his machines and all the machines he was in contact with – and there are probably hundreds of them – became zombies, doing the terrorists' work for them.'

By 2 a.m. the next morning, Camelot time, Neural Network and Techforce Ten had located eighteen terrorists in eleven countries – among them the Kingdom of the Euphrates, Afghanistan, China, Russia, Finland and Norway, via log files and IP addresses. Some IP addresses narrowed down the terrorists' location to a very small geographical area, some to areas so large that they were virtually useless. It was clear they would never be able to catch all the terrorists before the deadline expired. The aim had to be to catch enough of them to cripple the organisation.

In the far south of the Kingdom of the Euphrates Kraken glided mantled and undetected up the Persian Gulf towards Basra. Under cover of darkness it landed six actives and four miniature surveillance robots crammed with databanks of detailed information on the three terrorists they were looking for; in one case, a full physical description, in another, iris and voice signatures, and in a third – the crucial information that had brought Kraken to Basra – a geographical location and a mobile phone number. Moving fast, the mini-robots led the actives to a safe house in the back-streets of the city.

Two men were asleep, the third kept watch at an upstairs window. Spotting the actives before they saw him, he killed three of them with a burst of sub-machine gun fire. The three surviving soldiers burst into the house, rushed up the stairs and opened fire with their portables, Elimatting two of the terrorists. The third jumped from a window and escaped. The four mini-robots and the three actives made their way back to the pickup rendezvous where a Scuttle waited to take them back to Kraken. The surviving terrorist was tracked by a second Scuttle through the deserted streets of Basra. Not fast, but incredibly manoeuvrable, the bumbling craft was never far behind its quarry, riding high and swooping low over the sleeping city. About to take shelter in a warehouse, he raised a frightened face as the Scuttle loomed over him. A positron beam flashed down from the Scuttle's belly and the terrorist was Elimatted.

Though it was only a start, the news that three terrorists had been tracked down and killed galvanised the hunt. With the deadline fast approaching, two more were located in a Moscow suburb by Russian cyber security tipped off by Techforce Ten. One was killed immediately by an armed police unit, the second escaped. The whole incident had been observed and logged by Eclipse's on board computer network.

Minutes later, Eclipse relocated the hunted terrorist in the same suburb and dropped a destroyer robot programmed with the man's facial features, voice and iris signature, bone structure and skin-prints. As he sat working at his computer, a missile no bigger than a pencil drilled a neat hole through his head.

By 10 a.m. Eastern Seaboard time, two hours before the deadline, twenty-eight cyber-terrorists had been hunted down and killed, nineteen of them Elimatted by Camelot, the rest killed by security services working on information supplied by Techforce Ten. In these operations Camelot lost seven actives and three robots.

Locating and infiltrating the "zombie" computers had been a major breakthrough. Security forces considered it unlikely that any significant number of cyber-terrorists had survived. But although the terror group's body had been severely wounded, the head was still very much alive and as long as Ronin was at large, the group remained a major threat. It was feared likely that the next strike would be the biggest one so far, involving many casualties and major damage, and even at this late hour, with the deadline fast approaching, there was no clue to where it would be.

Fifty Two

The Hand of God

AGRAVAINE BROUGHT up on screen the last message from the terror group, a message he had read a hundred times, and still could make no sense of. *You shall know what it is to shed bitter tears. And your tears will engulf you.* Again and again he repeated the sentence that intrigued and puzzled him. *Your tears will engulf you.* How could tears engulf anyone? Was it simply an exaggerated description of grief? Or was there an underlying message? Suddenly, like an exploding firework, the answer burst in his brain, and for an instant dazzled him. No, it couldn't be. And then, yes, it had to be! 'That's it!' he cried, leaping off his stool and jumping up and down. 'That's it! That's it!'

'What is?' said Tich, regarding Agravaine with concern. Had Agro lost it?

'The next target!'

'What about it?'

'Don't you see! It's a dam!'

Arthur looked blankly at Agravaine. 'How do you know that?'

'Think what would happen if they breached a big dam! I mean a real biggie.'

'It could be a catastrophe,' said Arthur.

'Their tears would engulf them,' said Mordred.

'Exactly,' said Agravaine. 'That's what Ronin is saying. Obviously he's not going to reveal the target, but he can't resist telling us how clever he is. He gives us clues because he enjoys teasing and taunting us.'

Time was running out. Assumptions had to be made. It was their only chance. 'Right,' said Arthur briskly, 'let's assume that *The Hand of God* is going to attack a dam. The question is which dam. There are dams all over the world. The target dam could be anywhere.'

'I don't think so,' said Agravaine. 'Look how the message is worded. *When two days have passed by Eastern Seaboard time we shall demonstrate our power in a way our most arrogant enemy will never forget.* Ronin specifically mentions *Eastern Seaboard time* and *our most arrogant enemy.*'

'You are right,' said Arthur. 'He's going to attack the United States.'

'It's the Hoover Dam,' said Mordred, 'it has to be.'

'Let's have the data on it,' said Arthur.

In seconds, a mass of information on the Hoover Dam was on the table monitor. The three men leaned towards the screen.

'OK,' said Agravaine, 'let me summarise . . . The Hoover Dam is one of the wonders of the modern world – 726 feet tall, 660 feet wide at the bottom and 45 feet at the top. It weighs six million tons. This would not be a 9/11, 2001 situation. A building is far easier to destroy than a massive dam. According to experts it's highly unlikely that the dam could be breached by the impact of an aircraft.'

'Experts don't always take all possibilities into account,' said Arthur. 'What if the aircraft were loaded with high explosives set to detonate on impact?'

Agravaine put the question to Techforce Ten, and moments later the answer was on screen: *Large aircraft packed with explosives would have eighty per cent chance of breaching Hoover Dam.*

'Why would anyone want to attack the Hoover dam?' asked Tich. 'I can think of two small cities that might be affected by flooding – Boulder City and Las Vegas. And they would probably be evacuated before the waters reached them,'

'Hopefully they would,' said Arthur, 'though nothing is

certain. And remember, though terrorists aim for maximum casualties, they have other objectives too. According to experts, the Hoover Dam is one of the top five targets in the West. Breaching it would not only create major disruption, it would be an enormous psychological blow to the United States, bearing in mind that it was built at the time of the Great Depression of the 1930's. For many Americans, Hoover is not just a dam, it's a symbol of triumph over adversity, of hope in the future.'

Tich was not convinced. 'Flying a plane through the canyon would be a major challenge for any pilot, however good he was. The chances are that either the canyon walls or the transmission towers and lines would tear the wings off before the plane reached the dam. Why would terrorists go for a long shot when there are plenty of easier targets?'

It was 4 p.m. Camelot time, 11 a.m. Eastern Seaboard time – one hour to the deadline.

'How else could they breach the dam?' said Arthur, all too aware that time was fast running out.

'A missile?' suggested Agravaine.

'Anything's possible of course,' said Tich, 'but it's almost unthinkable that the US military would allow one of their missile sites to be compromised a second time. They must surely have learned a lesson from the White House disaster.'

The three men considered what other options there might be. Arthur paced the dimly-lit room waving his arms and talking to himself, Mordred sat head in hands, brooding, Agravaine fiddled compulsively with tissue boxes and rows of empty plastic coffee cups, Ian Tichgame produced playing cards from his nose.

'What if a missile were launched from another country,' said Agravaine.

Arthur shook his head. 'That would be interpreted as an act of war against the US, a step too far for any country, even the most daring rogue state. It would provoke an immediate and overwhelming counter-strike.'

The three men pondered.

Tich's eyes were suddenly bulging with excitement. 'Why does the aircraft have to be piloted?

Arthur stopped in mid-pace. 'Have we overlooked something?'

'We most certainly have,' said Tich. 'Everyone knows an aircraft can be flown on automatic pilot. What most people don't know is that the automatic pilot can be remotely controlled.'

'To do what exactly?' said Arthur.

'Everything,' said Agravaine, 'including taking off and landing. Though in this case,' he added grimly, 'landing would not be on the agenda.'

'What's more,' said Tich, 'an efficient guidance system would virtually eliminate errors.'

Silence, whilst the idea was digested. 'So the aircraft would have a fair chance of navigating the canyon,' said Arthur.

'I'd say an excellent chance,' said Tich.

That changed everything, everything but the fact that it was now 4.35 p.m. Camelot time, 11.35 a.m. Eastern Seaboard time – twenty-five minutes to the deadline.

The speakers crackled; it was Lancelot from Eclipse cruising at fifty thousand feet over Tehran. 'Have located Ronin and three of his aides in an Internet café in Tehran.'

Arthur's eyes sparkled. 'Is that a hundred per cent?'

'We have matching iris and voice signatures, plus the fact that Ronin is using the same server he has used before. It's them alright.'

Arthur gave his orders. 'Tell Techforce to contact the Americans. They are to shut down Las Vegas airport and all private airstrips in the vicinity. If any aircraft tries to take off, they must shoot it down.'

In seconds Agravaine had rapped out the message to Techforce Ten. Less than a minute later, the new US President was on videolink, his craggy face duplicated on four wall monitors.

'Arthur.'

'Mr President.'

'What's this all about?'

There was no time for lengthy explanations. 'We expect an imminent attack on the Hoover Dam.'

The President managed to look sceptical and fearful at the same time. 'We can't go blowing aircraft out of the sky for no good reason.'

'There *is* good reason, sir, you will have to take my word for it. If you don't act now, there could be a major disaster.'

'And if you're wrong,' said the President, 'I could be responsible for slaughtering innocent passengers on a commercial flight.'

'We believe the cyber-terrorists intend to fly an aircraft packed with high explosives into the dam. For many reasons, that is highly unlikely to involve a commercial aircraft with passengers on board.'

'I see.' The President exchanged a few words with someone out of camera shot. 'We've declared a five hundred kilometre exclusion zone around Lake Mead. If any aircraft breaches it, we'll destroy it.' He looked at his watch. 'How long have we got?'

Arthur consulted the wall clock. 'The deadline expires in approximately six minutes.'

Someone handed the President a note. 'I'm told there are no commercial aircraft airborn in the exclusion zone,' he said.

'There could be airstrips in the area your people don't know about,' said Arthur.

'We'll keep watching.' The President hesitated. 'I'm sorry to have to tell you, Arthur, but this is all theoretical.'

Arthur frowned. 'What do you mean?'

'Three fighter aircraft took off a couple of minutes ago, but they won't get there in time. Their ETA Hoover Dam is just over ten minutes from now.

It was the worst possible news. 'What about missiles?'

'The nearest missile sites have been alerted, but it's unlikely any suspect aircraft could be targeted in the time frame we have.' The President clasped his hands. 'I can only pray to God that you are wrong.' And with that his image faded from the screens.

Mordred stared woodenly at the blank screen where the President's face had been. Tich bit his inside lip until the blood ran. Agravaine shifted tissue balls around his desk.

'What do we do now, nuncle?'

'Get me Eclipse,' said Arthur.

In seconds Lancelot's face was on screen.

'Give me an update, Lance,' said Arthur.

'Ronin and three aides are still in the Internet café.'

'What are the aides doing?'

'Chain-smoking and drinking coffee. They seem nervous.'

'And Ronin?'

'Working at his computer and talking at the same time. He's very calm and focused.'

'Can you confirm exactly what he's doing on his computer?'

'No, sir, I can only make assumptions.'

It was all any of them could do. 'Anyone else in the café?'

'No one. Just self-service machines and computers. No waiters, no other customers.'

'Stand by to Elimat' said Arthur.

Galaxy's speakers crackled to life – another Techforce report. *Americans confirm large freighter aircraft just took off from unknown airstrip near Las Vegas. Now heading east. No indication of any crew on board. Believe on auto-pilot or under remote control.*

'Distance to target?' asked Agravaine.

Twenty-five kilometres.

The three men exchanged glum looks. Arthur asked what they were all thinking: 'Estimated time of arrival Hoover Dam?'

Twelve noon East Coast time.

There was no doubt now, if ever there had been. The target was the Hoover dam. Arthur could only pray that it was indeed Ronin controlling the aircraft, and not someone else in some other location. If it was Ronin, and if he were taken out, the aircraft would hopefully be out of control and veer away from the dam.

Galaxy's wall clock told the story: three minutes to the deadline.

'Do you copy, sir?' asked Lancelot from Eclipse.

'I copy.'

'Two women just entered the café. One is at the coffee dispensing machine, the other is sitting at a computer.'

'Any indication that they are members of *The Hand of God*?'

'Negative. They're carrying plastic shopping bags. They're laughing and chattering. No contact with the four men.'

Two minutes to noon, East Coast time. It was his decision, his and his alone. If he gave the order to target the café, everyone in it, guilty and innocent, would die. He could hear Merlin's voice. *The pain of loneliness is the vengeance of the gods. It is the price you must pay.*

Lancelot again, urgency in his voice. 'Permission to Elimat, sir?'

Before Arthur could react, Techforce was on speaker. *Aircraft on course for Hoover dam, now heading into canyon.*

As Arthur eyed the clock, Techforce Ten began the countdown. *One minute to deadline . . . fifty-nine seconds . . . fifty-eight.. fifty-seven . . .*

'Three more women entering the café,' reported Lancelot, his voice agitated. 'Two carrying babies . . . '

Forty-five . . . forty-four . . . forty-three . . .

Lancelot again. 'Two more men entering café, one with a small child...What do I do?'

Arthur stared straight ahead. *Twenty-six . . . twenty-five . . . twenty-four . . .*

'Your orders, sir!' cried Lancelot.

Fifteen . . . fourteen . . . thirteen . . . twelve . . . '

Five women, two men, one child, two babies . . . ten innocents. *Collateral damage* . . . could it ever be justified? If he slaughtered innocent women and children, was he any better than the terrorists he was fighting? Had his face become the monster's face?

Ten . . . nine . . . eight . . .

The scar on his face burned.

'For God's sake, nuncle!' Agravaine's cry brought him back to his senses.

'Elimat,' said Arthur.

Seconds from the deadline, the Internet café and its occupants disappeared for ever.

Had the aircraft reached its target? For a long time the speakers were silent. And then, from Techforce: *Aircraft crashed into canyon wall. Huge explosion.*

Arthur's voice was shaking. 'Is the dam intact?' Agravaine relayed the question.

From Techforce came the answer: *Dam intact.*

It had been a great victory, and it dealt a mortal blow to one of the most dangerous terror groups ever to threaten the world. The Sword that appeared in the sky the following day confirmed what most people already suspected – that it was Arthur who, yet again, had come to the planet's rescue. No one deluded themselves that the war against terrorism was won. One thing was certain, though; the world was a safer place than it had been before.

Arthur, a hero across the globe, and also in Camelot, willed himself to experience the exhilaration of the moment. Yet even that moment was tainted by the knowledge that innocent people had died, deaths for which he took responsibility. In vain did Leo Grant try to persuade him that fate had given him no option. 'You are a man of conscience, Arthur, and for that

I have always respected you. But nothing, not even conscience, can be allowed to stop you doing what you have to do. Yes, ten innocent people died, but who knows how many lives you may have saved?'

In the weeks that followed, three more terrorists, all self-confessed members of The Hand of God, were tried; one in France, one in Spain, one in Greece. All three were found guilty of terrorist activities and sentenced to long terms of imprisonment. The democratic world welcomed the harsh sentences. Yet within six months all three had "escaped" from prison. Not one of them was ever recaptured. It was rumoured, though never proved, that some kind of deal had been made with an Islamist government.

Arthur felt betrayed. When the terrorists had licked their wounds, who could say that history would not repeat itself? Was the struggle all for nothing? He needed Merlin, now more than ever.

Fifty Three

UNABLE TO MAKE contact with Merlin, and desperate to talk to him, Arthur flew to Somerset, landing his Scuttle in a field close to Merlin's cottage. Approaching it on foot, everything seemed normal, lawns lush, flower beds pampered, the gravel path leading to the front door immaculately raked. Parked outside was a big four-wheel drive.

Opening the door Nimue showed no surprise; it was almost as if she were expecting him. She was dressed simply; jeans and a white blouse, her dark hair piled high on her head. He had forgotten how beautiful she was.

'I'm sorry to disturb you,' he said, as she stood aside to let him in.

'You are not disturbing me.'

Standing in the kitchen, Arthur was overwhelmed with childhood memories. There in the corner of the room was the crib Merlin had laid him in when Uther handed him over for adoption, a story Merlin always delighted in telling. There was Robbie's basket, where on a winter's evening, Merlin's beloved labrador would doze in front of the fire, snoring gently, opening a sleepy eye now and then to reassure himself that Merlin was still there, and to the left of the fireplace, the Windsor chair Arthur used to sit in when he was a lad, listening enthralled to the Magus talking about everything in the world and out of it.

'Is Merlin in?'

'No.' She was looking everywhere but at him.

'Where is he?'

A shrug. 'I don't know. I got up one morning and he was gone.'

'When did this happen?'

Her eyes were wary. 'A few days ago.'

'May I look in his computer? There might be a clue.'

'Of course.'

Merlin's computer had been wiped clean. There was nothing on the hard drive, not even an address.

'Did you find what you wanted?' she asked, as he came down the stairs.

'No.'

She was tense, though still very much in control of herself. 'I'll be off home,' she said.

Where was home, he wondered. No point in asking; she would certainly avoid the question, or lie.

'What happened?'

'We'd been quarrelling,' she said, looking away. 'He walked out, that's all. Said he never wanted to see me again.' She fiddled with the strap of a soft bag lying on the table. 'He kept on about losing his powers. I think he blamed me for that.' She opened the front door, the bag over her shoulder. 'My stuff's in the car,' she said. 'I'll say goodbye, then.'

'Tell me the truth, Nimue. What really happened?'

She stood in the doorway with her back to him. 'I'm afraid . . . ' she muttered.

'Of what?'

'I'm afraid he may have killed himself,' she said, and closed the door quietly behind her. He heard the car start up and drive off. The sound of the engine faded to nothing. It made no sense. Merlin would never kill himself.

He went upstairs again, drifting aimlessly into a bedroom, a bathroom, a small library/sitting room – looking for anything that might offer a clue to Merlin's mysterious disappearance. Finding nothing, he returned to his office, checked the computer again – empty, suspiciously empty – and scoured every drawer and shelf for any software lying about. Nothing. No ornaments, not even a photo – no, wait a minute, there was one – a framed photo of Arthur on a beach, one he did not recall having seen before. And in the bottom left-hand corner an inscription in Merlin's handwriting: *From Merlin to Arthur*. Odd. Merlin was no photographer; he could not remember him ever owning a camera. There was that time on the beach years ago when Nimue had summoned him, and he had pretended to take a picture of Arthur. But he hadn't taken one, had he? There was no camera in his hand. Carefully, Arthur removed the photograph from its frame and examined it closely. The image was computer generated, and there was something odd about the feel of it, it didn't flex like photographic paper. Making an incision in the top edge, he turned the photo upside down and shook it. There, in the palm of his hand, was a paper thin disc.

In seconds, Merlin's face was on the computer screen, and the Magus was talking to him.

Remember now? The photograph on the beach, the photo I never took? A beam of triumph. I knew you'd find it.

Arthur's heart jumped in his chest, it was all so typically Merlin.

To prepare Camelot for you, Art, I needed a vast fortune. Problem was, I didn't have a bean to my name. I took various jobs involving cutting-edge science until finally I became the British Government's number one scientist and inventor of weapons and technology. Perfect cover for me. That was when I started hacking into the bank accounts of the wealthiest and most powerful drug baron in the world. Dionysus, he called himself. I never discovered his real name.

Over a relatively short period of time I relieved him of nearly a hundred billion dollars. As you can imagine Dionysus very soon discovered that his hoard of money was rapidly depleting, and tried to protect himself by shifting it round the world. But every time he did, he left a trail, and it wasn't long before I had traced the new accounts. With this money, and with the help of a few trusted men and women who shared my concern about where the world was heading, I set about experimenting with weapons and technology. When I bought the island of Camelot, I had already developed a prototype of Excalibur, the ultimate weapon and power source, and also of Eclipse and Kraken, Scuttles and Nimbles. Oh, I had twinges of conscience about using dirty money, but I consoled myself – and still do – with the thought that a bad thing can be used for a good purpose.

Unfortunately even Merlin makes mistakes. One day when I was tired, I left a 'calling card', a code that in the hands of a cyber expert would give away my location. I realised almost immediately what I had done and tried to cover my tracks. Too late. A few weeks later Nimue appeared. I suspected her from the start, of course. But she was bright, very bright, and a challenge to my intellect. She was also very beautiful. Despite myself, I fell in love with her, an experience entirely new to me and incredibly exciting. One day, I knew, she would rob me of my powers, one day she would be my nemesis. But because I loved her, I was unable to resist her. Oh, I know what you are thinking, Arthur. You warned me about Nimue. But then I warned you about Guinevere. And we were both helpless, weren't we?

If only Merlin were here in the flesh instead of a talking head on a computer screen. If only Virgil were there, sitting on Arthur's shoulder, hoo-hooing a greeting, nibbling his ear lobe. If only . . . He felt a stab of fear in his stomach, a premonition of disaster.

I was so in love, Art, that I agreed to reveal my secrets to her. She told me she loved me, and wanted to be part of my life for ever. To do that, she said, she needed to share my power.

And I believed her. I believed she had renounced the world she came from, and I believed she loved me. I convinced myself that she would never betray me. It was folly, of course, and I was deluding myself. I shut my eyes, Arthur, not wanting to see what was so obviously there. But then, Art, you of all people will understand how we allow ourselves to be betrayed by the ones we love most.

Merlin's words hit home, as no doubt they were intended to. At the same time, he had never felt closer to the Magus.

Soon, she was almost as powerful as I was, and it was too late to do anything about it, even if I had wanted to, which I didn't. But believe me, Arthur, I never revealed the secrets of Camelot. She tried to make me but she never succeeded. The other day I caught her at her computer talking to Dionysus, and to my horror, I learned he was her father. I believe that one day he will come for me and try to extract the secret of Excalibur. He will not succeed, I promise you. And in return, you must promise me that nothing – nothing, Arthur – will divert you from your great mission. Goodbye, my dear friend. I love you.

His heart beating fast, he played the disc a second and a third time, hoping that Merlin had left some clue to whatever had happened to him. But he had not. His disappearance remained a mystery. Had he run away and hidden? Or had Dionysus or his men taken him away? Even more of a mystery; why had he done nothing to protect himself, when surely he could have? How could he have allowed his love for Nimue to blind him? How could wise Merlin have been so stupid?

Waiting until nightfall, he flew to Tintagel, where, as a teenager, he had pulled the Sword from the Stone. Something told him that the secret of Merlin's disappearance lay there.

Landing the Scuttle by the ruins of the ancient castle, he

walked across the headland heights to the sculpture of The Sword in the Stone. It was a clear, bright night. The stars and the crescent moon softened the harsh landscape. Far below, was the sea, the crests of the Atlantic waves flecked with silver. Sitting on the plinth of the sculpture, he dreamed the years away, remembering how he had angered Keir and astonished Hector by pulling the Sword from the Stone. That had changed everything. Until that fateful day he had managed to convince himself that he was a boy like other boys. What happened then compelled him to acknowledge that he was different, that indeed, as Merlin told him, he had a special destiny. It was a heavy burden he had shouldered, a burden that had grown heavier with the years.

On the dark side of the headland, he made his way down the steep path that led to the beach and the entrance to Merlin's cave. It was not there. Was his memory playing tricks? Was Merlin? He walked up and down the beach in case he had mistaken the spot. No, there was no other entrance. He walked back again. This was where it used to be and should be still. Then he realised what had happened. The entrance to the cave was blocked by a huge boulder. Drawing his portable he fired at the boulder, Dematting it, and the entrance to Merlin's cave was revealed.

In the darkness he advanced cautiously. Every few seconds the incoming sea launched itself against the cave's outer walls, bursting through fissures and gullies in the rock, and streaming out again as the tide retreated. Softly he called, 'Merlin!' There was no response, only the echoes of his voice . . . *Merlin! Merlin!* An eerie, melancholy sound. Again he called, and again the echoes rebounded . . . *Merlin! Merlin!* as though they were mocking him.

Using his miniature power pack, he lit the cave. In the far corner, under an overhang of rock, lay Merlin's naked body, arms folded across his chest. Arthur experienced pain and shock such as he had never known before. Falling to his knees, he reached out and touched Merlin's face. The skin was translucent, the flesh cold and hard. Blinking away his tears, he saw to his horror that the bones of Merlin's feet and hands had been broken, finger and toe nails torn out. Laying his head on the Magus's chest he wept. 'Merlin, what have they done to you?'

After a minute or two he sat up, wiped his tear-stained face with his sleeve and looked again at the face of the Magus. It was astonishing. Merlin had been tortured, yet his magical green eyes were untroubled, their expression serene. What was it he had said in his last message? *I shut my eyes, Arthur, not wanting to see what was so obviously there.* No, that wasn't true. Merlin's eyes were always open, he had known exactly what was happening to him, and he was not afraid. Tenderly he closed the lids.

Where to bury him? Where to lay him to rest? Should he not take him back to Camelot, his creation, and bury him there with all the honour and love that his noble heart and mind deserved? It would be as much for his own sake as for Merlin's. For if he did not see Merlin buried, flesh and blood and bone, he would never believe that the Magus had died. For a few more minutes he remained in the cave debating the question before making up his mind. This was Merlin's cave. Some men said that this was where he was born. Certainly it was where he had died. Perhaps this was where he would one day rise up and be himself again.

After recording some images of Merlin's body, he switched off the power pack and stood for a minute or two in the darkness. The evidence of his senses told him that Merlin was dead, and yet he could have sworn that the Magus was watching him with those great green orbs of his. Merlin had taught him to believe in God, not the exclusive God men worshipped in church or synagogue or mosque, but the God who was in all things, in the stars, in the sun and the moon, in the wind and the rain, in trees and rivers, lakes and mountains, in birds and animals – in all

His creations. That God would never let Merlin die. But then his spirits, momentarily revived, sank again. He was deceiving himself. Merlin was dead. He would never see him again.

'Goodbye, old friend,' he said. Outside the cave he drew his portable and Rematted the boulder, sealing the entrance behind him.

Climbing, without knowing or caring where his legs were taking him, he staggered onto the summit of the headland, collapsed on the grass by The Sword in the Stone, and fell into a dreamless sleep. All that night he slept, waking with the dawn. When he opened his eyes the rising sun was turning the sky and ocean red. For a few seconds he forgot where he was, then with a sharp pang of despair he remembered. Down there was Merlin's cave where Merlin's tortured body lay. Nothing would ever be the same again.

Now, for the first time in his life, he was truly angry. Not for a single moment would he rest until he found Merlin's killers and punished them. In his mind the Magus's broken body was a symbol of the millions of addicted men, women and children whose lives had been ruined by drugs. There would be a reckoning for all those lost souls, those deranged minds and broken bodies, a reckoning for those who died, and for those who lived in torment.

And a reckoning for Merlin too.

Fifty Four

Mainline

THE FOUR DOUBLE DOORS clanged shut, the Guardian robots announced *Doors shut and secured,* and the Round Table was in session.

Members observed without comment that in front of Arthur lay the ceremonial sword, Excalibur. Already rumours had raced across the island, and the solemn faces around the table confirmed what everyone knew: this was the most important meeting in the history of the Round Table.

On four big wall screens Merlin's final message was projected alongside images of his tortured body lying in the cave at Tintagel. In the shocked silence, Arthur spoke.

'I have summoned you so that we can agree a course of action. My proposal is that we launch an attack not just on Dionysus and his drug empire, but on all major drug producers, transporters and dealers, whose activities threaten this, and all future generations. Our objective will be to wipe out the illegal drug trade – crops, production and distribution centres, the drug producers themselves, their weapons, their militias and major transportation facilities on land, sea and in the air. If we succeed, and I believe we shall, the message will go out to the world that drug dealing will no longer be tolerated. The code name for the party will be *Mainline.*'

There was a sharp intake of breath in the Great Hall. No one had been expecting anything quite as uncompromising as this, especially not from Arthur, still considered a dove by many.

Lancelot raised a hand. 'What you propose, sir, is a huge operation, our biggest yet. In my opinion we cannot afford half-measures. To have any chance of success, we need to commit all our resources.'

'I agree,' said Arthur. '*Operation Mainline* will involve Eclipse, Kraken, Nimbles, Scuttles, most of our actives and robots . . . and, of course, Excalibur.'

'Then I am in favour of it,' said Lancelot. The Commander-in-Chief's backing virtually assured Arthur of the support of the hawks at the Round Table. The doves, however, were not so easily convinced – amongst them, on this occasion, George Bedivere, normally hawkish, and one of Arthur's most loyal supporters. 'If we attack the drug barons on the scale you propose, many innocent people will die.'

'We shall do everything in our power,' Arthur assured him, 'to avoid killing innocent people. I admit, though, that in an operation of this scale, accidents can happen.'

'I am the last person to preach,' said George, 'but clearly there is an issue of morality here.'

'There is also the risk,' said Leo Grant, 'that so many people in so many different countries will be adversely affected that the world could turn against us.'

'There are risks, I agree,' acknowledged Arthur, 'but think, George, think Leo, think how many innocents will die if we do nothing. According to the World Health Organisation's latest statistics there are now at least two hundred million registered drug addicts in the world. The actual number is undoubtedly a multiple of that figure. Some estimates put it as high as one or two billion, and increasing even as I speak. Where will it end? When every man, woman and child in the world is an addict!'

Taking his time, Arthur looked slowly up and down the table. 'The human cost in terms of physical and mental suffering is incalculable. All efforts to deal with this enormous problem have so far failed. The drug trade is by far the biggest business in the world. There is so much money in it that across the globe thousands of politicians and businessmen, accountants and lawyers, drug enforcement officers and police are on the drug barons' payroll. What's more, Command Control and many security services have indisputable evidence that the drug barons finance worldwide terrorism. In summary, ladies and gentlemen, I am convinced that we have a moral duty to eliminate the drug trade, and if we succeed, that it may well be our greatest gift to mankind.'

There was no doubt that Arthur's powerful words had impressed the Round Table. 'Are you not afraid,' said Gawain, 'that any drug producers who survive will simply use their wealth to start up production again?'

'That could certainly happen,' said Arthur, 'if we allowed them to keep the rewards of their crimes. But we shall not. Command Control, Neural Network and Techforce Ten are already working to trace their bank accounts, wherever in the world they may be. That work did not start today, it has been going on for years. You will remember that three years ago we set up DTSG – the Drug Trade Surveillance Group – to infiltrate drug networks and steal their access codes. Their work is done. So not only are we confident we can destroy the drug barons, we believe we can also relieve them of most of their money.'

Galahad's colour alternated swiftly between deep red and pasty white. Clearly he had something to say, but was too shy to put up his hand. 'Speak up, Galahad,' said Arthur, 'you are among friends.'

'It is against God's law to kill,' said Galahad as Lancelot scowled at his son. Some in the Great Hall laughed openly at Galahad's naivety.

'I respect your beliefs, Galahad,' said Arthur, 'but in this case, I believe the end justifies the means.'

Galahad refused to back down. 'The use of force can never be justified, even against drug barons. Wicked men must be given the chance to walk the paths of righteousness. We must show them mercy, even as we ask God to be merciful to us.'

'We will show mercy wherever possible,' said Arthur. 'Those we take prisoner will be tried in a court of law, and given the chance to defend themselves.'

'God is the Judge of all things,' said Galahad. 'He has taught us that only through peace and goodwill can the kingdom of heaven be established on earth.'

'If that is what you believe,' demanded Gawain, 'what are you doing in Camelot?'

Many members nodded their agreement. Thumbing through his bible, Galahad seemed to be searching for the right text to support his argument, but then, sensing that the Round Table was against him, he snapped it shut, jumped up, and hurried out of the Great Hall. The hum of conversation quickly died as Lancelot raised his hand. His was a vital question, one asked before every operation.

'In what mode do we use Excalibur?'

'Elimat,' replied Arthur without hesitation. Coming from him, it was a surprising choice. Elimat mode was rarely resorted to, and its use had to be sanctioned by a majority of the Round Table. Not everyone agreed with him – Mordred for one. Diffidently, he raised his hand.

'Sir,' he said, 'will you forgive me if I speak my mind?'

'That is your right,' said Arthur, 'as a member of the Round Table. And as my son,' he added, smiling.

'Nevertheless,' said Mordred, 'it embarrasses me to express any opinion which differs from yours, knowing as I do how much I owe you.' Raising his voice and his arms to include every member of the Round Table, he added, 'how much we all owe you.'

Arthur inclined his head in acknowledgment.

Mordred went on to develop his theme. 'Since I arrived in Camelot, hardly a day has passed, sir, when I did not have cause to praise your infallible instinct for making the right decision.' Resting his hands on the table he leaned towards his father. 'Until today,' he said.

Not a member stirred. The silence had an edge to it.

'Forgive me, father,' continued Mordred, 'but it seems to me that you are allowing your very understandable anger to affect your judgement.'

The Round Table held its collective breath.

'You say we have a moral duty to eliminate the drug trade,' said Mordred. 'But with the greatest respect to you, sir, I suggest that *Operation Mainline* is not about morality at all.' The expression in his dark eyes was intense, challenging Arthur.

'What is it about, then?' said Arthur.

Mordred looked up and down the table, reassuring himself that he had the full attention of every member. 'It is about the need to avenge yourself on Merlin's killers.'

Whispered comments and astonished looks greeted these words. It was, moreover, clear from Arthur's face that Mordred's words had struck home.

It was the first time he had challenged his father at the Round Table, something he had longed to do from the day he arrived in Camelot. Exultant, he was also overawed at his own daring. His heart pounded, the palms of his hands were damp. 'Even if I am wrong,' he continued, 'and *Operation Mainline* is truly about morality, is it really the business of Camelot to make moral judgements? I don't think so. In my humble opinion, our business is to fight terrorists, not drug barons.' With that he sat down, his outward appearance calm, his mind in turmoil.

When members had recovered from their initial shock at Mordred's dramatic intervention, the debate, lively before, became even more spirited. As so often, it was a battle between doves and hawks. But when everyone had had their say, the Round Table voted overwhelmingly to approve *Operation Mainline*, and also, though by a smaller margin, the use of Elimat.

An hour later, Leo Grant visited Arthur in his observatory. 'I have never disagreed with you on any significant issue.'

'But you do now.'

'Yes.'

'Why didn't you say so at the Round Table?'

Leo's eyes softened. 'You are my son-in-law and my dearest friend. I have never openly opposed you, and I never shall.'

'Thank you for your loyalty.'

'This *Mainline* business is not well thought out,' said Leo. 'It will be costly in terms of lives, and it won't succeed. As long as people are stupid enough or weak enough to take drugs, there will be drug producers and drug dealers.'

'So there's nothing to be done? Is that what you are saying?'

'I'm saying this is not a job for Camelot. You and I have considered taking action against the drug barons at least a dozen times over the years, and we have always rejected the idea. What has changed?'

'Nothing,' said Arthur, 'except that the time has come to deal with them.'

'No, Arthur, be honest with yourself. What has changed is that Dionysus murdered Merlin. I hate to say so, but Mordred is right. As our leader, you have never allowed your heart to rule your head. You are doing so now. *Operation Mainline* is more about revenge than eliminating the drug trade.'

In his heart of hearts Arthur knew there was truth in what Leo was saying. Even so he was determined to go ahead. 'Nothing is impossible,' he said, 'if you really believe it can be done. Merlin taught me that.'

'Before you do anything,' said Leo, 'I urge you to consult world leaders. If you could convince the drug barons that the world is united against them, you might persuade them to do a deal.'

'What kind of deal?'

'I don't know – limit production, increase prices. Something that would at least reduce the flow of drugs.'

Arthur was unshakeable. 'It's too late, Leo. I've been there before. A united world? A fantasy, I'm afraid. The world is not united, and never will be. Its leaders are too weak or too self-serving or too corrupt to do what they should be doing; bringing peace and prosperity to the people they claim to represent.'

At the door Leo paused. 'So far you have charted a brilliant course, Arthur. You have never known failure. But now . . . ?' The panel acknowledged Leo's identity, the door clicked open. 'I fear for you. I fear for all of us.'

Fifty Five

Mainline

NEURAL NETWORK screened the files of information stored in data banks over the last few years before passing it to Techforce Ten and Command Control. In Galaxy, Agravaine sat with Arthur, Tich and Mordred, studying closely the data assembling on the big central monitor. As they watched, orbiting satellites, low-flying miniature unmanned air vehicles and surveillance land robots carrying micro-devices and sensors, pinpointed the world's main illegal drug producing facilities, crop-growing areas, distribution centres, refining factories, supply routes and warehouses. Scrolling down the wall screens were the names of every major drug baron and dealer in the world, their current, or last known location, the whereabouts and strength of their militias, and the exact position of their aircraft, helicopters, and ships. By late afternoon sufficient data had been accumulated and analysed, checked and cross-checked, to warrant the launching of Camelot's air, sea and land forces.

Arthur's words were relayed to all commanders: '*Operation Mainline* is under way. Good hunting and good luck to all of you.' It was to be the biggest party ever launched by Camelot. Eclipse, with Lancelot at the controls, rose from the launch pad, and from its underwater pen the dark, whale-like shape of Kraken, captained by Gawain, slipped silently into the grey Atlantic ocean.

The targets selected by Techforce were in twenty-seven countries on several continents – Afghanistan, the Bahamas, Bolivia, Brazil, Burma, China, Colombia, the Dominican

Republic, Ecuador, Ghana, Guatemala, Guinea Bissau, Haiti, India, Jamaica, Laos, Mauritania, Mexico, Nigeria, Pakistan, Panama, Paraguay, Peru, Senegal, Sierra Leone, Venezuela and Vietnam. The first indication that something extraordinary was happening was when, across the globe, major television networks were shut down and phone communications cut, the main purpose being to create confusion amongst major drug producers and dealers, but also to discourage any intervention by government agencies, friendly or otherwise.

Soon after sunrise, East Coast time, it was reported that in the Atlantic, Pacific and Indian oceans, in the Caribbean, the English Channel and the Mediterranean Sea, a number of cargo ships, sailing boats and motor launches were either blown apart or had simply disappeared. Not only ships at sea, but hundreds of cars, trucks and private, commercial and military aircraft, vanished into thin air. All had been positively identified by Techforce Ten as belonging to, or collaborating with, drug producers, and sensors had established that all were carrying a substantial quantity of drugs. Some were destroyed by Nimbles piloted by robo-pilots, some by Scuttles dropped by Eclipse or Sea Scuttles launched by Kraken, others by missiles fired by land-based destroyer robots.

Later that same morning, attacks were reported in all twenty-nine countries on nearly two hundred farms and private houses known to belong to major drug producers, on militias controlled by them, and on factories and warehouses. Some installations were destroyed by missiles descending mysteriously from the sky, most inexplicably vanished, neither they nor the people inside them ever to be seen again. In at least five countries Camelot's actives raided and destroyed military airfields and army camps, in the process killing a number of high-ranking officers known to be in the pay of drug barons.

Aware that many countries might panic and attribute these extraordinary events to a terrorist attack, Arthur appeared on TV networks around the world to explain what was happening, urging people to remain calm and patient for the next few days. At the same time he made it clear that no interference would be tolerated; anyone who tried to oppose Camelot's armed forces, or assist the drug barons or their allies, would be treated as the enemy.

In key production areas, Scuttles unloaded troops of Camelot's actives armed with portables in Elimat mode and also conventional weapons: bombs, grenades, hand-held missile launchers and automatic weapons. Bunkers, command posts, farms, warehouses and small factories that had escaped the attention of Eclipse and Kraken were destroyed. Anyone who resisted was Elimatted. Once they had completed their task, they swiftly withdrew to be evacuated by Scuttles.

Across the world the story was the same; drug producers, dealers and mafia bosses, all those whose businesses and activities were linked to drug money, were relentlessly hunted down and targeted. Those few fortunate enough to surrender were spirited away. Most were killed.

At 2 p.m. Camelot time on the second day, an enraged US President appeared on Galaxy's largest wall screen, patched in by Techforce Ten via the gravitational link. 'What in the name of fuck is going on!' he demanded, the veins on his forehead bulging, his colour dangerously high.

Arthur had no intention of allowing the President to bully him. '*Operation Mainline* is going on,' he responded coolly. The President's voice made an instant octave's leap to a manic shriek. 'Call it off, or by Christ, I swear I'll – I'll . . . ' His voice tailed off, as he lost confidence in what he had in mind to say. A relatively brief association with Arthur had taught him one thing; Camelot's leader was not impressed by threats. 'What the hell do you think you're doing?' he ended lamely.

'Dealing a mortal blow to the illegal drug trade,' said Arthur.

'And in the process destroying half the goddam world!'

'We are taking out drug barons, mafia drug bosses, militias, crops, drug producing and distribution centres, and, wherever possible, their means of transport,' said Arthur coolly. 'Nothing else, as far as I know.'

'Then you don't know much,' snapped the President, his mouth pursing waspishly. 'Your storm troopers are destroying thousands of crops, most of them grown by innocent farmers.'

'Farmers who grow plants for drug addicts. Farmers who destroy lives for money. How innocent is that?'

The President took a deep breath. 'Listen to me, Arthur. You will never destroy the illegal drug trade by force of arms. I know what you're trying to do, but you're going about it the wrong way. Take a tip from the USA. If we interfere in other countries' affairs, at least we try to do it diplomatically.'

'Like in Iraq and Afghanistan, you mean?'

It was a low blow. The US President bit his lip. 'I'll overlook that comment, Arthur. You and I both know the world has changed in the last three decades. And the United States of America has changed with it.'

'You certainly have,' said Arthur, 'you've gone soft on terrorists and drug barons.'

There was no one the President admired more than Arthur, nor anyone who infuriated him more. He slapped his right fist into the palm of his left hand, wishing it were Arthur's face. 'Listen to me, you stubborn bastard, force won't work.'

'What will, then?'

'Negotiation and more negotiation, talking to governments, doing trade deals with them, lending them money, encouraging them to clamp down on farmers and drug producers. We call it creative engagement.'

'Creative engagement.' Arthur smiled. 'One of those placebo phrases coined by diplomats. It sounds good, but what it really amounts to is turning a blind eye. The illegal drug trade is doubling every year, and that means more dealers, more drugs, more addicts, more deaths, more children's lives ruined.'

'Rome wasn't built in a day,' said the President. 'God knows, we can only keep trying. And believe me, we're getting there.

357

Let us get on with it. Call off your dogs, Arthur.'

'I will – when *Operation Mainline* has achieved its objectives.'

Though the President would have liked to slice Arthur up into small, bloody pieces, he knew that his only hope was to stay calm and convince him by rational argument. 'Do you truly believe that rampaging round the world killing people will change anything?'

Arthur gave an honest answer. 'I don't know. But there's one thing I do know – making shabby deals with drug barons and terrorists is not the solution. Camelot is fighting for the future of the world. Drugs are the greatest scourge mankind has ever faced. They destroy more lives than wars do. We have to act before it's too late.'

The President sighed the sigh of a defeated man. 'I'm getting reports from the FBI that some of our top Mafia bosses have disappeared,' he said.

Arthur looked innocent. 'Really?'

'Yes, really.' The President chose his words carefully. 'Here's what I'm saying, Arthur. We Americans like to take care of our own problems. We'll stay away from *Mainline*. You stay away from the United States. Agreed?'

Arthur considered the proposal; he did not like it, but if that was the price he had to pay for the USA's neutrality, then so be it.

'Agreed.'

Long after the US President's image faded from Galaxy's wall screen, Arthur was still wondering if he had not just concluded one of those shabby deals he had accused the President of making.

In conjunction with *Operation Mainline,* Camelot launched *Operation Detox* to relieve the drug barons of the wealth they had secreted in bank accounts throughout the world. Ian Tichgame in NIWIS, and Agravaine in Command Control, were in joint command of the money heist. Working in four hour shifts, teams of electronic gurus and house wizards conducted an intensive search for drug money, wherever in the world it might be, intercepting inter-bank messages and remittance instructions, "freaking" phone networks, zapping vital links and breaking into the electronic transfer systems of international banks by using security codes harvested from electronic and mobile communications.

By the fourth day of *Operation Detox* virtually the whole of the drug barons' software had been disabled, and Techforce Ten and NIWIS had used their knowledge of the codes in their possession to break into thousands of bank accounts and transfer billions of dollars, euros and pounds to secret accounts set up to receive them. From these accounts the funds orbited cyberspace, being diverted and rediverted from one account to another in a series of complex transactions, until the gurus and wizards were satisfied that it would take months, if not years, to track them down.

Reacting in panic, producers, distributors, transporters – all those involved in the international drug trade – rushed to their computers to check the status of their accounts, spewing out thousands of messages instructing bankers and bag men to shift funds from one account to another. To their horror, their computers refused to accept their commands. Phone links had either crashed or were crippled by "glitches", radio signals were blocked and electronic communications compromised. It was a unique and frightening experience for the drug barons who had lost control of their empires, their lives, and, most terrifying of all, their money. In their frustration they turned on business associates, competitors, hirelings, anyone near enough to be a target, accusing them of treachery. Many drug barons and farmers died in the bloodbath, some slaughtered by their own friends and family.

A few account holders succeeded in accessing their codes and transferring their money to new accounts seconds before Techforce Ten could lay hands on it. In at least two instances the new account numbers and access codes were extracted at gunpoint by actives in the field who forced the captured drug barons to reveal them. The great majority of account holders were unable to access their accounts for days, only to discover when finally they did, that their accounts were at zero, and that on their computer screens was an all too familiar image: a hand drawing a sword from a stone.

The panic of the banks whose protective barriers had been breached, was, if anything, greater than that of the drug barons. For them too, *Operation Detox* was a disaster. Despite their technical expertise, vast experience and great power, even the world's biggest international banks were unable to protect either themselves or their criminal clients. Having for years prospered from either knowingly or irresponsibly flouting the law, they were now faced with exposure and prosecution.

By the fourth day, Camelot's actives led by senior officers, had dealt with the drug barons and the militias whose task was to protect them. Eleven drug barons were taken alive, the rest were killed. All resistance had now ended. From Eclipse, Lancelot reported that amongst those captured was the most powerful drug baron of them all.

Arthur's heart missed a beat. 'Dionysus? The big man himself?'

'There's no doubt about it. We cross-checked his iris and voice signature with MI6 and the CIA. They're a perfect match.'

Arthur was satisfied. 'Our objectives have been achieved.' He ordered Camelot's armed forces to return to base. It was all over.

Within a few hours, Dionysus and his fellow surviving drug barons – Rematted and Dematted to Camelot via Scuttles, Eclipse and Kraken – were isolated in secure areas set aside for such a contingency. For days experts interrogated them, but since Camelot's code forbade the use of torture, little new information was obtained.

The next day the Round Table committed the prisoners for trial by the High Council.

Arthur visited Dionysus in his cell.

'I am Arthur.'

Dionysus was short, chubby and bespectacled; he looked more like a prosperous banker or a lawyer than one of the world's most notorious drug barons. 'I know who you are.' Dionysus spoke softly, with not a hint of resentment or aggression.

Apart from a bed and two stools, there was no furniture in the tiny room. Dionysus sat on one, Arthur faced him on the other. Dionysus broke the silence. 'An astonishingly successful operation,' he said, managing to look genuinely impressed. '*Operation Mainline*, I believe you called it.' His accented English was perfect. 'I congratulate you, Arthur.'

Familiar with the psychological games played by captured prisoners, Arthur was resolved to remain uninvolved and objective. He could not help noticing how white and even the man's teeth were, presumably the result of regular expensive dental makeovers; nothing but the best for the king of drug producers.

'It was all most impressive, although I'm afraid it's not going to achieve anything,' said Dionysus. 'Let me tell you why,' he added gently, as if he were explaining a simple equation to a child. 'You can destroy our fields and our drugs, you can destroy our warehouses, our transport, our networks, and yes, you can destroy us too. But there is one thing not even you can destroy.'

'And what is that?'

'The demand for drugs,' said Dionysus. 'There are people out there who need recreational drugs, need them like they need food or drink – or sex for that matter.' He spread his hands and shrugged apologetically, as though he were sharing with Arthur his distress at man's frailty. 'Personally I don't do drugs. Only fools do.' An indulgent smile. 'Fortunately there will always be plenty of those in the world.'

Arthur fought to control his anger. 'Does it mean nothing to you that there are billions of suffering men, women and children, all of them addicts because of you, and people like you?'

'You are mistaken,' said Dionysus, his eyes untroubled, his voice calm and reasonable, 'I don't turn people into addicts. They do it themselves. Do I force them to do drugs? Do I conceal drugs in their food? Do I bake cakes with drugs? Do I make soup with them? Do I stick needles in their arms? Do I lay lines of coke on their desks and toilet seats? No, Arthur, all I do is satisfy a demand. I'm a businessman. You may not like my business. Billions do.'

'You admit that you or your hit men murdered Merlin?'

A sharp look. 'Is that what *Operation Mainline* was about?'

Arthur ignored the jibe. 'Did you?'

'No, I did not.'

He was certain the man was lying, but he said nothing. What was there to say?

'What will happen to me?' asked Dionysus, a hint of anxiety in his voice.

'That is up to the High Council.'

'You dare not have me killed.'

'Dare not!'

'I have friends in high places,' said Dionysus, a hard edge to his voice, 'world leaders, men more powerful even than you. They will not allow you to harm me.'

'Why not?'

'Because, Arthur, I am much more useful to them alive than dead.'

Arthur stood, carefully replacing the stool where he had found it by the cell wall.

'Goodbye,' he said.

Dionysus followed him to the door. 'Let me go, and I'll give you anything you ask.' He grabbed his arm. 'I can make you wealthier than any man has ever been in the history of the world. I can give you millions. No? Billions! Still no? What about hundreds of billions? Don't tell me you wouldn't like to be the richest, most powerful man on earth. Think what you could do with all that money!'

Arthur knocked for the robot guard to open the cell door.

Shaking with fear, his mask of indifference dropped, Dionysus was babbling now. 'There are drug producers you haven't touched yet. I know who they are. I know where they are. I'll turn them in. I'll kill them myself if you ask me to, just give me the word. Listen to me, Arthur. In the name of Jesus, listen to me.' As the door opened, and the guard stood back to allow Arthur to leave, Dionysus screamed, 'What is it you want?'

'I want justice,' said Arthur. The cell door clanged shut behind him.

Dionysus's eyelids twitched uncontrollably, his body shook; first his arms and hands, then his legs. Lying on his bed he stared at the ceiling. Fear. He had seen it in the eyes of many men, men he had tortured, men he had killed. And though he had taken pleasure in their suffering, it had frustrated him too, not understanding fear, not knowing how it felt. Now, for the first time in his life, he knew.

By the morning of the sixth day, Camelot had accumulated over two hundred billion dollars of the drug barons' money in various accounts across the world. Agravaine was ecstatic, his eyes shining, his hands never still. Since the murder of his mother and Adrian Pellinore he had been aware of a certain reserve in his uncle's manner. Though Arthur had no proof, he clearly had suspicions. Agravaine hero-worshipped his uncle, lived for his praise. Now, he told himself, he would be his favourite nephew again. It was Tich and Mordred who dashed his hopes by telling him that substantial funds were still in the hands of the drug barons, most of the money controlled by one man: Dionysus.

'How can that be? It's not possible.' They had to be mistaken.

But they were not. Guiding Agravaine along devious cyber routes, Tich, aided by Mordred, uncovered the evidence. A number of large money transfers laid a trail that led finally to a series of firmly locked "doors" which, without passwords, could not be opened. It was now apparent that in the first hour of *Operation Detox* more than a hundred billion dollars had vanished via a complex network of transactions. The only clue to its whereabouts was a message decoded by Tich confirming that nine billion dollars had been entrusted to Dionysus by another drug baron.

Agravaine was puzzled. 'Why would he do that?'

Mordred explained. 'The man who remitted these funds to Dionysus was trapped by a troop of actives. Knowing that he and his men would be captured, he assumed they would be tortured, torture being routine in his world, and that either he or one of his lieutenants would be forced to reveal the details of his secret bank accounts. Like all drug barons in Colombia he owes allegiance to Dionysus who has always boasted he is too powerful and too well-connected ever to be killed, or indeed captured.

'So this hundred billion . . . '

'Is partly Dionysus's money, partly money belonging to drug producers who transferred their cash to him for safekeeping.'

Agravaine was devastated. He decided to pay Dionysus a visit.

An hour later, Agravaine, Tich and Mordred, working with Techforce, tracked down more than twenty substantial money transfers, arriving once again at the locked doors, this time, though, with the passwords to open them. One by one they gained entry to ten accounts that led them to another twenty, then to another thirty, and so on and on through a labyrinthine interweaving of accounts to the last door, and when that was opened, they found inside, not a hundred billion dollars, but over two hundred billion. In minutes the account was at zero, the funds wired through an intricate web of transfers to safe Camelot accounts.

That done, the three men danced round Galaxy congratulating each other – and especially Agravaine – on their brilliant success. It was the happiest day of his life. How proud of him Arthur would be!

Fifty Six

Mainline

THE HIGH COUNCIL found all eleven drug barons guilty of crimes against humanity; the production, distribution and sale of banned substances, murder, kidnap, torture, extortion and blackmail. Sentencing was to take place the following day.

Once the news was released, Arthur came under increasing pressure from world leaders, especially the US President, who had his own reasons for not wanting the drug barons to be executed; above all Dionysus.

Arthur found his arguments less than convincing. 'Whatever you believe, Mr. President, Camelot's High Council is an independent judicial body made up of highly experienced judges. Their decision will not be influenced by me or by anyone else.'

'I'm goddam certain,' said the President, 'that they'll be handing down the death penalty.' And when Arthur did not reply. 'Am I right?'

'No comment.'

'Look here, Arthur,' said the President, 'I'll do you a deal. Give me Dionysus. You can keep the rest. That's fair enough, isn't it? There's no hurry. You can ship him over here in a few months when the heat's off.'

'Why would I do that?'

'Why?' A few seconds pause whilst the President searched for an answer. 'So the world can see how justice works in the most powerful democracy on earth,' he said, hoping it sounded more convincing to Arthur than it did to him. 'And to demonstrate our commitment to the war on the drug trade.'

'Tell me honestly, Arvin,' said Arthur, 'why is it so important that I send you Dionysus?'

Out of excuses, feeling harried and persecuted, the President exploded with anger. 'Because, you mother-fucking, arrogant shit,' he yelled, his face and neck a dark choleric red, 'because I'm ordering you to!'

'Not good enough,' said Arthur calmly. 'I take my orders from the Round Table.'

About to explode again, the President managed to restrain himself. Losing his temper was not getting him anywhere. 'You and I are the boss men, Arthur,' he said, trying a touch of flattery by association. 'We don't take orders from anyone. Do it first and ask afterwards is what we do.'

'That's not how it works in Camelot,' said Arthur. 'I need to explain to the Round Table why you want Dionysus.'

'Why?' The wheels and cogs of the President's brain whirred in a frantic effort to find a way out. But there was none. 'Why?' He was cornered. He could see from the look on Arthur's face that no more excuses, no more prevarications would do. So desperate was he that he was tempted to do something he had rarely, if ever, done in his political life – tell the truth. 'Why?' he repeated yet again, rummaging his brain for some last-minute inspiration.

Arthur's gaze was unwavering.

'I'll tell you,' said the President, loathing himself, 'it's . . . it's because the United States government has given certain . . . ' – He cleared his throat nervously – ' . . . certain assurances.'

'To whom?'

'To the . . . ' The words stuck in the President's throat – to the Colombian government. We have made commitments to them. We – um – we have long-standing agreements.'

'What sort of agreements?'

'If you must know, the bottom line is that we turn a tolerant eye to the drug trade.'

'What does tolerant mean?'

'It means we hit the drug barons from time to time, but not too often, and not where it really hurts. They . . . well, they reciprocate.'

'How do they do that?'

'For chrissake.' The President was floundering, his eyes shifting evasively from side to side.

'How do they do that, Mr President?'

'They support us in the U.N., they put business deals our way, they exchange intelligence. A lot of stuff. Some I can't talk about. See here, Arthur, this is between you and me, it has to be.' He could not meet his eyes. 'Dionysus is big,' the President muttered, 'there's none bigger. He has the world in his pocket: politicians, generals, police, businessmen, they all owe him – their jobs, their money, their power, and yes, in some cases, their lives. They want him back, Arthur. Unharmed. And you know what? I've promised I'd make it happen. I'm committed. If I don't . . . ' He drew a finger across his throat in a dramatic gesture.

For a while Arthur said nothing, trying to absorb what the President had told him. 'When you were a senator,' he said, 'I was impressed by you. I thought you were on the side of the good guys.'

'I was,' said the President in a low voice.

'What happened?'

'They made me President.'

A long uncomfortable silence followed, the two leaders eyeing each other uneasily, Arthur sombre, the President shamefaced. 'This isn't your bag, Arthur,' he said finally. 'You are supposed to be fighting terrorists, not drug barons.'

'I fight anyone who threatens the future of mankind. No one poses a greater threat than drug producers.'

When all arguments failed, there was nothing left but to plead. 'Do this for me, Arthur. It's the last favour I'll ever ask of you, I swear it.'

There were no doubts in Arthur's mind. He would not, could

not, grant the President's request. At this moment, though, he did not have the heart to say so.

'Let's see what the High Council decides,' he said. 'We'll talk again.'

The High Council summoned the eleven convicted drug barons and handed down the same sentence to all of them – death. The executions were to take place the following morning at dawn.

When, a few minutes later, he heard the news, Agravaine rushed to the observatory.

'Is it true, nuncle? They are all to die?'

'Yes.'

'Dionysus too?'

'Certainly.'

'It was me who talked him into giving us the codes.'

'I heard,' said Arthur.

'More than two hundred billion dollars. Two hundred billion! How about that, nuncle!'

'Congratulations.'

'Dionysus thinks he's smart, but he's not half as smart as I am. I tricked him.'

'How did you do that?'

'I made a deal with him – his life in exchange for his money. And he believed me! Wasn't that clever of me?' To Agravaine's dismay, the look on Arthur's face was one not of admiration but of horror. 'What's the matter, nuncle?'

'You had no right to make any deal with Dionysus,' said Arthur. 'Not without my authority.'

The blood drained from Agravaine's face. 'But . . . '

'Didn't you know Dionysus would almost certainly be sentenced to death?'

'Of course I did. I fooled him. Didn't I do well?'

'No, Agravaine,' said Arthur, 'you did badly.'

Agravaine's jaw sagged. 'But I don't understand. I did it

for you, nuncle. What's wrong? What's wrong?' The words tumbled out faster and faster. 'I thought of all the good things Camelot could do with the money, all the bad people we could punish, all the good lives we could save. And we can, nuncle, I know we can. Tell me I did the right thing, nuncle, tell me I did right. Tell me you're not angry. Please don't be angry with me. Please, don't be angry, nuncle.'

'You lied and you cheated,' said Arthur sternly. 'You played a cruel trick on Dionysus.'

'But he's evil. Everyone knows that. Look how many millions of drug addicts there are because of him.'

'All that is true, Agravaine, but it's no excuse for what you did. If we do as the drug barons do, how are we better than they are?'

Agravaine's eyes filled with tears. 'You've been so cold to me since . . . ' – He gulped – 'since . . . '

Since Margot and Adrian Pellinore were murdered. So that was it. Now he knew for certain that what he had long suspected was true; Agravaine's hands were stained with blood. 'Go, now,' he said, turning his back on his nephew.

Agravaine pranced round his uncle, trying to make him look at him. 'What did I do wrong?' he asked plaintively over and over again, 'what did I do wrong?' As the observatory door closed behind him he cried out, 'Why can't you just love me, nuncle?'

A few minutes before dawn the eleven prisoners were handcuffed and led out of their cells to the prison yard. In front of them stood the firing squad – eleven members of the Round Table – each, bar one, having drawn the short straw. The sole exception, Arthur, had insisted on carrying out the sentence of death on Dionysus. As the time of the execution drew near, some prisoners began to moan and plead for mercy. A minute to go. George Bedivere looked at his watch, then up at the sky. There would be no sun to signal the dawn. A heavy bank of dark cloud hung over Camelot. The wind wailed round the prison walls.

Venom in his eyes, Dionysus spoke his last words. 'I told you I never killed Merlin. I lied,' he said. 'I killed him. And I tortured him before he died. My men held him down while I broke his arms, then his wrists, then the bones in his fingers and feet. He died in agony.'

'Merlin will never die,' said Arthur.

At a sign from George Bedivere, the execution squad raised their portables and fired in Elimat mode.

Nothing remained of the drug barons, neither flesh nor blood nor bone, nothing to show that they had ever existed.

Fifty Seven

THE SWORD IN THE SKY, seen yet again by billions around the globe, celebrated what many ordinary people considered to be Camelot's greatest achievement. As its image faded, Arthur appeared on TV channels across the globe. What Camelot had done was harsh, but necessary, he said. Sadly, innocent people had died, and that he deeply regretted. But *Operation Mainline* had succeeded in its goal of destroying the drug barons and rooting out the cancer of illegal drugs. It was now up to the nations of the world to ensure that the drug trade was never revived.

Following his speech, a world-wide debate began; and it soon became clear that not everyone agreed with Arthur. Some world leaders, in particular those whose territory had been invaded and whose nationals had either been Elimatted or killed by conventional means, condemned Camelot in the strongest terms, threatening serious consequences. For days the United Nations was in uproar. Religious leaders, whilst acknowledging Arthur's good intentions, questioned the moral justification for what he had done. The world's media generally saluted the spectacular success of *Operation Mainline*, but some questioned its long-term effectiveness, echoing Dionysus's observation; you can destroy the drug trade, but you can never destroy the demand.

The majority of the world's population, however, welcomed Camelot's victory over the drug barons, and in the wake of *Operation Mainline* there was a growing consensus to do what Arthur asked – to ensure that the deadly trade was never revived.

The most significant opposition came from those who, secretly, and sometimes not so secretly, collaborated with drug producers and dealers; senior police and army officers, politicians, businessmen, bankers, accountants and lawyers, all of whom had reaped vast rewards from active involvement in, or passive acceptance of, the drug trade. Hundreds of thousands of rich and powerful people had, as a direct result of *Operation Mainline,* lost money, power and prestige. They were the ones who most savagely criticised Arthur, accusing him of murder, fraud and theft on a massive scale.

The harsh truth was that the drug trade, tragic though its effects were, had provided a living for millions. Its elimination was destabilising, especially for third world countries whose economies virtually depended on street drugs. There were calls for the destruction of Camelot, and for Arthur to be brought to justice, though no one was able to suggest how that might be achieved.

Arthur himself was neither surprised, nor particularly concerned, by these adverse reactions. Yet he was beginning to have doubts. 'Did we do the right thing?' he asked Leo Grant.

'We acted in good faith,' said Leo. 'What we did, we did for the right reasons.'

'We?' Arthur was touched. Leo could easily have said, "I told you so." 'You never supported *Mainline.*'

'I had my reservations,' admitted Leo, 'but that's history now. As always, I am with you.'

So was the Round Table. Even Mordred was careful not to criticise his father openly. Though *Operation Mainline* might not have been an unqualified success, it had achieved many of its objectives. It was disheartening, therefore, that the reaction of so many world leaders was either lukewarm or downright hostile. More than ever, Camelot needed their co-operation.

A week later, Lancelot submitted a full report to Arthur. 'Our surveillance shows that at least ninety per cent of illegal drug supplies have been destroyed. That includes warehouse stocks, and drugs transported by air, ship, road and rail. We have also destroyed or incapacitated approximately the same percentage of processing plants.'

'And the drug barons?'

'According to our information,' said Lancelot, 'which by the way is confirmed by most of the world's intelligence services and narcotic agencies, there are no major drug barons left alive.'

This was more than satisfactory, better than Arthur could ever have hoped for. 'What about crops of coca, cannabis and poppies?'

'We have scanned the globe. There are no significant crops left.'

It was the answer to those who questioned whether the end justified the means. If only the world did its duty, there was a chance that the next generation would be free of the scourge of drugs. But then, as Lancelot was about to take his leave, there came the question he had hoped would not be asked.

'What about casualties?' said Arthur.

'We lost twenty-two men.'

By far the heaviest casualties they had suffered in any operation.

'So many.'

'I'm afraid so.'

'And other casualties?'

'They were proportionate.'

'Proportionate?'

'Well, as you know, we did all we could to avoid . . . '

Arthur cut in. 'The numbers, Lance.'

'Ah. Numbers.' Lancelot consulted his print-outs. 'Let me see.' There were columns of figures, many of which he would have preferred to forget. 'We estimate approximately – um – eight thousand, five hundred,' he said. 'Pretty much as expected,' he added, as if that somehow softened the blow.

Arthur looked shaken. 'How many of those were fatalities?'

Lancelot riffled through his notes, though in truth he had no need to. The numbers were branded on his brain. 'Those *are* the fatalities,' he said.

'We *killed* eight thousand five hundred people!'

'So it seems.' Lancelot shifted from foot to foot. 'What is that proverb about not being able to make omelettes without . . . '

'We are not talking eggs, we are talking lives,' said Arthur curtly. 'How many wounded?'

Lancelot shuffled his papers again.

'I asked you a question, Lance.'

'As we all know, the number of wounded always exceeds the number of fatalities,' Lancelot mumbled, 'by quite a large margin.'

'And that is?'

'Four to one,' Lancelot's glance wandered away from Arthur. 'I believe.'

'Are you saying we wounded thirty-four thousand people!'

'Give or take . . . '

Arthur sank back in his chair.

'I assure you, sir, we did the very best we could to minimise . . . ' began Lancelot, stopping abruptly as he saw the look on Arthur's face.

'I know,' said Arthur, 'I know you did. We all did.'

When Lancelot had left the observatory Arthur sank into a chair and stared disconsolately into space. There were times, he was thinking, when doing your best was not good enough.

There was, however, a measure of good news to come. It was only at the next Round Table meeting that its members were given the final tally of money extracted from drug producers and dealers, and deposited in hundreds of accounts opened by Techforce Ten around the world.

'Say that again,' said Arthur incredulously. 'How much?'

'One thousand, two hundred billion, eight hundred and seventy-five million, two hundred and thirty-eight thousand dollars,' said Tich. 'Or, if you like,' he added dryly, 'one trillion, two hundred billion, eight hundred million, and some loose change.'

For a long time not a muscle stirred, not a voice was raised. Members sat with mouths open, eyes wide. Then, beginning with a low murmur, the laughter grew louder and louder until it reached an hysterical crescendo. When it died down Leo Grant asked: 'What are we going to do with all this money?'

It seemed no one had given the question much thought.

Once the debate was under way, the Round Table was not short of ideas. 'Now that Merlin is no longer with us,' said Lancelot, 'we shall have to work even harder on research and development.' Agravaine wanted to commission more satellites in order to boost Camelot's lead over the rest of the world in communications and surveillance. Leo Grant proposed a second Eclipse and a second Kraken and doubling the number of Nimbles and Scuttles. George Bedivere – even more adventurous – wanted to construct a second Camelot on the other side of the globe 'to complement and expand our operations.'

There were those who opposed all these ideas. If a second Camelot would double their power, it would also double the security risk. As to more research and/or weapons, surely Camelot was already so far ahead of its time that it had no need to increase its arsenal or update its technology. So many ideas and so many points of view were advanced that finally it was agreed to reconvene in a week's time to consider the matter further.

After the meeting, Arthur summoned Leo Grant and George Bedivere. 'I'd like to have your opinion. What do we do with this obscene amount of money?'

'I don't know,' said Leo. 'We need more discussion.'

'I agree,' said George Bedivere. 'After all, there's no hurry. We should take our time and make the right decisions.'

Arthur's fingers brushed the faint scar on his cheek. 'In my opinion, there is only one decision to make.'

'And that is?' said Leo.

'Not to use it at all.'

Both men were close to Arthur. At a time like this, however, they realised how little they knew him.

'Explain,' said George.

'It's drug money.' Deep lines furrowed Arthur's forehead. 'Dirty money.'

'There's no such thing as dirty money,' said George Bedivere, thrusting out his big chin belligerently, 'there's only dirty hands. Your hands are clean, Arthur.'

'I see no problem,' said Leo Grant, 'as long as we use the money in a good cause.'

'A good cause,' repeated Arthur thoughtfully.

When his two friends had left, his mind focused on this new problem. A good cause, Leo had said. He was right. Whatever use they put the drug money to, it had to be for a good cause. His hands were clean, George said. If only that were true. Once, he would have been right. Not any more, though. He was tainted. They were all tainted . . .

. . . All but one.

Fifty Eight

THE DOOR PANEL BUZZED, the speaker crackled.
Name?
'Galahad.'
Enter Galahad.

As Arthur advanced to embrace him, Galahad first raised his hand as though it were a shield against an excessive display of intimacy, then extended it stiffly. Shaking it solemnly, Arthur waved the young man to a chair.

Galahad settled himself, crossed his ankles, folded his hands primly on his bible, and looked expectantly at Arthur.

'Are you enjoying your time in Camelot?'

'May I speak truthfully, sir?'

'I would expect nothing else from you.'

'I would like it better if my opinions were taken seriously,' said Galahad.

'You don't think they are?'

'No one listens to me.'

'I'm listening now,' said Arthur.

'On what subject would you like me to offer my views?' enquired Galahad gravely.

Arthur bit his lip to suppress a smile. 'I would value your opinion of *Operation Mainline*,' he said.

Galahad stroked his bible with his pale, scholar's hands. '*Vengeance is mine; I will repay, saith the Lord,*' he said.

'You think I should leave it to Him, do you?'

'I do.'

'I suspect that if I did,' said Arthur, 'He would do nothing about it.'

'Then that would be His will,' said Galahad.

'In which case,' said Arthur, 'He and I have different views.'

Sparring with Arthur did not appear to have weakened Galahad's resolve. He expressed himself bluntly. 'Force can never be justified.'

'Even when it is used to save millions of lives?'

'Even then.'

'If we don't stand up to the wicked,' said Arthur, 'they will destroy mankind.'

'It is not the power of Excalibur that will establish the kingdom of heaven on earth,' said Galahad.

'What will then?'

'The power of God's word,' said Galahad, his eyes bright.

'You really believe that?'

'I do. Excalibur obliterates as granite crushes chalk. God's word is like grass. It seeds itself, it grows and flourishes. You may think granite is stronger than grass, but it is grass that splinters granite and topples the castles of tyrants – even if it takes a thousand years.'

'I don't have a thousand years,' said Arthur.

'God does,' said Galahad.

Despite himself, Arthur was impressed. Some thought Galahad naive, and perhaps he was, but his eyes shone with the light of conviction. Such inner strength and self-belief was remarkable in one so young. Not only did he believe, he had the courage of his beliefs. Camelot needed those qualities, now more than ever.

'You heard the debate, Galahad. I want you to tell me what you would do with the drug money.' Before Galahad could speak, Arthur raised his hand. 'Take your time. Think carefully, and come and see me tomorrow.'

He could not get Leo Grant's words out of his mind. *As long as we use the money in a good cause.* Not more technology, not more weapons, not even a second Camelot could wash the dirty money clean.

Only a good cause.

Fifty Nine

Mission Grail

AS THE EIGHT Guardian robots declared the doors of the Great Hall *shut and secured*, members' eyes focused on Galahad, who, to the surprise of many, sat at Arthur's right hand, instead of in his usual seat next to his father, Lancelot.

'We are here to decide what to do with the drug money in our hands,' said Arthur. 'Since our last meeting we have polled members, and none of the proposals submitted at our last meeting has received the necessary fifty-one per cent of your votes. I would therefore like to introduce a fourth proposal – that of Galahad, whom I call upon to present it himself.'

A flurry of conversation, and Galahad rose to speak. 'We have taken from the drug barons more than a trillion dollars – a vast fortune. I propose we use it to search for the Holy Grail.'

This suggestion was greeted first with shocked silence, then with cries of disbelief and protest.

'A trillion dollars!' George Bedivere shouted mockingly above the din. 'That has to be the most expensive cup in history!'

A sally that was greeted with laughter and applause. Galahad was well enough liked, but he was young, and a bit too religious for most palates. The Round Table was making it very clear they did not take his proposal seriously. Yet, to the surprise of many, he seemed not at all abashed. Above the continuing rumble of dissenting voices his voice rose strongly.

'We must cleanse this dirty money. We must use it not to increase Camelot's power, but to help the poor, the disadvantaged, the sick, the mentally and physically disabled – above all the addicted, for they are the ones whose lives have been destroyed by drugs. Think what good we could do with a trillion dollars! We could offer hope to society's rejects, to those who suffer the torments of addiction wherever they are; in city centres, in the depths of the country, in drug colonies where addicts now collect, as lepers once did. We could build new rehabilitation centres, not just in the developed countries, but in Africa, in the Far East and South America. And let the ones we cure be trained to give others the strength to resist temptation, so that those who have not yet fallen will be saved by those who have. Let us shine the light of truth on the world, so that the dreadful scourge of drug addiction is banished from the planet – not by coercion, but by the will of the people.'

Looking at the upturned faces, Galahad could see that his words had made an impression on the Round Table. 'If we succeed, as I am certain we shall, not by threats, or by the use of force, but by appealing to the essential goodness in our fellow men, then the love and goodwill we create will be like a cleansing wind or a searing fire that will leave the world a better place – as pure and innocent as it was before the fall of man. When that day comes, we shall truly see in our time peace on earth and goodwill to all men.'

Then Galahad reached out his arms as if to embrace every man and woman in the Great Hall of the Round Table and smiled a smile so beautiful that for one ecstatic moment it seemed that the Lord himself was standing before them. 'When that day comes,' he said, 'we shall have found the Holy Grail.'

As he sat down, there was silence, a silence so deep that it was like a sentient, a living creature, filling the hall with its presence. And then, to the delight of Arthur and Lancelot, there was a burst of thunderous applause, members leaped from their seats, surrounded Galahad and thumped him on the back, offering their enthusiastic congratulations.

When the votes were counted, ninety-three members of the Round Table had voted in favour of Galahad's proposal, and only twenty-five against it.

Proud as he was of his son, Lancelot was secretly sceptical about *Mission Grail*. Much as he would have liked to share Galahad's messianic zeal, he could not. His instincts told him that it was not turning the other cheek that defeated terrorists, but advanced technology, highly motivated armed forces, and the ability to strike where and when you chose. What disturbed him most was that Arthur appeared to be enthused by the idea of *Mission Grail*. True, he had always been a man of conscience, but he was also a warrior. Once he had known when to extend the hand of friendship, and when to use the mailed fist. Not any more, it seemed.

Yet despite his concerns, Lancelot still desperately wanted to believe in his son. For most of his life he had stood apart from the crowd, aloof and proud. His affair with Guinevere had changed him, compelling him to acknowledge that he was as weak and fallible as other men; weaker in fact, since he had betrayed Arthur, the man who loved him as a son and had raised him to the highest rank in Camelot. Whatever his reservations about *Mission Grail*, therefore, he supported Galahad, in the hope that his son would become the man he had once aspired to be, and in the process, absolve him of his guilt.

Arthur was fired by a new sense of purpose. Though *Operation Mainline* may have been necessary, it had been harsh and bloody, and had made Camelot enemies. It was his hope that *Mission Grail* would make sense of all the killing and destruction. If it did, it would be the noblest of all Camelot's enterprises. Merlin himself would have approved of it. It was to this point, Arthur believed, that his life had been leading him. Justice and order were noble aspirations, and righteous causes to fight for. But there came a time when the killing had to stop.

George Bedivere was far from convinced. 'All this talk about searching for man's essential goodness is reminiscent of the flower power movement of the 1960s. "Make love not war" was a fine-sounding phrase. But what difference did it make?'

383

'It might have made a great deal more difference if the world had taken those youngsters seriously,' said Arthur.

Was Arthur going soft? George wondered 'Do you really believe that Galahad will find the Holy Grail?'

'I'm not sure what I believe,' said Arthur. 'One thing I'm certain of, though. No one has the right to stop him looking for it.'

Sixty

Mission Grail

AS THE TIME APPROACHED for the launch of *Mission Grail*, opinions in Camelot continued to polarise, the doves hoping *Grail* signalled the dawning of a new era, the hawks maintaining that the operation was ill-conceived. And not only Galahad's reputation was at stake.

In the early hours of a spring day, Galahad and a few trusted aides were transported to their pre-selected destinations around the world, and for over a year, little was heard of them. It was agreed there would be no involvement of any kind by Command Control, not even surveillance.

From time to time there were reports in the world's media of a mysterious and elusive philanthropic figure said to be donating large sums of money to worthy causes, though no one seemed to know who the phantom donor was. Here and there rumours erupted like flocks of startled birds; the philanthropist was a Russian oligarch, an American Internet billionaire, a Swiss banker, a reformed drug baron, the President of a third world country, a pop star, a prince. The amounts involved were said to be huge – millions, hundreds of millions, billions even.

Although there was a strict ban on any targeted surveillance of Galahad and his aides, Techforce Ten routinely monitored press, radio and television worldwide, and an increasing volume of coverage gave some clue to Galahad's activities. 'Journalists and newscasters are being more specific,' Agravaine told Arthur. 'They are talking about massive projects for new schools, hospitals and rehabilitation centres right across the globe.'

'Any mention of Galahad?'

'No, but it's him. Here's a quote from the Times of London.' *A twenty-first century messiah? Mystery Donor speaks of Peace on Earth.* 'Here's one from CNN news.' *Could the multi-billionaire be a spiritual leader?* 'And look here, nuncle – here's the clincher. It's from the BBC World Service.' *Dark horse donor talks of Mission Grail and asks all people of goodwill, whatever their colour or creed, to join him in the search for man's essential goodness.* 'What do you say to that, nuncle? *Mission Grail.* The search for man's essential goodness. It's got to be Galahad. He's doing a fantastic job. I had my doubts about him, but I was wrong. He's setting the world on fire.'

It was what Arthur was hoping for.

From many countries, rich and poor alike, thousands rushed to join what was now popularly known as *Mission Grail*, and a tide of optimism swept the world, silencing the doubters. In these difficult and dangerous times when people were starved of good news, *Mission Grail* was bringing hope to mankind. Politicians, religious leaders and businessmen were full of praise. A committee of show business personalities from thirty countries announced a forthcoming *Grail Day* on which, it was predicted, TV channels and radio stations would raise more money than had ever been contributed in the history of charitable ventures. In national forums, politicians made speeches in passionate support of *Mission Grail*, whilst at the United Nations General Assembly, representatives of almost every country on earth saluted the incredible generosity of the anonymous donor. People spoke of a new faith that was inclusive, embracing all nations, all colours and all creeds, a faith that appeared first as a tiny sapling, but had grown into a robustly healthy plant.

Arthur had never been happier. His belief in Galahad and in his own judgement had been vindicated, and Camelot's moral authority reasserted.

Sixty One

Mission Grail

EIGHTEEN MONTHS after the launch of *Mission Grail* Galahad returned to Camelot in triumph. As he entered the Great Hall, bible in hand, the members of the Round Table rose as one to greet him, the standing ovation lasting several minutes. At the end of it, Galahad made a short and modest speech, giving most of the credit for the success of *Mission Grail* to his aides. The most encouraging thing about the operation, he said, was the support he had received from ordinary men and women who believed, as he did, in man's goodness, and who shared his vision of establishing the kingdom of heaven on earth.

At the request of the Round Table Agravaine submitted an analysis of how the drug barons' funds had been spent, and though it was clearly impossible at this stage to account for every dollar, it appeared that in many countries projects involving new schools, hospitals, clinics and rehabilitation centres were either under construction or in an advanced planning stage, and that virtually all the funds were accounted for. It was agreed that after a few days well-earned rest, Galahad would return to duty in order to supervise the most important projects. Meanwhile, under the command of Lancelot and Gawain, Eclipse and Kraken left Camelot with instructions to assemble a more detailed report on progress, thirty orbiting satellites and several hundred mini-robots joining the surveillance operations.

That same evening the US President was on screen to Arthur. 'I don't know how to tell you this, Arthur, except to give it to you straight.' He waved a file. 'According to this report the Drug Enforcement Administration have just given me, there are at least fifteen major drug barons operating in Bolivia, China, Colombia, India, Laos, Jamaica, Mexico, Nigeria, Ghana and Venezuela, amongst other countries.'

'That's impossible,' said Arthur. 'We killed or captured every major drug baron in the world.'

'Maybe so, but according to the D.E.A. there's a new generation of drug barons out there, and those guys are moving significant quantities of illegal drugs. The billion dollar question – where did they get the seed money to revive the drug trade? They're financing farmers to grow crops, building warehouses, buying dedicated ships and aircraft, re-establishing supply routes, organising and paying militias and hiring lord knows how many sidekicks to do their dirty work. And let's not forget the pay-offs to bring politicians and police back on board. That's one hell of a lot of greenbacks we're talking about. Where did all the cash come from?'

'Crooked businessmen? Crooked banks?' suggested Arthur. 'Misappropriated taxes? Government loans?'

The President's fingertips beat a drum roll on his Oval Office desk. 'Not what I'm being told,' he said.

In a few days, Techforce Ten had the answer. Arthur, Tich, Mordred and Agravaine sat at Galaxy's big table monitor studying the incoming data. It made depressing reading. It now seemed that none of *Mission Grail's* projects had actually been completed; worse still, that out of hundreds of planned projects, only three had begun construction – a half-finished school in Brazil, the foundations of a rehabilitation centre in Colombia, and the first two floors of a hospital in Nigeria. On all three projects work had ceased several weeks ago.

Arthur sat shaking his head in disbelief. 'Then all that positive data brought back by Galahad . . . ?'

'Was fantasy,' said Mordred.

'Galahad doesn't lie,' said Arthur.

'He wasn't lying,' said Tich. 'He believed that everything was going according to plan. He was shown impressive spreadsheets,

388

architectural drawings, doctored photographs, you name it. I'll bet they showed him a couple of buildings under construction and told him they needed the money in advance for all the rest. From what we can see, he handed out money like he was giving sweets to kids.'

'We should have insisted on surveillance,' said Tich. Seeing the guilty look on Arthur's face, he tried to soften the blow. 'It wasn't just you, Arthur. We were all taken in.'

In the absence of Galahad, who had locked himself in his apartment, Lancelot faced a Round Table baying for his son's blood, holding him responsible for financing a new generation of drug barons.

Embarrassed, Lancelot defended him. 'I admit my son has been duped. The truth is, though, that he tried what none of us dared to do. He fought the forces of darkness, not with Excalibur, but with the only weapon he had – his belief in man's goodness. He fought, and he lost, as many of us feared he would. But the failure of *Mission Grail* was not his failure. It was mankind's.'

Despite Lancelot's brave words, *Mission Grail* had changed the upbeat mood of Camelot to pessimism and soul-searching. There were those who felt that Arthur's judgement was fallible. Some even questioned his right to lead Camelot. It was he, after all, who had sent Galahad on a wild goose chase, placing too great a burden on an inexperienced young man's shoulders. *Operation Mainline* had claimed many lives; had they all been lost in vain?

A week later, at Arthur's insistence, Galahad faced the Round Table. To a man, the hawks denounced him, accusing him of recklessness and naivety in squandering huge amounts of money that could and should have been used for the benefit of Camelot and the world. Though the doves were uneasy at the apparently disastrous outcome of *Mission Grail*, they found reasons to defend their champion.

Leo Grant spoke for them: 'Galahad acted in good faith. He

tried to do what he was asked to do, and we ought not to be blaming him for the failure of *Mission Grail*. Nor should we blame Arthur. If anyone is to blame, it is us, all of us. The Round Table sanctioned the operation, don't let us forget that.' His comments were cheered loudly by the doves, and booed equally loudly by the hawks.

Arthur waited for the Round Table to settle down. 'I take full responsibility for *Mission Grail*, and unlike some of you, I do not see it as a total failure. One way or another the nations of the world are politically involved in the drug trade. The mistake we made was to involve ourselves in politics. Politics is a dirty business, some would say the dirtiest business of all. We should not have soiled our hands. But whatever we did, we did it in a just cause. No one can deny that.'

'My emotions tell me you are right, father,' said Mordred, 'but my head is saying something else.'

'And what is that?' said Arthur.

'That Camelot has lost face,' said Mordred, 'even amongst our most enthusiastic supporters.'

It was clear from the Round Table's reaction that many agreed with him. Arthur was in two minds, torn between Galahad and Mordred. Mordred had a point; *Mission Grail* had failed in its objectives. Yet surely it could not be written off as a total failure? 'At the very least,' he said, 'we have shown the world that force is not always the answer to solving its problems, that there is – that there has to be – another way. Camelot lit a candle, and the light of the candle flickered and died. But in its place another candle will be lit, and another and another and another, until all the dark places of the world are illuminated.'

Inspired by Arthur's words, and stung by Mordred's criticism, Galahad jumped to his feet. 'Time will show,' he asserted defiantly, 'that *Mission Grail* was a complete success!' Angered by the laughter that greeted this claim, he brandished his bible. 'It is not for you to condemn me,' he shouted.

'Show some respect,' said Gawain. 'You are here to be judged by the Round Table.'

'Only God has the right to judge me,' cried Galahad. 'It was He, not the Round Table, who instructed me to establish His kingdom on earth.'

Groans and jeers greeted this response. So loud and protracted was the clamour that Arthur was compelled to intervene. 'Galahad has had the courage to appear before you. At least show him the courtesy of allowing him to speak his mind.'

When Galahad spoke again, his voice was calmer, his words more moderate. 'I ask only that you have faith in *Mission Grail*, as I do. The money will be accounted for. The hospitals and schools, the rehabilitation centres and the clinics – they will all be built.'

'What evidence is there of that?' demanded Mordred.

Galahad brandished his bible. 'This book is my evidence,' he proclaimed. 'On this bible men and women have sworn oaths, solemn oaths they dare not break, for fear of incurring God's anger.'

'Unfortunately,' said Mordred, 'oaths are all too often broken.' He held up his own bible. 'Even oaths sworn on this book.'

There was no doubt in Arthur's mind that he had been damaged. In the eyes of his friends and colleagues he saw questions that had not been there before. It would take time to rebuild confidence in his leadership. Against all his natural instincts he had persuaded himself that *Mission Grail* would succeed. Was it because he truly believed in it? Or because he felt guilty for the innocents slaughtered in *Operation Mainline*?

Never before had he allowed himself to consider the prospect of failure. Now he was all too aware of the widening divisions on the island. If he were to lose the support of the Round Table, what hope was there for Camelot?

Sixty Two

Whilst Mordred sipped coffee, Agravaine and Gaheris watched him uneasily, tense and upright in their chairs, their cups untouched. He was not the most sociable person in the world, this being only the second or third time they had been invited to his apartment. Why were they here now? Could it be something to do with their mother's death?

Observing his brothers' nervousness, Mordred made no effort to reassure them, chatting amiably for several minutes about the weather and world news, about anything in fact but the subject that must be – as he well knew – uppermost in their minds. Finally he laid down his cup and came obliquely to the point.

'I expect you are wondering why I asked you here.'

'We were rather,' said Agravaine, making a minuscule adjustment to the position of his cup and saucer so that it stood precisely in the centre of the coffee table.

'We were,' agreed Gaheris.

'It's because I need your help.' Mordred leaned back, amused by the look of relief on his brothers' faces.

'You have only to ask,' said Agravaine.

'I imagine you know . . . dammit of course you know, everyone in Camelot does . . . ' Mordred passed a hand across his brow. 'I am referring to the affair Lancelot is conducting with *my father's wife*.' It was clear from the distaste in his voice that he could hardly bring himself to speak Guinevere's name. 'You know what's going on, I take it?'

Agravaine was uncertain how to react. If he said no, he risked annoying his brother, and being branded a liar. If he said yes, and Mordred was only testing the waters, he might unwittingly be lending credence to gossip. He decided on compromise. 'We have heard rumours,' he responded cautiously, 'haven't we, Gaheris.'

Gaheris nodded his head vigorously, uncertain what he was agreeing to, but trusting his brother implicitly.

'I assure you we are talking about more than rumours,' said Mordred. 'The head of Camelot's armed forces is having an affair with Arthur's wife.'

Agravaine said nothing, hoping by his lack of reaction to suggest that he was, if not disinterested, then at least uncommitted.

'We must put a stop to it,' said Mordred, 'the three of us.'

Agravaine looked apprehensive, shaken by the unexpected turn the conversation had taken. 'I wouldn't want to create any problems.'

Mordred crossed the room and stood looking out at NIWIS. What was, and what seemed to be, were often very different, as he knew, not only from being Tich's assistant, but also from his own personal experience. For him life was a matter of interpretation, a shadowy, ambiguous country, full of delusions and misconceptions, a land of virtual unreality in which he saw himself as king. He turned, strode purposefully back and looked down at Agravaine. 'Family,' he declared, stabbing the air with his index finger to emphasise every key word, 'family you trust. Family you stand by. Family gives meaning to our lives. There is nothing, Agro, *nothing,*' he repeated, 'more important than family.'

'Very true,' murmured Agravaine, wondering where all this was leading.

'I love my father,' said Mordred, 'love him with all my heart. It hurts . . . ' – He thumped his chest and winced to demonstrate the point – 'it hurts me to see him being made a fool of. I cannot allow it to continue. Do you understand that?'

Agravaine mumbled something unintelligible that might have signified assent. Gaheris cleared his throat noisily.

'It is my duty,' continued Mordred, '*my duty* to protect Arthur against his enemies. Not just because I love and respect him, not just because he is my leader, but because he is *family*, Agro. *Family*.' He threw himself in his chair. 'I am certain you feel as I do.'

'Absolutely,' said Agravaine.

Gaheris scratched doggedly at a stain on his uniform.

'He is, after all, your uncle.'

'He is.'

'Then you will help me?'

Agravaine's forehead puckered. 'Help you do what, Mord?'

'Help me catch them in the act,' said Mordred, with a grin that disturbed only one side of his face.

'I'm not . . . I'm not sure it would be such a . . . g-good idea,' stammered Agravaine, wiping the sweat from his face with the back of his hand.

A resigned shrug. 'If that's how you feel . . . '

'I do,' said Agravaine. 'I'm really sorry, Mord, but you know how careful we have to be, Gaheris and I. Considering what happened when we . . . you know what I mean.'

'I know exactly what you mean, Agro,' said Mordred, examining his nails. 'And oddly enough, that delicate matter is – sadly – all too relevant to our discussion.' With a curl of the lip and a rueful shake of the head he looked like a man compelled against his will to unburden himself of something distasteful. 'I had hoped it would not be necessary to mention this . . . '

Agravaine crossed one leg over the other and jiggled his foot. 'What?' he asked, though he guessed what was coming.

'I gave you my word,' said Mordred, 'that I would never reveal to Arthur your involvement in that unfortunate business with your mother and Pellinore.'

Agravaine's foot juddered frenziedly.

Mordred patted the bible on the arm of his chair. 'You know me,' he said, 'so you know you can trust me. I swore never to reveal your secret, and I now renew that vow on this holy book.' He kissed the bible, looking over the top at Agravaine's ashen face. A full minute passed before he spoke again. 'Unfortunately there are those who . . . '

Agravaine lifted his head and gulped for air.

'Who cannot be trusted.'

Agravaine's heart stumbled in his chest. 'Who are you talking about?'

Mordred played the fish he had hooked. 'Who are making threats.'

'Who? Who?'

'Lancelot, for one.'

Agravaine's voice rose hysterically. 'What sort of threats?'

'He claims to have proof that you and Gaheris killed our mother,' said Mordred, 'and he's threatening to take it to Arthur.'

'He would never do that – not Lancelot,' said Agravaine. A pleading look. 'Would he?'

'I'm afraid he would,' said Mordred. 'Especially if he thought it would divert attention from his own somewhat – shall we say *exposed* – position with Arthur's wife.' He chuckled appreciatively at his own jest.

Agravaine's head was buried in his hands, Gaheris whined softly like an animal caught in a trap.

'One photo is all we need,' said Mordred.

'I can't do it,' Agravaine muttered.

'Believe me,' said Mordred, 'I take no pleasure in this sordid business. I know exactly how you feel. I feel the same way myself. But let's face it, Agro, it's either him or us.'

'Us? You mean me and Gaheris?'

Mordred left his seat and put his arms round Agravaine. 'I mean *us*,' he whispered in his ear. 'We are family.'

'Even so,' said Agravaine, pulling away, 'I can't betray

Lancelot.'

'You would rather betray Arthur?'

Agravaine looked at the floor.

'Camelot is founded on truth, honour and justice,' said Mordred. 'We all took a sacred oath to honour those high principles, did we not?'

Agravaine nodded dumbly.

'Tell me, then,' said Mordred, 'what truth, what honour, what justice is served when Arthur's wife and his Chief of Staff are screwing each other?'

Silence.

'Not only will we be doing our duty, we shall be doing Arthur a favour,' he insisted. 'As for Lancelot and Guinevere . . . ' – he raised his bible high – 'we shall save their souls, you and I, we shall rescue them from adulterous couplings, from lying and deceit, from treacherous assignations and guilty secrets. They will repent, and Camelot will be whole again.' He held out his hand. 'Are you with me, brothers?'

The two men looked at Mordred's hand, afraid to take it, afraid not to. Slowly, reluctantly, first Agravaine, then Gaheris, grasped the outstretched hand as gingerly as if it were an unexploded bomb.

Clasping his hands together and closing his eyes, Mordred bowed his head. 'Let us pray for guidance,' he said.

Troubled by his conscience, Agravaine went straight to his brother, Gawain, to alert him of Mordred's intentions, and Gawain passed on the warning to the one person he thought might be able to make Guinevere see reason.

Lanky did not try to soften her words. 'For your sake, Ginny, for all our sakes, give him up.'

'I can't do that.'

'For the love of God, girl,' said Lanky, 'we both know it will all come out sooner or later. Half Camelot knows what's going on, and the other half suspects it. One day, someone will do something about it. And that would be a disaster for you, for Lancelot, for Arthur, for all of us. Have you thought about that?'

Guinevere shivered. 'A million times.'

'I'm begging you, Ginny,' said Lanky, 'if you can't give him up, at least stop seeing him for a while.'

'I can't do that either.'

Much as she loved her friend, Lanky found her refusal to face facts exasperating. 'You're playing with fire,' she said. 'If Mordred gets his proof, he'll go straight to Arthur.'

'Arthur knows,' said Guinevere.

It was what Lanky had long suspected. Nevertheless: 'There's a big difference between knowing, and having it shoved in your face,' she observed shrewdly.

Signalling the end of the discussion, Guinevere's chin lifted in that stubborn gesture Lanky knew so well. She reported back to Gawain, who, in desperation, went straight to Lancelot.

'You must end this affair.'

Lancelot towered over Gawain. 'I don't see that it's any of your business.'

'Don't you?' Gawain's colour was dangerously high. 'Then let me disillusion you. Mordred is watching you. If he gets the evidence he's looking for, you and Guinevere will be disgraced, Arthur will be humiliated, and Camelot will be in turmoil. I'd say that makes it my business, wouldn't you?'

'I can't give her up.'

'For God's sake, man,' said Gawain furiously, 'you are Camelot's Chief of Staff. Your first duty is to Arthur.'

'You don't need to tell me where my duty lies,' said Lancelot. Through the window of his apartment he watched the sunlight draining from the white walls of Camelot's buildings as clouds inched their way across the sun. His spirits sank with the light. 'You are a good man, Gawain, but you don't understand. How could you? It's not Lancelot you're talking to. I'm like someone possessed. I've given up control of my life.'

'Then get it back.'

'I wish I could.'

'I can't protect you any longer,' said Gawain, his patience exhausted. 'If you and Guinevere are caught, I won't lift a finger to save you.'

Lancelot inclined his head. 'There's nothing I can do. It's fate.'

Gawain had other ideas. It was not fate that was responsible, it was a woman, a woman who had enslaved the two most powerful men in Camelot.

Sixty Three

WHILST ARTHUR WAS IN Command Control, Guinevere made her way to Lancelot's apartment, neutralising with her handset the electronic eyes and sensors lining her chosen route. Within seconds the two lovers were in bed, clinging together as if this lovemaking were their last.

First deactivating the electronic door panel, Mordred crept silently into Lancelot's bedroom, followed by Agravaine and Gaheris. Dozing in each other's arms Lancelot and Guinevere made an appealing picture. Mordred took several shots in rapid succession, then, finger to lips, pointed to the door. As Gaheris tiptoed out, his arm dislodged a framed photograph of Lancelot taking the oath of allegiance to Arthur. The noise awakened Lancelot. Leaping out of bed, he grabbed an automatic pistol from the bedside table. Gaheris stood his ground, Agravaine backed to the doorway between bedroom and sitting room. 'Don't kill me,' he pleaded, 'don't kill me.'

'Be careful what you're doing with that thing,' said Mordred, 'it might go off.'

'If you don't give me the camera, it will,' said Lancelot, advancing on him. Mordred tossed the camera to Gaheris. As he caught it, Lancelot threw himself towards him, one hand holding the gun, the other reaching for the camera. As the two men struggled, the gun went off. For a few seconds Gaheris and Lancelot stood looking at each other.

'You OK, Gaheris?'

The big man felt himself all over. 'I think so.'

Mordred looked round. 'Where's Agro?'

Agravaine was standing in the doorway.

'You OK, Agro?' said Lancelot. As he spoke, Agravaine's knees folded under him. For a few seconds he knelt on the carpet, supporting himself on his hands, then rolled over onto his back and lay still, eyes staring vacantly at the ceiling. Gaheris stooped and laid his hand on Agravaine's chest. 'Agro?' There was no answer. Gaheris lifted his hand and looked at it. It was covered in blood. 'No, Agro,' he said, 'don't die. I don't want you to die.'

Kneeling, Lancelot felt Agravaine's pulse, looked up at Mordred and shook his head. Guinevere stood half-naked in the doorway, eyes frightened, hair dishevelled.

The chest of Agravaine's uniform was damp, the gold insignia of the sword in the stone soaked in blood. Gaheris's breath grated in his throat.

'You'd better get dressed, both of you,' said Mordred to the lovers.

When the doctor arrived, he confirmed what they already knew; Agravaine was dead. The bullet had passed through his heart. Minutes later, a grim-faced Arthur rushed in. Told what had happened by an unusually subdued Mordred, he ordered the immediate arrest of Lancelot and Guinevere. Both were cautioned, and their rights read to them. Locked in separate cells in Camelot's prison, they were to remain there until someone decided what to do with them.

For the rest of the day Arthur shut himself in his apartment refusing to see or speak to anyone. Angry and humiliated, he was at last compelled to confront the fact that the woman he loved had betrayed him. If only he could find it in himself to condemn her, it might have eased his troubled soul, but he could not. Wandering aimlessly from room to room, he tried in his desperation to convince himself that he would find Guinevere making tea in the kitchen, or undressing for bed, telling himself over and over again that it had all been a horrible nightmare, that any moment he would wake up and she would be there, looking lovingly at him with those dark, beguiling eyes.

That night he slept a shallow sleep, his fitful dreams tormented by images of Guinevere and Lancelot entwined in the act of love, their heads turning to mock him even as they moaned their way to ecstasy. All night long they taunted him, their faces advancing and receding, grotesquely distorted and bloated by lust, until finally he could bear it no longer.

With a cry of rage, he grabbed the gun from his bedside table, waited for them to come close, and fired again and again. Throwing down the gun he rushed to the bathroom and peered at himself in the mirror. In his confused state, half-waking, half-sleeping, it seemed to him that his face, neck, arms and chest were drenched in blood. Tearing off his clothes he stood under the shower until the last trickle of red disappeared down the drain.

In the kitchen he made himself a coffee and sat clasping the warm mug, forcing himself to think clearly. However difficult the situation, decisions would have to be made. And he alone would have to make them. Every man and woman in Camelot would be looking to him for leadership, and he dared not let them down. One thing was clear; Lancelot must be brought to trial. He had killed Agravaine; whether accidentally or not was a matter for the High Council to decide. And Guinevere? She too must be tried. Though adultery was not a crime – not at least in the eyes of man – she was an accessory to a killing. The consequences were too terrible to contemplate. Would Camelot survive? Would any of them?

The first thing Lancelot knew of Mordred's visit was when the cell door clanged shut behind him.

'Before you say anything,' said Mordred hastily, 'I need to tell you how deeply sorry I am. I never dreamed it would end like this.'

'I thought you were a decent man,' said Lancelot. 'How wrong I was. You are a monster. This is all your doing.'

Mordred shifted his expression smoothly from penitent to offended mode. 'Why blame me? Did I go to bed with Guinevere? Did I kill Agravaine? I don't think so. All I did was take a couple of photographs of you and the lady in a compromising position.' He held up a print. 'This one came out well, don't you think?' he said, moistening his lips. 'I must say Guinevere's bum is rather cheeky.' Grabbing the photo, Lancelot tore it into small pieces and flung them in Mordred's face.

'Plenty more where that came from,' said Mordred.

It was the last straw. Lancelot laid his hands on his neck and squeezed.

'Aren't you in enough trouble?' gasped Mordred.

'What's one killing more,' said Lancelot. 'And this one I'm going to enjoy.'

'No, please, I can help you,' said Mordred, choking on the words.

'Why would you do that?' Lancelot's hands tightened round his neck.

'Let me speak!'

He relaxed his grip. 'Get out of here,' he said. 'You disgust me.'

Keeping a watchful eye on him, Mordred backed away. 'Just hear what I have to say.'

Lancelot pushed him to the cell door. 'Get out.'

'Let Gaheris take the rap.' A wicked grin. 'Just between us girls, of course.'

'What are you talking about?'

'I'll say he picked up the gun, and if it hadn't been for you, he'd have shot Guinevere.'

'Why would he do that?'

'Because she betrayed Arthur, and Arthur is his god. Because he hates women. Because he's crazy.' Mordred waved his hands dismissively. 'Who cares why? Motives are for the birds. We know Gaheris is a killer. He killed my mother, didn't he?'

'And that justifies accusing him of a crime he didn't commit?'

'Let's say it would be poetic justice.' Mordred's eyes glittered as the story unfolded in his mind. 'He was about to shoot Guinevere, you tackled him, the gun went off, and Agravaine was hit.'

Lancelot scowled.

'Don't you see, Lance, it's perfect! You weren't trying to kill anyone. On the contrary, you were trying to save Guinevere . . . Trying? What am I saying? You saved her! Arthur should be grateful to you. Alright, you fucked his wife, but what's done is done. And all's fair in love and war.'

Through the bars of his cell Lancelot looked across the island, past Command Control, NIWIS and the Robot Centre, across the landing strip to the clusters of white surveillance columns at the perimeter of the island. In the distance, as the land sloped away, he could see the Atlantic ocean. For an instant his spirits soared. A ray of sun penetrated a layer of cloud. High up, a wedge of geese flew in V-shaped formation.

He looked at Mordred with deep suspicion. 'Why would you lie for me?'

Mordred was prepared for that question. 'Because I like you, always have. And because Camelot needs you.'

'Then why are you trying to destroy me?'

A disdainful smile. 'I have no interest in destroying you,' said Mordred. 'You are my bait, Lance, my sprat to catch a mackerel.'

'And the mackerel is?'

'My father.'

'I don't understand.'

'Your affair with Guinevere was tearing Camelot apart. And all the time Arthur knew what was going on.'

Lancelot had no answer to that, knowing in his heart that it was true.

'And what did he do about it? I'll tell you what he did. Nothing. Just as he did nothing about my mother's murder.' Mordred spat out the words. 'I took an oath to respect

Camelot's principles. We all did. What a farce! What principles are we supposed to respect when our leader's life is one big lie?'

'And you want to replace one big lie with another?'

Mordred sighed. 'Don't be tiresome, Lance, you are in no position to lecture me. I'm throwing you a rope. Grab it, and you could be out of here tomorrow.'

Lancelot turned his back on his tormentor. 'I'd rather rot in this cell.'

'Then,' said Mordred, with a spiteful grin, 'that's exactly what you will do.'

Sixty Four

WHEN HE ENTERED her cell Guinevere could not look him in the face. Slowly, uncertainly, he moved towards her, and suddenly she was in his arms. For a time they stood there holding each other; then gently disengaging herself, she sat on the small bed in the corner of the cell, and he on a stool.

'I've brought shame on you,' she whispered.

'You should have left me,' said Arthur. 'It would have hurt, but none of this would have happened.'

He was surprised by the vehemence of her reaction. 'I would never leave you, never. I love you.'

'You love Lancelot,' said Arthur.

Guinevere's hands clasped and unclasped in her lap. 'I love you too,' she said. 'Don't ask me how I can love you both. I've tried to explain it to myself, but I can't.'

Lancelot with her heart, me with her head, he was thinking.

'Do you hate me?' she asked.

Arthur sighed. 'It would make things a lot easier if I did.'

'I'm sorry – truly sorry.'

He lifted his hands to silence her. 'No, Ginny, that's not what I want from you. You didn't mean to fall in love with Lance, I know that. Oddly enough, it changes nothing. To me you are still that girl I met in your father's house all those years ago.' His eyes dreamed back to those days. 'And then a few years later this amazingly beautiful young woman came into my life, and I fell in love.' He took her hands. 'I've been in love with her ever since.'

They sat looking into each other's eyes.

'Do you ever regret marrying me?' he asked.

'The only thing I regret is causing you pain,' she said, head down, shoulders shaking.

'Don't,' said Arthur. 'It will be alright. Everything will be alright.'

Gawain was torn between anger at the death of his brother and loyalty to Lancelot. Keenly competitive though the two men had always been, they were tied by bonds of mutual respect and comradeship that amounted to love. Yet whatever sympathy he may have felt for Lancelot, there was no doubt in his mind that he and Guinevere must be put on trial. What the verdict would be, he had no idea. One thing only he was certain of; if justice were not done and seen to be done, Camelot was doomed.

Lancelot begged him to save Guinevere. 'Her only sin was to fall in love with me, and for that we are answerable to Arthur, not to any court of law. She had nothing to do with the shooting. Mordred is spreading poison, saying she put me up to it. It's a lie.'

Gawain would not be drawn. 'It's for the High Council to decide.' He was struck by how dispirited his old rival was, there seemed to be no fight left in him. Where was proud Lancelot now?

'What will they do to her?'

Gawain tossed his head from side to side like a horse trying to throw off its bridle. 'I really can't say.'

Lancelot frowned. 'Can't, or won't?'

For a time Gawain looked through the window as if the answer were somewhere out there, blown on the westerly breezes. 'The word is she'll get a year or two.'

'But she hasn't done anything. Why should she be punished for what I did?'

'They'll say she's an accessory to manslaughter.'

'My God.' Lancelot's head sank into his hands. 'And me?'

'If they find you guilty of manslaughter, my guess is you'll get five years, maybe a bit less.'

Lancelot paced the tiny cell. 'I was set up by Mordred. I never meant to kill Agravaine. Why would I?'

'I don't know,' said Gawain.

'The truth is, I'm here, not because I killed a man by accident, but because God is punishing me for my presumption.'

'Why would He want to do that?'

Lancelot held out his hands, palms upward. 'You can't see it, but it's there.'

'What is?'

'The blood.' He thrust his hands into his armpits, 'It's on my hands and on my conscience.' In the twilight his dark eyes burned. 'They come for me every night,' he said, hunching his shoulders.

'Who does?'

'Ian Duncan . . . and now Agravaine.'

'Ian died in battle.'

'I sent him there. I killed him, just as surely as if I'd pulled the trigger myself.'

'That's not true.'

'All those men who died in battle, Gawain, my friends and comrades, they haunt me. I see their gaping wounds, their smashed faces, their torn limbs.'

'Soldier's nightmares,' said Gawain. 'We all have them.'

For a long time neither man spoke. 'How is Galahad?'

'Holding up well,' said Gawain. 'Still insisting that Mission Grail is not a lost cause.'

'Does anyone believe him?'

'There are those in the Round Table who see him as the only hope for the future – Arthur, for one.'

'I wish he would come and see me.'

'He'll come,' said Gawain.

'No, he won't. He has lost all respect for me.'

Gawain rehearsed a few words of comfort in his head, but

they sounded false.

'I hear he called me a murderer.'

'He's confused and angry now,' said Gawain. 'He'll be here, I promise you.'

'I'm not sure I want him to see me like this.' Crouched on his bed, hugging his knees, Lancelot rocked wretchedly from side to side, mourning his lost innocence. 'The shame of it, Gawain, the shame of it.'

Sixty Five

LEO GRANT WAS AT first convinced that his daughter's alleged affair with Lancelot was nothing but a vile rumour spread by Mordred. When, to his horror, Guinevere confessed her guilt, he bombarded her with questions. Did she not love Arthur? Did he not love her? Was he not a good husband? Had he not earned her loyalty? To every question her response was, yes. In that case, he asked, bewildered, why had she been unfaithful? To that she had no answer, partly because she was ashamed, partly because she did not know herself. Unwilling to condemn his beloved daughter, Leo blamed himself for the misfortune that had befallen her. It was he who had encouraged the relationship, he who had helped overcome her doubts about marrying Arthur.

When the Round Table met to consider the case against Lancelot and Guinevere, Leo pleaded with them not to send his daughter for trial. The members listened respectfully to the old man, but remained unconvinced, the overwhelming majority voting to refer the case to the High Council.

Approximately one month later, Lancelot and Guinevere were tried for the killing of Agravaine before a panel of three judges. On the third day they retired and, in less than two hours, returned with their verdict. Lancelot, they found guilty of manslaughter, Guinevere, of being an accessory to the crime. He was sentenced to six years in Camelot's prison, she to three. The news spread quickly round the island. Whilst there was satisfaction that justice had been done, there was also uneasiness about the future. This had been a humiliating experience for

Arthur. Had his authority been undermined? There were those who spoke of Mordred as his father's successor. Whatever reservations there were relating to his entrapment of the two lovers, a man who had brought about the downfall of Camelot's Chief of Staff and Arthur's wife could not be underrated. That he was Arthur's son made the situation even more intriguing.

A few days after the trial Gawain visited Lancelot in prison. 'I'll see to it you're looked after, Lance. And Guinevere, of course. In a few weeks, when the heat's off, things will be different, I promise you.'

'In what way?'

'You'll be given privileges.'

'What sort of privileges?'

'Longer exercise hours, better food, more visitors . . . ' Gawain's expansive hand gestures suggested that he was able to conjure privileges out of thin air.

'You are too generous,' said Lancelot, heavily sarcastic.

'It's just that for the time being we have to – you know what I mean, Lance, appearances are important.'

'Is that why I'm here? For the sake of appearances?'

'You are here because you shot Agravaine,' said Gawain coldly.

'I am being punished for a crime I did not commit.'

Gawain gritted his teeth. 'You killed my brother.'

'And for that I am deeply sorry,' said Lancelot. 'Believe me, if I could undo what I did, I would.'

Gawain said nothing.

Like a caged lion, Lancelot paced his cell. 'It's Guinevere I worry about. Three years! For what? For loving me. That's the truth of it.'

'She will not serve out her sentence,' said Gawain. 'Nor will you.'

'You can be sure of that,' said Lancelot.

In the silence that followed the two men exchanged looks, Gawain's concerned, Lancelot's defiant.

'You are not thinking of trying to escape, are you?'

Lancelot did not respond directly. 'I am a man with no hope and no future.'

'Listen to me, Lance,' said Gawain, 'if you try to escape, you'll be finished in Camelot. I strongly advise you to be patient. One day, I promise, the Round Table will welcome you back. When that day comes, I shall be happy to hand over command of the armed forces to the man who deserves to lead them. Agreed?'

'What is it you want from me?'

'Your solemn word that you will not try to escape,' said Gawain. 'If you give me that, I shall do everything in my power to make life easier for you, and for Guinevere too.' He held out his hand. 'Do I have it?'

Lancelot hesitated before taking the proffered hand. 'You have it,' he said.

For Arthur the future looked bleak. What would happen when Guinevere was released? Would their relationship ever recover? Would she want to come back to him? Would he want her to? And why had Mordred felt it necessary to do what he did? Yesterday Leo Grant had told him something disturbing.

'Your son is undermining your authority.'

'Who told you that?'

'I heard him – or rather overheard him – talking to several members of the Round Table. He's too smart to say such things in my presence.'

'What exactly did he say?'

'That condoning your wife's adultery was hypocritical, that we had all been contaminated by lies and deception, that he wanted to restore openness and truth to Camelot.'

'How did they react?'

'Some were convinced you knew nothing about the affair.'

'What did Mordred say to that?'

'He laughed. Said if you knew nothing about it, you were the only one in Camelot who didn't, which means you are not as

smart as you think you were. And if you knew what was going on, then you lied to yourself and everyone else. Either way . . . '
Leo could not say it.

'Go on, Leo.'

'Either way, you are unfit to govern.'

Was his own son plotting against him? Or were those harsh words spoken in a fit of anger? Whichever it was, there was more than a grain of truth in them. His love for Guinevere had clouded his judgement. Under siege, and feeling increasingly isolated, he was losing faith in his ability to fulfil his destiny. What kind of message was he sending to those who believed in him? How could he hope to make the world a better place if he could not even keep his own house in order?

Sixty Six

IT WAS NOW SIX MONTHS since the trial. As condemned prisoners, Lancelot and Guinevere were allowed to meet briefly once a day, but only with guards present. Their inner desperation showed itself in their downcast eyes and dejected bearing, Guinevere accepting her punishment as retribution for betraying Arthur, Lancelot continuing to maintain that he had been unjustly punished. Hardly a day passed when he did not curse himself for promising not to try and escape.

The longer Lancelot and Guinevere remained in prison, the more the men and women of Camelot sympathised with their predicament, wondering whether something should not be done to alleviate, or perhaps end, their suffering.

Talk of an appeal unnerved Mordred. What if the groundswell of sympathy were to grow? Now that the running sore of public outrage was healing, who could tell what might happen? An appeal with Arthur's backing might well succeed. If the sentences were substantially reduced, or if, heaven forbid, the guilty verdicts overturned, all his good work would be undone. People had such short memories. Lancelot and Guinevere would soon be back in favour, and Arthur's prestige and popularity fully restored. That must not be allowed to happen. It was essential that the two lovers serve out their sentences.

Or was there, perhaps, an alternative?

He chose Lancelot's birthday to visit him.

The chilly reception came as no surprise. 'What are you doing here?'

An unexpected answer: 'I came to ask your forgiveness. If

there is anything I can do to help you, I will do it. Trust me.'

Trust Mordred! Did the evil little monster really think he was impressed by that fawning manner and those obscenely hypocritical words? 'You are a devious bastard, Mordred. You have come here to gloat, that's obvious.'

Mordred pulled an untidily wrapped brown paper parcel from his coat pocket. 'I brought you a birthday present,' he said, tossing it on the bed.

'I want no presents from you.'

An airy wave of the hand. 'Give it away if you have no use for it.'

'Don't come back,' said Lancelot, 'or you'll live to regret it.' A meaningful look. 'Or you might not.'

Irritated by Mordred's obvious indifference to his threats, he added ominously, 'Just remember, Mordred, one day I'll be out of here.'

'That day,' said Mordred, 'could be nearer than you think.'

When he had gone, Lancelot unwrapped the parcel. Inside was a loaded semi-automatic pistol.

An appeal to the High Council on Lancelot's behalf was imminent. Concerned what his reaction might be if the appeal were rejected, Arthur gave orders that he was not to be forewarned. The day before the hearing, Gareth brought him his lunch. As he laid the tray on the bed, Lancelot drew the pistol. Backing to the cell door, Gareth closed it behind him. 'You are not getting out of here, Lance.'

'I don't have time to argue. Move away from the door.'

'This is crazy. Your appeal is being heard tomorrow.'

For a second Lancelot's attention was distracted. 'What appeal?'

'The appeal to overturn your conviction.'

'Nice try, Gareth.' Lancelot gestured with the gun. 'Now move away.'

Their faces were inches apart. 'You wouldn't shoot me.'

Lancelot held the barrel to Gareth's head and cocked the gun. 'I'm telling you for the last time, Gareth, move away from the door.'

Gareth moved, yelling as he did so, 'prisoner escaping!' As Gaheris rushed through the door and crashed into Lancelot, the gun flew out of his hand. Too dazed to react, Gaheris watched helplessly as Lancelot and Gareth wrestled, rolling over and over in a deadly struggle for the pistol. By far the stronger of the two men, Lancelot wrested the gun from Gareth and pointed it at him. 'On your stomach,' he ordered, standing over him, 'arms spread.' Crouching on all fours, Gareth froze for a second, then leaped at Lancelot's legs, bringing him down. There was a shot, a cry of pain, and Gareth fell back with a bullet in his chest. Gaheris, still dazed, pulled a gun and fired at Lancelot as he rose unsteadily to his feet. The shot missed, the bullet hitting the cell wall just above his head. Holding his pistol in both hands, Lancelot levelled it at Gaheris's head.

'Drop it,' he ordered, 'drop it, or I'll shoot.'

His chest heaving, Gaheris screamed, 'You killed my baby brother.' Raising his gun again, he took aim at Lancelot.

'For God's sake, Gaheris, don't make me do it.'

Gaheris began to cry. 'You're a dead man, Lance,' he whimpered, tears starting from his eyes, his finger squeezing the trigger even as the bullet from Lancelot's gun struck him in the neck.

When the medics arrived, Gaheris's lips were already turning blue. Gareth died on the way to hospital. Within minutes, George Bedivere reported the killings to Arthur.

'He used Gareth's key to let Guinevere out of her cell.'

'I must see her.'

'I'm sorry, Arthur, she's gone.'

'Gone?'

'She and Lancelot left the island together. He took one of the Scuttles. We can't find Lanky. It looks like she went with them.'

'I see,' said Arthur, his eyes vacant.

'They took off three minutes ago. The Scuttle has disappeared off the screen, but we have a pretty good idea where he's heading. He can't stay mantled too much longer or he'll run out of power. Sooner or later we'll get a fix on him.' He waited in vain for Arthur to say something. 'Just give the order and we'll send a Scuttle after them.'

Arthur's eyes were still blank. It was clear he had not fully grasped what George was telling him. 'Guinevere is where, you say?'

'She left the island.' George would rather have died than display any emotion, but he was close to tears now.

Arthur gazed intently into space, his eyes focused on something invisible to George. 'Lancelot too?'

'I'm truly sorry, Arthur.'

Arthur lowered himself into an armchair. 'I had such dreams,' he said, after a while.

'You'll make them all come true,' said George.

'Will I?'

George had known Arthur as comrade in arms and friend, and never for an instant had reason to doubt his strength and determination to handle the most difficult situation. Never, until this moment. In all the years he had never seen him in such despair. Not just his head but his whole body was bowed. Grief weighed him down.

The following day the Round Table met and voted that Lancelot be brought back to Camelot, if necessary by force, to be tried by the High Council. Some members argued that his presence in Camelot would be an embarrassment, and that he should be allowed to disappear. The majority felt strongly that in escaping from prison and killing Gaheris and Gareth in the process, he had expressed his contempt for Camelot and everything it stood for. Allowing him to go free would send the wrong signal to the world. How could they justify waging a war against the wicked if they themselves permitted wicked deeds to go unpunished?

Though Arthur had good reason to avenge himself on Lancelot, he had too much respect for the man to join the pack of wolves howling for his blood. As for Guinevere, how easy it would have been to allow his love for her to turn to hate. Yet, despite everything, he loved her still, and was haunted night and day by countless precious memories – the tender look in her eyes when he made love to her, the way her lips moved when she spoke, the smell of her body, the proud tilt of her chin.

In Gawain's mind there was no such conflict. Once, in another life, he had loved Lancelot. Now he wanted him dead. In a matter of months the man who had been both friend and rival had killed three of his brothers, first, the cleverest, Agravaine, and now poor, simple Gaheris, and sweet, innocent Gareth, Gawain's youngest sibling, whom he had loved and nurtured since he was little more than a baby. Gawain had his reservations about Mordred, but when he rose in the Great Hall to demand that 'Lancelot, the "serial killer", pay the price for his crimes,' he was the first to raise his hand in support.

And it was he, the natural choice, who was given the authority to lead the hunt. Before he left, he said goodbye to Arthur.

'I shall bring back Guinevere and Lanky.'

'And Lancelot?'

'He'll resist,' said Gawain.

'And if he doesn't?'

'I guarantee he will,' said Gawain, with black humour.

'In other words you intend to kill him.'

'You have a problem with that, uncle?'

'Yes, I do.'

'What do you suggest, then?'

'Bring him back for trial. Let the law take its course.'

'With respect, sir, this is between Lancelot and me. It's my brothers he killed.'

'I loved your brothers too,' said Arthur.

'Then let me do what I have to.'

'Will you promise to do everything in your power to bring him back for trial?'

Gawain avoided the question. 'Your idea of justice and mine are very different, uncle. You say you want the law to take its course, but the truth is that in your heart of hearts you don't want Lancelot punished.'

'And you, Gawain? What do you want?'

'I want revenge,' said Gawain.

'What about mercy?'

'What mercy did he show my brothers?'

'We must set an example to the world.'

'You know what?' said Gawain, 'I don't care what example I set. As long as the criminals are punished, what does it matter how we do it?'

'It matters,' said Arthur. 'Acting justly is what gives us the right to do what we do. What message would killing Lancelot send to the world?'

'I am not in the business of sending messages,' said Gawain, 'not any more.'

'This is Camelot, Gawain. We deal in justice, not revenge.'

'Do we?' said Gawain. 'What was *Operation Mainline*, then?'

Suddenly Arthur had the look of an old man, his skin ashen, his features lined and drawn, the light of his sapphire blue eyes dimmed. 'Who will go with you?' he asked quietly.

'I'm going alone.'

'I'm coming with you,' said Arthur.

'There is nothing you can do.'

'It's not a request,' said Arthur, 'it's an order.' The look in his eye told Gawain that there was no point in arguing.

'We leave in two hours,' he said.

Sixty Seven

AT THE LAST MINUTE, Arthur wavered; he should not leave Camelot at such a time. The trial and conviction of Lancelot and Guinevere, followed by their escape and the killing of the two brothers had left the island in a state of confusion. Who knew what might happen in his absence? In the end, forced to choose between his duty as leader, and his moral obligations as a man, he decided to go with Gawain. There was a life, perhaps two lives, to be saved, and that was what mattered most.

Someone had to be in charge whilst he was away. Not Mordred, who could no longer be trusted. Not Leo Grant, who was too old and tired for such responsibility. George Bedivere? A distinct possibility, especially if he had a man of unimpeachable integrity to support him. Summoning George, he offered him the job of acting Commander-in-Chief. After a token protest, he accepted, flattered at this demonstration of Arthur's confidence in him.

'You intend to bring them back?'

'Yes.'

George had a way of asking pertinent questions. 'Do you not think Lancelot would rather die a soldier's death than rot in jail?'

He was right. A shot to the head, or a split-second burst of Elimat from a portable, and it would be over; better for Lancelot, better in some ways for all of them. Nevertheless, George had missed the point. 'This isn't personal any more,' said Arthur. 'It's not about Lancelot or Gawain, or you or me. It's about justice. We have no choice. However painful, we have to do the right thing.' Taking a palm computer from his pocket he handed it to George.

'What's this?'

'The access codes to Excalibur,' said Arthur.

'Dear God.' Beads of sweat bloomed on George's forehead. 'I really don't need this,' he muttered.

'The codes have two main functions,' said Arthur, ignoring him. 'First, they give you the means to increase power at source.'

'Why would I need to do that?'

'The chances are you won't. Current levels of power are sufficient for our requirements. But in the unlikely event that you have to launch a major field operation, or should Camelot be under attack, you may need to increase those levels significantly.'

'And the second function?'

'The doomsday code – the code that commands Excalibur to self-destruct, and destroys the island with it. That situation would arise only if Camelot were about to fall into enemy hands and you decided to evacuate. Obviously you needn't concern yourself about that.'

George pondered. 'If something happened to me, the codes could fall into the wrong hands.'

'For that reason I have given duplicate codes to one other member of the Round Table.'

'Who?'

'Galahad.'

'Galahad! You can't be serious.'

'I am absolutely serious,' said Arthur.

George held up his steel right hand. 'A long time ago I lost this hand. If it hadn't been for you, I would have lost my life. For that I can never repay you. I would do anything for you, you know that.'

Arthur nodded.

'When have we ever disagreed about anything – anything that mattered?'

'Never.'

'Then trust my judgement now. Galahad is young and gullible, and he doesn't learn from experience. He's still rushing round the world trying to get rehab centres built.'

'What's wrong with that?'

'Nothing. Except that *Mission Grail* is dead on its feet.'

'Listen to me, George,' said Arthur, 'Galahad believes that all men and women are essentially good, which means that sometimes they let him down, betray him, mock him, spurn him. Does he give up? No, he keeps on trying. That's what he's doing now. Mission Grail is alive. It will never be dead. Galahad is young, and yes, he's naive too, but he's a good man, and he *believes*, he truly believes in the future of mankind.' Arthur's eyes shone with the light of conviction. 'Galahad is our future. If we lose faith in him, we lose faith in Camelot.'

Thoughtfully, George scratched his two day growth. He had always tried to do what needed to be done, done it right as he saw it, never thought too deeply about the why's and wherefore's, leaving that to Arthur. That's what he would do now. A grunt and a nod signified his assent.

'Bless you, George,' said Arthur. 'I shall tell the Round Table what we have agreed.'

As the two friends parted, George could not help wondering when, if ever, he would see Arthur again.

Sixty Eight

GALAHAD'S APPOINTMENT as joint acting Commander-in-Chief angered Mordred. George Bedivere's temporary promotion he could live with. An experienced soldier and former British Defence Minister, he was a man of maturity and common sense. What was Galahad? A religious fanatic who saw the world in black and white.

Moreover, it seemed to him that with Galahad's appointment, Arthur had anointed his heir. It was a signal that if anything should happen to him whilst he was off the island, Galahad was to take over. It confirmed what he had long suspected. For some time Arthur had made it obvious that Galahad was the chosen one, had said absurdly flattering things about him, things that to Mordred – and to Mordred's friends at the Round Table – were highly provocative; for example that Galahad was the future of Camelot. If that was so, it was not a future he wanted any part of.

In his view, by leaving Camelot – if only for a few days – Arthur had made two serious tactical, and quite possibly fatal, blunders. First, whilst he had hoped to secure his own position by appointing George and Galahad as his stand-ins, he had in fact left the field open to his son. Second, in anointing Galahad, he had demonstrated, better than any words could have done, that he did not trust Mordred. Why else had he not passed him the baton? It was a clear message, as he saw it; one intended to destroy any hope he might have had of succeeding his father, and it left him with no option but to take decisive action.

In the gardens of the House of Prayer was the only oak tree on the island, its branches distorted, its growth stunted by years of Atlantic storms. Around its trunk was a wooden seat where Galahad liked to sit reading his bible and communing with God. There Mordred joined him, lips moving as though in prayer, a bible open on his knees,

After a while he closed it. 'Do I disturb you?'

'Not at all.'

'I want to congratulate you on your appointment,' said Mordred. 'It's a great honour, and may I say, thoroughly deserved.'

'Thank you.'

Mordred looked up at the sky as though he were communing with some power above. 'I see you as Arthur's natural successor. And I am not alone in that opinion.'

'You are most kind,' said Galahad.

'I look forward to serving you.'

Galahad blinked nervously. That anyone should serve him was a new and rather unnerving thought.

'When the time comes, of course,' continued Mordred smoothly.

'That will not be for many years,' said Galahad, 'if ever it comes.'

'Mordred spoke softly but deliberately. 'There are those who would rather it happened sooner than later.'

Galahad shifted uneasily on the seat. He would have preferred to change the subject, but that was impossible. Mordred's words hung in the air, inviting – no demanding – a response.

'What are you suggesting, Mordred?'

Mordred drew in his breath, held it for a few seconds, and exhaled noisily, as if he were purging himself of some evil spirit. 'No man loves my father more than I do,' he said. 'I am his seed. His blood is my blood, his genes are my genes. You cannot imagine how much pain it gives me when I think . . . when I think what terrible things he has done.' Mordred rocked from side to side like a man in mourning. 'And the even more terrible things he intends to do,' he concluded unhappily.

Galahad was bewildered. Could this be Arthur, Mordred was talking about? 'What terrible things?'

Head in hands, Mordred was the embodiment of a man bearing the weight of the whole wicked world on his shoulders.

Galahad prompted him. 'What terrible things?'

Mordred sneaked a quick but penetrating look at Galahad. 'You agree *Operation Mainline* was a mistake?'

Galahad hesitated, fearing he was being drawn against his will to some unknown and intimidating place. 'Of course,' he said in a low voice.

'You may find this hard to believe,' said Mordred, 'but Arthur is convinced it was a triumph. The drug barons were destroyed, Camelot demonstrated its power, and he was the hero of the world. He appears to have forgotten that he killed many innocent people, or perhaps he considers it to be of no consequence. As for *Mission Grail* . . . you know what my father called *Mission Grail?*'

Galahad shook his head.

'A disaster,' said Mordred, hissing out the word.

Galahad opened his bible, hoping to find some comfort there, but there was none, only a blur of words. A soft breeze ruffled the pages, as though the hand of God had brushed them. Arthur might think *Mission Grail* a disaster. God did not. Of that Galahad was certain.

A voice intruded on his reflections. 'He admitted to me that he felt personally humiliated,' Mordred was saying. 'One day he was a hero, the next, a buffoon. He had lost face, and Camelot its reputation for being infallible. There was only one way to regain the world's respect, he said.'

'What way?'

'He intends to wipe out the new generation of drug barons. As soon as he gets back to Camelot, he will launch *Operation Mainline Number Two.*'

Galahad clasped his bible tightly. Fear wrenched his stomach. 'He cannot possibly mean it.'

'I'm afraid he does,' said Mordred, fixing on Galahad a gaze so searching that it seemed to reach into his very soul.

'I'll talk to him,' said Galahad. 'He'll listen to me, won't he?' His eyes begged for Mordred's agreement.

Mordred fingered his chin, as if unsure whether to speak his mind. 'I didn't want to tell you this,' he said, 'but I'm afraid it's too late for talking. My father intends to banish you from Camelot. He blames you for the divisions in the Round Table. You cause too much trouble, he says.'

'That isn't Arthur talking,' said Galahad. 'He's not himself. He isn't thinking straight.'

Mordred looked thoughtful. 'You could be right,' he said. 'I fear his mind may have collapsed under the strain of the last few months. I have been concerned about him for some time. So have many of his friends at the Round Table.'

Could that be the answer? 'The Round Table,' said Galahad. 'What about them?'

'He can't act without their support.'

'A formality,' said Mordred. 'The hawks are in the majority, and they'll vote for him.'

Galahad clutched his head despairingly. 'There must be something we can do.'

'The solution lies in your hands,' said Mordred.

'How can that be?' said Galahad. 'I am nothing. Arthur is the most powerful man on earth.'

'Not without Excalibur, he isn't,' said Mordred, savouring the effect of his words as they slithered like poisonous snakes into Galahad's brain.

The next morning he presented himself at the door of George Bedivere's apartment.

Name?

'Mordred.'

Enter Mordred.

'Good of you to see me,' said Mordred.

George grunted an acknowledgment, and waved in the direction of a chair. 'Have a seat.' Being a pleasant young man, and Arthur's son, George had always treated Mordred with the respect he felt he merited. On a personal level, he had relatively little contact with him.

Mordred seated himself in the armchair indicated, and, with great deliberation, placed the tips of his fingers and thumbs together, creating a triangle, over the apex of which he peered at George. 'I . . . I have – um – something of importance to share with you,' he said, his hesitant manner conveying the conflict in his head between the duty to speak and the fear of offending.

'Out with it,' said George, who disliked wasting time on what he regarded as waffle. In his view, Mordred had a tendency in that direction.

Sensing a certain reserve in his host, Mordred abandoned his planned indirect approach and came straight to the point, in the process separating his fingertips and patting the arms of his chair to add weight to his words. 'I am worried about Galahad,' he said, 'deeply worried. He is talking wildly, saying some very odd things.'

'He does have some strange ideas,' agreed George. 'But he's more foolish than dangerous.'

'Perhaps,' said Mordred. 'On the other hand,' – a series of pats accompanied his words – 'what could be more dangerous than the fanatical conviction that everything you do is sanctioned by God?'

'He talks a lot,' said George. 'I wouldn't take him too seriously if I were you.'

'I do hope you are right,' said Mordred, looking anxious, 'although if you are not . . . and he has some mischief in mind . . . ' He left the rest to George's imagination. The two men locked gazes, each challenging the other to speak.

In the end it was George who weakened. 'What kind of

mischief?'

'He has the access codes, doesn't he?' said Mordred, the insinuating look in his eye lending sinister meaning to his words.

George's stomach was suddenly queasy. In the small hours he had dreamed disquieting dreams, and Galahad figured in many of them. He had never approved the decision to leave the youngster the duplicate access codes, and had only acquiesced out of consideration for Arthur. What if something terrible were to happen? He would be responsible, answerable both to Arthur and the Round Table. 'Go on,' he said.

'The last time Galahad and I spoke,' said Mordred, 'he was sounding off about Arthur being a dictator with innocent blood on his hands, and how he wants to rule the world – a lot of crazy stuff like that.' He leaned forward in his chair, eyes blazing. 'You are not going to believe this, George. You know what he said?'

Tension gripped George's head like a steel vice.

'He claims that as soon as he gets back to Camelot, Arthur intends to launch *Operation Mainline Number Two* to kill off the new generation of drug barons! Now I ask you – knowing my father as you do, would he do such a thing?' Mordred lowered his voice conspiratorially. 'I don't like to say it, but to me he sounded deranged.'

'Maybe so,' said George, 'but he worships the ground Arthur treads on. Talking against him is one thing, doing anything about it is something else.'

'Exactly what I thought at first,' said Mordred, 'but then he started hinting he was going to do something really major. I kept asking him what, but every time I asked, he clammed up. Obviously he didn't trust me, so I decided the only way to win his confidence was to pretend to agree with him. If I hadn't, he would never have given himself away. And believe me, it's major. He wasn't kidding.'

George was becoming entangled in Mordred's web of deceit.

'Out with it. What is he going to do?'

'Destroy Excalibur,' said Mordred.

Whatever George was expecting, it was not that. 'My God!' A few moments reflection, and the full horror dawned. 'If he destroys Excalibur, he destroys Camelot with it. Does he know that?'

'I reminded him, and he seemed quite relaxed about it,' said Mordred. 'Says we'll have plenty of time to evacuate the island.'

The steel vice tightened further. George winced with pain. 'You are certain he is serious?'

'I was never more certain of anything in my life,' said Mordred.

'Then he must be mad,' said George.

'I fear he is,' said Mordred, as apologetically as if he were personally responsible for Galahad's mental condition. 'Arthur made a grave error of judgement when he gave him the access codes.'

'He has to be stopped. Perhaps I should arrest him on suspicion of plotting espionage,' mused George.

'If you think that's the way to go,' said Mordred. 'He would deny everything, of course. Besides, we can't be a hundred per cent certain he'll make good his threats.'

'That's true.' Under extreme pressure, George was doing his best to think clearly. 'I could talk to Arthur.'

Mordred appeared to give the idea serious consideration. 'Supposing Galahad is right, though. About Arthur, I mean.'

George nodded. Mordred had a point. This was a tricky one. On the one hand, Camelot could be in mortal danger. On the other, Galahad might just be ranting – about Arthur, and about his own intentions. 'I can't move without proof,' he concluded. 'When I have that, I'll do what has to be done.'

'I'll get you proof,' said Mordred.

'How?'

'When he decides to act, he'll tell me. And don't worry, I'll be there to stop him.'

George Bedivere had been in many life-threatening situations, but none as traumatic as this. One wrong decision could bring down Camelot. 'Too risky,' he said, 'he might give you the slip.'

'He won't do that,' said Mordred confidently. 'Remember, he thinks I'm on his side. I'll alert you the instant he makes his move.'

George considered consulting the Round Table, and decided against it. If he warned them about Galahad, Arthur would be severely criticised for giving him the codes. The effect on morale would be disastrous. 'I'm relying on you, Mordred,' he said, worry lines creasing his forehead. 'The future of Camelot may depend on us.'

'Trust me,' said Mordred.

Several floors below Galaxy, the Energy Control Centre regulated the energy source of all Camelot's communications and weaponry. In each of four rooms a dozen screens on a dozen computer terminals displayed current data measuring Excalibur's energy levels; energy consumed, and estimated energy required for the island, for air, land and sea craft, for weapons and communications, and for current and projected operations.

From the rim of an imaginary wheel, four corridors led from these rooms to the wheel's hub, Excalibur Control, a sparsely furnished, dimly lit room, with a single terminal in the centre, about the same size as the table monitor in Galaxy. The approaches to Excalibur Control were protected by four steel doors armed with surveillance panels, and at each door a destroyer robot programmed with the same instructions; no one, not even Arthur himself, was permitted to enter unless they knew the password of the day. Anyone trying to force an entry would be killed.

On the terminal's screen there was no data, only an image of a blue sky and reeds growing in a lake. Uninformative as this simple scene appeared to be, it nevertheless confirmed to those who knew, that Camelot's power source was operating smoothly. The scene never changed, the one small exception being that now and then the reeds swayed gently, and the surface of the water was ruffled by the lightest of breezes.

Galahad and Mordred sat at the command terminal for several minutes.

'Let's wait until Arthur gets back,' said Galahad, who was having second thoughts.

'Last minute nerves,' said Mordred. 'I'll help you. We'll do it together.' With his back to Galahad, he tapped George's wake-up alarm code into his mobcom.

'I need to talk about it some more.'

'Fine, let's talk,' said Mordred. 'You have it with you?'

Galahad produced a mini-computer from his pocket. As he accessed it, the computer's light painted his face an eerie green. On the screen, in six rows of five digits each, were thirty numbers.

'That's it, Mordred,' he said, his voice unsteady, 'that's the doomsday code.' Suddenly he was overwhelmed by the enormity of what he was contemplating. 'If I feed all those numbers in, Excalibur will self-destruct and Camelot will be torn apart.'

'Right,' said Mordred calmly, peering at the screen. 'The moment you do, we'll raise the alarm and evacuate the island.'

Galahad shook his head. 'I can't do it.'

'Of course you can,' said Mordred.

Galahad's head swam, his knees buckled. Grasping the desk, he steadied himself. 'I can't.'

Last minute nerves, Mordred had said. Now he was nervous too. For his plan to work, George would have to catch Galahad in the act, but if Galahad backed off, there would be no act to catch him in. It was now or never. 'Damn it,' he said, making a grab for the computer, 'if you won't do it, I will.'

Seconds later George Bedivere rushed into Excalibur Control to find Mordred and Galahad wrestling on the floor, each trying to seize the tiny computer.

'What the hell's going on?' he demanded.

The two men separated and jumped up. Mordred handed the mini-computer to George.

'He was trying to feed in the doomsday code,' he said, breathing heavily. 'Thank God, I managed to stop him in time.'

'That's not true!' protested Galahad. 'You told me to do it. I didn't want to.'

Mordred's face was a mask of outrage. 'I am shocked, profoundly shocked,' he declared, 'that someone who claims to be a man of God should be such a despicable liar.' Galahad opened his mouth to speak. 'But I never . . . '

'Don't say another word,' said Mordred, cutting him off, 'you disgust me.'

Bewildered and distraught, Galahad cried out, 'Why are you doing this to me?'

Mordred's eyes were ice-cold. 'I have done nothing,' he said. 'You have done it to yourself.'

Sinking to his knees, Galahad raised his hands and eyes to heaven. 'Forgive me, Lord,' he whispered, 'for I have sinned.'

'There's a confession if ever I heard one,' said Mordred triumphantly.

It was sufficient for George. 'Galahad,' he said, 'consider yourself under arrest.'

Galahad, shocked and bewildered, had nothing to say. Moments later a robot guard took him by the arm and led him away.

It was agreed that George would be the one to break the news of Galahad's arrest to Arthur who, it was expected, would return to Camelot immediately.

Sixty Nine

THE SCUTTLE PILOTED by Gawain and co-piloted by Arthur, landed in the middle of a deserted Yorkshire moor far from the nearest village. There they intended to wait until Techforce Ten got a fix on Lancelot. How long that would be, no one knew.

Nearly twenty-four hours earlier his Scuttle had taken off unmantled from Camelot, heading due south for approximately a hundred kilometres before mantling and disappearing from Command Control's screens. Techforce suspected a ruse. Lancelot had learned the arts of deception from Camelot's masters – Tich and Mordred. He could have mantled immediately after take-off, but had chosen not to. Why? Why would he fly unmantled for a hundred kilometres unless he were laying a false trail? And if he was, where was he heading now?

Techforce Ten, Arthur and Gawain, debated whether Lancelot's original course was a bluff or a double bluff. When he mantled his Scuttle, had he immediately changed course and headed north? (it was generally agreed that north was more likely than east or west). Or had he continued heading south?

For three days they camped out, Gawain spending most of the day on board Scuttle talking to Command Control, whilst Arthur went for long solitary walks across the moor. When he returned, Gawain would invariably still be in Scuttle's control room, becoming more and more frustrated as the hours and days passed with no clue to Lancelot's whereabouts.

Crouched on his heels, his back propped against one of

Scuttle's giant rear wheels, Arthur would wait for his nephew, half hoping he would find Lancelot, half hoping he would not, fearing that nothing he could say or do would stop the two men trying to kill each other. On the third day a pale autumn sun rose in a cloudless sky. By mid-morning, a mass of black clouds had rolled in from the east. A hundred metres from the parked Scuttle the small tent in which the two men slept flapped and tugged at its guy ropes.

Moving cautiously down the steps from the Scuttle's belly, Gawain grabbed the handrail as a sudden gust of wind threw him off balance. 'Arthur?'

'Here.'

Gawain joined him.

'Any news?' asked Arthur automatically, though he could read the answer on Gawain's face.

Huddled in the lee of the Scuttle against the chill wind, the two comrades stared unseeing into the distance.

'Techforce think he's somewhere up north,' said Gawain, 'though there's precious little evidence of it.'

Arthur plucked a handful of grass, tossed it in the air and watched it whirl away. The wind moaned round them, now and then gusting strongly enough to make even the big Scuttle shake. With a sudden pang of nostalgia he remembered how, when he was a boy fishing by Ponterlally bridge, he would throw handfuls of grass in the river and watch the green threads drift downstream in the current.

'You think they'll find him?'

'They'll find him,' said Gawain. 'They have four mini-satellites closing in. Techforce are certain he can't hide much longer.'

For good or ill, thought Arthur, it was probably true. Lancelot could twist and turn, but it was only a matter of time before Command Control located him. And when they did, Gawain would be after him like a hound let off the leash.

Back in the tent, they lay down and dozed. Arthur's earcom

433

vibrated, waking him. He touched the metal disc implanted in his earlobe. George Bedivere spoke. For a long time he listened, saying nothing, then cut the link. Gawain, awake now, was concerned. There was a look on Arthur's face he had never seen before. The wind dropped. It began to rain, the first drops rapping the canvas above their heads. Arthur looked defeated, as if the burden of living were suddenly too much for him. Something terrible must have happened. Flurries of rain assaulted the tent like avenging furies. The canvas slapped in the wind.

'What is it, uncle?'

'They've arrested Galahad.'

'Why, for God's sake!'

'It seems he was trying to use the access codes to command Excalibur to self-destruct.'

'I find that hard to believe,' said Gawain, more because he knew it was what Arthur wanted to hear than because he discounted the possibility.

Arthur told himself that Galahad was not capable of such treachery. Certainly he was against killing under any circumstances, had made no secret of it, but not against Camelot – never that. He believed in what Camelot was trying to achieve, even if, sometimes, he disapproved of its methods. It was inconceivable, therefore, that he would try to destroy Camelot's most powerful weapon. Unless . . . Galahad was not a man to compromise. Had his pacifist convictions overcome reason? Had the zealot in him taken over?

For Arthur, this was much more than a personal tragedy. The vision he had of a world peopled by men and women of goodwill was a noble one. Without that dream, man was no better than the animals. If Galahad had indeed turned traitor, if he were to be tried, found guilty and sentenced to a term of imprisonment, it would deal a severe blow, perhaps a mortal one, to Arthur's dream of saving mankind. Not for the first time, he suffered the pain of grief, and the pain of guilt too.

If he had stayed in Camelot instead of joining Gawain in the hunt for Lancelot, Galahad would not now be under arrest. He began to stuff his things in a backpack. 'We must get back,' he said. 'Camelot needs us.'

Gawain's jaw jutted stubbornly. 'Camelot needs *you*,' he said, 'not me.'

The tent struggled in the wind, as if desperate to be free of the earth's clutches.

'Galahad's arrest changes everything,' said Arthur.

'For me it changes nothing,' replied Gawain. His head told him it was his duty to go with Arthur, his gut instinct told him to stay, and that was a stronger pull. If he had been closer to Galahad, he might have felt differently, but he had never really warmed to him – a certain grudging admiration, no more than that. Poor Galahad. A young man not over-endowed with brains, with unshakable, not to say fanatical convictions. How could he have been so stupid? Hopefully there was some misunderstanding. Dismissing Galahad from his thoughts, he focused his mind on Lancelot.

Backpack slung over his shoulder, Arthur looked down at Gawain. 'Give up this hunt. No good can come of it.'

'My brothers will rest in peace,' said Gawain. 'And so will I.'

'If you kill Lancelot, you will never know a moment's peace in this life.'

'I'll just have to take that risk,' said Gawain.

The wind howled round the tent like a hungry wolf. Arthur had no doubt where his duty lay. Yet if he returned to Camelot alone, he would be abandoning Lancelot and Gawain to their fate. One of them, perhaps both, would surely die. Whatever he did, he would be taking a huge risk. He debated with himself, weighed the options, and made his decision; he would stay one more day. That could make little difference in Camelot, and it might just save a man's life. There was, of course, another reason to stay, one he scarcely dared admit to himself; the forlorn hope that he might persuade Guinevere to come back to Camelot with him. For despite everything, he still loved her. Nothing would ever change that.

He dropped his backpack. 'I leave tomorrow,' he said. 'Better check Scuttle's data bank again. See if they have a fix on Lancelot.'

Gawain tried not to show his disappointment. With Arthur out of the way, he would have had a free hand.

In the afternoon the wind dropped, and through a thin cloud layer a ghostly autumn sun illuminated the bleak landscape with a wan light. Gawain took a brief nap in the tent and went back to the Scuttle. Seconds later he rushed down the steps. 'They've found him!'

It was the best and the worst of news. Arthur's heart leaped and sank. 'Where?'

'He's holed up with Guinevere and Lanky in a derelict farmhouse. His Scuttle is on the other side of a big sand dune a kilometre from Bamburgh castle.' He was already back in the tent grabbing his gear. 'This is it. Let's go!'

Gawain put down the Scuttle between two massive sand dunes about a kilometre from the farmhouse. They had to assume that Lancelot knew he had been followed. Heat and movement sensors on his Scuttle would almost certainly have given their Scuttle's presence away as it unmantled. That night the sky cleared and the air was cold. Pitching their tent, they kept watch by turns. In the morning they would make their presence known.

Gawain slept like a baby, Arthur hardly at all. An hour before dawn he roused himself, made some tea and woke Gawain. For a while the two men sipped the warm brew, each committed to his own thoughts.

'I wonder what Lance is thinking now.'

Gawain stared into his mug. 'I don't give a damn,' he said. 'All I know is he murdered my brothers.'

'You should forgive him,' said Arthur.

Gawain's lips compressed. 'Even if I wanted to, I couldn't.

I have to avenge them, for their sakes as well as mine. It's my destiny, whether I like it or not.'

'Our destiny is what we make it,' said Arthur. 'Merlin taught me that.' For a few seconds he thought Gawain might be having second thoughts. But then he shook his head, indicating that the discussion was over.

An hour later Gawain knocked on the cottage door. In seconds Lancelot opened it. 'Won't you come in?' he said, showing no surprise. Gawain stood his ground. 'I'll stay out here.'

Lancelot shut the door behind him. 'Let's walk, then. Get some sea air.'

Leaning into the wind, they walked the shoreline. For a full minute neither man spoke.

'Why have you followed me here?'

'You know why,' said Gawain.

'To kill me.'

'To see justice done.'

'I have thought about that,' said Lancelot. 'If it's justice you want, let me be judged by the Round Table. I'll come back to Camelot with you.'

'I'll get no justice there. Arthur will save your skin.'

'Then it's not justice you want,' said Lancelot, 'it's revenge.'

Gawain did not answer. For a while the two men walked in silence, then Lancelot stopped and faced Gawain. 'If I were to remind you how much I loved your brothers, if I swore on my mother's life that I never meant to kill them, if I told you how bitterly I regret what happened, and that . . . not a day passes, no, nor a night either, when I do not pray for God's forgiveness – as I beg for yours now – would that change your mind?'

'It would change nothing,' said Gawain.

They walked on.

'How do you plan to kill me?' asked Lancelot, breaking another long silence.

'In a fair fight.'

'With what weapons? Ports?'

'That would not be a fight,' said Gawain. 'It would all be over in seconds.'

'You aim to prolong the agony, do you?'

Gawain would not be provoked. 'It will be a fair fight,' he repeated stolidly.

'What weapons do we use in this fair fight of yours?'

'Knives.'

'I don't have a knife.'

Gawain unstrapped a combat knife from his belt, laid it across his hand and offered it to Lancelot. 'You do now.'

Lancelot took the fearsome weapon and shuddered. 'This is not justice.'

'Nor is murder,' said Gawain.

A gust of wind blew salt spray in their faces. Turning, they retraced their steps, propelled now by the wind at their backs. A hundred metres from the cottage Lancelot fell on his knees in the sand and took Gawain's hand in his. 'I'm a proud man, Gawain. Never in my life have I begged anyone for anything, but I'm begging you now. Don't make me fight you.'

Gawain pulled his hand away. 'If you won't fight me, I shall cut your throat. Is that what you want? To be executed?'

Brushing the sand from his knees, Lancelot stood and faced his tormentor. 'Time?'

'Tomorrow, at dawn.'

'Place?'

Gawain pointed. 'The seaward side of that sand dune.'

As Arthur and Guinevere walked along the shoreline, he took her hand. Gently she eased it away. 'Don't,' she said, 'I'm too ashamed.'

'I want you back.'

'After what I've done to you?'

'I love you.'

'I love you too,' she said softly.

'And Lancelot?'

'I love him differently.'

'Come back with me, Ginny.'

'The Round Table would never accept me. I've broken the rules.'

'This isn't a game,' he said, 'there are no rules. All I care about is you – you and me. Won't you come back with me now? We could start our lives over again.'

Instead of answering, she asked, fear in her eyes, 'What will happen to Lance?'

What could he say? By this time tomorrow, Lancelot could be dead. 'I was hoping that perhaps . . . that you and he . . . that you...'

'That I would give him up?' The question hung in the air between them. 'I already have.'

Did that mean, then, that she would . . . ? He hardly dared ask.

'We have said goodbye,' she said. 'There's no future for us.'

He tried once more. 'And for us?'

She shook her head.

Until now there had been hope, a forlorn hope but hope nevertheless. That shake of the head confirmed what he had feared. There was nothing to hope for anymore. Without Guinevere there would be only a gaping emptiness that would gnaw at him, body and soul, for as long as he lived. 'Where will you go?'

'I don't know.'

'What will you do?'

'Something useful,' she said. 'Work with children, perhaps.'

'And Lanky?'

'We'll stay together. She needs me.' A sad smile. 'I need her.'

Fifty metres from the cottage they stopped.

'We were happy once,' he said, 'weren't we, Ginny?'

As happy as she had ever been, she thought. But then, had

she ever been truly happy? Or was happiness a dream, always somewhere out of reach? 'Happier than I had any right to be,' she said.

'I want you to know,' said Arthur, 'that every day with you was a precious gift.'

Counting her steps, he watched her walk away, still hoping that somehow this was not the end, that any moment she would stop and turn her head. Had she done so he would have run after her, taken her in his arms and kissed her a hundred times.

But she never did.

Seventy

THOUGH IT HAD TO COME, it was nevertheless a shock when it did.

'Tomorrow, you say?'

'With combat knives.'

'Madness.'

'His madness, not mine.'

'You must call it off.'

'I can't do that.'

'Then I'm coming with you.'

'What for?'

'To see fair play,' said Arthur. 'I won't interfere.'

It was not true, and they both knew it. Arthur would use all his skill and cunning to stop the fight, and that could prove embarrassing and quite possibly dangerous. Gawain had far too much respect for his leader to be involved in a quarrel with him, more especially a violent one, and undoubtedly Lancelot would feel the same. Which meant that if Arthur were present, there would be no fight, and Lancelot might well escape with his life.

The two men climbed into their sleeping bags.

'Where?'

'Near the farmhouse.'

'When?'

'An hour after dawn,' said Gawain. 'I'll wake you.'

Arthur set the alarm on his wristcom, turning away from Gawain so that he could not see what he was doing . . . a precaution in case he "forgot" to wake him.

Shivering in the cold morning air, the two men stripped to the waist, jumping on the spot to stimulate circulation. Blotting out the few remaining stars, a bank of menacing black cloud moved relentlessly in from the sea towards the shoreline as if it were a portent of some imminent disaster.

Directing the point of his combat knife at Lancelot, Gawain spoke. One word: 'Ready?'

Lancelot had no desire to kill, much less be killed. He planned to stay out of serious trouble, accepting that sooner or later he would probably have to take a hit. Hopefully one hit would be enough to satisfy Gawain's bloodlust. 'Ready,' he said.

Peering into the gloom, the two men circled each other warily, weighing each other up, both of them studying how his opponent held his knife, how he moved, how he breathed, straining to catch the warning sign that would signal an attack; a change of expression, a tensing of lips, a spark in the eye, both knowing that the enemy was formidable, skilled in hand-to-hand combat and in the age-old art of deception.

As the minutes passed, Gawain grew more and more impatient. When he leaped forward, Lancelot sidestepped. When he thrust at his opponent's chest, Lancelot swayed back, avoiding the clumsy blow.

'Fight, you bastard,' he growled

'I am fighting.'

'Call that fighting? You're running away.'

'You want me to stand still and let you cut me?' said Lancelot, taunting him.

'You're a coward.'

'You know that isn't true.'

'Then fight like a man.'

'I don't want to fight you at all,' said Lancelot, lowering his knife.

Gawain lumbered forward. 'Hold up your knife.'

'You can't make me.'

His temper flaring, Gawain slashed at Lancelot's upper arm, the wound spurting blood. For a second or two Lancelot was tempted to retaliate. But then, restraining himself, he threw down his knife. 'First blood to you. The fight is over.'

'The fight will be over when you are dead,' said Gawain.

'You want me dead? Then get it over with.' Lancelot closed his eyes and thrust his head back, exposing his throat.

Gawain hesitated. He was being driven where he did not want to go. This was not the way it ought to end, certainly not the fair fight he had planned. Yet what choice did he have? It was his duty to avenge his brothers. Nothing else mattered. Tensing the muscles of his right arm he laid the sharp tip of his combat knife on Lancelot's carotid artery.

Hoping that he could, at the last minute, persuade Gawain to abandon his vendetta, Arthur had his best night's sleep for a long time. When the alarm buzzed, he opened his eyes and looked across at his nephew's sleeping bag. It was empty. Tearing open the tent flaps he blinked in the early dawn light. No sign of Gawain. Pulling on his clothes and boots he ran aimlessly here and there, shouting 'Gawain! Gawain!', though in his heart he knew it was a waste of time. No one answered. He had been tricked.

Lancelot waited for the end, praying it would come quickly. When seconds passed, and Gawain's knife had still not done its work, he opened his eyes and saw the indecision on his face. Deciding that his only hope of a swift end was to make him lose his temper again, he chose his words carefully. 'You are shaming your brothers' memory,' he said.

For a moment or two nothing happened, then with a roar like a wounded animal Gawain raised his knife and slashed Lancelot's face from forehead to chin. As the blood streamed into his eyes and down his cheeks Lancelot retreated, half blinded, holding up his hands to shield himself from another attack. Not knowing where he was going, he backed to the top of the sand dune and stood there swaying whilst Gawain looked up at him, stunned and sickened by the terrible wound he had inflicted. For the first time in the fight, he felt a twinge of pity for his opponent. But then he was looking not at Lancelot's bleeding face but at his baby brother, Gareth, lying on the floor of Lancelot's cell, blood oozing from the bullet wound in his chest. Climbing slowly, menacingly, to the top of the dune, he transferred his knife to his left hand and with his right punched Lancelot in the face with all his strength, once, twice, a third time, accompanying each successive blow with the words, 'That's for Agravaine, that's for Gaheris, that's for Gareth.'

Lancelot's face was sheathed in blood, the exposed bone of his brow and cheeks glistening in the first rays of the rising sun. His knees folding under him, he sank to the sand.

Gawain stood over him. 'I'll give you five minutes,' he said. 'Wash yourself in the sea . . . whatever.'

Lancelot mouthed his words with difficulty. 'You can give me till doomsday,' he said, 'I won't fight you.'

Gawain knew that he could kill Lancelot any time he wanted to. But where would be the satisfaction in that? His brothers' memory demanded that Lancelot died in combat. Besides, Lancelot was a soldier, and a soldier deserved to end his days fighting, not slaughtered like a pig.

'For the love of God, fight.' He was pleading now.

The pain was unbearable. All Lancelot wanted was a quick end to his torment. 'Your brothers got what they deserved,' he said.

Gawain grabbed Lancelot's neck with his big hands and squeezed. Somehow Lancelot found the strength to wrench Gawain's hands apart and retreat a few steps down the sand dune before Gawain hurled himself at him and knocked him down. Astride Lancelot, he seized his neck with his left hand, and raised his knife. 'Die, you bastard! Die!' Confronted with imminent death, Lancelot reacted instinctively. With the strength of desperation he threw Gawain off him. Still clutching his combat knife, Gawain somersaulted backwards and landed face down at the bottom of the dune.

Pushing himself to his feet, Lancelot staggered step by painful step and fell on his knees beside him. Gawain lay still. Laying his hand on his back, he shook him. Gawain did not stir. Gently he eased him over. He had fallen on his combat knife, the blade buried to the hilt just below the rib cage on the left side of his chest. He felt his wrist. There was a pulse, a weak one. Gawain opened his eyes.

'You're going to be OK,' said Lancelot. 'I'll call an air ambulance.'

Gawain coughed blood. 'No one can help me now.'

'I'm so sorry.'

'Not your fault,' whispered Gawain, sweat beading his brow, even in the cold morning air. 'You did . . . what you could . . . to stop me.' With his last remaining strength he raised his hand a few inches from his chest, and Lancelot grasped it. 'Forgive me,' he said, 'forgive me the wrongs I have done you and your family.' Blinking his eyes in acknowledgment, Gawain breathed a long, low sigh as the spirit left his body.

Kneeling in the sand Lancelot prayed to the God who all those years ago had brought Daniel Shalott back to life. 'Grant me this one last miracle,' he whispered. 'Let Gawain live.' Lost in his own thoughts, he did not see Arthur until he was standing over him. Dropping to his knees, Arthur felt Gawain's wrist and neck.

'He's coming to,' said Lancelot. 'Look, he moved his fingers.'

'He's gone, Lance.' Gently, Arthur smoothed shut the lids of Gawain's eyes.

'See that,' said Lancelot, 'he moved his hand again. He's trying to open his eyes.' Grabbing Gawain by the shoulders, he shook him hard. 'Open your eyes, Gawain. Open them.'

'He's dead,' said Arthur.

'I saw him move,' cried Lancelot. 'He's not dead! He's not

dead, I tell you!'

When they had loaded Gawain's body onto Arthur's Scuttle the two men walked along the shorefront.

'It was an accident,' said Lancelot, after a while. 'He fell on his own knife.'

Arthur walked on, saying nothing.

'You believe me, don't you?'

'I believe you.'

'And yet there is something in your eyes that tells me you blame me for Gawain's death.'

'It is not for me to judge you, Lance.'

Lancelot stopped and faced Arthur, eyes blazing in his bloodied, battered face. 'Why not? Why in God's name not? Who has a better right to judge me than you? I stole your wife, I killed your nephews. Strike me down. I won't lift a finger to defend myself.' Drawing his combat knife, he offered it to Arthur. 'Do it now. Kill me. I deserve to die.'

Far out a cargo vessel plummeted deep in the ocean, rode high on the crests of the waves, and plunged again. Like a man's fortunes, thought Arthur.

'There's something I have to tell you, Lance.'

'I know,' said Lancelot. 'You are taking me back to Camelot for trial.' A resigned shrug. 'Do what you have to do. I don't care what happens to me any more.'

'I'm afraid it's bad news.'

'Things couldn't get any worse.'

'It's Galahad.'

'What's he been up to?'

'They've arrested him.'

Lancelot stared blankly at Arthur. 'For what?'

'He was trying to destroy Excalibur by activating the self-destruct code.'

'Destroy Excalibur!' said Lancelot. 'Impossible.' Talking to himself, he paced back and forth on the sand. 'He needs me.

I'm going back to Camelot'

'The Round Table will not allow you to do that,' said Arthur. 'Nor will I.'

'Don't do this to me,' pleaded Lancelot. 'Don't banish me now.'

'I'm sorry, Lance, you can't come back. Not now, not ever.'

A truculent glare. 'You can't stop me.'

'You wouldn't get anywhere near the island.'

If Arthur gave the command, the Scuttle would either be destroyed or diverted, and Lancelot knew it. 'Let me clear my son's name,' he said, 'that's all I ask. When I've done that, I'll surrender to the High Council. They can do whatever they like with me. Or if you prefer, I'll leave Camelot for good.'

For an instant, Arthur was tempted. Then he shook his head. Lancelot had too many crimes to answer for. This time he would not be allowed to escape justice. If he came back, he would rot in a prison cell for the rest of his life.

'I'm begging you as a father, let me come back with you.'

'I can't do that,' said Arthur, feeling Lancelot's pain. 'It's a matter for the Round Table now. They must decide if there's a case against Galahad to answer.'

'You believe there is?'

'I am sure there isn't,' said Arthur, 'and I give you my word that I will do everything in my power to help prove his innocence.'

With that assurance Lancelot had to be satisfied.

They had reached the foot of Scuttle's stairs. 'You understand that I must destroy your Scuttle on the ground,' said Arthur.

'Yes.'

'Where will you go?'

'Somewhere no one knows me, or what I have done – if such a place exists.' He saluted his Commander-in-Chief. 'Goodbye, sir,' he said. 'I pray that one day you will find it in your heart to forgive me.'

'I forgive you now.' Arthur put out his hand.

Lancelot knelt and kissed it. 'I don't deserve to be forgiven.'

'Which of us does?' said Arthur.

The Scuttle rose vertically into the blue sky, disappearing as it mantled. Seconds later a positron beam Elimatted Lancelot's Scuttle. Slowly he walked back to the cottage knowing that in this life he would never see Arthur again.

Guinevere opened the door. Shocked by his terrible wounds but thankful he was alive, she studied his face, her eyes questioning his. 'What is it?'

'Gawain is dead.'

'Oh, no.'

With frightened eyes she watched him fill a backpack with his few belongings. 'Where are you going?'

'I don't know.'

'How did it happen?'

'What does it matter? He's dead.'

Her eyes rebuked him.

'If you must know,' he said savagely, 'he died with a knife in his guts. That's four deaths. I'm cursed, Ginny. Everyone around me is cursed. Including you.'

'That isn't true.'

'They've arrested Galahad.'

Her hand went to her mouth. 'Why?'

'They say he was trying to destroy Excalibur.' A bitter smile. 'It seems treachery runs in the family.'

'You don't mean that.'

'No,' he said, 'I don't. Galahad is innocent . . . unlike his father.'

'Please don't go,' she begged.

For an instant, standing there with his head down, he seemed moved by her plea. But then he straightened up and crossed to the door. 'I shall always love you,' he said, over his shoulder.

'Is this it?'

He nodded. 'Where will you go?'

'I have a friend who runs a children's home,' she said. 'Ever since I was a little girl I have always wanted children. Now I shall have them.'

'Lanky?'

'She's coming with me.'

He opened the door. 'Goodbye,' he said, and walked quickly away.

In the gathering storm the ocean heaved and fretted. On a secluded beach in the lee of the wind, the water, embraced by two rocky headlands, was calm. For a long time Lancelot stood looking out to sea, his mind and body drawn by a powerful undertow of despair. Out there his mother was waiting for him. He could hear her calling his name. 'Lancelot! Lancelot!'

Seventy One

THE CONTROLLER GUIDING the Scuttle towards Camelot gave no indication that anything was amiss, yet Arthur's instinct told him something was wrong. Still mantled, he circled the shoreline twice looking for signs of unrest; there were none. The island was as calm and beautiful as ever, its white buildings glowing in the afternoon sun, the scanning antennae on their elegant columns waving a greeting – or so it seemed to him – hovercarts criss-crossing the island, robots bustling about their daily business. Demantling, he banked, lined up the Scuttle with the gravitational beam, and lowered it onto the landing pad.

Mordred and George Bedivere were waiting for him on the airstrip. As Arthur descended the Scuttle's stairs Mordred rushed forward and threw his arms round him. 'Thank God you're back, father' he said, kissing him on both cheeks, something he had never done before. 'You can't imagine how much we have all have missed you.'

Arthur murmured his thanks.

Then came a no nonsense shake of the hand from George, and a brisk, 'Welcome home.' Displays of emotion were not his thing. 'These are yours,' he said, greatly relieved to be handing over the two mini-computers containing the access codes. And then, in a low voice: 'I can't tell you how sorry I am about Gawain.'

Arthur did not react. 'I have summoned the Round Table,' he said. 'We meet in two hours time.'

Gawain's body was unloaded to be taken to the morgue. 'I leave you to make the necessary arrangements, George,' said

Arthur. 'Tomorrow we bury him with full military honours.'

'Yes, sir.'

The hovercart moved off with Mordred at the wheel. 'Drop me at the prison,' said Arthur. 'I want to talk to Galahad.'

'Let me come with you,' said Mordred.

'I'll see him alone.'

'If that's what you want.' For some reason Mordred seemed ill-at-ease.

'It is.'

Face drawn, eyes ringed with blue, Galahad sat disconsolately on the bed of his cell. Arthur's heart went out to him.

'Do you want to talk?'

'What is there to say?'

'I am here to listen,' said Arthur, 'not to accuse, not to blame.'

'I am guilty,' said Galahad.

'Of what?'

'Of whatever it is they accuse me of.'

'Mordred says you tried to destroy Excalibur.'

Galahad stared at the stone wall.

'I need to hear it from you, Galahad. Is it true?'

No answer. There was about him an obstinately perverse look that Arthur found hard to interpret. Was it the look of a guilty man ashamed to admit his guilt? Or the look of an innocent man too proud to defend himself?

'Well?'

Galahad muttered sullenly, 'I don't remember.'

Deciding that nothing would be gained by prolonging this tense exchange, Arthur left Galahad in his cell to reflect on whatever it was he had done or not done.

On the way to the observatory he stopped off at Command Control and took the escalator all the way down. In the dim light of Excalibur Control he stared at the familiar image confirming that all was well with Excalibur: blue sky, reeds growing in a lake, and now and then a breeze ruffling the lake, stirring the reeds; a calm scene, oddly out of sorts with these troubled times.

He checked the main terminal's computer, then both mini-computers, fed in the first four digits of the doomsday code and immediately cancelled them. Everything was functioning normally. Finally, he checked the main computer again, rechecked a second and third time, took the escalator to ground level and walked across to NIWIS.

'I need your help, Tich.'

He grinned. 'There's nothing I would rather give you, sir.'

Arthur checked his wristcom. 'You have just one hour before the Round Table meets.'

'To do what?'

'First, I want you to check that all portables are in the armoury and accounted for.'

'I'm sure they are,' said Tich. 'The code is clear. Ports are only handed out for a military operation.'

Yes, the code was clear. At a time like this, though, the code counted for little. Tensions at the meeting would be high. If tempers frayed, and violence erupted, wounds inflicted by guns and knives could be treated. Elimat was forever.

'Do as I ask, Tich. Check.'

'I will, sir.'

'One more thing,' said Arthur. 'Here is a list of twenty names – the names of those members of the Round Table I would trust with my life.'

Tich spoke forcefully. 'You can trust every man and woman on the island with your life.'

'No doubt,' said Arthur. 'And Tich . . . these twenty men and women are to bring fully-loaded automatic weapons into the Great Hall.'

As he shook his head, Tich's double chins swayed in disapproving unison. 'Now that is strictly against the code.'

'There comes a time, Tich,' said Arthur, 'when rules have to be broken. This is one of them, take my word for it. Make sure the weapons are well concealed. Oh, and Tich, no one else is to know about this. Hopefully, no one ever will.' For a few moments he was preoccupied, considering possible scenarios, however unlikely they might seem. 'One final thing. No other commands but mine are to be obeyed. Is that clear?'

Tich's big face crumpled with concern. 'May I know what this is all about?'

'Best not,' said Arthur.

Back in his observatory, he settled into his favourite armchair for a few minutes relaxation and meditation before the Round Table convened. For years, the observatory had been his own personal brain centre, his private Command Control where he drew up plans for military operations and made decisions affecting the future of Camelot and the world. It had also been a retreat, where even in the darkest hours he had preserved his mental equilibrium by studying the stars in their courses and observing the universe in action. Here he had wandered in the quiet places of his mind and found sanctuary from turmoil, death and destruction. No longer. There was no quiet place to hide any more, no sanctuary from what was about to happen. Chaos threatened.

Seventy Two

As the doors closed, and the echoes of their closing reverberated in the Great Hall, members took their seats. The Round Table was in session.

Looking about him, Arthur was surprised at the number of empty chairs. Lancelot had fled, the four Lotte brothers, Gawain, Agravaine, Gaheris and Gareth, were dead, as were thirty-three other members killed in military operations over the years. In his head he made a quick calculation, and concluded that more members were absent than he could account for. Of the hundred and fifty seats at the Round Table, approximately seventy were unoccupied, meaning that about thirty members were missing, amongst them his brother, Keir. Where were they?

Addressing the meeting, he came directly to the point. 'We are assembled here today to decide whether or not Galahad should be sent to the High Council for trial.'

Galahad, escorted from his cell by a robot guard, stared unseeing at the bible on the table in front of him.

'Who wishes to speak first?' said Arthur.

Mordred and George Bedivere exchanged glances. George nodded, and Mordred raised his hand. 'I cannot tell you how distressing it is for me,' he said, 'to be compelled to speak out against a beloved colleague and friend. Sadly, I have no choice. My loyalty to the Round Table – and to you, sir . . .' – Arthur inclined his head in acknowledgment – 'is paramount.' Mordred paused, ordering his thoughts. 'Whether Galahad understood what he was doing or not, I do not know. What I do know is that he acted like a traitor.' He sighed. 'Those are the facts. I only wish they were not.'

'I hope you understand, Galahad,' said Arthur, 'that this is an inquiry, not a trial. We are here to get at the truth. To do that, we need your co-operation.'

Galahad continued to stare at his bible.

Next, Leo Grant put a question to Galahad. 'Am I right in thinking that you are in principle opposed to violence?'

Galahad muttered an inaudible response.

'Answer the question,' said Arthur.

'I am opposed to violence,' confirmed Galahad, his voice expressionless, his manner as detached as if he inhabited another planet.

'Then I find it difficult to understand,' said Leo, 'why you would want to do what you are accused of doing. Destroying not only Excalibur but also the island of Camelot is the most violent act you could possibly imagine. It might well have resulted in significant loss of life, and it would certainly have ended our dream of making the world a better place.'

Galahad stirred himself, lifted his eyes from his bible, and opened his mouth as though to speak. But then he folded his lips, and remained obstinately silent.

'Please explain yourself,' said Arthur.

Opening his bible, Galahad leafed through the pages, seeing and saying nothing.

'The truth is,' interjected Mordred, 'there is nothing to explain. It grieves me to say so, but Galahad is . . . ' how to put it? – he is not fully in control of his mental faculties. How else can you interpret his actions?' – A furtive glance in Arthur's direction – 'I am sorry to have to say this, but . . . ' He stopped, looking embarrassed.

'Go on,' said Arthur.

Mordred addressed his next words to the ceiling. 'Was it prudent to entrust such a man with the access codes?'

The Round Table stirred. It seemed not only Galahad was under investigation.

Leo tried once again to coax him into some kind of explanation for his conduct. 'Many of us have our doubts about this allegation,' he said. 'We believe there may have been a misunderstanding. We are here to help you. But we cannot help a man who will not help himself. My question is, did you really intend to destroy Excalibur?'

For the first time Galahad responded. 'Yes, I did,' he said.

A sigh of disappointment from Leo.

'But . . . but . . . ' stammered Galahad.

'But what?'

A long hesitation. 'I changed my mind.'

Leo's pulse quickened. 'When did you do that?'

'I don't remember.' said Galahad, his eyes wandering in Mordred's direction.

'I think you do,' said Leo quietly. 'Let me ask you again. When did you change your mind?'

His relentless but sympathetic interrogation was beginning to produce results. Though Galahad was still nervous, he seemed more inclined to co-operate. 'In Excalibur Control,' he said. 'I was holding the mini-computer . . . and then . . . Mordred attacked me.'

'What else was I supposed to do?' cried Mordred, appealing to the Round Table. 'He was feeding in the doomsday code.'

'Were you?' asked Leo.

Galahad laid his hands on his bible as if to draw strength from it. 'I told Mordred I could not do what he had asked me to do.'

Leo's voice was low and hypnotic, his eyes never leaving Galahad's. 'And what was that?'

'Must we listen to any more of this rubbish?' cried Mordred, his arms thrown wide in appeal. 'The man is clearly deranged.'

'He asked me to destroy Excalibur,' said Galahad, ignoring him.

'Lies!' protested Mordred, waving an accusing finger at Galahad. 'I took you for an honourable man, a man of principle.

How wrong I was.' He continued muttering angrily to himself as Leo renewed his questioning.

'And you agreed to do it?'

'Yes.'

'Why?'

'Mordred said it was the only way to stop Arthur launching a second *Operation Mainline*.'

'Isn't it always the way,' protested Mordred. 'You try to be nice to people, and what do you get? Lies. You have let me down, Galahad. You have let us all down. You claim to be a man of principle, and then you perjure yourself like this.'

As if he had not spoken, Leo put his next question. 'Did you really believe Arthur would do that?'

Unable to meet his interrogator's eyes, Galahad mumbled, 'At the time I did – to my shame.'

'In the name of God, Leo,' said Mordred, 'can't you see what he's up to? He's trying to shift the blame onto me because I stopped him blowing us all to kingdom come. I warn you, if you let him go, he'll try again. And next time I might not be around to stop him.'

'I am giving a suspect the chance to defend himself,' said Leo, unimpressed by Mordred's dire warning.

'Fine. But he's lying. Ask George. He saw what happened.'

'Tell us what you saw, George,' said Leo.

'I saw Mordred and Galahad struggling on the floor.'

'Anything else?'

'Mordred grabbed the mini-computer from Galahad and held it up.'

'Is that all?'

'That's all,' said George.

'So you did not actually see Galahad feed in the doomsday code,' said Leo.

'No.'

From the back of Mordred's throat came a harsh sound that was part protest, part cry of anguish. 'Why are you doing this to me, George? You saw him! You know you did!'

George's eyes were expressionless, his face wooden. 'I did not see him feed in the doomsday code,' he said.

It took no more than a few seconds for the Round Table to draw the obvious conclusion: it was now Mordred's word against Galahad's.

Mordred turned to Arthur. 'I ask you, sir,' he said, 'who are you going to believe? Your own son who loves you, and serves you loyally and devotedly? Or a deluded religious fanatic who believes he's God's personal representative on earth?'

First taking time to consider, Arthur addressed Galahad. 'Having heard Mordred,' he said, 'is there anything in your story you would like to change?'

'Nothing,' said Galahad.

'And you, Mord,' said Arthur, 'is there anything in your version of events you would like to alter?'

'With respect, sir,' said Mordred, 'it is not my version of events – it is the truth.'

'You still maintain you saw Galahad dialling in the doomsday code?'

'I most certainly do,' said Mordred, adding artfully, 'why else would I try and stop him? You know me, father. Am I the sort of man who goes around attacking people for no good reason?'

Arthur produced a mini-computer from the top pocket of his uniform and held it up. 'This is one of the mini-computers containing the Excalibur access codes.'

All eyes were focused somewhat apprehensively on the tiny computer.

'Access codes consist of combinations of digits, different combinations being used, for example, to regulate Excalibur's energy levels. We do that on a daily basis.'

The Round Table was alert, listening intently to Arthur's every word.

'As each number is dialled on this mini-computer, it is stored

458

in the main computer's memory bank, together with the date and time it was fed in; a routine that enables technicians to carry out checks, and also as a matter of basic security. The same would apply . . . ' – Arthur chose his words carefully – 'if someone were to feed in the doomsday code, *or any part of it*. Every number they dialled would be recorded in the main computer's memory bank.'

Excitement radiated through the Great Hall like a charge of electricity.

'When I returned to Camelot,' continued Arthur, 'I checked the main computer. And I found . . . ' – looking directly at Mordred – 'I found that there were no doomsday access code numbers in the computer's memory bank, neither for the date in question, nor for any other date.'

Mordred was dismissive. 'Computers malfunction.'

'The data on the main computer is backed up several times,' said Arthur. 'There was no malfunction. Galahad is telling the truth. He never tried to access the doomsday code.'

'Now really, father,' said Mordred indignantly, 'how can you say that? Would I lie to you? . . . I love you . . . I love Galahad . . . I love him like a brother . . . everyone knows that . . . ' Blustering for a few seconds, he fell silent.

Arthur's eyes were unforgiving. 'You love no one, Mordred,' he said, 'no one but yourself. From the day you came to Camelot you plotted to overthrow me and take my place. You are a liar and a hypocrite. I should have seen it long ago. I was a fool ever to trust you.'

'Now, now, father,' said Mordred soothingly, 'you are upset – and God knows, you have good reason to be. But this – this is paranoia. You are blaming me for your own – shall we call them, *misfortunes*? Is that the right word?'

'Explain yourself,' said Arthur.

This might well be his last opportunity to do just that, Mordred was thinking. He could not afford to waste it. Rising slowly to his feet, he addressed the Round Table.

'My father has had his successes, his glory days,' he conceded. 'But they were in the past. We are dealing with the present. My mistake has been to be loyal to him – too loyal – and too generous with my support. The time has come to correct that. From now on, I promise you, I shall be guided not by my heart, but by my head.' A melancholy shake of that head and an audible sigh was designed to impress on everyone in the Great Hall that standing before them was a man of integrity, compelled by circumstances to reveal the painful truth about his own flesh and blood.

'In recent times,' he continued, his voice sharper, edged now with bitterness, 'Camelot has been made to look foolish, worse than foolish, brutal. In *Operation Mainline* we slaughtered thousands of innocents. *Mission Grail* – the brainchild of Galahad and my father – was a disaster that made us the laughing stock of the world.'

There were loud protests from the Round Table. Waiting for the hubbub to die down, Mordred continued as if nothing had happened. 'This man,' he said, waving a contemptuous hand in Arthur's direction, 'this man who accuses me of hypocrisy – this is the same man who condoned his wife's adultery for years.'

A shocked intake of breath greeted this accusation. 'And what was the result of turning the other cheek?' asked Mordred. 'Let me remind you. Murder! Brutal, cold-blooded murder. Lancelot, the adulterer, murdered my darling brothers, Agravaine, Gaheris and Gareth. And now, we are told, he has . . . ' – Mordred's voice broke – 'he has murdered Gawain too.' For a time he seemed unable to speak, and then, his voice hoarse with emotion, he continued. 'And what has our great leader done about it? . . . ' He looked about him, as if inviting an answer to his rhetorical question. 'I'll tell you what he has done. He has allowed Lancelot, a psychopathic serial killer, to escape.'

He paused, his chest heaving. 'I ask you, ladies and gentlemen, why did my father leave the island at such a time? Was it on Camelot's business?' His fierce gaze ranged the Round Table. 'Was it?' There was no reaction. 'No, my friends, it was not. It was in pursuit of a personal vendetta – to revenge himself on his wife's lover.'

The members of the Round Table were in two minds. Undeniably there was more than a grain of truth in what Mordred was saying. Yet for a son to condemn his father so brazenly and vindictively was both disloyal and cruel. Though he sensed the mood in the hall, Mordred calculated he had nothing to lose. He had shown his hand; there could be no going back now. As though he were a barrister in a court of law, he summarised his case.

'My father is guilty of dereliction of duty. First, he put his need for revenge before his duty to Camelot. Second, his failure to confront his wife and her lover led directly to the death of my four brothers. Third, he gave the Excalibur access codes to a man known to be both a religious extremist and a pacifist who opposed the use of force in any circumstances. That, I say, constituted gross negligence on my father's part, and very nearly led to catastrophe. Had I not stopped Galahad, he would have destroyed Excalibur, this island and everything on it. If he had succeeded, none of us would be sitting here today.' Mordred rested his hands on the table, and such was the hypnotic power of his personality that several members, reacting spontaneously, inclined towards him.

'The question we have to answer is a straightforward one,' he concluded. 'Is this man . . .' – directing a contemptuous look at his father – 'fit to govern us? I say no.' And with that dramatic pronouncement he sat down, looking around him as he tried to assess the Round Table's reaction to his words.

For a time there was silence, and then a low murmur of voices, as members, disturbed and puzzled by what they had heard, exchanged views. For Mordred they had little or no sympathy. What did he expect of them? Yes, there had been setbacks, and the running sore of Lancelot and Guinevere's affair. Yes, Arthur's reputation had been tarnished. All true. But there was one greater truth. There was only one Arthur. Who could take his place?

Arthur looked around at his friends and comrades, men and women who had served him loyally, trusting him, obeying his every command, and they looked back at him, their eyes expressing their devotion. Turning now to his son Mordred, he spoke without a trace of bitterness or resentment. 'You say I joined Gawain to avenge myself on my wife's lover. That is not so. I joined Gawain for one reason only – to prevent bloodshed. That I failed, is for me a matter of deep regret.'

Mordred tried to intervene but was shouted down.

'You say I was negligent in leaving the access codes with Galahad. You omitted to mention that, as a precaution, I gave duplicate codes to George Bedivere. Had it become obvious that Galahad intended to use the doomsday code, George could have used the intercept code at any time. What I did not, and could not know, was that a member of the Round Table would poison Galahad's mind.'

A sneer distorted Mordred's face. 'What are you suggesting, father? That it was me?'

'I am certain it was,' said Arthur.

'That is slander,' said Mordred, 'vicious slander. I demand that you withdraw it.'

'It is the truth, Mordred,' said Galahad. 'You know it is.'

'Who is going to believe a crazy man,' jeered Mordred. 'The Round Table knows who is telling the truth.'

Breaking the silence that followed this assertion, George raised his hand. 'Then let the Round Table be the judge,' he said.

It was a challenge Mordred could not ignore. 'Very well, I put to the Round Table the motion that my father, Arthur Pendragon, has brought Camelot into disrepute, and should be ordered to stand down as our leader.'

Arthur spoke the traditional words: 'Those in favour of the motion, raise your hands.'

One hand was raised – Mordred's.

Every face in the hall now turned towards Arthur.

'I propose that Mordred be arrested,' he said, 'and charged with high treason and conspiracy to murder.'

With one exception, every man and woman sitting at the Round Table raised their hand.

'The motion is carried,' said Arthur. 'Mordred, you will be sent to the High Council for trial.'

'All against me?' said Mordred. 'Not one of you on my side?' A doleful shake of the head. 'How very disheartening. I have to say I think you are all making a huge mistake. Still, if that's the way you want it . . . '

He tapped his wristcom twice. In seconds, the massive doors of the Great Hall burst open, and thirty men in dark blue uniforms, faces masked, automatic guns drawn, ran in and took up positions around the Great Hall.

Several members jumped to their feet, twenty of them reaching for concealed weapons.

'Now, gentlemen,' said Mordred, patting the air with his hands, 'don't do anything rash. I suggest everyone stays in their seats and puts their hands on the table. This is one of those tricky situations that could so easily get out of hand. Don't you agree, father?'

Arthur nodded. 'Do as he says.' If there was to be a fight, now was not the time. He and his supporters would be cut down.

George Bedivere swung his steel right hand high, and brought it down on the Round Table with a loud bang that made the already nervous members jump. 'You, Mordred are a disgrace to the name, Pendragon. You bring shame to your father and to the Round Table. As for you . . . – a dismissive wave at the masked men standing against the walls of the Great Hall – 'you are traitors and cowards, all of you. You don't even have the guts to show us your faces.'

'To be fair,' said Mordred, 'the masks were my idea. I thought they would make things more discreet. But of course if you don't like them . . . remove your masks, gentlemen.'

As they did so, there were gasps and groans from the Round Table as members recognised the friends and comrades they had fought alongside. One of them, Arthur acknowledged with particular dismay.

'You too, Keir?'

Keir hung his head and said nothing.

'What do you hope to gain by this, Mordred?' said Arthur.

Mordred considered the question carefully. 'Do you know,' he said, 'at this point I'm not entirely sure. Let's see how it plays, shall we? Meanwhile a robot guard is on the way here to take you to prison. After that, we shall see . . . A trial? An execution? Several trials? Several executions? Who knows? Anything could happen. In the lap of the gods, as they say.' A malicious grin. 'I always think a touch of uncertainty is the icing on the cake.'

'Any dispute between us,' said Arthur, 'can be settled by talking.'

'Talking?' said Mordred. 'How boring. No, I'd much rather execute you, father – and a few of your chums, of course – well, quite a lot of them, actually. One by one would be good – until the Round Table sees sense and puts me in charge.'

'That will never happen.'

'Let's not waste time arguing,' said Mordred. 'You want to talk? So let's talk. The first thing you will do is order the Round Table to dismiss you.'

'They have just voted on that motion. They will not alter their decision.'

'I think they will,' said Mordred, pulling a gun and pointing it at Arthur. 'Do as I say,' he said, cocking it, 'or this is where it ends for you.'

Before anyone could stop him, Galahad leapt from his seat,

seized the barrel of Mordred's gun and wrestled it from him. 'Tell your men to drop their weapons,' he shouted. Mordred snapped his fingers, half turning to catch the gun thrown by one of his men. For a few tense seconds they confronted each other, Mordred smiling, Galahad anxious, the gun unsteady in his hands. Then Mordred opened fire. Blood spurting from his chest, Galahad was hurled back dead on the Round Table.

Screaming his rage, Arthur seized Galahad's gun and fired. As Mordred fell, hit in the thigh, his left shoulder and arm shattered, he fired a long burst. Arthur staggered and collapsed, shot in the shoulder and lower abdomen. Every gun was firing now, the noise deafening. In thirty seconds it was all over, the Great Hall eerily quiet. Almost every member of the Round Table lay dead, some still upright in their seats, some half-sprawled across the table. A few, having run, ducked, twisted and turned in a vain effort to escape the hail of bullets, lay on the floor in the distorted attitudes of death. Leo Grant died in his chair, his head shattered by bullets. On the floor beside him, Ban lay dying. Close by was the body of Ian Tichgame, the flesh ripped from his face. A few wounded survivors broke the silence with their moans.

Arthur looked in horror at the dreadful carnage. Mordred limped aimlessly about the Great Hall, his supporters dead or dying, except for two who had been pursued out of the hall and shot by George Bedivere. Keir lay huddled against a wall with a bullet in the shoulder.

Legs astride in conqueror's pose, Mordred stood over Arthur, smiling mockingly. 'You see what a caring son I am,' he said. 'I told my men not to finish you off.' He thrust his gun at his father's head. 'I wanted to keep it in the family.'

Arthur did not flinch. 'For the love of God, Mordred, just tell me why.'

'I'd like to oblige, father, really I would,' said Mordred. 'The thing is, I don't have the time to go into all that. What does it matter anyway? You've had your day. It's my turn now.'

This day is yours, Arthur. My day will come. The black knight's prophecy had been fulfilled.

'I am not afraid to die,' said Arthur, 'but if you pull that trigger you will never be at peace. Killing your own father is a mortal sin.'

'Dear me,' said Mordred, feigning horror, 'a mortal sin! Is it really? You surprise me. It's not one of the Ten Commandments, is it? *Thou shalt not kill thy father?* No, it doesn't sound right, does it? Galahad would know, but dear me, it's too late to ask him. You know what? I don't think there's anything in the bible about not killing your father. I seem to remember something about oxen and asses. But fathers? Not a word. If I remember rightly, it does say *Thou shalt not kill*, but let's face it, no one takes any notice of that any more, do they? Certainly not you. And while we're on the subject, is killing your father any worse than killing your son?'

'I never did that,' said Arthur.

'No, but you had a damn good try. And it's my mother I have to thank for saving my life, not you. Not so?'

Arthur's chin sank onto his chest

'Cheer up, father, at least you've had a good life. Well not good, exactly, but interesting, wouldn't you say? A damned sight more interesting than most men's.' Mordred consulted his wristcom. 'Six o'clock already. My, my, time passes quickly when you're having fun.' His finger tightened on the trigger. 'This is it, father. Sorry and all that. You'll be with your dead groupies in a moment or two.'

As Arthur closed his eyes and prepared himself for death, a voice across the hall cried, 'No!' Mordred whirled round. 'What's up with you, Keir?'

Wincing with pain, Keir pushed himself into a sitting position. 'You never said anything about killing him.'

'Didn't I? Naughty, naughty, smack hand, it must have slipped my mind.' Clutching his left arm, Mordred limped back across the hall to Keir. 'What's eating you? You'll be as happy

466

to see your brother dead as I will.' A grin and a knowing look. 'Oh, I get it,' he said, 'you want to do it yourself.' He licked his lips. 'Well, why not? Go ahead. I'll watch. Should be quite a turn-on.' Retrieving Keir's gun, he handed it to him. 'He's all yours.'

'I won't kill a helpless man,' said Keir.

Mordred shrugged. 'Suit yourself,' he said, 'I'll do it.' As he limped his way back to Arthur, he heard a gun being cocked. Spinning on his heels, he saw to his horror that Keir's gun was pointing not at Arthur, but at him. Even as he hurled himself to the floor, the bullets struck him in the stomach and chest. 'God damn you,' he groaned, 'what did you do that for?' Mortally wounded, he fired, and went on firing at Keir's body until the magazine of his gun was empty.

'God grant you peace, brother,' said Arthur.

Blood oozed from the sides of Mordred's mouth. 'What a mess, eh, father?'

They were dying, father and son. It was time for the truth. Weaker by the minute from loss of blood, Arthur dragged himself across the flagstones to his son. 'Why do you hate me, Mordred?'

The light in Mordred's eyes was fading. 'I wanted you to love me. And you never did.'

It was true. Try as he might, he had never been able to love his son. 'Forgive me, Mord,' he said. 'It's not too late for forgiveness.'

'Forget the deathbed reconciliation, father,' said Mordred faintly. 'It isn't going to happen.' They were his last words. His breath rasping in his throat, his limbs racked by two violent spasms, he fell back, dead.

Arthur sat by his son's body, tears streaming down his cheeks, thinking of what was, and what might have been.

Seventy Three

SHOOTING DEAD THE two fleeing actives, George rushed back to the Great Hall where Arthur, bleeding profusely from his wounds, sat by Mordred's body. Stooping, he put his arms round him. 'I'll carry you to A and E,' he said. 'They'll fix you up.'

Arthur squeezed George's arm gratefully. 'There are more urgent matters to attend to.'

'What could be more urgent than saving your life?'

'Listen to me carefully, George,' said Arthur, 'this is what you must do.'

Drifting in and out of consciousness, Arthur opened his eyes, and there, in blurred shades of white and yellow, was a barn owl. Fluttering onto his shoulder, Virgil tugged gently at his earlobe.

Fingers straying to the scar on his left cheek, he murmured, 'I was a fool to think that I could change the world.'

'As I told you a long time ago,' said Merlin, 'you can change many things, but you cannot change man's nature.'

'Then what is the point of the struggle?' said Arthur.

'The point *is* the struggle, Arthur. Even though we can never win the war, still we have to fight it. Remember how, when Pandora's box was opened, sickness and plague, death and destruction, despair, depression and loneliness were released, condemning man, Zeus's frail creation, to an endless war with himself. Remember too that something else was released from Pandora's box, something that did not fly away when

468

it was opened.' Merlin's green orbs glowed. 'Hope, Arthur – Prometheus's last gift to man, the gift that gives life meaning, the gift that makes it impossible for us to give up the struggle.'

'What hope can there be,' said Arthur, his strength failing, 'if we are doomed to an endless war with our own nature?'

'The hope,' said Merlin, 'that every time we confront evil, the closer we are to redemption, the hope that one day when the wicked are vanquished, the meek truly will inherit the earth. You did what you were destined to do, you fought the battle against evil, and the echoes of that battle will reverberate down the years. Take heart, Arthur. You have searched for the truth, the indestructible truth at the centre of things, and you have come close to finding it, closer than anyone before you in the long and troubled history of mankind.'

Arthur shook his head wearily. 'All those men and women I sent to their deaths,' he said. 'Every night I see them in my dreams, and every night they ask me the same question. "What did we die for?"' He seized Merlin's hand. 'What can I tell them, Magus?'

'Tell them,' said Merlin, 'tell them they died to keep hope alive. And tell them, Arthur, tell them that in the end, all men die, but hope never dies.'

Arthur was comforted by Merlin's words. 'Does God exist, Magus?'

'I believe he does.'

'What if he doesn't?'

'Then God help us,' said Merlin, with a glint and a glow of mischief.

'Is this the end?'

Bending to kiss Arthur's forehead, Merlin replied, 'When the world needs us, we shall walk again on Glastonbury Tor, you and I.' With a wave of his hand he summoned Virgil to his shoulder, and together with the owl faded slowly from Arthur's sight, his green eyes still glowing long after the rest of his body had disappeared.

When George Bedivere returned, he was shocked to find Arthur lying unconscious on the floor of the Great Hall. For a moment he thought he was dead. Fearfully, he touched his shoulder. Arthur opened his eyes. 'Is it done, George?'

'It is done.'

'The island is evacuated?'

'We are the only ones left.'

'The wounded?'

'In a mainland hospital.'

'And the rest?'

'Making their way to friends and families on the mainland.'

'Memories?'

'Excised in the memory bank as you instructed.'

'The Scuttles that flew them there?'

'Elimatted on the mainland as soon as passengers disembarked.'

'The motor launches?'

'Waiting for us on the beach as you ordered.'

Arthur was satisfied. 'You have done well, George.'

George bent over Arthur and slid his strong arms round him. 'There's a hovercart waiting outside. I'm taking you to the regeneration unit. I'm no expert, but I'm sure I can patch you up – well enough at least to get you to a hospital.'

'It is too late,' said Arthur.

George released his hold and stood back, the first tears he had ever shed rolling down his leathery cheeks. Never had he thought to hear those words from Arthur.

'I have one final task for you.'

'What must I do?'

'Destroy Excalibur.'

Was loss of blood affecting Arthur's brain? 'What are you saying? If we destroy Excalibur, we lose our power.'

'If we don't,' said Arthur, 'and Excalibur falls into the wrong hands, billions will perish, whole continents will be destroyed, perhaps even the planet itself. It must be done, George.'

George nodded unhappily.

'The computer is in my inside pocket. Take it now.'

With great care, fearing to hurt him, George eased the mini-computer from Arthur's blood-soaked uniform.

'Go to the terminal in Excalibur Control and feed in the doomsday code. When you have done that, come back and tell me what you saw. There is only a thirty minute delay before self-destruct, so there'll be no time to lose.'

In the dim blue light of Excalibur Control, George stared fascinated at the scene on the monitor: a lake bordered by reeds swaying now and then in the light breeze that ruffled the water's surface. Nothing could have been more tranquil, or more incongruous. For this was the monitor of the computer that controlled Excalibur, the most powerful weapon on earth.

Laying his hands on the keyboard, he consulted the palm-computer and prepared to type in the doomsday code. But his fingers would not move. It was as if they were glued to the keys. Did Arthur really know what he was ordering him to do? Had he foreseen the consequences? He was a dying man, confused, not in full control of his faculties. Camelot was surely the only hope for the future of mankind. There would be a new Round Table, and they would need Excalibur. If he were to destroy it now, mankind was surely doomed, and the world would slide into chaos. Pocketing the palm-computer, he hurried back to Arthur.

'Did you do it, George?'

'I did.'

'What did you see on the screen?'

'A lake . . . and some reeds.'

'Is that all?'

'Yes.'

'Nothing else?'

471

'Nothing.'

Arthur frowned. 'You have lied to me,' he said. 'Go back, feed in the doomsday code, and tell me what you saw.'

George considered protesting his innocence, but thought better of it. What would be the point? He had never been a good liar, and Arthur, dying though he was, would see right through him. Murmuring an apology, he rushed out of the Great Hall.

A second time he sat in front of the monitor. He had never disobeyed Arthur, yet in this situation was it not his duty to do so? Why must he destroy Excalibur? No, he would not, could not do it. Arthur assumed that no one could take his place. But what if someone were to pick up his sword when Arthur died? For a while he daydreamed, seeing the death of Arthur, the return of all those men and women who had fled the island, the recruiting of new members, and his election by the Round Table as Camelot's leader. Yes, that was it. He, George Bedivere, Arthur's old friend and comrade, would carry on his great work. Who else could do it?

'Is it done, George?'

'Yes.'

'What did you see on the screen?'

'I saw a lake . . . and some reeds.'

'Anything else?'

George had his answer ready. 'From time to time I saw the reeds sway in the breeze.'

'Nothing else?'

'Nothing.'

'Then you have lied to me again,' said Arthur angrily, and when George looked ashamed, added softly, 'we have been friends and comrades for years, George. Do not betray me now when I need you most. Go back again, and do what I ordered you to do.'

A third time George sat at the Excalibur terminal, his fingers resting on the keyboard, the mini-computer on the desk in front of him. Was Arthur right or wrong? Who could say? Obeying or disobeying him had reduced itself to a simple matter of loyalty to the man who, of all men, George most admired, the man who once saved his life. He made his decision; he would do what he had been ordered to do, he would not betray Arthur. Consulting the code on the illuminated screen of the palm-computer, he took a deep breath and began to tap in the numbers.

'Is it done, George?'
'It is done.'
'You fed in the doomsday code?'
'Yes.'
'What did you see on the screen?'
'I saw a lake. I saw reeds swaying, and the surface of the water ruffled by a breeze.'
'Anything else?'
'I saw a sword turning in the air, its blade gleaming like fire in the sun. It was about to fall into the lake when a hand broke the surface, caught it by the hilt, brandished it three times, and drew it under the water.'
Arthur nodded, satisfied. 'You have done as I asked you.'

The hovercart made a soft landing on the beach below Castle Rock. Weak from loss of blood, Arthur's eyes were dulled by fatigue and pain, the skin on his hands and face translucent.

Two motor launches tethered on the beach rose and fell with the ebb and flow of the tide. Lowering Arthur gently into one of them, George made one last effort to change his leader's mind. 'Let me take you to a hospital on the mainland. When your wounds have healed, you will summon the Round Table and lead us as you did before. Camelot will rise again.'

'Not in this life, George.'

Frustrated by Arthur's intransigence, and already grieving at the prospect of losing him, George snapped impatiently, 'In the name of God, Arthur, don't you want mankind to be saved?'

'I live and die in that hope,' said Arthur, his eyes dreaming.

George laid a gentle hand on his shoulder. 'Forgive me.'

'There is nothing to forgive. You have been the best and most loyal friend a man could ever have.'

George brushed away a tear. 'Shall we never meet again?'

'There is no such thing as never.'

'I wish I could believe that.'

'Believe it, George,' said Arthur. 'We are all immortal. Think of it. Everything began with a speck of dust. That's what we are, specks of dust. That's all the planets are, and the stars and the galaxies. Though we live only a few brief years, we are made of star stuff, you and I. We are stamped with the secrets of the universe.'

Far out to sea the gulls mourned, crying their sad tale. 'I have one last request,' said Arthur, 'before I leave you. All other memories but yours are in the memory bank and will be destroyed. Whatever happens, Camelot must not be forgotten, or nothing will ever change. You are the only one left to tell the world our story.'

'I will do it.'

'Swear,' said Arthur, holding out his hand.

George knelt and kissed it. 'I swear,' he said.

Looking into his old friend's eyes, Arthur was satisfied. 'It is time,' he said.

George pushed the boat into the sea as Arthur tapped the engine to life. The voice-activated computer stirred. *Destination?*

'Avalon,' said Arthur.

A second's delay, and the computer responded: *Error. Avalon does not exist. Error. Avalon does not exist.*

'Must be a technical fault,' said George. 'Key in the co-ordinates.'

'I don't know them,' said Arthur over his shoulder, as his boat headed out to sea.

'How will you find it, then?' George called after him. 'How will you find this Avalon?'

'Avalon will find me,' Arthur called back, waving a last farewell.

George watched Arthur's boat move steadily west into the afternoon sun. In a few minutes, Excalibur would self-destruct. He did not know exactly what would happen when the deadline expired, only that he needed to put a couple of kilometres between him and the island before then. He looked at his wristcom: ten minutes to go. Arthur had made him promise to wait a full minute before putting out to sea, and when he did, that he would not follow him, a promise he now regretted making.

Jumping into his launch, George started the engine and glided smoothly across the ocean's smooth surface heading in a south-easterly direction towards the mainland. A kilometre ahead, Arthur had changed course, heading north now, from time to time veering west-north-west. Was he on auto, or was he steering the boat? If he was, did he know where he was going? Avalon, he had said. Where was this mysterious Avalon? Did it really exist, or was it the creation of a fevered imagination, the last delusion of a dying man? If so, the promise he had made was hardly binding.

Altering course, he followed Arthur. If only he could get him to the mainland, there was still an outside chance of saving his life. Opening up the engine he found himself almost immediately in a low bank of mist, with visibility no more than thirty metres in front of him. Throttling back, he peered ahead, listening for the sound of Arthur's boat. But he could hear nothing, nothing but the sea slapping the sides of his own boat. Silence and the mist enveloped him.

Sensing a menacing presence, the hairs rose on the back of his neck, his skin crawled. For no apparent reason, he was afraid. Breathing deeply, he tried to slow his racing heart. As he emerged from the mist, something made him look up, and there, hovering over him, keeping pace with the boat, was an eagle, its massive wings spread wide, its fierce yellow eyes glinting like gold in the sun. His heart pounding, he cut the engine, stopping the boat dead in the water. The eagle circled, banked, flapped its wings lazily and sped away inches above the sea, heading directly for the boat ahead. Fearful that the deadly raptor was about to attack Arthur, George restarted the engine and followed at speed, the launch bounding across the sea, churning the water white. As if in response, the eagle lifted effortlessly from the ocean, soared into the blue sky and disappeared.

When he was no more than a hundred metres from Arthur's boat, the light of the sun was blocked out as the eagle stooped in an almost vertical dive, its curved beak and deadly talons reaching down towards George's upturned face. Certain that his end had come, he threw up his arms to protect himself, but at the last second the eagle braked and turned away, its tail feathers brushing his face. Terrified, he swung the wheel so sharply that the engine stalled, the boat heeled over, righted itself, and wallowed helplessly in the water.

Seeking what shelter he could, he crouched down, expecting the deadly raptor to attack again. Next time he might not be so fortunate. Seconds passed, and nothing happened. Cautiously, he lifted his head and peered over the gunwale. There, half a kilometre away, was Arthur's boat, and circling above it, the eagle. What could it mean? Why was the eagle that attacked him, so protective of Arthur? And then the answer came to him. The great raptor's intention had been not to harm him, but to warn him not to follow Arthur. Restarting the engine, he turned back to Camelot, and as he did so the eagle's cry floated across the water: Kluee! Kluee! Kluee!, a sound so melancholy that it seemed as if nature itself was mourning Arthur.

Two kilometres from the island he cut the engine, waited and watched. Camelot's white buildings, its pyramids and squares, its columns and spires, its rectangles, hexagons and spheres, shimmered in the afternoon sun. Sadness enveloped him like a shroud. Never again would he see Command Control, the Robot Centre, the Computer Network, Satellite Control, NIWIS and all the rest, never again fly in Eclipse or Scuttle, or take to the sea in Kraken, never again sit at the Round Table. A quick check of his wristcom: in precisely one minute Excalibur would self-destruct. A bank of black cloud moving in from the west obscured the sun, a light breeze touched his face, the boat rocked gently. Holding on to the gunwale, he looked at his watch – ten seconds to go.

As the cloud moved over the island, the light died on Camelot. A strong wind blew, the Atlantic waves leapt high and thundered down on Castle Rock beach, the boat heaving so violently he feared it might capsize. The cloud began to revolve, slowly at first, then faster and faster, and from the bowels of the island came a howling like the cry of a thousand devils in hell, growing louder and louder until island, ocean and sky seemed to be screaming in unison. Blocking his ears with his hands, George tried to shut out the terrible sound.

Then the howling stopped and the black cloud disintegrated. Looking about him, he shook his head incredulously, looked, and looked again, his brain reluctant to accept the evidence of his eyes. For where the island of Camelot had been only a few seconds before, there was now nothing but the untroubled ocean gleaming in the afternoon sun.

Tapping the engine to life, he set course for the mainland.

The End

Until the next beginning